'*Madwoman* is a feminist page-turner – sharp writing meets daring plotting and defiant truth-telling. The result is a firecracker of a novel, an exploration between two covers.'

**Tayari Jones, author of *An American Marriage*,
winner of the Women's Prize for Fiction**

'Run a live wire straight through the human heart and you might get close to what Chelsea Bieker has done in *Madwoman*, an astonishing, edge-of-your-seat story about an image-obsessed housewife trying to hold her violent childhood at bay. Darkly funny, heart-smashing, and absolutely unforgettable, *Madwoman* is a masterpiece.'

Rachel Yoder, author of *Nightbitch*

'Chelsea Bieker is an absolutely crackling talent.'

Lauren Groff, author of *Matrix*

'Much like motherhood itself, *Madwoman* is a book of beautiful contradictions – shattering and funny, thrilling and nuanced, heartbreaking and life-affirming, scathing yet sincere... I devoured every perfect sentence about the scars we carry both from and for the ones we love. A truly stunning read – this is my book of the year.'

Ella Berman, author of *Before We Were Innocent*

'One of the most essential books about domestic violence I've ever read – *Madwoman* is a breathtaking adventure, a fun house, a house of horrors, and ultimately, a love letter. Chelsea Bieker will break your heart and stun your senses. Chilling, satirical, and grip-your-seat daring, Bieker is a marvel, peerless in her storytelling; you won't be able to turn away from this book, not even for a second.'

T Kira Madden, author of *Long Live the Tribe of Fatherless Girls*

'Unputdownable. Harrowing while somehow also being deeply funny and furiously wise. Chelsea Bieker is a daredevil and a wonder.'

Claudia Dey, author of *Daughter*

'*Madwoman* lives at that harrowing edge where despair and violence collide. A story of deceit, delusion, love and terror, this novel is a scream at dawn, an impossible-to-forget story told by an author whose work I will now forever adore.'

Rachel Louise Snyder, author of
Women We Buried, Women We Burned

'Electrifying and vital, *Madwoman* is literary suspense of the highest order – a page-turning study of motherhood, memory, and the menace of an untold past. Chelsea Bieker's propulsive, unsparing take on generational violence is potent and stylish, rendered in prose that's beautiful and devastating all the way down to the heart-stopping and unforgettable end. Sexy and turbulent, witty and whip smart, this is a brilliant novel from a blazing, singular talent.'

Kimberly King Parsons, author of *Black Light*

'This intense, propulsive novel takes an age-old story right up to the minute. In portraying the exhausting attempt to overcome violence and safeguard loved ones, Bieker writes with urgency, integrity and emotional acuity.'

Caoilinn Hughes, author of *The Alternatives*

'*Madwoman* is brilliant. The rare kind of book that lives in your bones, as riveting as it is intimate. This is emotional suspense at its best… Fresh, urgent, and darkly comic. A novel hasn't consumed me like this in a very long time.'

Ashley Audrain, author of *The Push*

'An indelible portrait of what living with intergenerational trauma and a legacy of abuse can look like. In the guise of a suspense story, Bieker delves into the heart of what it really means to survive violence.'

Kirkus

MADWOMAN

CHELSEA BIEKER

ONEWORLD

A Oneworld Book

First published in the United Kingdom, Republic of Ireland and Australia
by Oneworld Publications Ltd, 2024

ISBN 978-0-86154-788-3 (hardback)
ISBN 978-0-86154-910-8 (trade paperback)
eISBN 978-0-86154-789-0

Printed and bound in Great Britain by Clays Ltd, Elcograf S.p.A
Book interior design by Marie Mundaca

This book is a work of fiction. Names, characters, businesses, organisations,
places and events are either the product of the author's imagination or are
used fictitiously. Any resemblance to actual persons, living or dead, events
or locales is entirely coincidental.

Oneworld Publications Ltd
10 Bloomsbury Street
London WC1B 3SR
England

Stay up to date with the latest books,
special offers, and exclusive content from
Oneworld with our newsletter

Sign up on our website
oneworld-publications.com

This book is for my mother,
who lives in every line.

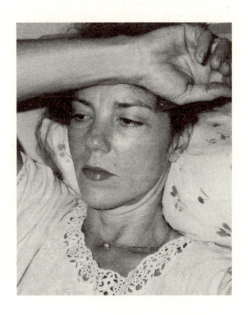

I pray her life will be different than mine.
Let me live dear father.
Don't leave her motherless like me.

—Mary Louise Glim, Waikiki, 1992

MADWOMAN

CHAPTER 1

The world is not made for mothers. Yet mothers made the world. The world is not made for children. Yet children are the future. Or so I've seen on posters at pediatric offices. Pro-life campaigns. PBS maybe. When I was in school, we spent our lunch hour foreheads pressed to the table while a small twitchy principal bellowed into a megaphone for silence. This was before the internet and secret viral videos and conscious parenting. He and the lunch ladies swatted at us but never hit. I don't remember telling you about it. I'm sure it seemed irrelevant to me at that time in my life, meaning my entire childhood, when all we cared about was surviving my father. My head on the cool table, solemnly eating Tater Tots, probably seemed like heaven.

Do you get Tater Tots where you are?

Now I'm the mother of Nova and Lark, seven-year-old girl, three-year-old boy, and I sense I'm coming to something important. Or rather, something important is coming to me. It will serve us both to bear witness. The world is not made for us — certainly it's not; just try to afford preschool — but this thing I'm starting to understand, transforming from felt to known, it's about the energy of violence. The way violence shrinks women, makes us feel lucky for things that aren't lucky. Even when we think we've outrun it, look back—see its long reaching fingers touching every choice we've made.

For many years, despite all I'd seen and all I'd survived, I thought I had evaded those long fingers. That life was about wise choices. For instance, if I did motherhood differently than you, if I ensured a peaceful family life, then I could leave the past behind. No. Not just behind. I could annihilate it.

I would not, for example, burden myself with recalling the time you put a flat of plastic bottled waters in our shopping cart. They were marked down, what we'd been waiting for. You had decided women with plastic water bottles poking out of their purses were living at the height of luxury. You even had me excited to carry one around in the mini backpack we'd stolen from Mervyn's. "Don't make eye contact," you'd said as we left without paying for it. We never felt bad about stealing. Life owed us minor rewards. But stealing from a grocery store was a non-option. "Not the *grocery store*," you'd said, exasperated once when I'd gone to pocket a candy bar. I asked why not. "You don't bite the hand that feeds you," you answered. I didn't understand. The same way I didn't understand why bottled water, Crystal Geyser to be exact, had become such a preoccupation. Now I know it was easier to fixate on small externals than address the fact that we did not know if we would live to see the next day.

We might have gotten the waters that afternoon had my father not come with us, might have been able to expertly hide them around the apartment, maybe even have a moment of total enjoyment, tipping our heads back and drinking in a place where others might observe, think, *Who is that extravagantly loved and enormously worthy mother and daughter consuming such pure water?* But my father had been home for a week nursing an injury, mashed his middle finger during a mining shift, something to do with looking away when he'd needed to look. He was slowed down on pain pills but that morning declared he was sick of being inside. "Goodbye, peace," you'd mouthed to me as we got in the car.

He was slowed down, but not as much as you'd estimated. He picked up on your desire in the store and made quick work of it, throwing the waters from the cart, crashing them into a display of baked beans. Cans everywhere. Snarled in your face that you were a poverty-stricken bitch and bitches like you drank dirty dog water. That's how he did most of the verbal stuff, not so much yelling, not so much screaming. More of a low demon growl meant to be heard up close.

You tried to pick up the cans but there were too many. People stared. I felt angry at you, not my father—which is part of the disease of all of this, I know, and we're getting there, I promise—but what made me so mad was the way you took care of the onlookers instead of defending yourself. Now I know you didn't want the pity of strangers. At that time, I was only newly attuned to the life-sucking energy of pity, the way it stretched the canvas for shame. Young, eight maybe, still possessing hope that someone would do the right thing and shoot my father between the eyes.

We put diseased animals out of their misery, we don't want them to suffer, to infect the rest of the lot. We let men live.

You angled your head down, saying, "It's okay, it's okay," as we walked out single file behind my father, having purchased nothing.

In my pocket, though, a pack of gum. Something I could not, would never, show you. *Is this betrayal?* I wondered as my father steered the Jimmy to Burger King, a public place so he wouldn't strangle you. Sometimes we could wait these things out, strategize safety, my father an active participant in the game of our survival. The next day, you woke to a bottle of Aquafina by your bedside. You held it to your chest. I started to point out it was the wrong brand, but you said, "See, he loves me." I shook my head at your stupid ability to forgive. "I know what you're thinking," you said, putting the prized bottle in your purse. "You're thinking one day you'll grow up and do everything better than me."

I thought having babies, soft mobile extensions of my body tucked sweetly in organic linen slings, would help me escape all that. That as a mother I would ascend and actualize into who I was meant to be. Babies, the ultimate distraction. No time for memories with a mouth at the breast, tracking infant weight gain and defecation. Unbridled happy exhaustion, new life in arms. Sometimes I thought it was working. But now my babies had transformed into kids. Walking, talking individuals, holding up mirror after mirror, and in those mirrors I saw my own face, and it was not as I'd hoped. Instead of healing and transformation due to all my wise choices, I saw my father's face just under my skin, so similar in structure, his eyes my eyes. And behind him, you, Mother, looking at me with something like expectation, sorrow, and in my worst visions, a roiling and motivated anger.

I'll carry the burden of you and my father and everything that happened on the island for the rest of my life. But I vowed to carry it in silence. So many lies I've told to ensure it would be my secret forever. Mine to death. I really had things figured out.

Until the morning I got your letter.

CHAPTER 2

I had the day planned, chores to do. It was the first day of summer break for Nova and the first day Lark would no longer be breastfeeding. The night before we had sung a special song and talked about how this was his last time for what he called *Nonnies,* that he'd done such a great job drinking all the milk. All the milk was gone, and it had made him big and strong. He had just turned three. It was time. I wanted to say good night with a kiss and not a full feeding session that was by now purely recreational—the kid put down more food than I did—and I wanted him to stop pulling my boobs out of my shirt in public.

The morning had gone okay so far; he'd asked for Nonnies once but was easily distracted by a glass of hand-strained—my hand—almond milk with cinnamon and vanilla. With school out, his sister would be home all day to direct and delight and torment him, a total change to our quiet one-on-one rhythm. But change was good, I told myself, and on the other side of summer Lark would be officially weaned and I would no longer be *touched out*. I might have a sliver of space in my brain again, something I was looking forward to.

As I got the kids dressed I thought of you in little blips, images coming and going, how you started the day with a Diet Coke and a splash of vodka, or was it vodka with a splash of Diet Coke? So different from my cold-pressed celery juice. You thought I had been dead for so long, sixteen years, while I was simply alive, urging my children to go potty before we got in the car. I saw each detail of my life two ways—what it was, and then what you would think of it. It wasn't a choice.

First, we went to Earthside Grocery and ate a leisurely breakfast of hot-bar eggs and sprouted-grain French toast on the upstairs patio. Lark crunched nitrate-free bacon; Nova drank a power-greens smoothie. Moments before, they had both produced real wet tears when I'd denied them a unicorn-shaped piece of cake on a stick at the checkout line, but now we were back on track. I metabolized my annoyance and focused on the fact that they were adequately fueled. Content. We all loved the grocery store—I was proud to have passed this love down to them, one of the only good and pure things I could give. The rest of my genetic offerings were fucked.

And perhaps this summer the two of them would finally bond, really bond, after so much struggle. Siblings are lifelong companions, my husband said often, as if reciting a line from some handbook only he had access to, and I sucked it all down, not knowing any better, not having anything to compare it to, overlooking the fact that he rarely spoke to his siblings, that his brother had recently posted a photo of his toddler son holding a rifle at a gun show and we had deemed them unsafe to visit. I had wished for a sibling, but you told me it was lucky you never got pregnant again. Why add another to the pot of suffering? Now I must say, you were right about that.

I loved that two children seemed so ordinary. A nice, even number, a sturdy team of four. But while the other mothers told you BOB made the best double stroller, they failed to mention what to do when your older child resented you for your younger child's existence. Those been-there-done-thats only looked at you honestly once you had already joined them, like when a mother at preschool pickup said to me flatly, "One is fun, and two is ten." Where had this advice been before? I was a miner of advice, watching others for clues on how to build a life, a real and good one, with an intense, propulsive need to educate myself on everything I didn't know. The sense that I was always catching up to common knowledge plagued me. Or drove me, to put it more positively, and being positive was important, was a marker of the kind of mother I wanted to be.

Now, sitting in our favorite place, looking at my children's cute faces, I saw picnics. Long U-pick days, marionberries and Hood strawberries, sandy feet jammed in puffy rubber sandals, nights of heavy sun-steeped sleep. Nonnies safely packed away in hopes of rehabilitation. It had been a nightmare Portland spring with almost no break from rain, no break from the winter-like dark and bone-deep cold. But today. Sun. Warmth. I put my full-length puffer in the basement.

"It's so nice, right?" I said to them. "Blue skies!"

"I want ice cream," Lark said, putting down his forkful of eggs. He pushed his plate away. "Ice cream now."

"We aren't going to have ice cream at eight o'clock in the morning," I said. I did the smile. The one that pushed down the untoward feelings a dishonest woman like myself was not allowed to have. I had formed, at some point in early motherhood, my own laws of the universe applicable only to someone like me, who had lied the way I had. I knew if I wanted to keep all my good things, keep them safe and untouched by my past, I was allowed no common fuckups. No ordinary parental outbursts. No shoddy decision-making. And no trusting others to take care of the souls assigned to me. I'd used up my allotted amount of luck and grace, shot that wad early in life. You'll see.

The day before my bleed, though, at the apex of luteal anguish, I did allow myself a ten-minute cry in the bathtub followed by a single throat-shredding scream into a pillow after my children were asleep and while my husband was doing his rowing machine. Then I would lick hazelnut cacao butter off a spoon and read erotic novels that made my pelvic floor ache. But that's it. Otherwise, my dead father who circled the block in the Jimmy would take me back to where I belonged. And where was it I belonged? Oh, I pictured hell. Hell was an empty movie theater playing my childhood over and over forever. No one could see my father but me. Who would believe me if I told them he was waiting for the moment I'd slip, yell at my kids, take their safety for granted? Some days I felt I was doing a good job, but on other, harder days, when my children wouldn't stop fighting, or Lark, my dear, sweet son, would punch his sister for no reason I could see, I'd feel the terror of what I'd done, a terror so consuming it would one day lead me out of my house and into the night, where my father would be idling. He wouldn't force me in. He'd merely lean over and open the door. Inside on the seat would be a box. I imagined the box wrapped in velvet, a ribbon tied in a bow. I would hold it in my hands. I would lose all power to run. He would wait for me to open it. The box. There was something inside I needed to see.

But no, I could avoid this, I knew I could. Some days I even laughed at myself. There was certainly no dead father cruising in his Jimmy, and the best distraction from all this foolishness was to buy something. Smile and push down the urge to yell at my children — *Shut up, you have it so good! All you have to cry about is not getting a unicorn cake pop for breakfast!* — until I could get to my favorite sustainable secondhand clothing site and claim an eco-Spanish-wool cardigan with polished horn buttons, maybe a linen romper the exact color of sand, and while I was on my screen why not send for a synbiotic vitamin subscription that had a three-month waitlist, endorsed by Gwyneth Paltrow. My smile was a mouth smile, my husband had recently noticed. Not the full face. The dance of managing both motherhood and trauma was slowly eroding me, but I could not say that. I could scarcely think it. Instead I researched the world's most perfect trench coat.

Lark continued begging for ice cream in a high-pitched squeaking voice, and the seed of a headache rooted behind my eye. He snatched his sister's leopard purse and she screamed and slapped his arm.

"Do not hit," I said. Calm, I was calm. "We do not hit in this family. Say it back to me." I could tolerate a lot, but I could not tolerate violence.

She shook her head no.

"Say it right now. *We do not hit.*" Wait, wasn't it bad to talk in the *we* to kids? Wasn't it emotionally demeaning? Eternally damaging? As bad as saying *good job,* which I did all the time? "Say, *I do not hit my brother's body.*"

"He hit me in the face this morning. I guess you don't care about that."

"Of course I care. Why didn't you come to me when it happened? I could have helped."

Lark curled up in my lap for his second small breakdown of the morning, then resettled and finished the eggs. "I want both of you to come to me before you get to the top of anger mountain. Hitting is never the solution."

Nova glared at her brother. "It's not my fault his favorite job on this planet is to push me up the mountain!" Tears formed behind her anger. What anger didn't have tears just behind?

"Chill," I said to her. "Chill," I said to him. "Just chill, alright?"

A woman alone with a laptop at a nearby table raised her eyebrows at us. Imperceptible, almost, her judgment. Perhaps she was signaling my dead father right now to park the Jimmy, letting him know I was ready to leave this nice life, that I had failed. Good try, but not good enough. I shook the thought away. There was context, I wanted to tell this woman, and the context was that despite my cycle breaking and self-reinvention and doing everything you and my father did not, doing it all better, my kids still had very little to no chill. What did the books and podcasts call children like mine? Ah yes, *spirited*. If this woman only knew the daily negotiations, the monkey-bar swings from one emotion to the next so that by the time six o'clock rolled around I could nearly understand my father's need to punch holes in walls...I smiled with a full face at her. Things were fine. I was in control. It was summer and I could still try for the post office, where I planned to mail off a dress I'd sold online so I could afford to buy another dress I'd later hate and sell. It was a major risk to sneak in a purely adult activity with both of my children in tow, but. The sun was out. My PO box called to me.

Day to day I couldn't predict the number of packages coming in, the bills, the general warfare of my compulsions. The PO box kept everything separate. My husband didn't need to know I had just done a balance transfer of eight thousand dollars to yet another credit card, the same debt following me around no matter how many online English classes I taught, the only job I could retain while being a full-time caretaker with a degree in creative writing. I kept buying dresses and jumpsuits and expensive supplements. Spending recklessly at the grocery store on a near-daily basis. If I lived within my means, making instant oatmeal and sad bagged teas at home, I could possibly catch up to my debt, but it would strip me of something vital. You and those bottled waters. Didn't I deserve the abundance of a credit card after all we went through? In truth, it was hard to know what I deserved.

But I was in deep by now, addicted to self-improvement, each new supplement pulling me further away from my past. The safety of radiant health was something I found great meaning in chasing. Unfortunately, it cost a lot of money. But the cost of confessing the debt to my husband was higher, even though I dreamed about it, and because he literally worked in finance, managing rich people's wealth, he would create a simple and straightforward way out. But this way would not involve my continued devotion to $395 ethically constructed canvas sailor pants or the $200 designer billowy blouses I tucked into them. He would lose trust in me, see the first crack, and then start looking for the rest of my lies. And these lies were not like the debt. No, they were not the sort you overcame in marriage counseling. These lies were the never-talk-to-me-again, the I'm-taking-custody, the do-I-even-know-you-at-all sort. The kind that lands a good, wholesome man like my husband on *The Maury Povich Show*. Well, that's what you and I watched when I was little. I don't know what the equivalent is now, but I could imagine the camera zooming in on his conventionally attractive and dismayed face, the audience sighing their sympathy.

Nova eyed me as I opened my special box with my special key.

Normally she was at school when I brought Lark to the post office. And hadn't Lark just been a baby in the Ergo mere weeks ago, asleep or halfway there most of the time? But life had transformed again. It was my first summer with two *children*. And children were different from babies. Children might report how many packages their mother picked up at the post office to their father.

"It's where Santa is going to drop your presents and Daddy's presents around Christmastime, so don't mention it to Daddy." She looked skeptical. I had made it too memorable by mentioning Santa, a man she revered as God.

"Presents don't fit in there," she said.

"No, see? We take these little slips of paper to the people behind the counter and they get the big stuff for us."

"Is there something in there for me today?"

"Well, no, not today."

"That sucks," she said. She was big into the word *suck* lately. I tried to ignore it. Lark echoed her, "Sucks, sucks." I took the stack of envelopes and slips, so many slips—what had I even ordered?—locked the box, and followed Lark, who by now was bounding ahead of us toward the long line.

Nova observed him with menace. "Say the word and I'll leash him up for puppy time."

Puppy time was a borderline sadistic game Nova invented that involved tying Lark by the wrist to a doorknob and serving him food and water in bowls on the floor and then leaving him there while she did something else entirely, a game they both loved for very different reasons. I let it go on because it was one of the few things they did that offered me a chance to take an alone shower.

"No public leashing," I said to Nova, walking faster now because, yep, Lark had opened the glass cabinet that stood alongside the line. Normally the cabinet housed dusty stationery sets featuring jazz musicians or past presidents, maybe Marilyn Monroe, but they had changed it up. Today, an impressive display of a to-scale Lego post office had been erected, complete with tiny postal workers and customers holding wee brown boxes with white string. How convenient for me, a mother of a very curious three-year-old, that it was unlocked. I closed it. He opened it. I set my bag down, handed my mail to Nova. I'd need two arms to wage this war. He would not just *look with his eyes.*

I picked Lark up, straining my back, releasing against my will a teaspoon of pee into the canvas pants even though I had peed before we left the grocery store. Lark flailed and screamed. He had been doing a new shriek lately, a total ear stab. A woman of grandmotherly age got involved, saying "That's a no-no" to the wailing Lark as if she alone had invented *no-no.* You used to say to me when I was young, "You're pushing the lemon!" But now, as I pinned Lark's arms to his sides, coaching him to pause and take a deep breath, it occurred to me you had been saying "You're pushing the limit." Of course, it was *limit.* I'd heard it one way, but it was always another.

I set Lark down, squatting next to him to rifle through my purse for something tantalizing. My left overproducing breast started to leak. For the last year my left breast had been two full sizes larger than my right. The right had given up but the nipple still tingled, reaching out for cellular communication with the other. Lark tried to free the left from my high-necked white blouse but couldn't get in there. "Nonnie!" he cried. "*Nonnie!*" No, I wouldn't give in like I had so many times. I wouldn't sit on this post office floor and untuck my beautiful shirt and let my three-year-old nurse until he calmed. I was ready to graduate from Nonnie. It was time to transition into being like the mothers I'd seen at the park with their books, looking up every so often to make sure their children hadn't been abducted, and no more.

"Not right now," I said. "Nonnie is sleeping."

"Just give it to him," Nova said. "Precious baby gets whatever he wants anyway."

I stared into the disappointing entrails of my purse. A dragon-fruit juice had opened at some point that morning and leaked out all over the expensive pink leather. Maybe if I just kept looking, I'd find a manuka honey sucker or some of those dried fruit buttons every kid loved. I didn't want to hand him *Daniel Tiger* on my phone because I would be judged for that too. His need to touch the Lego persisted. And not just touch — dismantle; destroy. It was Lego or nurse. Lego or nurse. His endurance amazed me, the way his cries only got louder, his face redder, the sands of logic sifting through a bottomless hourglass until nothing existed but noise.

"What's the Central California Women's…Faculty?" Nova asked, holding a piece of paper, the torn envelope at her feet. She repeated the question, but I barely heard her because just then Lark scratched me hard across the cheek. Hot blood. I raised my hand to the wound, and he broke free, slamming the glass door open, grabbing the Lego roof, collapsing a side wall. A tiny customer lay scandalized on its side.

"Dear Clove," Nova read. "I guess that's what you're calling yourself these days. I feel like I gave you a fine name, but it makes sense why you don't use it."

I was not understanding. I was still hung up on *faculty* and *Central California*. I looked down to see my blouse had ripped.

"I know you don't want to be found. But I found you." Nova's voice boomed and I was momentarily impressed by her clear enunciation; the performing arts classes I'd charged were totally paying off, I thought, as she added a reverent tremor to the line: "Because you're my child..."

I snatched the paper out of her hands. "What is this?" I said, or maybe I roared. Everyone was looking now, if they hadn't been before. The contents of my purse lay scattered, my stash of bills and slips fanned out at our feet, Nova crying along with Lark because I'd grabbed the paper from her in a not-nice way, Lark trying to rip the hole in my blouse larger so he could tunnel his way to Nonnie, then giving up and slamming open the glass cabinet once more, and me, holding your words in my hands in this public space. *Facility*, not *faculty*. The woman working the counter leaned over, pointed at Lark, and said, "Do you think you can stop him from opening that?"

All the years of feeling judged while navigating public spaces that were not meant for me and my children, like a post office, for example, and the fear I carried day to day that we would not be able to make it through simple tasks, like mail a package, grocery shop, "run in" to any store, the terror I had of showing frustration or anger lest my very normal life be snatched away from me...all of it came up now into my throat, and I said, "Do you think you could put a lock on this child-height display of Lego? Or better yet, why have a Lego display at all? Instead, you could have a shelf with kids' books on it and they could go to town reading while their parents wait."

She blinked. "The guy who built that was on the *LEGO Masters* show. He's local."

"Well, thank god he's local," I said. She winced at my deadpan delivery, but it turned out I was not done. "Who is this for if not for a child? It makes no sense." The grandmotherly woman edged away from me as if realizing she might be in a hostage situation. The room blurred. "I mean, come on. What kid doesn't want to play with colorful plastic? He's three! Three years on this planet. That's nothing! Imagine being…three!"

"He won the show. He's a very talented architect."

"Well, now," I said to her, sliding the glass door open. "My son has a real interest in architecture." Lark smiled, his eyes crazed with giddy disbelief, and started rearranging the minifigs, doing cute voices with them. *Any time's a good time for imaginative play.* I stared ahead. Was the circular nature of caretaking what made it so hard for you to leave my father? Motherhood pinned you in place, made everything feel impossible?

Nova tugged on my pant leg, said, "Let's go." But as terrible as things were in that moment, I knew once I walked out the doors and into the sunshine, they would only get worse. For I was now a woman who held a letter from her mother.

"Uh, hey." Could it be? The college-age boy before me was going to offer up his place at the front of the line? "Can I get that pen?" he said, standing a step too close, looking at Lark, who was now using one of several chained post office pens as an airplane for the small Lego people to ride, content and quiet at last. "I need to write an address on this."

I slipped into the place where violence lived. I pictured my father's hands, the way he would remove the grime from his shifts with corn huskers lotion and a pocketknife over the kitchen sink. How one of his hands could grip your whole neck. "You want the very pen that's keeping him occupied?" I asked. I felt my mouth creep into a weird smile.

The young man nodded, exuding a full-bodied confidence.

"Is this boy's mother here to tell him to maybe use a different one?" I called out to the line. "Anyone? His mother? Is she here?"

He looked at me with contempt. Who was I to tell him anything, me, this woman who held no sexual promise for him whatsoever?

"Use a different one, shitbag," I said. Lark tensed as if I was a stranger. And I was, wasn't I, my father's words in my mouth. *Shitbag, haybag, whore.*

The college boy breathed *bitch* and sulked back to his place in line. The older woman made a show of producing a pen and a peppermint from her purse, pressing them into his hands. Such a peppermint might have worked on my three-year-old minutes before, but no. Her eyes tried to shame me for failing to accommodate the young man, but I stared ahead. *Central California Women's Facility.*

By the time it was my turn at the counter, my tears fell freely and my breasts cried milk. Two wet circles bloomed over my nipples. Faintly, I could smell my own urine. The same woman who had asked me to control Lark was now before me pressing buttons and printing my shipping sticker while liquid poured from all my places and my face itched with resentment. I worried if I opened my mouth to speak, some deformed bird might plop out.

The woman went to the back, returning with an armful of brown boxes and puffy white mailers. She slid them across the counter, all my secret treats. "Anything else?" she said, expressionless.

I mustered dignity—"That will be all"—then piled the packages into my reusable shopping tote and herded my children out the door to the car, your letter gripped in my hand. If I didn't get home soon, something bad would happen. I strapped Lark in his car seat—Nova could do it herself by now, a small gift—and then tried to calm down by doing breath of fire, focusing my eyes on the tallest point of a Doug fir in the distance.

I wanted badly to text my husband, tell him what was happening.

19

Maybe he could come pick us up and take us back to the grocery store for lunch, a safe place.

Out of the question, though, seeing as our entire relationship was bolted to the foundation of lies I'd fed him on our first date, namely, that you and my father had died in a car accident when I was seventeen. That you and my father were a regular mom and dad, and prior to your deaths, I'd had a regular life. He'd questioned the logistics very little all these years, but every so often he would catch me in a moment of spellbound adoration for one of our children, gazing at their sleeping faces from the doorway, or that time at Nova's holiday recital when she ran to the front of the stage at the end for an impromptu solo, delighting the adults in the room with her bravado, and he'd lean over, his mouth close to my ear, and say with so much confidence I could almost believe it, "They'd be so proud of you." Meaning you and my father, if you were alive, would be so proud of me now, the mother I'd become. At such times I'd feel two distinct ways toward him: first, grateful for his understanding that grief crests equally in times of joy and in times of difficulty, and second, annoyed. Who was he to imagine he knew you and my father? But the annoyance could only be rerouted inward, of course. It was mine to bear.

When I met my husband, I was already on my path of reinvention. Already knew what I wanted—a kind husband and adoring children, a blue house with a porch, family movie nights, no eruptions of anger, no long sleeves in summer, no 911 calls. But to get there from where I had been—I was not naïve. I was pretty enough to convince a man to fall in love, but I knew once he found out about my past, it would be ruined. The first man I fell in love with at seventeen proved this to be correct. With time, he could no longer look at me without seeing it: my story. To him I would always be the girl whose mother had murdered her father. The orphan, more archetype than person. His pity rotted our love from the inside. After him, I knew it would not serve me to walk through the world so obviously damaged. I'd have to start over, build a self from scratch.

It amazes me now that I did it.

I watched my future husband all semester our senior year of college in an elective drama class. By then I was restless to meet the one who would pull me out of the floating half-life I'd been living, suspended between the horror of my childhood and the blissful future I spent no less than one hour a day visualizing in a meditative state, blindfolded with binaural beats.

He was an econ major, which utterly bored me but would be useful for future stability. My pheromones vibrated over the perfect ball of muscle above each of his knees. And legs aside, there was a goodness about him. He kept his head down, appearing to take furious notes as the professor assigned parts to students, but from the seat behind him I could see he was only drawing Stussy signs. He seemed nervous to perform, which was good. I didn't want someone who harbored artistic intentions, who investigated the world with too much curiosity. Who might one day turn that curiosity toward me.

As the class shuffled around, getting in formation for a read-through of *The Taming of the Shrew,* I leaned forward, whispered, "Come with me." I gestured to the stage, where we could slip behind the curtain unseen. The professor was distracted, answering a student's question. *Come on,* I thought. *Follow me.*

He glanced around and then got up. I pulled him by the wrist into the rest of his life.

"We could kiss back here, and no one would know," I said, taking my shot, a long one considering most of our conversations to that point had been about due dates. He didn't reply right away. *Probably has a girlfriend,* I thought.

Then: "I'd rather take you to dinner first."

It's something we still laugh about, how I put my hand out and we shook, like making a deal.

By the time class was over, I knew he was a Safe. There were Safes and Unsafes, and if you knew what to feel for, you could tell which a person was within ten minutes of meeting them, often sooner. It was as subtle as a current in the air around them. My future husband's current was smooth and glowy as he carefully put his binder away, drank from his Klean Kanteen with the RESPECT MOTHER EARTH sticker on it, the ONE LOVE sticker. Outside after class, a bee landed on his arm. He grew very still, communicated to the tiny animal something of the world's purest care.

You told me most women, if they possessed even a shred of intuition, could tell when a man wanted them, that one day I would be wanted and I'd have to ask myself if I really wanted the man back, or if I was just in love with the fact of his wanting. How the two could look remarkably alike but were in fact different. I told you it seemed like the wrong question to ask. You threw your head back and laughed. "Oh, daughter," you said. "You're too wise."

You, Mother, were not wise, and this was your downfall. The right question had nothing to do with a man's wanting, or even my own. It had only to do with looking at his deepest insides and testing the hot core of violence within. Would he or would he not one day grip my neck and let my toes dangle? Would he or would he not sneer into my ear that I was worthless? Shred my clothes with his hands and remind me of the gun behind the headboard. These were the only questions that mattered.

The bee flew away, unscathed.

22

★ ★ ★

The next night my future husband took me to a lively place off campus with patio seating and ordered us grilled calamari tacos, and I let him tell me about seafood even though I had spent a good portion of my youth eating poke over rice in Waikiki, later eating crabs people had carelessly discarded into San Francisco trash cans, still full of flesh. "I've never had something so delicious," I told him, and that wasn't true either. The shave ice I ate with you outside the Royal Hawaiian after school was more delicious than anything I had eaten or ever would.

He said he liked to play soccer on weekends. His biceps popped when he pulled out my chair. His body was solid and sculpted but not overbearing. We were about the same height, so he would never glower down at me. He had a biggish nose that was slightly crooked and he had perfect teeth and his eyes were sandy green and a little close together and his eyebrows arched severely, making him look clever. Boyish brown hair in a thick mop. A plain T-shirt. Birkenstocks. My father had perfect teeth too, but not a crooked nose. My father's eyebrows had been bushy and his lashes long. My father wore a gold signet necklace hung low on his hairy chest, and when he was not wearing a hard hat and greasy dungarees, he'd wear white slacks and half-buttoned hibiscus-print shirts and the gold chain glinted in the sun. I wore his necklace on the date, my father's necklace I still wear today. You had it made from an heirloom Hawaiian golden nugget someone from AA gave you when you celebrated one year of continuous sobriety during a stint when my father allowed you to go to meetings, and, afraid of accepting a gift for yourself, you took it to a jeweler and had them press his first initial into it, string it on a long gold chain. Of your belongings, I have nothing.

What did they do with all our stuff after everything?

I dreamed one day I would see that floral dress you loved walk up to me in a coffee shop on another woman's body. I'd play out the scenario: if she didn't give it to me, I'd tear it off her.

On our date my future husband ordered a beer and my hopes dimmed. I considered going to the bathroom and not coming back.

"Does my drinking bother you?" he said.

I arranged my face into calmness. I couldn't tell him the smell of beer on a man's breath meant a fist was coming later. In that moment, I sensed the depth of my mission. If I went through with it, this very real and no longer imagined man would never know me. I didn't yet understand the cost of this.

"I'm happy to not drink," he said, "if you'd be more comfortable. Hey, I'll never drink again if you don't want me to. Maybe one last Guinness right before I die, and that's it. You can spoon it to me in our nursing home."

"What else would you never do again for me?" I said it with some sex.

He got a bit flustered. He didn't realize I was a wise crone inside the body of a college child. I'd lived several lives by then and maybe he felt my own current: jagged, love questing, and hot with need. "Anything," he said. On autopilot he lifted his beer to take a sip and I raised my chin. He dropped the glass, actually dropped it, realizing his mistake. It spilled across the table and onto the floor. A waiter came to clean up the mess, but we could gaze only at each other.

He told me about his un-divorced parents who loved him and his siblings, how every year they went to their lake house, how he'd called his mother Tootsie from the time he could talk and no one knew why but it stuck and now she introduced herself by it. How every year they took a family camping trip.

I sat up straighter, pushed my chest out a little, when he said camping. The thought of a family who functioned so highly — could make it out the door, set up a tent successfully, char meats on a portable grill. It was beyond anything I could fathom, and to imagine myself with them, part of it all…I leaned over, wiped a piece of cilantro from his lip.

He had tasted sadness, though, a high school friend who died on the football field of a heart disaster.

"A heart disaster," I'd repeated, enjoying the two words together.

"That's what his mom called it." He sighed. "She was never the same. Life is so hard for people, but it doesn't have to be. I feel like, it's all about perspective, you know?"

It was confirmed then: he had never lost anything. My legs tingled with erotic anticipation. It was like witnessing a just-born fawn stumble about a war zone, eyes fixed only on the puff of clouds above.

My foot grazed his under the table. "One hundred percent."

He liked that. "So. Who is Clove?"

Here it was, the moment I could step into a new life with this normal man as my witness. I was making my vows to him right then, but he didn't know it. I vowed to keep my secrets and keep myself hidden.

I told him when I was seventeen you and my father were killed in a car accident on a mountain road in Kāne'ohe. It had been night, and you were driving to pick me up from a friend's house. How it was quick and final. I twirled my father's necklace as I spoke, a nervous habit. Noticing my future husband's eyes on it, I held it up so he could see. "It's the only belonging of my father's I have," I told him. "Saved from the wreckage." He leaned over the table and regarded it as tenderly as he had the bee.

I concluded the sad story with some nonsense about focusing on the good years we'd had together instead of all that was missing. Stuck the landing with some semblance of the actual truth: how after the tragedy, I moved to San Francisco.

"At seventeen? Alone?"

"I worked at a grocery store," I said, as if it explained something. "Grocery saved my life."

"Grocery?"

"Think about a grocery store," I said. "No one could survive without grocery stores. It's very important work."

Work I still did then at a small co-op nearly every day when I wasn't in class—me and my aisles—before returning to my cold studio whose windows looked out on the brick building crammed up next to it.

"Cheers to grocery," he said. I turned down my intensity. We clinked water glasses. His brows relaxed. He stared, piecing me together: My story was not uniquely tragic. I was not uniquely broken. It was a story he might have encountered in mainstream media, a common child's nightmare. He reached across the table like in movies and held my hand. I felt his subconscious desire to redeem the loss of my parents through his own stability and love.

And while it was true I had debated with myself whether or not I needed a man at all for my new life, I understood innately that a man, a *good* man, a nonviolent man like the Safe before me, would opt me out of the terror of dating, the exhaustion of over and over having to predict a man's potential for control, for cunning, for violence. No woman could create, could dream, could mother, under those conditions. And I wanted to be a mother, I knew that by then. Motherhood, the ultimate healing modality. Did my eyes communicate all of this to him then? I like to believe they did.

Finally, he said, "Honestly, you seem so normal," and blood rushed to my clit.

"Let's talk about something else," I said. My voice was smooth. The hardest part was over.

He asked if I had dated anyone seriously before. My first love's face hovered next to his, but I pushed him away. No time for heartbreak or hauntings.

"Oh, one guy when I was seventeen. Nothing serious." Untrue. "But mostly I've focused on school. I've never been with anyone, like, in bed. I don't want to get pregnant with the wrong person's baby."

My first love and I had sex in the meat locker at work, on every plausible surface in the apartment we shared, once in a park as the sun slipped behind a hill. I released these details into the past.

"Well," he said. He thought maybe I was being funny. "I'm glad you didn't become a mom to the wrong person's baby. Then we'd have never met."

"I've been holding out for you." I was pretty enough to say these things and for them to be heard the way he needed to hear them.

You said you wished you'd lied to my father in your early days of dating. Before the first time my father ever hit you. Well, he didn't hit you, he'd remind us. It was your fault for talking in passing about the guy who'd taken you to your senior prom. You were both tipsy walking out of a bar. My father lifted you off the ground. You thought he was being playful—you'd just had a great night—and you'd squealed in mock protest. Then the shock, the confusion, when he hoisted you into a dumpster. The pain of your sprained ankle, the cuts on your hands from the broken glass. You harped on that moment. How important it was, not because it was the moment you should have left him, but because it was the moment you should have lied. Had you lied, you might have allowed my father to think he was your first and only, your past, present, and future. Prevented all that was to come. You were never a very good liar.

But I was.

My children's voices came rushing back to me. "Drive, Mama, drive!" I was still in the post office parking lot and I had to drive us home. And then, once home, once alone, I had to read your letter. Of course, there was no telling my husband I'd received a letter from a women's prison and my un-dead mother had written it. But where was aloneness in our house? My children occupied every corner and filled every silence. The thing about motherhood was that everything was happening all the time.

Dread gathered in my chest, its usual nesting ground. At least by now I knew I was not dying of a *heart disaster* when this happened; it was just wild, unmanaged anxiety. But my body lashed out nonetheless, my foot pressing too hard on the gas, my eyes playing tricks. How did you find out I was still alive, Mother? And what did you want?

But I couldn't wonder too long because now Lark wailed for his Grover book that had fallen onto the floor under his feet. "Give me my book! Give me my book! Give me my book!"

I turned, contorting myself to grab it. I handed it to him, glanced at his red puffed face. He looked exactly like my father. When he pinched his sister, when he clenched his little fists, and when he looked up at me moon-eyed and said, "I love you." My life's work was searching for hints of future violence within my children and snuffing them out with feelings wheels, praise of tears, and endless correctives: "We do not hit!" My daughter, who was now shrieking at me, "Stop! Stop! Stop!" looked exactly like you. A great cosmic joke.

"What?" I said, turning back to the road. But it was too late. I slammed on my brakes, everything flew forward, and we crashed into the car in front of us.

Body checks, body checks. I scanned my children's bodies. "Everyone okay? Everyone okay?" I considered speeding away — this was a terrible moment for a car accident — but then I saw I'd hit a woman alone. I followed her onto a neighborhood street. Only once I was completely stopped did I notice the car itself, an old pristine powder-blue Chevy. My father knew every make and model of car there was to know. His brain was often lovely.

I turned off my engine and got out. The kids seemed fine. But were they? I hadn't been going very fast. "Fuck, fuck."

The woman emerged from the great blue leathered cavern. Was it you? Her hair sat coiled on top of her head and was the same shiny copper you dyed yours. But this woman was anywhere from twenty-five to thirty-five? Dressed in flared Levi's and a crop top. Her stomach was as flat as yours had been, concave really, and something about her movements, her long toned arms. A memory enveloped me, the way it felt when we hugged, how I loved your embrace, but *bone bag* was what my father called you. I often mistook other women for you, Mother.

"I'm so sorry," I said. "Are you okay? God, I'm mortified."

She waved my words away. "The truck in front of me stopped to let a dude with a leashed cat into the road. Not even a crosswalk. Don't get me started on drivers in this city. Or people and their pets."

"I turned around for a second. To get my son's book. Hold on,

I need to check on them." My brain did its terrorist work: *internal bleeding, concussion, organ failure.* Constructed a headline…*Seemingly normal fender bender takes a fatal twist*…My worst fears lived in the realm of unexpected complications long after the main trauma, once you were settled and relaxed. Don't ever look up *dry drowning.*

The woman came up next to me and peered into my car. Vanilla and neroli came off her taut and moisturized skin. Your smell was cheap coconut sunscreen. And her nose was not your nose. Hers was long and expensive-looking, while yours was buttoned-up, natural. "They look pretty good to me," she said.

"My mom is getting ready to shed her uterus," Nova informed her from her booster seat. "It makes her crazy."

The woman smiled, revealing a row of lined-up whites that made me think of pageant-girl flippers. I imagined her clicking them in and out. You had a wide gap between your front teeth my father called your missing tooth. You'd pull your top lip down over it, self-conscious, but when we were alone and you'd laugh your real laugh, I loved watching it be free.

"Wow, smarty," she said to Nova with real enthusiasm.

"Not my uterus," I corrected. "The lining."

"Whatever," Nova said. She looked at the woman with the casual authority she projected onto everything and everyone. "Do you have snacks? Our mom forgot to pack us something to eat, and this has been a lot." Lark echoed, "Fruity snackies?"

The woman continued smiling at my salty children, emanating the energy of love. Had you died and been reincarnated as this woman? I often wondered if you had died in prison—I'd have no way of knowing—had even comforted myself with the thought that if I developed psychic powers, I could learn to find a deep and satisfactory connection to you through flickering lights, ladybugs landing on my sweater sleeves, and angel numbers on the micro-wave. Most people would consider this a morbid desire, but I knew you understood death and its benefits.

However, you were very alive—I held a recently sent letter from you. It was then a strong premonition came over me: I was on a path to lose my mind.

"I can't wait to have kids," the woman said dreamily. She looked skyward as if addressing her future children's spirits. "I mean, the priceless things they say. It must be so much fun. So meaningful. Hope you're writing all this down." I'd written nothing in a very long time.

"Are you sure you're okay?" I asked her.

"I was just at a yoga class, so I'm all Zenned out." There was a tiny wave tattoo on her collarbone. Nails freshly shellacked like little nubs of opalite at the end of each finger. I wanted to see her eyes behind the huge sunglasses so I could confirm they were not your eyes, so I could puzzle together how they fit in with the very straight nose and fake-looking teeth. Her crop top was vintage and aspirational, the kind of thing I did not have the time or quiet to find and would therefore spend hundreds of dollars on imitations of.

I held out what I was pretty sure was my insurance card. "Cool top."

She ran a hand over the gauzy fabric. "It was my mother's, from before she had me."

"Well, your mother must have been very fashionable."

"Not really." I waited for her to say more, but she left it, took in my milk-stained and torn shirt, glanced at Lark, who was chanting, "Nonnie time, Nonnie time," and making the hand signal for milk. "My mother nursed me until I was five. Rotted out all my baby teeth."

"This is day one of weaning for us," I told her. "He just turned three. But I felt done six months ago."

"It's not good for kids to get everything they want. Especially a nice-looking little man of privilege like him. That's how serial killers get made."

I thought of my father, who had also been a nice-looking little man. Privilege was questionable. Oldest of five in a two-room shack. Father a World War II vet. Beat them all to hell and back every night, you had told me. As soon as my father was old enough to enlist, he did. Vietnam. It might have been safe to say he'd gotten nothing he'd wanted as a child.

"I thought serial killers were made by neglect."

She considered this. "Oh, maybe I'm talking about narcissists. Can't keep them straight."

I wanted to talk about violence, where it came from, where it started. Did she know, could she tell me?

"I'm so sorry again," I said instead.

"You think your day is going one way, and then, boom, someone runs right into you. A reminder the universe has a higher plan."

The cool thing would be to agree that somehow this car accident was a more exalted outcome than, say, just getting home in a normal fashion, or to summon a spiritual tidbit about synchronicity from my hours upon hours of esoteric podcast listening, but I found myself unable to reply. I didn't yet want her to make her mind up about me. I inspected the Chevy's beautiful silver bumper. There was no damage to her car. She took her phone out. I wondered if she was going to ask for my number. I imagined sitting across from her in a coffee shop discussing our sex lives, our childhoods. Discussing things I desperately wished to discuss in detail with another woman, but this intimacy felt out of reach, fleeting, and hard to achieve at, say, a children's play café. Hard to achieve when you'd opted out of a past, like I had.

"I better take a picture of your information, you know, in case I wake up and can't walk. My mother always said you can't trust anyone." She tapped her forehead. "Her voice is always in here."

I held out my license for her to photograph, noticing for the first time that I'd never updated my address on it since moving to a bigger house after Lark was born. Same with the insurance card, another thing on my list of tedious tasks that technically weren't hard, yet in the day to day with my children seemed impossible. Especially now, considering your letter, alive and waiting, in the pocket of my sailor pants. Yet around this woman, the rush I'd felt to get home minutes before faded. Maybe I could stop time, make a day out of this. Head to Earthside for a snack, let the kids play in the little miniature house with the wooden fruit and veggies. I had a feeling I could really distract myself with her.

"My father used to say the same thing," I said.

"Your father sounds neurotic."

The muscles in my shoulders gripped. "He struggled."

She touched my elbow lightly. "You look like you've seen a ghost."

I willed the image of my father in his Jimmy, blasting Van Morrison, out of my mind. He loved your big beautiful brown eyes. "It's been a weird day, I'm sorry."

"Saying sorry a bunch of times doesn't change the fact you hit my car," she said. "So stop saying it."

Intimacy, honesty. This was someone existing in a different way than most, free from the drain of small talk that prohibited true human interaction. I tried it out. "But it lets you know I understand what I did. It lets you know I care. It creates meaning between us."

You and my father had never apologized to me for any of it. I wondered what it would be like to hear those words from you, if the acknowledgment would feel like love, or if it was too late for love.

"Okay, Celine," she said gently. "I hear you."

I put my hand on my car to steady myself. No one called me Celine. I went by Clove exclusively. "How do you know my name?"

She looked at me like I was as crazy as I felt. "Your license. Just now."

"Oh." I came back to earth. Of course, Celine was the name on my license. My legal name. How I tried to forget. All my energy left me. This woman was not you. She was a random person. Nothing was miraculous. "Right."

"Well, good luck." She waved goodbye to the kids and turned and got into the Chevy, a car so beautiful it looked like a fake off a movie set. Together they didn't seem real. I wanted to ask my children, *We hit someone, right? She was just here? A copper-haired woman in a dream car?* My license plate was bent a little. My neck already stiffening. I reached in my pocket to feel your letter, still there. The life I'd constructed began to slip away. What would you make of me now, Mother? What would you do to me?

CHAPTER 3

At home, despite your intrusion, there was lunch to be made. SunButter and jam on sourdough, something my children loved yesterday but today would hate. I felt real blistering danger each time they refused to eat, some leftover primal instinct. Or maybe, as I often suspected, my children sensed there was something wrong with me, couldn't explain why they didn't want food from my hand, could only push their plates away. I imagined the Chevy woman eating a salad of surprising edible flowers and bitter endive while she researched insurance claims and how to get a series of free massages, perhaps planning a lawsuit that would send us into financial ruin. But the way she'd looked at my children, the amused and adoring way you might, Mother, if you were here to see them. If the Chevy woman was at this table, she would get them to eat.

I set the sandwiches down in front of my children, complete with sliced strawberries and cut-up baby carrots, each bite sculpted to reduce the risk of choking, then I stepped out onto the porch and threw up in the rosemary bush. Gingery immunity shot and the

35

remainder of Nova's power-greens smoothie I had sucked down on the way to the post office, back again. I looked up to see our next-door neighbor watching, holding a limp garden hose. I'd once heard her husband yell at her in a way that caused me to snap the stick of incense I'd been lighting in half. Caused me to come out onto the porch and stare him down. I'd never heard him do it again. But I didn't need to. Once was enough to properly categorize him: *Unsafe.*

"Oh my," she said pleasantly. "Are we expecting again?"

After Lark's birth she'd rung the doorbell on two separate occasions to say, "Tell me if there's anything I can do to help," when what she should have done was quietly place a fully cooked rotisserie chicken on my porch and run.

I wiped my lip. Straightened. "I'm doing a cleanse," I said. "This is part of it."

It was true on our block that I was known for my "extreme" health consciousness, bringing microgreens salads or elaborate gluten and refined-sugar-free desserts no one but me liked to the annual block party.

"I saw on *Dr. Oz* those health cleanses are silent killers," she said.

She knew nothing of killers, silent or otherwise. "I feel amazing."

"Have some protein!" she called out as I scurried back inside, locking the door behind me. I needed to read the letter, but where was safe? This was where motherhood baffled me, quite literally trapped me. It seemed insane to have to work this hard to have a moment alone, and yet. I headed to the refrigerator. A chorus of "I want mac and cheese!" followed me, and "This sandwich is gross," at which point another of your phrases flew to mind, then, to my surprise, out of my mouth. "If you don't like it, lump it!" Their little faces were stunned—where was their mother?

Where was mine? They had never asked about you before. I assumed one day they would register that I had never mentioned a mother of my own, and they would ask. I planned to tell them how beautiful you were, how creative, how funny. I planned to tell them how much I loved you. How much I missed you. How life isn't fair, but not to worry, it would be fair for them. I'd leave out the rest.

I stood in the glow of the refrigerator, all my gorgeous berries, my grain-free tortillas, my broccoli sprouts—more nutrient dense than actual broccoli, by the way—my chia pudding made with blue spirulina, my probiotic coconut yogurt that was $9.99 per tiny portion. I tried to breathe diaphragmatically, let my items soothe me. I cracked open a sparkling burdock-root elixir, tuned my children out, and read your letter.

I had done my best to be untraceable, created a world in which you had no choice but to presume me dead—but now you say a *feminist lawyer* has taken up a mission to redeem the battered women the system threw away. And it's you she wants to help first. Your case that seems the most unfair. She came to see you, the first personal visitor you've ever had beyond the few desperate women who've slipped in as distant cousins but were really after husband-killing advice. Held your hand as she told you I was still alive. She had become obsessed with your case, had a real heart for it, was so moved by your bravery. Explained we had arrived at a crossroads where the understanding of domestic violence was possibly, for the first time, intersecting with justice. That what you did, what happened that night, wasn't seen as self-defense back then, but it might be now. And she thinks, she's sure in fact, that if your daughter— *That's you, honey,* you wrote, as if I could forget—came forward with an eyewitness account of that night, told the entire story, you could be granted a retrial and freed. But it needed to be you to reach out to me, not her, she said. *She'll respond better to you because you're her mother.*

You've been doing your research like she instructed. You feel shaken awake by these women on TV, in magazines, speaking their truth, getting their chance. Feature upon feature, memoir after memoir—survivors being heard. Couldn't you be one of them? *They aren't always believed,* you noted, a vast understatement. *But I deserve the chance. Don't you think I deserve the chance?*

The lawyer said to tell me I'd have the summer to consider it. She will give me that time, the summer and no more, before she brings the case to the world. She said things would be easier for me if I complied. If we all formed a *united front.* You told her I was a good girl. I'd want to help my mother.

But there's so many parts to this you don't know. Things this lawyer couldn't possibly understand.

The letter ended with a simple *xo, Mom,* and I realized I had never received a letter from you, had no idea what your favored sign-off was. *Xo.* You liked to say my father could do anything to you, bruise you, break you, but how much could he really take away? It was all surface damage, you said, and none of it could change the fact that you were my mother, and I was your daughter. But my father's violence stood between you and everything. Most often, it stood between you and me.

I put the letter back in my pocket. Anger overcame me. I took a large bite of artisanal dark chocolate. Enough time had passed that we didn't know each other anymore. Or rather, you didn't know me. Had you ever?

Before you ask me to tell your story, you should know mine.

You should know what my help would cost. Because it's

impossible for me to help you without taking myself down. I guess that's how it's always been between us.

I took another bite of chocolate and then walked out to my husband's converted garage office. Stood before his large desk. Reggae played softly in the background. I looked at him and thought of all the time that had passed during which he still hadn't hit me, shoved me, gripped my arms too tight. He'd never yelled at me, controlled me, isolated me. Called me a name. Love surged in my chest. But under that love I felt a disorientation that was hard to pin down. What would it have been like to explore without fear? Have a motivation beyond finding someone who would simply not abuse me? The voice that wondered who I would have been without my past had gotten louder over the years, but it could be quieted. It was, after all, a small price to pay for safety. I tucked away my fear and did my best to engage normally.

"I barfed," I said to him. He was clearly busy, but no one could deny the seriousness of vomit.

He took his headphones off. "Huh?"

"I puked just now. Something's wrong with me. I need to lie down. Can you break?"

"I'm working," he said. "I'm about to get on a call."

"Can't the finance bros understand the need for maternal breaks every now and then? Family flexibility?"

"Are you calling me a finance bro?" He made a cute face.

"That depends. Are you going to take a break so I can have half an hour to myself?" Half an hour seemed a small thing to ask, yet would impact me greatly, would allow me to stand under scalding water in the upstairs shower while I figured out what to do.

"I know I'm in the backyard, but I'm still at work. I'll try to come in later."

"Later I could be dead, your children pestering my ghost to open Popsicles."

"You really could have been an actress."

"Could have been something." It came out flatter, meaner than I'd intended, and he dropped his smile.

"What's going on?" I heard him say, but I was already walking back inside. Once you and this feminist lawyer revealed all my lies, he would leave me. Once he'd heard everything, he would see me as a stranger. You have to know that, Mother. The walls narrowed in my beautiful house. I would soon be cast out. I had long feared my father circling the block, but now I had to manage you, too. You had come to collect.

My body roiled with the need to *do something,* but there was no thirty-minute silent shower retreat to be had, and there was no advice line for this particular situation. My husband *on a call,* my children's bodies cloying against my chilled skin. So cold on such a warm day — was I in clinical shock? — but no time to wonder; they needed me to fill the water bottles they were now thrusting into my hands. And they needed a trip to the park. And then they would need a snack. And then they would need crisis mitigation because someone would draw on the face of someone else's American Girl doll. And then they would need dinner and then they would need a bath and then they would need books read and songs sung and then they would probably wake at three a.m. and stand at my bedside and ask for a glass of water, and where, Mother, was the time for me to deal with you? So I went through the motions of caretaking instead. I did what good mothers do.

★ ★ ★

When night fell and they were finally asleep, my mind turned to the one person who could have revealed me to this feminist lawyer. Who must have approached her, in fact, because there was no way she could have found me on her own. Yes, my first love held the key: knowledge of the missing daughter who was not so missing. But why now? This was what I couldn't parse out. What was in it for him and why would he want to hurt me?

Well, perhaps because I'd hurt him.

That was all so long ago. But time can change a person. There was a time in my father's life before he'd ever hit a woman, just as there was a time in my own life before I'd become a missing person. Perhaps my first love had become a drug addict; perhaps he thought there was money to be gained in this somehow. Maybe he wanted me back and would stop at nothing. Or, more likely, he felt sorry for you and the weight of memory had become too much for his conscience. Maybe he'd signed a petition to *end intimate partner violence,* which seemed to be what they were calling it now — I wanted to spit on the ground when it was called anything less than terrorism — and thought, *Hey, I know how I can really help!*

Had he also been disturbed by the recent famous woman who lost her case against her more famous husband? Had he been stirred by this injustice and then thought of me, his old girlfriend and all her baggage? All she had confessed to him? Maybe he was in a twelve-step program and had reached that pesky ninth step where you upended other people's lives under the guise of making *amends.* That was the step you always stumbled on, Mother. The step you told your sponsors over the years was just too much. You'd stop going to meetings, and then I'd find you taking swigs from a bottle in a paper bag while you made spaghetti. But the step itself wasn't why you stopped AA, abandoned your own recovery. It was my father. He insisted on attending your meetings. He'd sit next to you and sigh and drum his fingers loudly on the big blue book as others spoke their deepest truths. Your body would shrink into your seat. When people applauded you for accepting your chips, *30 days, 60 days, 90 days,* my father seethed. Terrible beatings followed those chips. He knew if you hung around there long enough you might get clearheaded, you might make friends, you might leave him. I didn't understand your relapses at the time. But now I do.

Of course this lawyer became obsessed with your case, Mother, how interesting it all must have seemed coming from my old love's mouth, all he would be able to tell her. He knew almost everything. Almost, but not quite. I told him enough that I had to leave him.

Dawn crested and still I had not slept, because when I closed my eyes I was in the ocean with my father, dark water churning around us. What could I do about any of this?

By the time my husband and children were awake, the day's bustle under way, I realized while the current version of me did not know what to do about you, Mother, a future, better version did. I had transformed before and could transform again. Uplevel as wife and mother: Clove 2.0. A Clove who would be full of light and love, a total embodiment of the life I had created. Someone who was capable of writing you back the perfect letter to make you see me, and then to make you forget me. I saw now, there was much work to be done.

I took a handful of adaptogens that promised to improve alertness and focus, two prebiotic fiber gummies, drank a glass of water with an electrolyte powder mixed in to restore mineral levels, and finished it off with five drops of highly absorbable vitamin D_3 *now with K_2,* then stood before my husband in his office and told him I was headed into the chrysalis, about to embark on a great spiritual metamorphosis. He spread real cream cheese on a gluten-ass bagel at his desk despite my warnings about inflammation.

"Right on," he said.

"Okay. Great." I clapped my hands. "Maybe with me undergoing this transformation and all, you can take a longer afternoon break or something now that school's out. Just for the summer."

Sometimes I got soft and imagined a day when he would finally see my truth, he would just know. Maybe it was happening now. I rolled a selenite wand across my forehead.

"You know what I woke up thinking about?" he asked. Chew chew chew. He got up and walked past me, arranged a cone of paper inside his slow-drip coffee maker. "How sad it is that only two Beatles are left. Time passes," he said. "Every second of every day."

"The remaining Beatles have made you realize you want to take more time off to give me a break?"

"I was just thinking of life in general. You know, sometimes I think of your parents and all they're missing of you. I wish they could see how amazing you are."

Why was he mentioning my parents now of all times? Usually this sort of comment was reserved for Mother's and Father's Days, my birthday, maybe Christmas. I needed to shut this down. "Not right now. I don't have time to feel sad."

"Oh, come on," he said. He tried to hug me, maybe get something started. He loved the idea of doing it in his office; we'd only done it once and it was almost as bad as shower sex, the sad instability of his OfficeMax rollie chair, I couldn't come right, had half an orgasm, worse than no orgasm at all. He came fine, though, thought it was all pretty hot, a difference of perspective. I stood stiffly now, offering nothing.

"You have no follow-up questions about my spiritual metamorphosis, huh?"

He stepped back, did a little sigh. "Even if I had follow-up questions, you'd get all weird and evasive. You already assume I wouldn't understand because I didn't read that book about human design or north node journeys or whatever."

Occasionally it hit me with a sudden shock — *Maybe my marriage isn't going well and I don't realize it because I don't know what a normal marriage is like* — but the great thing about having kids was that we could barely form a full thought in the noise of their needs, let alone have a complex conversation with each other.

I couldn't dissect my marriage now, anyway, when all I could think of was your letter. The lawyer, my ex. My car crashing into that Chevy. My old life and my current life. Which was real? His phone rang. "Chrysalis," I said. "Just know that."

"Does this mean you're going to ban grains from the house again?" He put his headset on.

"You thrived," I hissed, half out the door, "on a grain-free lifestyle."

I went back into the kitchen and texted my few real-life mom friends not to contact me until I reached out again. *Needing a lot of spaciousness right now...*They responded with gold-dust emojis, crystal balls. *I'm feeling celestite for you!* alongside a photo of a beautiful blue crystal. One of my postnatal yoga friends wrote *Do this!* offering a link to an enticing regimen where each day you only ate foods from one color group at a time that corresponded with your seven energy centers. One sent me a picture of a butterfly she claimed had just landed on her knee. *It's a signnnnnn.* No one asked if I was okay or could use some childcare, a meal dropped at the door, a psychiatric evaluation perhaps, and that was just as

44

well. I needed everyone off my back if I was going to turn this around.

But how could Clove 2.0 emerge when all day the kids infiltrated every corner of my consciousness? They begged for treats and television time, things I usually didn't give in to but under these circumstances began to hand out freely to get some moments to myself to listen to my wellness podcasts hosted by women with waist-length hair and confounding income sources, as they accessed the Akashic records and processed their sensitive natures born of the fact that they were not human at all, but starseeds. One spoke of a practice called earthing, something that seemed relatively easy to do and a very effective upleveling tool, not to mention free, so I dumped a bin of Magna-Tiles onto the rug and snuck away to the backyard, where I lay flat on my back on the grass, arms outstretched. I tried to let my mind fade, see my rapid and terrifying thoughts as passing clouds, the electromagnetic fields of nature making me good.

Not ten minutes into this practice, my children came outside and began kicking balls of various sizes and weights into and over me, whooping and whining. I tried to force myself deeper into a meditative state, which is impossible to do. Force has no place in activating the parasympathetic nervous system. But from the outside I must have looked admirable, meditating while my children played, perhaps a skill I could create an identity around. Maybe an old-school blog. *Meditation Mama*. When I'd chosen this life of secrets, I had of course not considered the ways it would stunt my creativity. I often dreamed of writing, but I had only one story, and I knew it. It was the one I could never tell.

Lark jolted me out of my thoughts with his pain scream. I sat up to see my husband standing over me holding my tear-stricken boy. "Clove," he said. The sun blared behind him, making him look headless. "Clove, hello?"

"What?" I snapped.

"Did you see what just happened?"

My eyes adjusted. Fresh blood colored Lark's lips and teeth. He grasped his father's neck. "They were fine a second ago," I said. I got up and tried to pry him from my husband's arms.

"Me want Nonnie," he said sadly, burrowing into my husband's chest. It was true that usually I would give in to Nonnie for such an ouchie. But a parenting podcast I listened to had likened a good mother to a ship's calm captain. Lark needed to see I was in charge of this vessel. A no-no is a no-no.

"Second day having them together at home and it seems like it's not going well, chrysalis-wise," my husband said. "Maybe it's time to revisit the idea of a nanny." He used his shirt to dab blood away from Lark's lip.

"I'm earthing." I nuzzled Lark. "Mommy was earthing, hon."

"Sissy kicked me in the face with the ball."

"Accident!" Nova screamed from inside. She was hiding in guilt, looking on from the kitchen window.

"I wish you'd accept I have to work, that I can't be putting out fires all summer." My husband gestured to his office. The office I sometimes wrote in, or tried to, sitting at his desk imagining his life, what it would be like to be gone eight hours a day advancing a career unburdened by caretaking but still enjoying all the rewards and high points of parenthood.

"You put out one fire and now you're the fire master, huh?"

"Okay." He set down Lark, who then clung to his legs. "I see we're not going to have a productive conversation here."

"I needed a minute," I said. "There's a lot on my mind."

"Like what?"

Oh, buddy. "I need a little space sometimes. But it doesn't mean a rando should watch my kids. Things go wrong with that all the time. Read the news."

"I will never understand your thing against other people watching them. What do you think is going to happen?"

Hit by a car, gas explosion, fatal choking, molestation, broken neck, psychological damage, electrocution… "We can't afford a nanny." I tried it out. Usually it ended the conversation because he loved any impression we were saving money, and of course, I was the best source of free childcare there could ever be.

"We can't afford for our kids to kill each other while you're earthing."

I wanted to hit him. The line between people who acted on impulse and people who did not seemed as slim as a mouth smiling without eyes.

"Think about it. Ask your friends. Maybe there's someone from the bulletin board at Earthside. You say you want to write, you want to do your yoga."

"*Your* yoga? Could you be any more condescending?"

"It's not a sin to ask for help. The miserable Martha thing isn't your best summer look."

"Look at you and your alliteration."

"My mom said she thinks it's because you never really found your thing in life, and I told her, Clove is a writer, and she was like, well, why doesn't she write? And she sort of had a point. I think you'd be a lot happier if—"

"Earthside!" Lark interrupted. "Me want to go to Earthside!" Lark knew we went to Earthside at the slightest hint of distress and he wanted to soothe his mother, sweet boy. I held his beautiful hand.

"What's your mother's thing? Was she not a stay-at-home mom?"

"Well, yeah, but she did major scrapbooking. She was really into it. With you, you're not doing the thing your artistic soul wants to do and now it's affecting all of us."

"Your mother saved your braces and had them melted down into earrings that she still wears today."

"The soul wants what the soul wants."

I thought not of my artistic soul then, but of how impossible it would be to write you back, convince you and the feminist lawyer to leave me out of this, unless I had time to think, form a plan. I saw then my problem was twofold. There was the outer issue my husband could plainly see — my textbook motherly exhaustion, my need for independence that had boiled over — and then there was the inner issue, known only to me, this sudden forced mission to escape my past yet again.

Both issues might be solved by the presence of a nanny. The presence of help. I pressed my hands to my breasts, which felt full again. *Go away, milk.* "Maybe you're right," I said. My mind flashed to the Chevy woman, the way she had smiled at my children. The way she reminded me of you. "I'll find her."

CHAPTER 4

The next day, my husband texted me links to nanny profiles from places like Care.com and I sent back emojis of knives next to little baby angels and he sent back question marks and then I sent back *NOT TRYING TO END UP ON DATELINE* and he sent back *I see you more on 60 Minutes.* He did not understand that being on Care.com for me was total psychic overwhelm: trying to interpret the potential for violence and negligence based on photos, on internet vibes alone. The criminal weight of responsibility I held in my hands. The shame of forgetting to ask the Chevy woman's name, her number.

For all I knew she might be a career nanny. Maybe between jobs. The exact person I was supposed to meet and I'd fucked it up, too stunned over your letter to function. My husband pinged back into my phone with another profile, the main picture a drawing of a toad in a crocheted bonnet, hobbies: being an atheist, cooking shows. *Seems creative,* he wrote.

I threw the phone onto the couch, considered popping by every yoga studio in town to orchestrate another run-in. I had to do something. The nanny idea was imperative now, something I couldn't table any longer. Your letter burned me, pulled energy from my bones, called out from the innermost pocket of my immense Baggu. I needed quiet, a different kind of quiet than I got from sending the kids to the basement to watch a show. That was momentary and I could still hear them. Their lives still depended on me. I needed a deeper stillness that would only be achieved by separating myself from them. In some ways, Mother, I could appreciate that your appearance back into my life was forcing me to do something most mothers did with ease. Maybe if I reframed things, this was you mothering me.

The sun cast rays through the hanging clear crystals in my windows, sending dots of light across the floor and walls. I organized a shower for myself, sending Nova to her father's office to color, Lark coming in with me. He stared at my chest in mourning. In the warmth and wet, my nipples relaxed toward the drain. I couldn't tell if I was peeing or not peeing. Lark cried when water got on his face, then cried again when I said we were all done. He was laughing by the time I'd wrapped us in towels and did "the basket" where I held him tightly in a ball, my fingers clasped under his knees while he cupped my face in his hands and stared without self-consciousness into my eyes. Was this what my father was like as a boy? Sensitive, wanting connection above all? My father rarely lapsed into narrative. Things were one way. His childhood was *bad*. His mother was *sad*. And his father was *mad*. He never spoke of what defined madness or badness, sadness or happiness, but you shook your head, chided me for asking. "It was awful for him," you said when we were alone, allowing a little shiver to run up and down your body. "And then don't get me started on the military. May as well be the Ivy League for becoming a wife beater."

I asked you if my father had ever killed another person, and you said you really did not want to know. I wanted to know.

Lark broke the basket and scampered off to his room. I could hear him slamming his blocks together. "You die? I die!" He had become attuned to death lately, but I couldn't figure out the source. *The source is you,* my mind whispered. *You're poisoning them all. Best to just get in that Jimmy and go back where you belong.* I considered the science of what connected us: Your body holding mine, and meanwhile tucked inside my fetal ovaries, all the eggs I would ever produce in my lifetime. You carried me, and also, the beginnings of my two children. All of us together as my father beat you. "Die, man!" I heard Lark say. Neither child was a peaceful sleeper, drifting from their beds in the thin hours after midnight, looking for me, holding me tight, whispering nightmares, flushing with fear. "Where do your scaries come from?" my husband asks them. I stay quiet, holding them close. I have some ideas.

But enough of that. I ran to my laptop and pulled the trigger on an expensive lipstick from a clean beauty brand my social media ads had been shoving down my throat. It was a darker color than normal for me, and only after it was safely purchased did I realize it was just like the color you wore religiously, Revlon's 457 Wild Orchid. The color that was stamped on every cup, and often on your teeth. The color on your lips the last time I saw you, your mouth open, howling.

"You seem sort of down," my husband said that night after the kids were in bed. He sounded far away. He pulled me into his chest. "What do you need? A special treat?"

I felt comforted by the sure fact of his body, that if I asked, he would throw on clothes and drive to Earthside to buy me a raw vegan cheesecake slice. I could lose all of this by summer's end.

Could and would. "I've been really consumed imagining the plot of a novel I want to write. It's kind of a thriller."

"Yeah?" he said. He seemed happy to hear this. He really *was* an encouraging husband, the sort I could effusively thank in the acknowledgments if I ever did write a book: *And for you, baby, the one who believed in me from day one!*

I nodded, slipping between the sheets. "If I look distracted, trust I am deeply in my creative process."

"See, even the idea of a nanny is starting to shift things for you. Imagine how much writing you'll get done."

He wasn't wrong about the writing. I had been writing late into the night, the laptop glow turned way down, forgoing sleep. And I was writing in my mind, all day long. But not a novel. I was writing to you, Mother. I had to make you see. Make you understand that sparing me was best. Let me go for good. We can let each other go, can't we?

My husband fell asleep within minutes, his arms heavy around me, his boner twitching against my back. The boner was endearing, how it persisted no matter what state I was in, no matter how many nights we'd slept in the same bed. Endearing but still representative of another need to fulfill. I scooted away from it, only for it to find me again. His love language was touch. Mine was secrets.

I scrolled through pictures on my phone, stopping on a selfie I had taken as Lark nursed for the very last time. I edited the lighting and cropped out a messy corner of Lark's room and brightened the hair that obscured my face. Of Lark's face only an eyebrow and long eyelashes against his round cheek were visible. I never showed our faces on social media. No identifying factors, never ever, but despite anonymity it was enough to amass nearly forty thousand followers over the last several years. I'd played with some hashtags after Nova was born, something to do while pinned to the rocking chair at all hours of the day and night as she nursed, and the mom followers came in droves. *#slowparenting #purechildhood #unplugged-parents #letthembelittle*

I didn't know what had compelled me to add these tags to my posts aside from the fact that when I clicked one I was taken through a magic portal where all the squares spoke to my fantasy of what safety and normalcy must look like, and I wanted to be a part of it. I might have no idea how to be in a family, but my device reflected that I was doing a good job, that my life looked like other lives I would enjoy. It was close to slow fashion and grocery stores on my list of self-soothers.

I wrote the caption now: *Someone's done nursing! #bittersweet #slowchildhood #fedisbest*

You had to add the "fed is best" hashtag or off with your head. While I worried in real life I was ruining my children, I had learned to play motherhood mostly correctly and inclusively on social media.

I considered my profile and what you might think of it. How it would show you only the smallest shred of my lived experience. What had begun as an account for landscapes and rivers and pictures of my hand in my husband's hand had transformed into a curated collection of edited and artistically inclined motherhood-themed photos with captions that were a little self-damning and a lot inspirational. Lots of dramatic forests and my kids from the back skipping down narrow dirt paths.

Now I required confirmation from these internet women to know I was choosing the right products, the safest and most tested vitamins, the purest shampoos, the correct brand of sustainable prairie dress. Organic cotton wasn't enough anymore; it needed to be grown on a regenerative farm and handstamped with plant dyes.

The dress should be compostable. You weren't around to advise me, Mother. I'll admit that as I read your letter, so much had come hurtling back—terror, thrill, anger, love, my messy untamed devotion, but also a feeling of *what the fuck*. You didn't once ask how I was doing.

Responses to the weaning post rolled in quickly, some congratulatory, some stunned I had still been nursing Lark at his advanced age. There was one *gonna make him a boob man* comment, and someone with a peace sign for a profile picture said, *well you're a woman, not a cow.* They didn't matter in the face of all the nice comments, all the pretty little hearts. But then something from a photoless MamaCandy291: *Watch out for the weaning sads! Good luck, it totally fucked me up. You'll probably be fine. But if not. Godspeed.*

The weaning sads. What did she mean? Could it have something to do with the fact that since I'd cut off Lark's supply I'd been obsessively googling the statistical risk of a child dying from meningitis, a relatively rare disease that my children showed no current symptoms of? What about my newly heightened preoccupation with metal utensils and power sockets, my plans to replace all our silverware with bamboo sporks—my shock that I hadn't done this years ago! Maybe my mind *was* crazing in tighter circles than ever before, even for me. What were the fucking chances that the day I'd weaned, I'd also received your letter? Your letter had certainly shoved me into despair, but now on top of it I was also contending with the very real hormonal shift from weaning? Great. No one had told me this could happen. I knew about postpartum anxiety, but post *weaning*?

MamaCandy's profile was private. I went back to the photo to see if she'd added any details, but her original comment was gone. I tried to return to her profile, but it had become lost among the many MamaCandys of the world. I wondered briefly if the comment had been in my imagination, felt terrified by this notion.

I took a strong dose of magnesium but then fought through the relaxation it brought, googling *can you die from too much magnesium?* And as a new day announced itself through the blinds, I found myself in a much more dangerous place. The place I'd forbidden myself all these years. I'd arrived in the sordid world of our headlines, the many articles and message boards and photographs starring my father's death.

All along they'd lived just clicks away, version after version of our story, all unable, no, *unwilling,* to capture the truth. Beyond not wanting to allow the energy of the past in, this is why I'd never read about us: I knew my father would carry no blame and you would carry all of it. *A horrific tragedy. Father killed in cold blood. Woman murders innocent husband. Justice served—madwoman gets life in prison.*

I wiped my search history clean. Went downstairs and made a cup of tea, counting the minutes until the Portland Women's Clinic of Obstetrics and Midwifery opened. "What's the issue?" the scheduler asked.

"I'm having a bad reaction."

"To what?"

"To my father's murder."

"I'm sorry, you broke up," the voice said. I looked at my phone, saw the seconds ticking by on the call. I was really talking. I had really just said that. "Hello? You still there?"

"Weaning. Sorry. Weaning has become a problem. I think I'm allergic to it."

A small sigh wafted through the phone, the opposite of comfort. "I will write that down, but I don't think it's a clinical possibility."

"Listen," I pleaded. "It's an emergency."

CHAPTER 5

The news reported you shoved my father. In a swift, savage move, you heaved yourself at him hard enough to send him over the rail of our lanai and down thirty-three stories to an instant death. These details were accompanied by a photograph of my father looking like a 1970s Kenny Rogers, holding me as a chubby toddler. They said these things as if he'd been out there sipping an iced tea and you'd executed a premeditated lunge. Logistically nothing they said made sense. Did no one think to look into how a man as large as my father could be *thrown* by a much smaller person? Unless of course he was teetering on the ledge to begin with... They didn't know that was one of his favorite ways to torture you, keep you ever vigilant to the possibility that if you pissed him off enough, he'd jump. Of course, only after he'd sent you over first.

The high-rise itself was a method of my father's control, a constant threat that could be consummated at any moment. "A dark traveler comes over me, Alma," he'd say. You would position yourself a few feet away from him when he'd start in, erratically jumping up onto the ledge, back down, then up again. You had to be close enough to talk him down, but far enough away to be out of his reach. That concrete ledge, ten inches wide if I'm being generous. When we'd moved in, the landlord warned us that while it would be tempting, it was best not to line it with potted plants, that over the years too many had fallen during storms, narrowly missing pedestrians below. I imagined my father falling and what would happen to his body, to his veins and vessels, the solid mass of him having no choice but to liquefy on impact. "The only way to get rid of it..." he would say, sitting up there, one leg dangling off, looking out at the sea as if it held the answer. "The only way." And you would cry and beg, "Please get down, please come back inside, we love you, we need you." He said he dreamed all the time about leaping off. "You and your mother would love that, wouldn't you?" But with time, his dream evolved into all of us going over the edge together, a final end to our suffering. A final act of love.

The articles dismissed you as nothing but a waitress, but you held so many jobs. Full-time mother and manager of death. Yes, all the work we'd done to prevent death—mine, yours, and his for so many years—totally off page. When I was little you taped signs all over our apartment in my toddler sight line—red pen: CALL 911— and coached me to dial that number if things got really bad. No mention of that. And when I think how all you wanted was to go to adult school at night, take some writing classes. You can see, Mother, why it's easier to try to not think of you at all.

Then there was the most mysterious piece: the teenage daughter who disappeared the night of the incident. True crime message boards schemed that you were involved in my disappearance, a mother gone insane, killed her husband *and* child. I went missing without a trace, presumed dead, and, blessedly, eventually forgotten, it seemed, but for the few devotees who sporadically graced

YouTube with a "Whatever happened to Calla Lily?" speech, always with too much hunger in their eyes.

Mostly, though, the articles lingered over the *Do You Have Battered Men's Syndrome?* informational pamphlet that had been found in my father's glove box. *It doesn't just happen to women...*Then the narrative became a cautionary tale for men. Don't fall prey to a black widow. The pictures of you they chose for these stories were curious. Your face painted green on Halloween when I'd begged you to be a witch to my princess. Your tall black hat from the dollar store and a simple black shirt with a jack-o'-lantern on it, your hand curled up as if casting a spell. The one used most often was of you reading me a bedtime story. My floral pillowcase visible behind your head, but who was looking at that when there were your brown eyes, your thick lashes cast half down, presumably looking at a fairy tale. Your arm up shielding your face. You didn't like your photo taken. You felt ugly, embarrassed about bruises. But that time my father captured something in you just before you could object. On my screen now, so many years later, I'm startled by the simple clarity that we are, in this way, the same: we both need our mothers, and there's no way to relieve the need.

But most people probably looked at the photo and saw a sad, beautiful face. What privilege were you granted for your beauty? Your beauty made it easier for them to trample you.

No one reported that my father didn't believe you were in labor with me, so a neighbor drove you all the way to Fresno, the nearest city to our little mountain town, and dropped you off at the main door of St. Agnes Hospital. He'd kept you from going to your prenatal appointments, so you had no context for that place, no familiar doctor. Between contractions you called my father at the Barge, where you knew he would be. Told him you forgot your Anita

Baker tape and it was all you wanted, to hear Anita's voice while you swayed and shook and moaned. He swore he'd bring it but when he showed up he had no tape and you'd been cut in half, and I was nearly a day old. He was mean drunk and said, "That baby better look like me, you whore."

Welcome to the world, baby girl, a nice nurse had written on the dry-erase board on the door to our room.

You said those days recovering from your C-section were the most peaceful of your life. Us alone, nurses bringing you meals. The closest you ever got to a five-star resort. They refused to let my father see you after his display. They offered you a visit with a social worker. When she came, she asked if my father ever hurt you, if you felt safe at home. "Do you think he would harm the baby?"

You thought, here's my chance to escape. But you already believed there was no such thing as escape so long as you both were alive. And a new fear: what if they took your baby away from you? They would see you had nowhere to live other than with my father, no job beyond waitressing, and how could you do that anyhow with a newborn? If you told them how bad things really were, surely they would give me to a better couple. And where would that leave you? Alone with him again. At least now you weren't alone. You clutched me to your chest, the baby you hoped would change everything. Said, "He would never hurt us."

That wasn't the first time you lied for my father, but it was the first time your lie was written down, beginning years of documentation that would later be used to criminalize you. But before that, it bound us together in our secrets. From my first day on earth, I would serve as the primary witness to your pain.

The news did not report that my father had been beating you at regular intervals since you first started dating, since you were only nineteen. Your own mother had been beaten by your father and you swore it would never happen to you. You were sure you had learned from her. You resented her and you loved your father because you said that with him, even though there were awful times, he was able to come out of them and be lively and fun. Able to say he loved you. But your mother's depression was boundless, timeless, without end. He shut her down, it was his fault, yet you couldn't deny that when his attention turned to you, when he shone the face of love upon you, you lit up from within. You wound up being mad at your mother for getting knocked around, a great stupid irony. I think you told me this so I wouldn't come to resent you, so I wouldn't favor my father. So I'd be reminded what a monster he was, and so I'd never leave you.

You liked to tell me how my father never hit you in the stomach the whole nine months I was inside you. You said it like a love thing.

Before Hawai'i, we lived in the mountains above Fresno in a small beige apartment complex, The Pines, backdropped by a craggy hill full of skinny wild dogs that roamed the roads at night. Mainly miners up in that little town and the people who fed them, made them drinks, slept with them. You tended bar. You spotted him one night, he was fresh. His skin still looked clean. You locked eyes, and then he came for you. He was older, had a string of crazy exes. A reputation as a lady-killer. You did coke all night together and the next day you were an item. When a mine collapsed on him, crushing his ribs and nearly killing him, he told you he'd had a vision—that it was to be you and him forever, and a blond baby girl. You were already pregnant with me but didn't know it yet. "I couldn't go through with leaving him once you were in the picture," you'd say, wistful, looking into the mirror as you applied your Wild Orchid. "I couldn't deprive him of fatherhood."

Around the time I was ten, my father's buddy Cuddles convinced him to take up work in Hawai'i on a major interstate tunnel project in the Ko'olau mountains. My father was math-minded, could become an inspector if he worked his way up, could leave Central California for the first time. Cuddles wrote my father letters about his new life in a Waikiki high-rise apartment with his wife, Sugarcookie, how they loved the views of the ocean, boy did they. Even sent a photo of him and Cookie posing on their lanai, all blue behind. "Come on, SD!" the back of the picture said. SD was what the miners called my father, but those were not his proper initials. It stood for Spider Dick. "I hate that tattoo on him," you said. "Right on his ween. Can you believe it? Anyway, don't repeat that, or everyone'll think your daddy is some kinda freak."

I didn't repeat it. For a long time, I did just what you said.

I remember eyeing that photo of Cookie and Cuddles. They did look happy, their hands raised making a sign I didn't recognize. "What's this mean?" I asked you.

"If it's not a thumbs-up or the bird, I have no idea."

"Hang loose," my father said. "That's what everyone does there." He held his pinky and thumb up, shaking his wrist back and forth. I did it back and he tapped me lovingly on the nose. I watched you take us in and instinctively moved away from him. I knew you collected these happy images to later use as reasons for why we couldn't leave.

But maybe with Hawai'i on the horizon my father would learn to hang loose, adopt a laid-back lifestyle of no more wife beating. Things had gotten worse lately. He'd begun keeping you inside. Not letting you go to your waitressing job. Convinced you were sleeping with mountain men, men at the gas station, men he made up, men in his dreams. He covered your body in dark blooming roses. You coughed blood in the morning. But in Hawai'i. Things would have to be different in a place that beautiful.

Once the transfer was confirmed, you became obsessed with ground-level dwellings, my father obsessed with views. The higher the better, he told HR, just like the place they set Cuddles up in. You called them back after he'd gone to celebrate at the bar and asked, and then begged, not to be put up in a high-rise. You blamed it on having a child. "Haven't you heard 'Tears in Heaven'? Clapton's son fell out of a window. It can happen to the best of us."

On a ground floor, you told me, a gurney could be wheeled in with ease, and on a ground floor there would be foot traffic outside, people to hear you scream. Reasons to not fight. Proximity to what you called the *public influence*. As if being in public would safeguard us from him. There was certainly not enough public influence in the mountains, yet we considered it before any outing with my father. What was the level of public influence that time of day at the lake? The diner? You were convinced my father was possessed by a demon. That his violence wasn't him. He approved of this idea too, that his violence was something outside of him, something we all needed to take part in combating. He even agreed to go to a healer before we departed for Hawai'i to rid him of his dark traveler, leave it behind in California.

We waited for him outside the healer's trailer, straining to hear what was happening. You cast long glances at me every few minutes, holding up crossed fingers. A few times I thought I heard my father release a sob. We'd worn clean sundresses for this blessed day of his transformation, and you allowed me a little of your lipstick. If things went well, you told me, we'd go out for Mexican food in

Fresno. I could have an horchata. You'd heard of something called fried ice cream.

But he came out snarling. "Another woman and her bullshit." You followed him to the car with your kicked-dog gait, but I stayed glued to the trailer. What if I simply didn't follow? Could I move in with the healer? Could I forget you? Leave you alone with him? Maybe you wouldn't notice I wasn't in the car and you'd drive away without me.

The healer woman looked warily out of her little window. She didn't see me, didn't save me. Her eyes locked instead on my father's car. She touched her fingers to her temple and closed her eyes. Offering a curse, a blessing?

Wherever I was, I felt alone. I still feel this way now, as if the things I've seen have created a barrier between me and the living world, and there is nothing I can ever do, no supplement I can take, no inner-child meditation strong enough, deep enough, to remove it. Though I keep trying. But that day, I gave up and got in the car. My father opened the glove box and took out his handgun, held it to his head. "You want me to do it? You probably want me to do it, Alma." This went on for a while, you pleading with him to put the gun away, me lying on the floorboard of the back seat like you'd taught me to do. Finally he put it on his lap and tore down small roads home.

"What happened?" I'd asked you later that night after he'd fled to the Barge to drink.

"Well, clearly," you said, nursing a new wound on your face, "that healer was a fraud." You stayed in bed for days after that and my father took to calmly packing our things. "Hawai'i," he kept offering as I watched him bubble wrap the cheap dishes he normally threw. "In Hawai'i it will be different."

The first time we walked into the thirty-third-floor unit at the Lani Apartments I expected the clouds to drift in through our window. You paced the new rooms, said, "I'm seasick this high up."

"No," I corrected you, my eyes trying to make sense of the impossible blue view. "You're skysick."

It was a simple apartment, stuck in the seventies with worn shag carpet, spots of dried candle wax in the fibers. My father loved it. He smoked a cigarette on the lanai, leaning against the waist-high railing overlooking the sea like in Cuddles' photo, unaffected by the height that made our insides churn. He kept kissing you on the top of your head, the sins of California forgotten. Played the same song over and over as he worked his way through two six-packs. *Don't tell my heart, my achy breaky heart*...turning it up and swinging me around the room. He was smiling so big I could see the glint of his gold back teeth when he said, "This is heaven."

Even you couldn't hide it—despite the high-rise, you were hopeful.

On the day of my father's first shift you told him we would stay in and clean, but he was feeling jovial and said we could explore a bit if we wanted. You already had a job interview lined up the next day at Marie Callender's, where you said, if hired, you'd be eligible for one free pie a week. My father didn't want you to work, of course, but since he routinely unloaded full paychecks at the bar, we needed everything we could get. Daytime work at what he called the old folks' home seemed like a low threat level and something you could do while I was at school. I could barely process my thrill over exotic key limes, banana creams, lemon meringues, this enchanting new place, and now the unexpected option to *explore.*

He looked to me and said, "Keep an eye on your mother." It was then a shift occurred, slight but felt: in Hawai'i he saw me differently. Perhaps as a peer, a newly solid leg on our dysfunctional chair. In the moment, I took it as a good thing.

The beach, the beach, I begged you, but you said it was more important to begin our public influence work, walk the halls of each story to meet neighbors. If they knew us, maybe later they would feel compelled to call for help if something happened. And if we got lucky, you told me, there might be another woman nearby who could really be on our side if things got ugly.

"Let's hope for a single mother," you said. We held hands like we often did when my father wasn't around.

"Why a single mother?" I asked.

"Part of the reason things got so bad in California was because there weren't enough mothers around. Mothers without husbands in the way understand things differently. They can move mountains."

Sugarcookie was in a different high-rise building down the street and that was just as well. "I'm not saying all miners' wives are stupid." You gestured to yourself. "But that one. Well, there's no helping her." I loved when you talked like this. Around my father it was best that you stayed quiet, agreeable, and neutral to all things, ready to align with what he thought on a particular topic. But when we were alone I could see the real you, all your feist and humor and cunning. The spark of who you might have been if not for him. The things that probably made him love you to begin with.

We took one more look around the thirty-second floor and were heading toward the staircase to try thirty-one when a woman came out of her apartment. You nudged my ribs. "Go," you whispered. I skipped toward her in my purple terry-cloth dress. "Hi!" I said. "My name's Calla Lily. What's yours?"

You caught up to me, feigning breathless apology. "Oh gosh, she's so social. Didn't mean to bother you." You introduced us, explained we'd just arrived from California and knew no one. The woman was petite, wore an ankle-length sack with fluttering sleeves. Perfect posture. Thin dark hair cut in a sharp line at her shoulders with close-cropped bangs. When I looked at her I thought *illness*. She took you in, your California bruises, which had faded to yellow by then, the one on your cheek nearly invisible, but I could tell she clocked it. She glanced nervously from her door to the elevator as you spoke.

"She'll be up from her nap soon," she said. "I've got to get this shopping done."

"Oh, a baby?" you said.

"Might as well be." She looked at me. "But no. She's probably around your age, actually. How old are you?"

I hadn't had many friends in the mountains. Wasn't allowed over to anyone's house to play after school because my father was convinced there were *too many nuts in this world*. And no one was allowed at our house on account of him also being a nut. But in Hawai'i he said if I was good, I could have more freedom. The idea of another girl my age below us thrilled me. A place to go, to hide, a person to weigh the world with. "Ten," I told her.

"Oh, my daughter is ten too. Nearly eleven. But she's not healthy like you. Caring for her is the one job Goddess has bestowed upon me, and I am bent on doing it right."

"What's wrong with her?" I asked. *Who is Goddess?* I also wondered, but I'd save that for another time.

The woman braced herself like she'd been caught in a strong wind. "Well. That's a very personal question."

"I'm so sorry—" you started, but she went ahead.

"She's a very sick child. Immune compromised and born with a very rare—I mean verrrrry rare—disease that produces internal lesions that have disrupted nearly every normal functioning of her vital organs."

You put a hand on your heart. "Oh, poor thing."

"And what about me? My life, every second. The responsibility."

"No mother should have to watch her baby struggle," you said. "I cannot imagine what you've been through. You're certainly an angel."

The woman relaxed a little. Reached out and grasped your arm. You put your hand over hers and patted it. She was shorter than you, peered up into your gaze. "See," she said. "You understand what we women are up against."

I didn't like the intensity that was building. I just wanted to go to the beach with another kid, damn.

"Can she play?" I interjected. How sick could she really be? I was going to have a friend. I'd already decided.

"Honey," you said to me. "We don't even know this nice woman's name. Sorry, Calla Lily has a lot of energy."

The woman took me in. "I'm Christina," she said finally. "Any recent viruses?"

"I don't get sick," I said, and it was sort of true, I realized. Who had time to get sick around you and my father?

You stood in thrall to this new woman. She was tense and abrupt but—I think you felt it then too—we shared a similar marrow. I could feel her daughter reaching out to me from behind the door. We had all glimpsed death yet walked among the living.

Christina smiled, revealing purple-tinted teeth. She pulled out a Tupperware of dark liquid from her shopping basket, shook it, and then took a long drink. You hadn't had a drink since we'd landed on the island, a promise you'd made to me, that you would stay clearheaded and vigilant. You eyed the liquid. I prayed it wasn't wine, that this woman wasn't a drunk.

"Grape juice," she said to my stare. "I just love it. I can't get enough. Gives me the bump I need to caretake."

"Well, we all need a little boost every now and then," you said.

"You got a man?" Christina asked. "Pretty woman like you, I bet the answer's yes. No one would leave you single for long. And you!" She grabbed my chin with her clammy hand. "You look like someone, but it isn't your mama. You must look like daddy. Bet he's a looker. But the real question is," she said, glancing back at her door again, "is he a good one? A good one's rare. Impossible almost. Most women are sleeping with the enemy. So is he? A good one?"

She looked to me for some reason. I turned to you. I didn't want to ruin the moment. "No," you said. You smiled bravely. "He's not."

Christina became your best friend after that. And her daughter, the girl behind the door, became mine.

CHAPTER 6

I sat on the exam table at the midwifery clinic and explained my emergency to the woman who had once pushed aside my cervical lip when I was stuck at eight centimeters with Nova, the woman who had held up baby Lark in his first seconds of life and deemed his skin "dusky" and put him on oxygen because he'd inhaled meconium. Had patted my back as I'd cried for you, contracting.

I spoke in my own private code, keeping things focused on my physical body, hoping she might decipher what I really meant, which was that the bottled rage that lived in my chest for every man who beat or killed a woman and got away with it had finally burst its container. Not even my father had received proper punishment, despite the fact that he was killed. And was he *killed*? I guess that's the question that needs re-answering.

But killed or not, I don't believe as he fell my father thought, *What have I done?* but rather, *What did she?*

The midwife settled into the role of the passive listener as I described my newly intrusive thoughts, my sleepless nights, my heightened fear of accidental poisoning and disease. How only the night before I'd taken all the knives from their stand on the counter and pushed them to the back of drawers. "Low-hanging fruit," I'd explained to my husband when he caught me.

"For who?" he'd asked.

"Your optimism is a huge liability."

You knew to keep knives tucked away, to never hang heavy decorations my father might grab off the wall. You taped foam to the corners of our tables as if we had a perpetual toddler running around prone to head bonks. We had a whole system of potential safety, and since reading your letter that system had come back to me. How much sense it made to protect oneself from violence. From oneself.

I didn't mention this to the midwife.

"Sounds like you have death goggles on," she said. "I see it a lot postpartum, you know, the bringing forth of a life being inextricable from the fact that the life will someday end. You really give birth to little ticking time bombs, right?"

"The goggles still apply post weaning?" I asked.

"The goggles are always there, we just trick ourselves into believing that we aren't wearing them." She spoke with a casual airiness that was beginning to annoy me.

"The thing is, it's a bad time for my body to be doing this," I said. "I have a lot going on and really need to focus. How can I make it stop? Take the metaphoric goggles off. I mean, not everyone wears them all the time. So. Must be something I can do." *Tell me the right fucking herbs.* I didn't mention that before I'd come to the appointment I'd tried to see if Lark wanted to resume nursing. We could go back to it for six months, get those stabilizing hormones pumping again, and then I'd wean once everything had settled down. But no dice. Seemingly overnight he'd attached to his new big-kid cup, and Nova had taught him to pour milk from the refrigerator into it.

The midwife crossed her arms. "Maybe you're overthinking it. Our bodies do wacky things all the time."

I thought of *Wacky Wednesday,* a book I'd read no less than one thousand times to my children, imagining that instead of the child waking up to find shoes on walls, they were confronted with me, the mother, Nonnies on my back, one coming out of my forehead while I feverishly hid the household sharps. *Close your eyes and Wacky Wednesday will soon go away.*

"Wacky things?"

"Sure, your body is changing every second. That means it can become out of balance and then regain balance. You might try herbs."

"Yes! I've been thinking herbs are definitely the answer. But which ones, you know? There's so many."

"Hmm," she said. "Maybe there are some teas you could try. Chamomile?"

Surely she was joking. "I'm a little beyond chamomile."

"Beyond chamomile? It's a wonderful tea."

"I was thinking more along the lines of, say, the herbal version of Valium. Or something."

She clicked around on her computer, hopefully looking for a way to redeem herself from chamomile.

"Maybe you can put some specific stuff to try in my chart," I encouraged her. "You know, links."

She stopped her clicking. "Have you tried ancient Chinese medicine?"

"I need something I can take that will make me feel better, like, right away."

"How about a low dose of Xanax?"

"I can't entertain that level of intervention when magnesium is freaking me out. Like, I'm scared of taking too hot a bath and passing out and drowning."

She stood up from her stool. "Maybe try to have more orgasms. Find ways to love bomb yourself."

Love bomb. I knew the term from somewhere else. *Stay in the moment, Clove.* I took a deep, bitchy breath. "Don't you see this in your practice? Don't other women come in here asking what the hell happened? The milk runs dry and they lose their shit? They start remembering things from childhood, things that don't matter at all anymore?" *And in a stroke of truly malevolent timing they get a letter from their mother after years and years of silence threatening to upend their entire life as they know it?*

"We don't usually see women much beyond their six-week appointment. I actually assumed you were coming in because you were pregnant again."

"Don't you think it would be worth following up with new moms, say, two years down the line, to make sure they aren't wandering by the highway pushing an empty stroller?"

Now she was annoyed. "What sorts of childhood things do you mean?" she asked. "We have a few more minutes if you'd like to spend them on that."

Out the window behind her, a tree. I tried to focus on it, but its lush leaves melted into a green blob. I thought of Christina, how not only her teeth but her skin, too, had a purple tint from all that grape juice. How we fell almost immediately into an unspoken routine, coming down a floor to visit Christina and her daughter, Celine, whenever my father was at work or out drinking. We kept a basket full of old clothes there in case we heard his footsteps above unexpectedly. We could just rush home, feign that we'd been in the laundry room.

"I named her after the greatest singer of all time," Christina had said when she'd introduced Celine to us, wheeling her out into the living room in her special chair. The chair was pink, even the hardware, and decorated with sparkling Lisa Frank fantasy animals.

"Whitney is the greatest," you'd countered, "but we're very happy to meet you."

Celine's skin had not seen sunlight for some time; she was nearly gray. But she perked up when she saw me. "Do you like *Jerry Springer*?" she asked, clicking the television on. I looked at you for permission, but you were already laughing, deep in a debate with Christina—Houston versus Dion—and I settled in front of the massive screen that took up most of the wall with this girl who was my age but seemed several years younger based on size alone. Her dreamy gaze floated over me, then back to the screen. "I'm gonna host this show one day," she said with solemn reverence, as if promising to cure the very disease that ailed her. A man who barely came up to Jerry's pelvis toppled a woman with fake breasts the size of honeydews. "Jerry will die a natural death and I'll take over."

"Do you have a lot of friends?" I'd asked like an idiot.

She looked at me and smiled. "You."

I'd never seen a truly sick child before. I saw it then, why she couldn't go to the beach. I stood. "I want something cold," I told her, feeling like I might suffocate. I already loved her, already felt the weight of her desire for talk-show-host stardom, the painful fact that she would likely never achieve it. In the kitchen I opened the freezer, which was full of frozen grape logs. There in the midwifery clinic I could almost hear Christina's wooden spoon hitting the side of her glass pitcher as she mixed a fresh batch of juice.

"How's your cycle?" the midwife asked, but I was still in Hawai'i, newly thirteen in Christina's bathroom, which looked exactly like our bathroom except in theirs everything was pink down to the cotton swabs, my first bleed showing up on the toilet paper as I wiped. I'd yelled, "It's here!" You and Christina crowded in the doorway, Celine in her chair crammed close behind. Christina advised me to only use pads so I could really inspect the quality of my blood for health, not to mention avoid the toxic shock of tampons, and you all watched as I pressed one into my underwear. The arrival of my blood warranted a chocolate cream pie from your Marie Callender's shift that night, but when, a few days later, Celine improbably started her period as well, Christina was enraged.

"If you're raped," she said as she paced her small galley kitchen, waving the mixing spoon around, "now you and Celine can get pregnant with your rapist's child. And at least *you* can try to defend yourself. But Celine would be done for. She should have never started her period. She's emaciated. She's on death's door and now she can be raped and carry life?" She looked up at the ceiling and scolded Goddess. "You just keep hitting me with challenges, don't you?"

You tried to comfort Christina, said, "But isn't it a good sign she's bleeding? Maybe her body is getting better?"

"She isn't getting better," Christina snapped. "It's a miracle she's been alive this long. Don't you see that? Medical studies are done on men's bodies. What do they know about her? I'm alone in this, Alma." Christina swung her face at me. "No one believes women. They don't believe you if you say you're sick, they don't believe you if you say you've been raped. Hell, look at your mother." She gripped my shoulder. "I've seen police come and go. You think they can't see what your scumbag father does to her? And nothing! You can have the bruises all over you and they'll say, 'Must have

74

done something to provoke him.' And now Celine is going to be treated like all the rest. She'll get little tits and then when I take her to the doctor, he can feel those up too."

"Oh, for god's sake," you said. "You're terrifying them. Girls, you are perfectly fine."

"Perfectly fine," Christina repeated in a high-pitched, mocking voice. She was often fired up, drilling into our heads that our main job as women was to fight the systems that held us down, but after we got our periods the lectures intensified; at the same time, some new awareness of an incoming womanhood of our own sparked within us. Celine and I began trading notes in a spiral-bound notebook: musings about our mothers, the many things wrong with them, and our vows to one day be different. I wondered if being a feminist meant I would end up like Christina, trapped in a high-rise in the most beautiful place in the world, the curtains drawn against the postcard view, and Celine wondered if it meant she would end up like you, beautiful, broken, a monument to lost potential. I would scribble in the notebook that I didn't think you were a real feminist, otherwise you would leave my father, but Celine took a different view. She thought there was something valiant in your refusal to give up on him. Something romantic about it, brave, which incensed me.

Christina went on, and you reached over and held Celine's hand, not mine. At some point, someone muted the rational voice of Jerry Springer and that day's oil-wrestling bimbos, their bodies slipping and sliding silently around an inflated ring, fighting for their man.

"You are the last person these girls should listen to," Christina snarled. "You, a woman who has squandered her beauty, her talent, her own daughter—everything in service to that man you claim to love. You don't love him, though. You love being a victim."

Celine wiped away tears. I worried this meant we would no longer be able to come over, would lose our secret clubhouse that my father knew nothing about. But after that day, things deepened between the four of us, and while this would become a typical weekly argument, Christina berating you and you mostly taking it—"I know, I'm sick, too," you would say—it was a relief to have everything out on the table. Things were getting worse with my father, but the edge of new possibility had taken hold of me—I was changing, and you were staying the same.

Christina and I began to talk about you when we were alone, Celine napping, you at Marie Callender's. I'd tell her the things he did to you and how you would excuse it all away. Blame yourself: "I shouldn't have said that, I'm always pressing his buttons." How sometimes it seemed you *would* press his buttons, turn sullen just as he was turning fun, get too drunk, say, "Go ahead, hit me." My father bemoaned your alcoholic ways and accused you of breaking up our family with your drinking while actively thwarting your attempts at sobriety. Every time the cops came, sure enough, you'd have booze on your breath, and nothing, nothing was worse than a drunk mother. In this way, there was record upon record of you disturbing the peace and of my father trying to help. "Alcoholism is an ugly disease," he'd say to the officers apologetically. If I ever tried to interrupt, you would tell them I was a liar. But Christina listened to me. Believed me. For the first time, someone saw our life the way I did, and put language to it.

In the notebook Celine wrote that your biggest problem was that you just wanted to be loved. But that couldn't be it. I loved you.

"Clove?" the midwife said.

I blinked, tried to focus on her round glasses. "Everyone has

stuff," I said. "Hard things, *trauma,* or whatever. Everyone is traumatized. I'm not special."

"I don't consider myself traumatized, actually," she said softly.
"And I know plenty of people who wouldn't necessarily describe
themselves that way."

"What would they say — 'mother, sister, wife, warrior'? Look, I
was fine before this. I just want my hormones balanced again."

"You could ask lactation about these issues. They're the experts
on breastfeeding. It's a whole world unto itself."

"Don't you want to take my blood? Check vitamin levels?"

"Your primary can do that during your annual checkup."

"But I'm here now. And alone, a rare treat."

But she was already on to the next. Tears threatened me. She
was a midwife. If she couldn't help me, what hope was there?

A nanny would help, I could hear my husband saying.

"Do you want to talk to our social worker?"

"Can she get me past chamomile?"

"She's not really versed in Eastern medicine —"

I cut her off. "You know, you did a real shitty job sewing me
up." I gestured to my crotch. She pressed her palm to her chest and
leaned back. Maybe she thought herself a supreme labial architect,
but I was here to tell her she was mediocre at best.

I walked out. Perhaps I stormed. This was not my usual way.
I was a smiler, an easygoing gal, a helper, and a stuffer. A good
wife and mommy. But your letter had awakened something in me.
The waiting room was full of women coming down the production line. Look at them, oh to be them. To think I knew what I
was talking about again. To think I could fathom all that having
children would mean, what it would provoke. How many of them,

like me, thought being a mother would repair something? Prevent something.

"Watch out for weaning," I announced to the room. Some glanced up. "They don't know shit about it in there, but maybe someone does. Start looking now." A sign on the wall said TELL YOUR DOCTOR IF YOU ARE NOT FEELING LIKE YOURSELF AFTER HAVING A BABY...What an idiotic sign.

I saw you sitting in a chair in the waiting room, young and pregnant with me. Scared but happy. You said despite every bad thing about being with my father, you were so happy to be having a baby.

I slapped the sign and you disappeared, replaced by a woman who was not you, her large hard belly pinning her to the chair. "Don't ruin it for us," she said. The other mothers looked at their phones.

In the car I closed my eyes and there was my father's dead body. I never saw his remains. Though it dawned on me now there were pictures somewhere in a file. That you must have had to look at them in the courtroom. I'm sorry I wasn't with you for that.

I searched *post-weaning anxiety* on my phone and scanned the screen for help, but all that came up was an ad for flower essences in mystical green glass bottles made in small batches by a onetime famous movie star in Sweden. Energetic medicine. I ordered one called *Release* via the credit card I had vowed not to use again.

Likely therapy could help, but therapy involved too much honesty, and frankly at this point, too much time. *You have the summer and no more.* By law therapists were supposed to keep secrets, but my particular secrets went beyond the scope of doctor-patient confidentiality. I had tried energetic healers, psychics, and tarot readers, who all more or less had the same feedback. I was very, very blocked. I was carrying a lot of "not me" energy. One said simply, "Your parents…not good." I left promptly after that, concerned she would pull too much from me. It was best to keep focused on the health of the body. Safer, and still a viable path to healing if it was true that everything was connected.

I could not let myself succumb to depression like you had, Mother, and like your mother had before you. You would retreat to your bed for days at a time, and even my father would not rile you, respecting something about your own demon when he saw it, taking me to Colonel Sanders, the only one on the island, for a bucket of fried chicken.

"Your mother's sad," he would say.

Because of you, I did not say. The key to peace between my father and me was to pretend he was not the source of our pain. I counted myself lucky that he only shoved me if I stood in his way to get to you. I'd play along when he'd call women crazy, as if I was not also a woman.

Not also crazy. I *was* a different person than you—look at this life I had created. Sure, I had not been spared a short bout of what I could now see as postpartum anxiety after having Nova, where I could not sleep more than one hour at a time and I had the urge to keep moving, walking miles and miles, stroller and carrier and stocked diaper bag in tow. Nova would nap on my chest while I walked and chugged water and drowned out the past with podcasts about meditation or manifestation or crystals or plant-based lifestyles. Solid weeks devoted to learning about food sensitivities and diagnosing myself with them, throwing myself into the work of elimination, of achieving systemic purity. The voices of the podcasts were what I needed so I could not hear my own voice, which was telling me only terrifying things, telling me insane things like maybe my newborn had swallowed a coin from my purse, even though I had no coins in my purse, even though I had not taken my eyes off her for one second, unless you counted when I ordered my tea at the tea place, and maybe it had happened then. Around five p.m. I would walk us home, drenched in sweat, lay out unrelated items from the fridge on the table, and my husband and I would eat them, or maybe just share a bowl of cold grapes, my skin crawling with nerves. Some nights he would leave and come back with fried pickles from the place down the street and Nova would sleep and for a few minutes I could imagine we were still intact, that we were not parents.

At my Friday new moms group I'd held my floppy-bodied Nova close to my chest and described a light version of the fear I was having, and a woman propping up a moist-looking baby with a shock of red hair and mean eyes turned to me and said, "Some moms drive off the road if they don't get that shit figured out." She had paused and sort of nodded at the circle of stunned-mother faces. Added for good measure: "With their babies in the car."

After that, I stopped going to the new moms group and began to meet up with more *like-minded mamas* I found on Facebook when that was still a thing, who centered yoga and clean eating and mushroom coffee as a means to keep us *elevated,* aka sane. Forget 3D consciousness when we were ascending to 5D. We arrived at each meeting with thermoses of steaming bone broth. It was all about remineralization. We didn't need to delve deep into our psyches when we could fill our nurseries with rose quartz and black tourmaline, salt the corners of each room. And while my husband may have cocked an eyebrow at the many bubble-wrapped crystals coming into the house, the decks of intention cards, the angel cards, the tarot cards, the archetype cards, he was happy I was happy. He liked looking in on me holding Nova in the rocker. Once, he stood in the doorway, stared a while. "You're a natural," he said, and I realized I'd yet to receive a real compliment before that moment.

But I was no natural. I had not ascended for shit. As I drove home from the clinic my mind fixated on the bottle of ibuprofen we stored in the top cabinet. How the week before, Lark had climbed up on the counter to pull down the "sick supplies" and play with the thermometers, shaking the bottle of pills to make music. I had simply put the supplies away again, but not before giving the bottle a silly shake myself, making him laugh. Had I somehow communicated it was fine for him to play with ibuprofen? What if he ate it like candy and died before I could get home? What if he ate it and then wandered into his room and passed out on the floor? And my husband would be like, *Oh, he's so tired,* and close the door. Maybe all of this had already happened, and my husband was too distraught to call me. An ambulance would be waiting in the driveway. *Stop. Stop, Clove.* But there was a price to pay for each moment alone, wasn't there?

I raced inside to find Lark and Nova with their father playing on the living room floor. I went to the kitchen without saying hello and threw all the anti-inflammatories away. And vitamins were lethal in high doses, iron overdose being the leading cause of children's death, so what were we playing at having delicious children's gummy multivitamins shaped like bears right in our cabinets? Trash.

"Everyone's okay, right?" I asked them. They blinked up at me. Fine to the naked eye, but who knew? Swallowing a button cell battery is fatal within two hours. *Two.* By the time you realized they had swallowed it, if you ever did, it was too late.

"I gotta go back to work," I heard my husband say, but I was already down the hall, snapping up all those annoying books with button cell battery audio voices in them from their rooms. The talking doll, goodbye. How dare the world make toys with lethal weapons inside?

My husband watched as I shoved things into a big dumpster bag. Packages of dried seaweed were so clearly the enemy, those moisture-absorbing sachets waiting to be gnawed on, and who could trust the meager offering on the packet that said *harmless*. No one cared about the mortality of my children, not a soul, except me. No one cared about protecting them like I did. These were the things I could control. The only things, because of course I could not control what was coming, what you'd set in motion, Mother, with this feminist lawyer—whom I felt like strangling, by the way—not to add violence to violence—but really, I was feeling some things, some anger. I was angry.

"Button cell," I said to my husband, whose mouth hung open as I threw away a Polly Pocket. It made a splashing noise when Polly jumped off the diving board.

A Polly I would have died to have as a child. In Hawai'i I was allowed to scour the bins at the Goodwill warehouse Saturday mornings if my father was working. We would leave grimy-armed, you gushing about the vintage designer items you'd found but never purchased. Before my father, you loved fashion magazines. You were taking classes at the city college in theater and writing. You really liked to write, you said. You thought maybe you would write for those fashion magazines you loved, but who were you kidding? Not everyone finds their way.

If you came home with something new, even something basic—a new white T-shirt—my father would accuse you of dressing up for other men. But in those Goodwill dressing rooms, which weren't rooms at all but an open space with no dividers, we would enter our own fashion show. I zipped tight dresses up your back, watched you wriggle into vintage Guess, cropped tops that showed your tanned and toned stomach that was never full of food, always too nervous or too hungover to eat. The employees knew us. They watched and commented on your beauty. You would come alive and I would sink into my own hungry sadness, my vision of the life you could have had if you had not met my father. I saw it all so clearly, but you no longer could. Your drinking put it all at a swimmy distance.

"I have nowhere to wear any of this," you'd say to whoever was working. "But why not?" and you'd carry the bundle out, pretending to be on your way to the register. Then you'd look around before dropping it all back in the bins. From there we'd survey the toys, but by then you'd have mentally departed, all the clothes you'd put back reminding you that a drink would soon be needed. You'd rush me. "Pick something already." Safety was far from your mind; it only mattered that I find something we could lie about, say we discovered at the beach, tourist droppings.

I felt my husband's arms around me now, heard my children screaming and crying for their toys. The present moment rushed in. "It's okay, it's okay. We'll get new, safer toys. I'm so sorry Mommy didn't catch these before."

"Did the midwife tell you to do this?" my husband whispered.

"The midwife does not give a fuck."

"I believe you once said a midwife should be president. Are you okay?"

I wondered how many times this man would ask this same question before he 5150'd me. His arms closed tight, but not in an embrace. He was stopping me. He had taken the garbage bag away, I realized, but I wasn't done. I needed to stay in motion. We were safe right now, but what about in five minutes?

"Maybe you need to take a walk," he said, looking at the kids as they stared on, then warily back at me.

I broke free and snatched the bag from his hands. "Don't you ever hold my arms down like that."

"Are you kidding me?" he said.

"I will leave you so fast. I will take them so far away you'll never be able to find us."

He stepped backward like I was pointing a gun at him. My father had once pointed a shotgun in my face. He was half asleep and drunk, caught up in his nightly visit to Vietnam. He banged on the door a few times; I'd said to wait. I was inspecting my changing body with a laser focus, was that a new hair? Was one tiny breast-lette larger than the other? Was this the clitoris I'd seen in the health class diagram? When I finally emerged, there he was with that gun, ready. Later, in place of an apology, he said he thought I was an intruder, that he was protecting us. In any case, I know what it's like to look down two barrels and see the end. My husband and children did not.

Lark cried for his toys in his father's arms. I put my shoes on and Nova cast a cold stare my way. My kids now hated me, but at least they were alive. Okay, outside. Big breath. I shoved the bag in the trash bin. When I closed the lid on all that wreckage, I heard it. A clock ticking, unmistakable. I sped down the sidewalk as fast as I could go without peeing myself; move or die, like before. But this moving was different; I had no baby in an Ergo. Now it would be a lone rove. And a distinct thought rose to greet me: I could really get myself into trouble.

CHAPTER 7

Now for what you don't know, Mother. The part after my father fell. The part where you could do nothing but scream, when you ran senselessly into that elevator, down thirty-three floors to the ground where he lay. And for the first time, I didn't follow.

I bought a red-eye ticket to San Francisco instead. Told the clerk I was an unaccompanied minor. Showed a paper with a supposed signature of permission. The clerk seemed weary. Looked a long time at Celine's social security card and birth certificate. Because I was her now. That's how it had to be. Her name wasn't too far from my actual name, Calla Lily, a name you insisted on never abbreviating. Something you'd gotten from a film called *Stage Door* with Katharine Hepburn you'd watched in a film class at that community college. "Your father made me drop out of school," you told me. "But I get to remember it every time I say your name. Our secret."

The line grew longer behind me. The clerk looked at every traveler with disdain, informed a passing fellow employee it would be her break soon. "I dream of dinner," she said to me, or maybe to herself. "Take it now," the other employee said. She looked me over one more time. Lifted her shoulders in a tiny shrug, *life*. "It's cold where you're going," she said. But I was already on my way, streaming through the airport, astonished at each turn that no one was stopping me. Not even when the news started showing scenes of police cars swarming our high-rise, then gave way to the first photo they would use of my father's face, a friendly-looking smile from his company ID. I can't describe to you the feeling of being in that airport filled with Kona coffee for sale, grass skirts with coconut bras, boxes of chocolate-covered macadamia nuts, the same stands we'd walked past together when I was ten, thinking this was our clean slate, this was our new life, and how my father bought fresh flower leis and placed them around our necks. Heartbreaking, the way he had also bought himself a lei, as if it would protect him from himself. I kept my head down past the stalls this time. Imagine, Mother, your teenage daughter alone, trying to find that gate number.

Christina had been right. This was my only chance to leave, when the facts were still coalescing, when I wasn't technically missing yet. No alarm went off as the plane accelerated and no one paid me any mind aside from the sunburned man next to me, who emitted a fecal smell and asked if I wanted a Cuba libre. The man on my other side in a bad suit finished his magazine and then donned a sleep mask. I pretended to be asleep as the sunburned man rested a hand on my knee, lifting it every time the attendant walked by, then resting it again. You weren't around anymore to excuse the behavior of men, to soften it, talk it away. I knew as I picked up the ballpoint pen from bad suit's tray and turned to the sunburn, held the pointed end against his neck and whispered, "Don't fuck with me," that we were in fact quite different from each other.

★ ★ ★

San Francisco was Christina's idea. She had written down an address on Bessie Street, just south of the Mission, in Bernal Heights. *Maternal Bernal* she'd called it. "Lots of lesbians with big dogs. You'll be fine." It was the house of a woman she'd once known, who she thought might be able to take me in. Christina had grown up in San Francisco and had escaped her home to live with this woman during what she called her *hell summer* as a teenage girl. Christina had told me many stories from her life and I doubted they could all be true. But here was an address. A place she'd really been. She said her shitty childhood was why she wanted the opposite for Celine. It was why she clung so closely to her. Cared so very much.

I had your Marie Callender's tips in your fanny pack. Almost five hundred dollars in ones and fives and tens. I didn't feel bad taking it. I earned it.

Christina had told me that from the airport I should use BART and get off at Twenty-Fourth and Mission. Walk the rest of the way. To ask someone how it worked if I got confused, but how could I ask anyone when my face was now quite literally on most of the television screens as I walked through the airport. Christina had given me a pair of large sunglasses to wear and a straw hat, but the hat looked wrong so far from the island now. I threw it away and felt thankful that the girl in the photo they were using was sea swept and vibrant, long wavy hair, pale blue eyes still young. I would never look that way again after what I'd seen just hours before. And the mirror in the airport bathroom confirmed it: at some point during the flight it seemed my eyes had shifted from light aquamarine to the deep-sea blue of my father's. I knew then I had not come alone across that ocean. My father's traveler was with me.

The morning outside was cold, as I'd been warned, and hazy

with fog. Taxis streamed by. I was intimidated by the train, had no idea how to use it. I watched a man in a plaid suit lift his hand up to flag a yellow car and get in, speeding off into the mist. I copied him, surprised when almost immediately a taxi stopped in front of me. Surprised I was still a person people could see. I opened the door. My swimsuit cut into my skin underneath a pair of Christina's sweatpants and oversized sweatshirt. I looked like an inmate of sorts, in solid gray, except the sweatshirt said LIFE IS GOOD across the chest. I wore your flip-flops with the outline of your bunions etched in, sand still gritty between my toes. I fumbled through the fanny pack for something to do with my hands, and there, in the small pouch, was my father's gold signet necklace, the chain broken. You must have been carrying it around with the intent to get it fixed. Jewelry repair people could probably identify their domestic violence customers easily. Most people don't snap their jewelry by accident on a near monthly basis.

"You got money to pay for this?" the driver said. "I ain't going until I see you have money. I been put out too many times."

"I have money."

"Can't pay with that necklace, sweetheart."

I put it back in the pack and held up some of the cash. Good enough for him. He pulled away from the curb and the airport disappeared into the fog. He lit a vanilla Sweet Dream and his ash flew back, landed on my sweats, my face. My father smoked like it was his job in the front seat of the Jimmy. I had several little circular scars on my chest from his windblown cherries.

"Can you put that out?" I said.

The man turned in jags through narrow streets, finishing the Sweet Dream as if he hadn't heard me, and maybe he hadn't. Had I spoken aloud? I was so tired. I kept bracing and catching my breath, thinking we were about to hit pedestrians, so many people walking in the streets as if they believed they were invincible. We crested an impossible hill. I closed my eyes and entered a zone that would come to be familiar in the following weeks, the floating place of the undecided spirit, prompting me to choose: continue this human experience or end it. Surely not all lives were worth living. Surely not mine, ruined so young.

When I looked up, we were on a street called Valencia. My father was dead and you were in the trap of whatever would happen next to a woman found over the remains of her husband's body. How would you find me when they released you? In that moment, I assumed they would in fact release you. But I remembered what Christina told me when I'd showed up at her apartment stunned and shaking, as I explained my father was dead. Celine was asleep down the hall and Christina sat me down at her kitchen table, poured me a glass of grape juice I did not touch. She was silent. Then finally, I saw something coalesce in her mind. "Start over," she said. "Forget your mother. Give yourself a chance." She laid out the plan, handed over her daughter's documents. "Most importantly," she said, "don't waste Celine's life."

How can I leave my mother? I'd almost asked, but there was no time. As I walked out of her apartment, I knew Christina had schooled me all those years in preparation for just this moment, when I would be given the chance at a life of my own, and be able to claim it.

The taxi stopped in front of a row of houses in vibrant colors and trims. I'd never seen houses like this, pressed right up against one another, tiny steep driveways and wrought-iron gates in front of the doors. I got out, just me and the fanny pack. I don't remember how much I paid the man, but I handed over some bills and he left. Down the street: a grassy park, an Italian market, a coffee shop. My father said his mother took him to Pier 39 once, let him eat clam chowder from a bread bowl, let him try a crabcake. His mother died when he was young, leaving him alone with his father. He didn't like to talk about his father. Still, their ghosts lived in his bones and in my bones.

I considered how I would kill myself. The little Italian market on the corner would have painkillers. I could take them all at the park and lie down in the tunnel slide. But then I pictured a child bumping into me with their feet. The mother with the child, and what she would have to do to explain it. How the child might be convinced the person in the slide was just sleeping, but every time the mother went to a park, she'd think of dead bodies in slides. Might even stop going to parks. I didn't want to shrink a woman's world. I did know that.

The door to the Bessie Street house opened and two teenage girls walked out link-armed, one very tall and one very short. They wore ripped black tights and safety pins everywhere and short pleated skirts with shiny stack-soled burgundy boots. Their hair was in shocks of bright platinum and ink. They stopped when they saw me, gave dirty looks to my dreary sweats.

"No way," the short one said. "There is no more fucking room in this madhouse."

The tall one stared with vacant eyes. I knew intuitively she would never commit to either living or dying but remain in the between life. But I could still decide. I could emerge or not. I knew I was not interested in half measures. "I'm supposed to ask for Velvet," I said. She took her headphones off. "She better have you sleeping on the floor," she said, but she held open the door as if to say, *Fine, go in.*

They walked up the street, hanging a left back toward the congested traffic area I'd just been driven through, and I went in the house. The dark front rooms were cluttered with floor pillows and blankets and the television played a muted soap opera. The hall gave way to a large open kitchen with a massive picture window framing the city skyline. Everything around me conjured a picture of warm chaos; the dishes piled high in the sink, the smell of cheap floral body spray, the ten labeled hooks on the wall where backpacks and shoulder bags hung. On the dining room table, several open bottles of Wet n Wild nail polish emanated their chemical fumes. A headache bloomed near my left temple. I would associate all future headaches with this moment, the feeling of my new reality sinking in. A deck of terrifyingly illustrated tarot cards lay fanned out near the polish. I picked up a card with ten swords skewering a skeletal bull, one sword through his sad-shaped eye sockets. I stared at it for a long time. Eventually a voice behind me said, "Destruction, ending, perhaps a betrayal. But, somehow, a gift."

I dropped the card and turned to see a woman who could only be Velvet in a rhinestone-embellished tracksuit made of blue velour, her bleached hair in long ringlets, her demeanor young but her skin cut with deep wrinkles and very tan. Later I'd discover the tanning bed in the garage, where she partook of her daily meditation.

"It was just here," I said of the card. "I didn't choose it."

"The cards choose us," she said casually. Her lips were lined far outside her actual mouth, so it looked like she was smiling even if she wasn't. She seemed expectant, waiting for me, I assumed, to introduce myself. But Christina said not to say who I was, to only say her name and that would be enough. To not get sad and confessional to anyone. Not even Velvet. *Don't open the door a crack. You never know what might get through.*

"Christina sent me," I said to Velvet.

"I've had more than one Christina over the years."

How to describe her? "Grape juice," I tried.

"Ahhhh yes. Last I saw her, she was walking out the door you just came in. I don't waste my time wondering what happens to my girls once they leave." She stepped closer and held her hands over my head and closed her eyes. After a time, she said, "You've seen some scary stuff." She lit a bundle of pale green leaves and heavy smoke bloomed around me. I willed myself not to cough.

"You won't get rid of it," I said. It was there in the room, my father's traveler.

She snuffed the bundle out in a little ramekin of sand. "No," she agreed. "But one day you might."

She fed me a microwave dinner of chicken enchiladas and waved the other girls away when they passed through the room. "I feel it would be in your best interest to change the way you look. Most of my girls benefit from a makeover, practically and psychologically."

I wondered if most of her girls were also on the run.

"They're like you one way or another. Not a one of them wants to be found."

"Are you reading my mind?" I asked.

She shrugged, her big breasts moving up and down. I forced my thoughts to stay on the food, close her off from the truth of what had brought me here. When I finished eating she led me upstairs to her bedroom, a black-walled casino-themed monstrosity, complete with what seemed to be a fully operating slot machine—*cherry cherry cherry*—next to the bed in lieu of a nightstand. She sat me at her light-studded vanity, where she cut my sandy-blond hair to my chin, *spun gold,* you called it. But now it was painted with maroon dye, eyebrows to match. By the time she was done with me I was no longer Calla Lily. "What should we call you?" she said. I started to say *Celine* but stopped myself. I had Celine's social security card, I had her birth certificate, sure, but using her name felt wrong, would be too much of a reminder. How would I start completely over if I had to hear a name from the past all the time? "Call me C."

In the house there were chores to be done, and I was diligent about doing my share, still fearful a messy house could be grounds for a beating. Once I finished, I did not lounge on the floor pillows like the other girls. I kept moving. If I paused, thoughts of my father falling would creep in, his body in pieces, blood staining the sidewalk. So I walked the length of the city and back again. With my new hair and skinny body and dark eyes, I was not scared. People did not look at me; they looked through me. I lived on things I found. There was food at the house, but I didn't want to be accused of taking too much, of the other girls forming a case against me. The world was built on exchanges, and I was offering Velvet nothing but liability. At Pier 39 I ate myself sick on pale red crabs still full of meat and the softly melting Cherry Garcia ice cream cones tourists threw carelessly into dumpsters. I'd stare out at the water, going over and over my internal debate on whether to live or die. Living seemed too painful. But something began to happen on my walks. I started to understand the choice to keep living was possibly not about the past, but rather a potential for some completely different future. That is, if I chose it.

About six months into my stay at Velvet's, a letter arrived from Christina, written sparingly, but I knew what everything meant. She hoped I was fine. She wanted to let me know that Celine had passed on finally that morning and that a few days prior, she herself had received a diagnosis she'd long suspected, and would forgo treatment. *I've seen enough of the medical system to know I want no part in it. Tomorrow, I'll take us both out to sea. I will report nothing.* There was a second envelope inside on which she'd written *She Rests in Peace.* I opened it to find a polaroid of Celine on her bed, illuminated by the light of the ever-on television, her arms folded limply over what at first I thought was a cross, but on closer look was the remote. She wore a too-large white sundress I'd passed down to her. On the back: *I had a nice ceremony for her, don't worry. Don't spend your life worrying. It's not what she would have wanted.*

I dropped the picture. Dry heaved. I tried not to consider the logistics of how Christina would get Celine onto a boat, out to sea, but I couldn't help imagining Celine's small, dead body collapsed and covered with blankets inside her rolling grocery cart, disappearing into the belly of a sunset cruise ship. I filled in the blanks, how Christina would pay for a ticket with a fake name, then when the time came, she would take them both off the side in the dark, stones weighing them down. I knew however she did it, she would do it right. *You can breathe easy. Everything will be complete, the path clear for you. Make us proud with your life and don't let any fuckheads get in the way. Fuckheads,* her favorite term for shitty men. I picked the photo back up and forced myself to be with it. It was only right to pay my respects. That's why Christina had sent it. It mattered to her that people acknowledge the truth. This was something I could do privately for them, a small thing, considering all they had given me. That night I was bowled over by grief, yes, but also relief—I possessed all the documentation of a real, supposedly alive person who held no relation to you or my father. Now Calla Lily could truly vanish. I kept the photo of Celine in my wallet, fingers brushing it every time I pulled a dollar out. One day it was gone, and I didn't go looking for it.

By then you had received a life sentence for first-degree murder. You pleaded it was self-defense, your body covered in bruises new and old, hair missing from your scalp and a shattered cheekbone. But no one saw it that way. There was too much against you.

When I'd seen your sentence on the news, I knew my fantasy of our reunion was stronger than I'd realized. Christina's warnings had slipped away. I could have both. What did she know? I could have a new life *and* my mother. Velvet was teaching us all about abundance mindset. One plus one could equal more than two. But you were taken from me yet again. Even with my father dead, you were still unreachable. I had no one to blame but myself. At night my guilt kept me awake, and Velvet would give me bitter blue pills that brought me to an empty place, void of joy and void of sadness.

Our case was still all over the news. When the girls at Bessie Street talked about it, they'd theorize. Maybe you'd had a lover you wanted to be with. Maybe you were a natural-born killer and offed your daughter too. Maybe you were simply insane.

"Maybe he was going to kill her," I said when I couldn't stand it anymore, kicking the coffee table. "And she got to it first." They all went silent. Then finally one girl said, "No doy," reaching up and pinching my calf. "Let us have our fun. We know it's just the same sack-of-shit man doing the same sack-of-shit thing."

They didn't recognize me as the missing girl in the story. Between the changes in my body from grief, the deepening of my eyes, and Velvet's handiwork, I really was a different person. Terrifying and exhilarating that such a complete change was possible. After my outburst, Velvet forbade us from watching the news, clicked the television back to a soap, and put an end to the discussion. Tapped me on the shoulder. "It's time, I think," she said, "to get you a job."

CHAPTER 8

Two weeks had passed since your letter arrived, since I'd crashed into the Chevy woman. Two weeks of Nova out of school invading Lark's daily routine with constant fighting, bickering, contestants in a pageant show for my undivided affection. The families on our street with children Nova's age, children she normally played with after school, who distracted her from her little brother, were off *summering* at second homes on the coast, second homes in the mountains. They were all proficient in snow and water sports. The women bonded over skiing injuries while I floated away, imagining myself with you on the sand. I couldn't identify a wakeboard in a lineup. This was something I hadn't anticipated being an issue when we'd moved onto a street where everyone was richer than us. I thought we were doing okay, thought my husband was relatively successful, felt fortunate I only worked part-time from home, but quickly the scale had changed. Well, at least I'm beautiful, I thought, but I was realizing that beauty was a fickle currency. Certainly, beauty had done nothing for you. And now, after being ravaged by endless nights of lost sleep, I wasn't *that* beautiful.

"Why don't you send her to summer camp? She's old enough now, right? Don't you have some money from your teaching stuff?" My husband offered this the night before when I'd mentioned my grievances about Nova's absent playmates. He didn't realize to get Nova into a day camp you had to sign up months prior and each one was $350 plus for a single week of partial days led by strangers in matching shirts promising children experiences away from their parents in the woods foraging mushrooms, learning to boulder, or worse. My paranoia was much too high to handle the separation I desired. Besides, I'd spent my online teaching money before it had even hit my account. How else did he think I was affording my growing collection of designer cottagecore dresses?

I hadn't been back to check the PO box to see if there was another letter from you, couldn't fathom returning my kids to that public arena for another Lego showdown—but I knew you must be growing impatient. Maybe you were assuming the first letter hadn't reached me, and it was time to send another to my home address, which certainly the feminist lawyer was smart enough to have discovered if she had been able to find the PO box. I didn't want to think too long about how she figured that one out, seeing as they aren't listed. She was working with skill, of course she was. Perhaps she was watching me now.

The kids wailed for the park, wailed when I denied them, but grew compliant when I suggested they spend some time with PBS Kids. Maybe the television was not the enemy but in fact a free summer camp. *Sure, Mom, yes, Mom. Me lubs you, Mama.* Television, my newest ally. Besides, what choice did I have? I couldn't go to the park at a time like this.

Not when I had to watch for the mail from the dining room table. The sounds of show after show jingled up through the vents as I sat with my laptop filling online shopping carts then clicking out of windows before I could *buy now!* Each time I didn't buy something I felt I had saved money. All this saving would backfire the next day at the grocery store when I felt rich for no reason. Just as I was about to justify a rather homely but sort of chic housedress, the mailwoman came. She was not a pleasant woman. My husband was like *What's her deal?* but I understood her implicitly.

"I'm so sorry to bother you," I said, coming out onto the porch. "But I have kind of a weird situation."

She didn't flinch. She was probably fifty, a long gray-blond braid down to her butt and icy pink lipstick. "I cannot be shocked."

I lowered my voice. "Well, there's someone who might send me a letter from a prison. And I want to keep things very confidential, and…"

"You'll have to speak up. I got half-working hearing aids and I can't get an appointment to replace them for three months. Doesn't matter I'm an essential worker."

Next door, the neighbor and her husband were evaluating their berry bushes, but could they be listening?

"I might be getting letters from a prison. An institute. Also, maybe a law office. I don't want anyone to see them. Well, but me. I need to see them. Just anything that looks prisony or legalish. I need to see. And only me."

"My sister married a guy in prison. Never seen her so in love. I said, don't you care he did all that bad business? But she was stuck on his innocence. She reads those true crime books like they're bedtime stories. I told her you better knock those off, they mess with your brain."

"This is a bit different," I said. She looked at me blankly. "I guess I'm wondering if you'd be willing to put the special correspondence, if there is any, just in the bush here and not the mailbox. Hold on. I have an idea." I ran to the kitchen and retrieved one of the very expensive silicone storage baggies I bought and lost at alarming rates. "Use this," I said cheerily.

She plucked it from my hand, then shifted her eyes to the tiny Melissa & Doug piano at our feet. "I got a grandson living with me. He's two. My daughter lives with me also and I put food on the table for all of us including Rex."

I didn't want to know about Rex. "Would your grandson like that piano?" It was one of the few toys Lark actually played with, but I would rather deal with that than the prospect of my husband finding things he shouldn't.

"Looks a little beat-up," she said.

"So you'll do it?"

"What you're asking is illegal. So I can't say if I will or won't, but it would be nice to find some lunch money in that mailbox."

"I think we're understanding each other." I hoped to Goddess.

She shuffled through my mail and kept one envelope aside, putting the rest in the box.

"Something like this what you're talking about? Central California Women's—"

I snatched it from her hand. She was so loud. "Oh my god. Yes. Yes, exactly right. See, I had a feeling something was coming today."

"I don't wanna know," she said, carrying the small piano under her arm to the mail truck. But before she drove off, she nodded at me. She did understand. People, most of the time, will try to meet you halfway if you ask. But you only learn that by asking, and you only ask if you're desperate.

★ ★ ★

I took the mail upstairs and shut myself in my closet. I wondered what you'd say this time, so eager, you couldn't even wait for my response to the first one. But it wasn't you.

Hi Clove,

That's a weird name, isn't it? But easier to say than Calla Lily that's for sure. "Wonder why she chose Clove," your mother keeps saying. She's in shock since she found out you're alive. She really did think you were dead. That's what they told her, why would she think any different? They said, ma'am, your daughter was never found, and when that happens it most likely means she's gone, as in IN THE GROUND.

Anyway, here we go. Your mom doesn't know I'm writing to you but I felt like why not? I got time. So I'm Selby, and me and your mom are tight in here. We share a room. I call it a room but it's a box made of cement. Been very close for a while. I think it's sad you never visited her. You ever want to come visit her? She'd like that. She told me she hasn't heard back from you but it took a lot of courage for her to write that letter so it's messed up to ignore it. She's been laying around all depressed. We got your addresses from that lawyer and your mother was bent on not sending you anything at home, but I told her, I bet your girl doesn't check a PO box. Only weirdos or celebrities have PO boxes. So why not help your mom out? We're all hoping for the dream in here. It wouldn't be too hard. You could really tell them the truth about your dad and everything. We keep seeing women coming forward on the TV. I say to your mom, I say, that could be you up there, finally telling your story. And then here comes that lawyer. Meant to be. Your mom's so sure she can't do it without you. Even this lawyer thinks that's the case. If it were me, I'd mow down anyone in my path to get out. If there was even one small chance I could. But your mom seems to love you for no reason that I can see. I'm not one of those moms. I know my kid's a piece of shit. Alright. So do the right thing, why don't you? Your mom needs you. How you gonna sit around in your nice house knowing your mom's rotting in here? You evil or something?

Selby McGee

I put Selby's letter in my bag with yours, in the deep inner pocket, and headed to the fridge. I opened my coconut probiotic yogurt and ate it in measured bites, admiring the zing and slight effervescence of the cream. The clock turned up in my ear. I didn't have much longer. I hated what I had to do next. Once I did it, all this would be real. But there was no other choice. I had to make sure it was him.

CHAPTER 9

Velvet took me to the thrift shops on Valencia, tight, crammed spaces with no discernible organizing principle, but she was like you, adept at combing the racks quickly and efficiently, right away unearthing a moody floral silk bias-cut dress with long sleeves that flounced at the wrists. She first held it up to herself, and the width of it barely covered one side of her chest. She handed it to me. "You might need to dress up sometime, you know."

Something about the pinks and purples reminded me of your favorite dress, the one you wore if my father's mood could withstand it. We kept it hidden in my dresser so it wouldn't be in reach when he'd rage through your closet looking for things to destroy. Yours wasn't silk; it was cotton. Yours was made by your mother before she died when you were fifteen years old.

I checked the tags. Designer. "This is a quality dress," I said.

"How would you know that?" she asked with genuine curiosity.

"My mother loved *Vogue*. We used to go to the Goodwill bins a lot."

She stopped and stared at me. I had never spoken of you, and this small detail hung between us. I felt you there almost, what it would be like for you to come up behind me, put your arms around me and your chin on my shoulder like you did.

"You miss her," Velvet said, pulling me close, the dress pressed between us. The loss of you would kill me if I let it. "I see it. I know it's hard."

I pulled back. "Why do you do all this?" I asked her. We didn't pay to live with her. She had her rules, but I couldn't see what we possibly offered her.

She seemed caught off guard, looked at me strangely. "Hardly anyone ever asks," she said. "I guess the short story is, I inherited the house, and I inherited some money when my father passed. He was a cold man. He made my life into something that would allow me to understand girls like yourself, and I thought, well, I don't have any interest in being romantically involved with anyone. I don't want children of my own. And so what can I give? I give this. That's really all it is."

I felt the urge then to tell her everything, to explain what happened to us, and I started to, but she shook her head. "I don't need to know. In fact, it's best if I don't. I have love for you, but I don't love you. Imagine if I let myself love each of you. I'd have jumped from the Golden Gate by now."

Of course, I thought. She was not going to replace you. I smiled, accepted it outwardly. But inside I felt panicked. Was this how life would be from now on, striving to find maternal love and failing each time because what I really yearned for was you? The one person I could never have? And now, never even see again.

"I understand," I said to her.

She nodded. We didn't mention you anymore. She bought me low-rise bootcut jeans that were in style and a striped V-neck shirt. I still wore your fanny pack everywhere with my father's broken necklace inside. I refused to take the pack off even when she told me kindly that it was dorky. The dress came with us too. I wished I could have handed it to you. Taken you out to a seafood dinner.

At Bessie Street I put it on to find it was a perfect fit. And in the mirror was a glimmer of my future adult self. I pretended the dress was a gift from you, had once been yours, that my burgeoning beauty was also yours even though my face was so much my father. Velvet did my makeup, covered the dark circles below my eyes. Her touch almost put me to sleep it felt so safe. "I can tell you were very pretty before everything, and you can be pretty again," she said.

"I don't want anyone thinking of me in terms of prettiness." I would later reverse this thinking entirely, but then it felt like an important stance to take.

"Well, I didn't say you're Miss America. All I'm saying is you're pretty enough."

I laughed then, a real laugh, my first since I'd arrived, and she clapped. "See, there you are! Some life in you yet. And just in time, because once my girls hit eighteen they're on their own, and it's best to get a plan going early. Not wait until your birthday like some of my lazy bums. Like I say, I'll help my girls one time toward their future, but the rest is up to you. And the best way to get going in this world is to stop thinking so much about your own problems and start seeing yourself as someone other people can rely on. And so when I meditated in my sun bed, it came to me all at once, like the best ideas do." She swiped my lips with gloss. "For you, grocery."

★ ★ ★

When Velvet was satisfied with my transformation, she walked me to the little Italian market on the corner. The girls loved to go there for pastel-wrapped candies and sea-salt chips, but I never went with them. The inside was cavernous and full of things I'd never seen before, red and green packages, dried pasta in many shapes and colors, and along the back wall, a glass case of red dead meat, slippery chicken breasts, sausage links, and racks of ribs. Head-sized globes of mortadella and honeyed ham. A young man stood behind the counter, handing over a white-wrapped package to a beautiful glowing woman with a stroller. She whisked by us and the man grinned at Velvet.

"How can I help you today, ma'am?"

"I have someone here looking for a job. She's dependable, she's easygoing, she's a great listener, and she's—"

"Not hiring at the moment." But he stepped out from behind the meat counter anyhow. His apron was covered in blood. He surveyed me as I stood next to Velvet, who wasn't going to give up. I felt suddenly very out of place in the glamorous dress; I wanted to strip it off, wear what he was wearing.

"She can start for free, like an apprenticeship or something."

"The last time didn't go so well," he said.

"Trust me, this one is nothing like that one. This one isn't gone yet."

They deliberated about me as if I wasn't there until I couldn't take it anymore.

"I have experience," I said, my voice too loud for the space. It was a lie. Sort of. I did have life experience, had run a home with you, Mother, making sure everything was just so for my father, reminding you of forgotten items at the grocery store, loving the safety of when we'd be inside under those fluorescent aisles without him, dreaming up possible meals that might protect us. A dinner idea to set a mood. To control a feeling.

Velvet went along with it. "Yes, she has work experience. And she can start right away."

"No drugs," the butcher said, turned to me. "I see drugs and you're gone. No conversation about it, nothing. Just out. You got it? The last one stole from our register, overdosed in the back. The whole nine."

"I don't do drugs," I said. "I never have and I never will."

He looked at me. No Miss America, but I was young and had my father's smile. I used it then. "I'm fine," I reassured him. "A normal girl." And with total clearness, as if the butcher and this market had conjured it, I decided: I would not kill myself. I had not made it this far just to die. My whole life had been about surviving and now I had, hadn't I? Might as well work at a grocery store.

He went to the back and Velvet squeezed my arm. He returned with an apron and a paper to fill out. I took him in, his low ponytail, the tattoos going up his forearms, mermaids and nautical symbols, a simple sailboat. A sketched black dog crept up his neck. I'd never had boyfriends in Hawai'i, never been asked on a date, something my father wouldn't have allowed anyway. Celine and I would imagine what sex might be like in our journal—*I think it would be like scratching a really bad itch,* she'd written—but neither of us had so much as held hands with someone, aside from each other. Yet now this man locked eyes with me and I opened, held his gaze. The ghost of my father faded. Only for a time, of course. Only for a time. But I didn't know that then.

★ ★ ★

The market was a mom-and-pop-type place that sold fine deli items, cans of dense red sauce and fresh pasta, made-to-order sandos with thick-cut salami and cheeses I had never seen, along with every sort of dead animal that stalked the earth, and the Butcher was in charge. He didn't own it, not yet, but it was like he did. The owner lived above, an old man with a bulging glass eye who checked on things once a week, and all I had to do was be cool when he was around. The Butcher said he'd been in grocery since he was fourteen, when the old man had taken him up on his offer to work for nothing, and now he was twenty-three. According to Celine's birth certificate, the only one that mattered now, I'd turn eighteen in a matter of months.

During that first shift he set me up on a project of entering new items into the inventory, then took a break and stood outside smoking, leaning into the wall, talking to some cute woman in leather pants with silver hoop earrings. The way she tilted toward him, how she laughed. Sex pulsed between them. The image bewitched me and filled me with rage.

That night I told Velvet about my first day, and then about him and the woman.

She huffed. "Your mother made you hate yourself."

"What do you mean?"

"Well, right now, you're so convinced you aren't as good as this woman, this woman he seems to like or tolerate, but you have no reason to think she's any better than you. I bet your mother walked through the world thinking she couldn't do any better. Don't take that on. Turns a woman's life from this"—she held her arms out in a big orb—"to this," and she shrunk the orb down to nothing.

"If she hated herself, it was because my father made her," I said. "It was because she didn't have a choice."

She smiled at me sadly. "It was probably long before that. Her own mother probably passed it on to her, and the men she chose were just the right ones to make it all true. I don't let women get away with things, as you might be able to tell about me. I say it straight. Men are monsters, no question, but your mother, I have a feeling, lay down and died in it."

"What do you know? You don't let anyone in. You don't even love us."

"Well." She put her hands on her hips. "That was a mouthful."

I went quiet. My body ran through anger, and when that died down there was only the truth of Velvet's words left behind. For I did know what she meant; these were the thoughts I'd had of you that shamed me the most—that you kept us in the shit, kept us trapped when we could have been free. But I could never be sure. There were so many things I didn't understand about how to leave, things you told me were much too hard. Money, escaping without being found, the overwhelm of starting over. If we took it too far, he'd kill you. I, more than you, Mother, understood that he would do it.

"I bet her own mother died young," Velvet went on. "The energy you're putting out is a lot of violence, and a lot of maternal loss."

Velvet's own motherloss hung in the air between us. She'd had a bad father, sure. But I could tell she'd had no mother. I didn't even have to ask. That was the real reason she ran the Bessie Street house.

After my shifts at the market I continued wandering the city, but now I went inside places. Spent money on books and trinkets, finally asked the Butcher where I should get my father's necklace repaired and paid a jeweler to fix the chain. Kept it around my neck, a talisman to ward off men like the one who had worn it. My own evil eye.

I learned how to stock shelves, make special orders, slice deli meat, package anchovies and tapenade. Each day the Butcher would teach me something new about handling meat, characteristics of certain cuts and how to approximate the weight of bulk sausage before slapping a mound of it on the scale. Customers didn't like when you overestimated and had to put the excess back into the case. Even if it was a subconscious issue, he told me, it would influence if they came back, how frequently, and how much they'd spend.

Meanwhile I learned about lust. About feeling things for another person that had nothing to do with you or my father. Intoxicating, how the stares between me and the Butcher grew heavier. He started spending his breaks talking to me while I worked rather than outside smoking with the leather-pants woman. It was all well and good, my mood had lightened considerably, but Celine's birthday was fast approaching, and I didn't make enough to live on, afford rent. I knew I was in trouble.

So I asked the Butcher for a meeting. A professional meeting, I said, to talk about my future. We sat down on overturned buckets in the back alley, facing each other, his legs spread apart in black denim. He lit a cigarette and I watched the muscles in his arms tense and relax. "What's up?" he said. "What do you need?" He frequently offered me things from the recently expired stock that would get thrown out anyway, saved me especially tantalizing confectionary. "This week I got some of those chocolate bars with the dried roses on top you like, got some pig ears, couple jars of alfredo, more cannellinis?"

I laughed. Velvet's house was stocked now with about eighteen cans of expired but still fine cannellinis. "No, it's not about food."

"You're a real good worker, C," he said. Tears sprang to my eyes unexpectedly, and I hid my face in my hands. "Oh no, are you quitting on me? Got a better job lined up? I'll give you a raise. Wouldn't want to lose my best girl."

"Your only girl," I said. I meant it to come out light, a joke, the only girl working in the shop, of course, but we both heard it the other way.

He bit the corner of his bottom lip. "My only girl."

I took a deep breath. "I have no family, no friends, and soon, once I'm eighteen, nowhere to live," I told him.

He must have already known all this because he didn't look surprised. He knew Velvet and what she did. "Well," he said, "my roommate joined a communal farm up north so I have some space. Was gonna live alone for a while, but I might be able to help you. You know, see how it goes. But first, tell me your real name."

My face burned. I'd written Celine's name on the hiring paperwork, copied down her social and birthday. But I knew he probably hadn't looked at any of that. I'd seen him hand it straight to the glass-eyed old man. "C works."

He didn't look so sure. "You're more than just one letter."

I was surprised at what I said next. "I won't live with you if you have a girlfriend."

He smiled like he knew something I didn't. "Are you saying you like me, C?"

I stood up. My legs shook. How could any of this work? I had made a mistake in not ending my life. This would be too hard. "Forget it," I said, turning to gather my bag. "Just forget it."

He got up too, knocking his bucket over. He tossed the cigarette. "Forget what?"

"Me."

He took my bag and set it on the ground, our faces close. "Well,
now, that won't be possible."

That night we climbed the hill up to Cortland Avenue and he took
me to dinner at a pizza parlor where I peeled all the greasy cheese
off my slice and pushed it around the plate. Like second nature he
scooped the lumps of cheese after I was done with them into his
mouth. He asked me lots of questions about my life. Under his spell,
I went against Christina's advice, telling him the general logistics
of what we'd gone through with my father. I didn't get too specific, but I said enough to have him nearly in tears. Was this a kind
of power? He seemed to not recognize my story from the news. I
would come to learn he read no news sources, watched no television. It littered his mind. He preferred music, entire albums played
in the order their maker intended, books on Zen Buddhism and
poetry collections about men in love and men under trees, *Love Is a
Dog from Hell*.

I cried as I unspooled myself, drunk on the relief it brought.
He would wait until I caught my breath, and then he'd ask another
question. He put his leather jacket around my skinny shoulders. It
was after this gesture of kindness that I made a huge mistake. I told
him of a girl I'd once known and her mother, what they had done
for me. Not their names, just the basic facts of their deadness, how
it was thanks to them I was in San Francisco at all. During that first
dinner, though, he remained far more fixated on my father.

"Any man who does that is trash." He looked like he wanted to bite something, but it wasn't anger; it was passion. "Your father was scum, the worst scum of the earth."

I was surprised at how shaming it felt to have another person name it. I didn't like that the Butcher now thought of me this way, as the daughter of scum. Scum didn't seem to account for the good things about my father, which I found myself daydreaming about now that the immediate danger he imposed was gone—his humor, his charm, the way he sang "Blue Suede Shoes," whirling me around the apartment. Who he was without the dark traveler wasn't scum.

But how to explain this to another person? To explain that I felt love in my heart for my father. The night turned on me. I was sick with the desire to take back my words, to have never told this outsider anything about me, about my past, but it was too late.

"I've never had sex before," I said, wanting to acknowledge that I was aware of the currency it would take for me to have a roof over my head. I felt very mature in doing this, in getting ahead of it.

He leaned back in the booth. He had hair growing out of the top of his white shirt. He looked different when he wasn't wearing his butcher's clothes. He had taken his ponytail out and brown strands fell in his eyes. He looked like the Jesus portrait in Velvet's dining room, except in tight jeans.

"You don't have to pretend to be inexperienced for me to like you."

"It's the truth."

I could tell he didn't believe me. "When the time comes, it will be good between us."

"How can you know?"

He reached across the table and traced his finger on the back of my hand. "I can tell there won't be a day from now until I die that I won't think of you. That's a fact."

But I could not be at ease.

"If you ever hit me," I said. "Or even yell at me. Call me a name. Control me. Anything. I'll leave you. I won't stand for it. I won't make the same mistakes as my mother."

He considered this, turned it over. "No. That's not it," he said finally. "I won't make the same mistakes as your father."

The Butcher lived a few blocks up from the market in a tiny one-bedroom, the windows strung with Tibetan prayer flags. In the kitchen, a set of vintage blue floral Pyrex mixing bowls like you had of your mother's sat on the counter. I thought maybe it was a sign from you that I was doing the right thing. I tried to kiss him that first night, but he wouldn't let me. "You're not eighteen and I want to do this right," he said.

"I turn eighteen so soon."

He nodded. "So soon, then. It's a date."

From there we lived and worked side by side, and during our shifts I imagined what it would be like once we finally slept together. I wanted to just do it. I would wake up next to him in his bed, throbbing from dreams where he would bring me to the edge and I'd pull his hand toward me to finish things, but he wouldn't do it. "I'm not going to tell anyone," I'd beg. I had no one to tell.

I thought falling in love meant having sex, but soon I discovered it meant dropping a jar of tomato sauce that splattered all over his kitchen floor and having him pick me up and set me on the counter to make sure I didn't step in the glass and kiss my nose and clean it all up. Love was when he didn't grip my hair and bring my face close to the mess and snarl, *Look at how fucking stupid you are.*

On Celine's eighteenth birthday he made me a perfectly round olive oil cake and put a *1* candle on top, because, as he explained, it was the first day of my life. My real life, the life I could choose. My life with him. We ate the entire cake at the little table and he sang to me, and then we slow danced to the music he was introducing me to, gentle folk ballads I'd never heard that seemed to unlock the centers for love and possibility in my brain. I was so attracted to him. Those pure pheromones behind his ear.

That night he took me through all the motions he thought I could stand. We moved through my pain together and then beyond pain into a place where I felt determined to master what we were doing. First high. Who knew this could happen between two people? It didn't cost a thing.

"I don't want it in my mouth," I said at one point when he paused on his knees on the bed and I was on my back. His tongue had just been inside me; he was opening me up slow.

He smiled, started doing unspeakable things to my neck. A neck could feel good. A neck could be something other than strangled. I believed him when he said I was beautiful.

We spent the rest of the night in a trance and fell asleep as the sky brightened. When we woke, it was warm in the room, afternoon, and we were both late for the market. My burgundy hair had begun to grow out and a few inches of blond roots could be seen. There was color in my cheeks and I'd gained weight from all the pasta and good cheese.

"I'll name you. I'll name you right now," he said dreamily. He appraised me. "I've got it. C-Love."

I laughed. "C-Love. How creative."

But I loved it. It flattened the past and all I'd seen. It meant something to me. He probably never knew how much.

* * *

For a while our sex was so visceral no bad thoughts could get in. We would do it at work in the refrigerated meat lockers. The smell of cold meat pressed against my senses, but I was wild for the touch of him. Slowly, though, I started to see my father.

There he was, pinning you to the wall in the kitchen. The sound of him spitting, the dead-end thud of his boot colliding with your stomach. I'd gasp for air and open my eyes and I'd see the Butcher over me. "Come back," he'd say. He knew when I left myself. I learned to keep my eyes open all the time. In my head I'd chant *blank blank blank*. When nearly a year passed, and the Butcher never became my father, when he never threw a meal I had made across the room, broke dishes over my head, I was happy to learn that not all men were the way I thought they must be. How I longed to report this breaking news to Christina, to you, and to Celine most of all. That her ideas of romance were in fact possible.

The problem I began to identify, though, was that his expression of love was tightly entwined with pity. He felt bad for me. Little orphan he had saved. I had pitied you my whole life, so I knew how it worked. There was no power in pity. Here I had thought he was able to see me clearly, to love me in my entirety, but it wasn't quite that. He looked at me and saw my past. Saw you and my father.

Soon I didn't like how we slept naked pressed into each other, and even on the coldest of nights when the heater would flatline and the sheets felt like ice, I started to yearn for distance. Who was I? I wondered as I fell asleep. He seemed sure of who I was. Was it enough? He'd curl into me and around me and I'd smell the smell of the meat we handled every day, the acid of nightshades and garlic in our throats. When we woke, he would look at me as if staring into the sun, ask, "How are you, darlin'?" Sometimes when he would go down on me he'd come on the sheets before I could even touch him.

And he smoked cigarettes, nearly a pack a day.

I told him I hated it, that you and my father smoked constantly. But he said he would never quit. It was the one thing he would not do for me. He loved it too much. I said, "I'll leave you if you don't," and he looked over at me and grinned. "You won't."

During my shifts at the market I took pleasure in watching people, what they purchased, what they filled their bodies with, and what made their lives. Food really was the most primary part of a person, and its effects were curious to me. Most curious of all was that beautiful glowing woman I'd seen on my first day pushing her stroller, someone I soon recognized as a regular. Everything about her was clean and elevated. Clear-glossed fingernails and lintless sweaters that hung exactly right, shoes that appeared new and leather satchels with gold buckles. She did not rip her cuticles until they bled. She did not forget to moisturize. She bought things with total abandon, throwing overpriced colanders and whisks from the endcaps into her basket, buying yet another ten-dollar canvas tote with the store's logo when she realized she'd forgotten the one she'd bought last time. She carried around a mason jar full of bright green liquid, which she sipped through a stainless-steel straw as she paced our aisles, as I packaged her chuck roast.

"You eat meat?" I asked her one day, eyeing the juice.

"When I'm nearing my moon cycle. For the iron. But all this stuff"—she gestured to the expensive cheese and crackers and fresh ropes of pasta and jars of sauce — "this is all for my husband. He's Italian. He's really proud of it."

I didn't care about her Italian husband. "What do you eat?" I asked. My admiration was shot through with envy. But envy was better than pity. Envy was a useful tool to show me what I wanted. Her baby mewled and she lifted its plump body from the carrier and turned it sideways to her chest, where she pulled down her tank top to expose her dark brown nipple and the baby latched on, sighed into it. The Glowing Woman did all this while standing, considering my question.

"I don't eat anything processed. So, whole foods. Bright colors. No dairy, or gluten. Absolutely no refined sugar. I take a high-quality probiotic with warm lemon water every morning. No caffeine. I live for the bitterness of cacao. I do Pilates. Classical, of course, not modern."

I felt as if she'd just spoken in another language. I'd had gritty off-brand instant coffee that morning with the Butcher in bed, Frosted Flakes swimming in sugary cow's milk. I considered the market's barely there vitamin endcap, which included heartburn tablets and Tylenol PM and metallic-smelling multis. "I don't think we carry probiotic," I said, not knowing what such a thing was.

She popped her baby off her nipple and a little milk glistened on its lip. The baby had rolls on its arms and legs and was very happy. She was clearly doing life right. She kissed the baby's chin and slid her back into the carrier on her chest. Took the roast from my outstretched hand. "This is only one stop for the week. I go to Right Life on Cortland every day. That's my real spot. That's where they have what you need to build a solid foundation. Once your gut microbiome is right, everything else falls into place."

★ ★ ★

That night after my shift, instead of going home to the Butcher, I walked up the steep-hilled streets to Cortland Avenue and into Right Life. City smells left and were replaced by eucalyptus rising from a bamboo diffuser. Incandescent pink salt formations stood at each checkout stand. Glistening bunches of rainbow chard and pyramids of limes overwhelmed my eyes. I paused at the pineapples, remembered Hawai'i, the stands where we'd buy halved papayas filled with pineapple slices and coconut snow. I walked on. I couldn't afford to ruminate. I still didn't trust myself not to run to the nearest police department and turn myself in, no longer be Celine, no longer be a *missing person*. The lie felt unbearable at times, but if I could focus on the present, on the future, I could make it recede.

There were three aisles dedicated to vitamins and they were organized by aspiration. Little handwritten signs spelled out things like *Feeling down in the dumps? Try St. John's wort, nature's antidepressant!* A whole wall just for gut health as the Glowing Woman had promised. *Your gut is your second brain!* A young woman with dreadlocks and a Right Life apron, HELLO! I'M: SAGE, restocked the magnesium (citrate, glycinate, malate, carbonate). She glanced up at me. "Want a sample?" I nodded in reverence, and she handed me a little packet of something called *Relax*. "This one isn't my favorite, like, there's better forms out there, but they're really pushing it this week. You can try anything you want. Just ask one of us. We're happy to open anything at all. We're not like other grocery stores."

"What's magnesium?" I said, opening the packet. It looked like sugar. I dipped my finger in and brought it to my tongue. "Wow, that's sour," I said, trying to downplay my shock.

She laughed. "You have to mix it with water," she said, then smiled warmly without judgment.

"I've never been here," I said. "I've never taken any vitamins." I'd long hated pills. They reminded me of the many orange-bottled varieties Celine had to take each day. But vitamins seemed the opposite of that. Vitamins, by the looks of these aisles and the people perusing them, were full of promise.

"Then let me set you up with something special."

She crouched down and unlocked a cupboard, began filling a cloth bag with samples of natural sun creams and neem toothpaste and women's once dailies and fish oil, and cod liver oil and vitamin D_3 gummies and something called *200 mg of Zen*. Suntheanine and reishi powder and lion's mane and mucuna and Vitamineral Green. Liposomal vitamin C. And a week's sampling of a *powerful* probiotic. Handed the bag to me and smiled. "Welcome."

Looking at my loot, I wondered if you and my father had discovered such vitamins, had restored your health from the inside out, would that have kept us safe? It made a kind of intrinsic sense. The Butcher liked to say *as above, so below* and I never understood what it meant, but maybe it had something to do with this. What went inside the body would manifest outside of it. I had discovered the epicenter of all solution.

I floated away from Sage, light and clear, felt myself smiling as I collected a refrigerated carton of raw hemp milk and a bulk-bin bag of oat bran and a dark kale salad from the deli full of something called *pepitas* and raw shredded beets and little gleams of pink grapefruit. Raw forms of foods seemed preferred, but there was also a hot vat of something called *kitchari* you could dole out into recyclable cups. There was a bench against the wall next to a lending library full of secondhand books on spirituality. I sat and thumbed through one about astral travel and felt the torn seams of my life start to mend together. Possibility expanded around me, more glowing women like the one from the market gliding through their days, embodied and awakened. I scanned their limbs for bruises, handprints, scratches, the shakes, and found only vitality. They weren't skittish; they moved with confidence, no black eyes, no shell-shocked expressions. One of them asked an employee if the bread she was holding was true sourdough, which had to mean there was false sourdough out there masquerading as the real thing! I wrote it down. So much to learn. Out from under you and my father, I wanted to learn things. What might I learn to desire if I sat here in the belly of all nourishment? What might I learn about myself?

I watched men assess stone fruit, weigh bags of sprouted nuts, consider fair-trade coffee. These lean-limbed Teva-clad dads with babies in hiking backpacks and leather bracelets on their tanned wrists also possessed the mysterious glow of health. I clutched my bag of samples and my eyes filled with tears. I wanted this life. I wanted the Right Life. And none of these people here had a story like mine. I just knew it. The Butcher knew too much about me and would always smell of it. I loved him, I really did. But I would not be able to take him with me. I had to start completely over. Christina had been right.

The next week I saw the Glowing Woman in the market—which seemed positively dismal now next to Right Life. I asked her what advice she would give a woman of nearly nineteen. "I'm taking *a* probiotic now," I assured her.

She smiled, leaned in. "Go to college," she said. "Either get a career to pay for the life you want or meet a man there who will."

This advice seemed old-fashioned to me even then, but also realistic. I had no wealth. I had no safety at all. "Which did you do?" I asked.

She shrugged happily. "Both. I knew I wanted a family. I'll go back to my career once she's in preschool, but for now, this is perfect. I get to be a mom and be supported and still have the education to do what I want when the time is right. But you don't have to have kids. Lots of my friends don't."

"How did you know you wanted kids?"

"Oh, probably because my parents were divorced and I guess I wanted to do things differently. Raise a kid in a happy home. Reprogram my own bad childhood by experiencing a good one through her. I read a great article on neuroplasticity and it all made sense. It's really the ultimate healing, having a positive opposite experience to rewrite the old one." She kissed the baby's head.

Reprogram…neuroplasticity…positive opposite experience. I made a mental note to look these up later. "I don't have a family," I told her. "I mean, I have him." I gestured to the Butcher. He was helping someone understand pesto. "We're in love."

She smiled. "You have no idea how young you are."

"I'm about the age my mother met my father. I know it all counts."

"Aha," she said. "That's very wise. And I suppose very true."

I looked at the Butcher and wanted to cry. I loved how his eyes glowed hazel and saw me so deeply. I loved the veins that ran up his forearms. How his forearms could send me into a near panic of sexual need. How a few months prior, he'd gotten his nickname for me tattooed across his knuckles.

But it wasn't as if I'd never given anyone up before. You had rushed down to my father's dead body, and I'd walked purposefully to Christina's, accepted my new life. I took the elevator down, hiding under her floppy straw hat, those oversized sweats, and glanced back only once at you, howling over my father, before turning down Ala Wai toward Lewers to catch the bus to the airport. A small group of people had amassed around you. I thought stupidly you were being taken care of.

If I could walk away then, I was capable of anything.

"Listen," the Glowing Woman said, pulling me back to the market and to her. "You should spend some time journaling, really think about your wildest dreams. If you could be anyone. Who? People don't understand, you really can change everything."

I wanted to tell her how I'd done it once, that I could do it again. Better this time. I smiled instead and she turned to leave.

"Wait," I said. "Where did you go to college?"

"Oh," she said. "A little school in Portland, Oregon."

The Butcher told me he wanted to one day own the market. He infused me into these fantasies, too, mapping our future every day. I could manage the employees and do the ordering and we could have lunch breaks together. And then one day we'd open more locations. It was hard for me then to imagine this becoming lucrative. I thought of the old man who owned the market, his meager dwelling and shabby clothes.

"Do you want kids one day?" I asked him.

"Nah," he said. "Let's do other stuff."

"Well, I want kids," I challenged. It came out clear and true. I wanted to be like the Glowing Woman, finding the ultimate opposite positive experience. "I want to know what it's like to have a family." And what she hadn't said, but I knew, was that without kids it would be me alone all day subsumed by memories, the truth of you and my father ever present and inescapable. New souls around me seemed important.

"We're young," he said, brushing my words off. "We have time to figure all that out." The way he was standing there, his hand on his hip, a cigarette between his fingers. For a second he reminded me of my father.

The next day while the Butcher worked I went to the library, where a kind librarian helped me figure out how to take a GED test so I could apply to community college in Portland. From there, I'd transfer to the little college the Glowing Woman had gone to, a redbrick dream with its own forested walking trails. "Why Portland?" the librarian asked as she clicked around with speed. "Rains a lot there."

"I need somewhere new."

"I can understand that. Well, there are certainly similarities to San Francisco. I bet you'll like it." She didn't know I'd forever long for humidity on my skin, palm trees swaying overhead, the sudden explosions of blue ginger, Mango Man sitting still on the street corner on our way to the beach. That waves lapped the shore inside my ears and always would. But there was nothing to fill the trench of my longing for Hawai'i, or for you, Mother, so I walked alongside it, making sure never to look down.

I left the library with a stack of printed forms, information to read. Back at the apartment, the Butcher had left a note on the pillow as he often did. *C-Love, you are my whole world.* As I filled out the paperwork and made calls, I paused each time at my name. It didn't seem smart to change it legally from Celine to something else. The last thing I wanted to do was draw attention to myself. But what was the harm in using a different name on the *preferred name* line? In truth every time I wrote *Celine,* I felt her ill body in the room, sensed I was living out some version of her life. But Christina had implored me not to feel bad, had called this one last act of love from Celine, some purpose for her abbreviated and difficult life, said she was more than happy to offer herself, especially for her one and only friend. Toward the end, Celine had seemed sicker than ever, a total dimming of her personhood. There hadn't been time to say goodbye to her that night, but I wished I had gone into the dark of the back bedroom and kissed her cool forehead. Apologized for leaving her. I tried to remind myself the dead didn't care about formalities like a social security number. But a name felt sacred. I told myself I wouldn't use it if I could help it.

I glanced at the Butcher's note again, the way his small handwriting made everything look like one stream of connected letters. I let my eyes unfocus. *C-Love. C-love. C love, Clove.* I wrote it on the line. Said it aloud again and again, an invocation, "Clove."

According to the library, Portland, Oregon, was tree heavy and rugged, verdant and wild, rushing rivers and roses and winding hidden trails where owls perched on high branches twisting their haunted heads. The Butcher didn't have a car that was reliable enough for us to even leave San Francisco; despite his love, he would not come searching for me in an entirely different state. I'd get an apartment all my own where no one knew me. I would edit and manage my story until it sang. I would never be pitied again.

* * *

"How you doing, darlin'?" the Butcher would say. "Fine," I'd tell him. Fine, after passing my GED in secret. Fine, while securing an apartment over the phone, wiring a down payment. Fine, I said on the morning I knew I was leaving him and not going to the laundromat like normal, nearly two years since I'd arrived on Bessie Street. I walked out the door with all our laundry in a sack, the few things I was bringing tucked inside. This now struck me as needlessly cruel. I could have taken his laundry back to the apartment after he left for his shift; I did not need to dump it on a street corner. But my parents were gone and the Butcher would continually want to process it, talk about it, remind me incessantly that whatever feeble life he offered was so much better than where I'd come from. He would always feel he had the upper hand, even if he would never call it that. A few nights before I left I'd overheard him talking to his friend in the living room, a joint floating between them, slowing the Butcher down, making him sound bewildered—"Her dad beat up her mom all the time, then her mom fucking killed him. She was right there when it happened." The friend whistled, said, "That's some real damage. That's a full-time fucking job." The Butcher said, "Yeah, but she doesn't want to acknowledge any of it. She doesn't want to do the work." I couldn't see him from the hall, but I knew he was doing the thing where he put two hands in that long thick hair, pulling it away from his face and letting it go. The friend inhaled deeply. "No, I meant for you. That shit's gonna be *your* full-time job."

The Butcher sighed. Didn't say anything else. The sigh was enough.

I took a final look at the Butcher's clothing strewn on the corner. I was doing him a favor by getting rid of his clothes that would carry my smell, absolving him of the job of me. The fog hung heavy. A silver glint in his shirt pocket caught my eye. A packet of Nicorette. I sat on the curb and allowed myself to cry. I could just go back. I picked up one of his tight white shirts I loved, smelled it. But no. I could not afford to be sentimental. There was a job to take up, but it wasn't as the Butcher pictured.

I felt in every moment of my life that I was running out of time. I had to cut away, cut away, while I still could. So I was a blade slicing toward the train station, off to become undamaged. I was Clove.

CHAPTER 10

I never looked the Butcher up online, despite my intense curiosity. Even as social media exploded and became a free offering of falsely intimate details about anyone and everyone, I had abstained. I loved the way I'd trained myself, how once I had decided something, it was so. You and my father could never hold yourself back from anything, so I made myself different. I didn't drink alcohol. I didn't take mind-altering substances. I smiled through anger, and I didn't stalk my only ex.

But now my life was full of exceptions.

His profile said he still lived in San Francisco, likely still in Bernal Heights, according to the photo of him in Precita Park, paces from our old place, holding hands with what looked to be his daughter, their dog alongside. He hadn't wanted kids, but here he was with one. He hadn't wanted to quit smoking, but there had been that first sign, the Nicorette in his pocket. I had the destabilizing sensation that I'd stepped to the side of the life that was meant for me. Everything in the photos felt familiar, as if I'd taken them. As if the daughter was my own. She was about Nova's age and didn't resemble him but for the eyes. He still looked like the man I'd once melded my soul to, but now there was a certain refinement to him. Money was no doubt involved. Perfectly fitting jeans cuffed at his ankles, loafers, no socks, and a snug hemp dyed T-shirt that was either great vintage or very expensive, probably both. He still had long hair, but it wasn't too long and his beard was trimmed but not too trimmed, and the light wrinkles around those hazel eyes suited him. He wore a silver chain necklace and several rings and a few beaded bracelets. I loved jewelry on a man when it was good jewelry. Shoes when they were good shoes. I wanted to grab that chain, *mine.* A photo of him close up revealed C-L-O-V-E still on his knuckles and I couldn't help imagining those fingers inside the women who came after me, my letters disappearing between their legs. The thought heated me up in multiple directions—possessiveness, arousal—but I had come for a purpose and it was best to stick to it.

But no harm in looking for a wife in the photo grid. There had to be a woman, or several. Jealousy boiled in my bloodstream, a concoction of misery and motivation. Deep down, I understood my father's disposition. I, too, wanted to be wanted, only me, the most, forever.

I wondered if the Butcher had ever searched for me before. But it was hard to search for *C,* and even if he stumbled on my profile by sheer accident, my face was nowhere. Just limbs and nature and backs of heads. He never knew I took the name he had given me. I tried to see my profile through his eyes. My most recent post was a picture of my hand holding a green juice in front of my face, recipe below. Posted right before I received your letter, when things were still normal, when I was concerned with likes and shares.

I could not locate any of the Butcher's potential women, but my, he had a lot of grocery content. Pictures in the aisle of a store that looked almost identical to Right Life, the kind of natural food oasis I would travel many miles in order to tour like a theme park. I had tried to convince my husband years before to move to Los Angeles so I could live near Erewhon, the mecca of all my desire, pints of Harry's Berries and adaptogen smoothies named after celebrities, *add sea moss*—but only halfheartedly. California would undo me. It was too close to where I'd grown up before Hawai'i, and now, apparently, where you had been transferred.

It took me some time to realize the Butcher was the owner of the natural food store in his photographs, but once I confirmed it, I felt a scary longing for this San Francisco life. I'd gotten everything wrong. I ventured over to the Butcher's company page, Home Grown, and it was impressive. The cold-pressed glass-bottled juice display alone rivaled anything Earthside was dishing up. I saw myself next to him in the company photo. The honesty between us would be the highest form of eroticism I could know now. To think when I'd left him I thought it was the opposite. Remembering our sex, my heart felt heavy. I had been too young to know that kind of chemistry didn't waltz around everywhere. I was too overcome by my desire for anonymity. For new beginnings. I'd never get fucked like that again. By which I mean fucked with honesty, where the other person knew the real me, and still wanted it.

But not so fast. As quickly as I could recall our sex, I could hear him saying, *God, just think of your mother in there. It's so unfair. She was just defending herself. I can't believe you won't help her.* I had to know if he was the one who had gotten all this rolling; I had to know each thing he'd said. Trying to remember the details I'd once told him was impossible. I drank back then on occasion before I realized that was a no-no, and there were a few blank nights, nights I knew I'd been hysterical and crying into his chest after we'd had too much. Perhaps I'd given him your full name. Yes, that was probably it. Your name haunted him until he couldn't stop himself from taking up your cause. And oh, he loved to take up a cause, spending his off days in a vest in Golden Gate Park gathering signatures to save dolphins. Maybe he'd emerged from a meditation feeling called by a higher power to save you. I remembered filling out those employment forms at the market. I'd left behind everything one would need to track me down. To hand me over to the nearest feminist lawyer he could find. I began typing.

There's no easy way to do this. So I'll start by saying I'm sorry. I'm sorry for so much, but mostly that I left like I did. You did not deserve that. I hope you can believe me when I say I had my reasons. It's really nice to see your profile after all these years. It looks like you're doing well. Congratulations on the store. Your daughter? Beautiful.

I'm writing because recently my mother reached out to me from prison and said a lawyer had told her I was alive. Had given her my address. She is wanting a retrial. Wanting my help. I've never told anyone else about my life but you. I have to ask, are you somehow involved? Did you go to her? And if you did, why? Are you intent on ruining my life? I have worked very hard over the years to remake myself and find goodness. Find someone who didn't see me as damaged. It has been a full-time fucking job. I knew you thought it was unreasonable that I did not find a way to let my mother know I was alive, find a way to see her. You thought I'd given up hope on the truth and you imagined a fool's world where she could be free and happy and we'd be reunited. You knew nothing of violence or how it worked on the brain, probably still don't. You thought the truth would prevail if only I tried, but I knew better than that. I really wish you had not meddled. But if you did, I need to know. And if you didn't, I need to know that even more.

CHAPTER 11

In the morning my husband hurried me out of the house, suggesting I head to Earthside. "We're running low on stuff," he said, but we both knew that thanks to my habit we were rarely low on anything. He was not a good liar. And why should he be, when the world was made for him? I would not have become the liar I was today had Christina not taken me through her advanced course. I learned as I watched her schedule Celine's appointments with specialists with two-year waitlists, negotiating and bending the truth, *creating* the truth, to get what they needed, and fast. She said for women to be taken seriously, we had to tell people the story they wanted—needed—to hear. And the most important thing was that you had to believe what you were saying.

I had trusted my own lies in the early days with my husband. By the time I met him, Clove had become a real and full person to me, the resilient child of parents who had died together tragically, the ever-growing, self-improving adult. Substance-free, with an early bedtime, a morning run and evening yoga routine, meditation, the cleanest of eating. Grueling shifts at grocery stores, no room for nightmares of my father and me in the middle of the ocean, only room for item codes. *Fennel bulb 10223, head of radicchio 10557.* Then, when I married and left grocery, I filled my head with the consumerism of impending motherhood, researching things to buy, *NoseFrida, DockATot, balm for everything from nips to lips,* preparing the way for the arrival of a new person who would be a glimmer of myself, but so much better: they would never know you or my father.

But then Nova arrived, and along with her, my father cruising around my block in his Jimmy. I remember the first time I saw him, one week home from the hospital, my husband and I had been sitting on the couch, zoning out, as we'd done every night since we had returned home as parents, Nova's six-and-a-half-pound body languid across the Brest Friend, my eyes dry, everything feeling taken apart and put back together by a thumbless mechanic, were these even my eyes? They were wrong in my face now.

"Holy shit, this woman just pushed her husband off a balcony," my husband said.

I came to, sort of. "Are you talking to me?"

"It's that *Snapped* show," he said, gesturing to the screen, where a bad dramatization of a scrambling fight was taking place, a man's body flopping over a skinny metal railing that, sure, looked like some of the neighboring high-rises' lanais, but not ours. Ours was thicker and solid—more a wall than a rail. Still, only a waist-high wall to hold us back from the pull of all that blue that beckoned and tortured my father?

I looked from my husband to the television and back a few times. It couldn't be. The screen showed the fight and the fall again, this time in slow motion. My two worlds filled our living room. Then a real-life photo of you and my father with a young version of me appeared. My husband stared at our faces. Did he recognize me? I'd never shown him a childhood picture because I didn't have any. The show listed the many police reports of your drunken displays, your "routine disruption of the peace." *Goodbye, peace.* The weight of my baby pressed into me.

"That woman looks..." he said. Paused. Looked back at me. Here it was. I'd been caught.

I wrenched my pinky into Nova's mouth like the nurse said I could, which felt like a crude thing to do but was the only way to force-release her mighty jaw. I handed her sloppily over to him and she grunted out a warm batch of seedy yellow newborn poop that seeped right out of her diaper, which we hadn't done up very well, apparently. I scrambled for the remote but couldn't find it, so much baby shrapnel in my way. Our story played on.

"She doesn't look like me," I said.

"I was gonna say she looks sad," my husband said, laying Nova on the changing pad on the floor. Your granddaughter, whose eyes were open now, stared into my soul. *I know exactly who you are.*

The remote was gone, lost to the ether. The television continued: "He fell thirty-three stories...unthinkable act of violence... neighbors say they often saw the woman drunk in the elevator going up and down, heard the daughter crying for help."

"This is crazy," I said to the room, to this moment. I felt like I'd been injected with speed.

My husband watched on as the television displayed another terrible reenactment of the man who looked nothing like my father being thrown over the railing. "Imagine how awful things would have to be for her to kill her husband like that," he said.

I stared at him in disbelief. Was it possible he understood why a woman would do this? That she was no madwoman at all, but a Mad Woman, a for-years-and-years abused woman? Might he understand what you and I had been through?

"Yeah," I said. "Things would have had to be pretty bad."

He finished the diaper job and kissed Nova's forehead. "She did seem to have a lot of problems, though," he said. "Why didn't she just stop drinking? Or ask for help?"

Panic, hell, back in the high-rise with you and my father. "I don't want to watch this shit," I said, my voice too loud. "I want to watch *Desperate Housewives*."

"Put the ladies on, then." He knew I loved my ladies. Their perfect homes on Wisteria Lane. I'd discovered them alone in my little apartment during college on nights when sleep would not come. So many episodes it seemed I'd never reach the end of the stream. The women became my mother, my best friends, my sisters, my enemies. People died and houses burned down and mysteries were left unsolved, yet by each episode's end, things were more or less hopeful. But even once Gaby and Susan and Bree and Lynette had taken over the screen, playing cards around Susan's cheerful table, a full pot of coffee between them, I felt a charge. I couldn't let *Snapped* go.

"I bet every single one of those women were being tortured for years and years before the moment they finally...*snapped*," I said, using air quotes, barely able to spit out the word.

As Gaby took on a failed-from-inception job as a child pageant coach, my husband said, "I don't know, she seemed sort of nuts the more I think about it."

"If you simplify it that way, you're part of the problem. A huge part."

Nova whimpered and he handed her to me. That was our MO. At the smallest hint of a cry we'd pop her on my boob. She clamped down on my nipple, a shallow latch. I clenched my jaw. "Why are you crying?" he asked.

I touched my face and it was wet. But everything was wet; I was drenched in sweat and milk and the bloody sludge still filling my *mama diapers*. "Domestic violence," I choked out. I hated calling it that, a public service announcement. "Ever consider it?"

"Seems like it's a money thing," he said thoughtfully. "Like, lack of resources breeds desperation breeds violence. I'm sure there are studies that show that correlation."

"You sound like an idiot," I said. "You sound like a fucking anti-feminist idiot. You hate women."

He stared at me. "I honestly can't tell if you're joking right now," he said. "All I'm saying is poverty plays a role. How could it not? Those people" — he gestured to the TV, meaning us — "didn't it say she worked at a pie shop?"

Your favorite floral dress, your cracked plastic drugstore products in your shabby little makeup bag, dollar-store sodium laurel sulfate shampoo in neon colors staining our tub. Our grasping attempts at pleasure and luxury seemed so sad to me now. Hello, familiar coat of shame. On my infant's skin was an organic handmade cream that cost thirty-eight dollars for two ounces.

"He would have tortured her rich or poor," I said.

I got up and walked to our living room window, cradling the baby, who was still latched, the nursing pillow hanging from my waist. I stared into my own reflection. Apart from my perfect new daughter, apart from my husband who knew just how to rock her to sleep, I was still a girl waiting for my mother to come back to me in that high-rise apartment, trapped forever in those moments before I ran to Christina's. No matter what I did in life, how far I got, I'd still be waiting for you, Mother, in that apartment. And that's when my own reflection faded and out the window I saw my father idling.

"Hard to know," my husband said, coming up behind me. I couldn't speak, my fear blocking my throat. Did he see the Jimmy too? But he put his face in the crook of my neck, admiring Nova, who had released my nipple and was now in a deep sleep. He lifted her out of my arms and carried her off to our room. When I looked outside again, my father was gone.

Now in the entryway, my husband handed me my purse. "When you come back," he said, "we have something for you." The kids zipped through the hall in pajamas scream-laughing, seemingly fine without me. Okay.

I closed my eyes and saw the Butcher. That morning I'd awoken feeling the intensity of our love in my body. I pushed it aside while I smiled at my family. I was a mother, a wife. I was Clove. No matter what the feminist lawyer knew, no matter what the Butcher would say in his response, I was still Clove. And Clove was real, a lie that had transformed into a truth, as real as my two children who looked at me with assuredness: Mom.

On the drive to Earthside I checked my Instagram messages at each red light to see if the Butcher had replied. After several checks, *seen* appeared under what I had sent. "Oh my fucking god!" I screamed. I put the phone away deep in my bag. But this was good, I reminded myself. Now it wouldn't be long before he would write back, and then I could deal with all of this logically and efficiently. Maybe there was even a chance the Butcher could go back to you and the lawyer and convince you both I was in fact not needed. You always did value the opinion of a man.

Inside the grocery store I collected myself in front of the immunity shots display, which boasted a new sign: THREE PER CUSTOMER.

A betrayal really. I refused to accept this limitation. I put three into my cart, then selected three more off the shelf, downing them in quick succession. If accused of stealing, I would blame my mind half gone on weaning. Maybe soon someone would wrap me in a weighted blanket and I'd be taken to an inpatient hospital for a thirty-day stay and when I came out I'd realize I was simply Clove and all the rest had been a hallucination, some weird chemical reaction to motherhood.

As the ginger burned down my throat, a memory hit me from a few days prior, in bed with my husband. He had been talking. Something about his mother, Tootsie. A potential visit. I was having a hard time absorbing information lately due to the constant din of my anxiety, but now I considered, what if his mother was the surprise? I had made no progress in finding a nanny—well, finding *her,* the nameless Chevy woman—and now he'd taken matters into his own hands. A part of me was impressed, but the rest of me felt bitter imagining his mother coming into my home, making it hers, the air smelling of holiday-themed synthetic fragrance collections despite the summer season.

Everyone wants to support you, Clove. He'd said something like that. *We just don't know how. If my mom came you could really focus on finding a nanny, interviewing them or whatever it is you need to do.* Yes, I remembered telling him I was still on board with the nanny idea but that it was taking time. *I'd never want to put your mom out,* I'd maybe said. In truth it gave me pleasure to imagine her inconvenienced, but I didn't want the inconvenience to be me.

I checked my messages again as I steered the cart toward Wellness. The hell of a lone *seen*. Of knowing the Butcher had betrayed me by talking to the feminist lawyer. But in my favorite section, I started to calm down, step into the vibration of solution.

137

Somewhere, on one of these shelves, was a product I needed. A product that would fix this, fix me. That was one of the first lessons the Butcher taught me at the market, that everything in a grocery store was the answer to a problem. A vital piece of the whole. The whole was the day, and the day was the life. I ran a finger over the elderberry lineup, the amber jars of health honey, new brands and promises every day, when a voice chimed in—"I know you."

It had finally happened. The supplements were talking.

But no. It was an employee. Wide blue eyes and faint freckles. Indecipherable age. Energy field like a vacuum. I had to catch up to myself here, because of course a part of me knew right when I heard her voice who she was. But the place was wrong, her hair down instead of up. And most importantly, I knew everyone who worked at Earthside, and she definitely did not. And yet, an employee apron. Name tag: JANE. A badge: I'M NEW! BE NICE TO ME!

Confused, I muttered something about the new immunity shots rule. "I would not recommend imposing a customer limit on these." I gestured with my eyes to the empties in my cart.

She smiled. Her top, her jeans, her belly button with its two sparkling diamonds the size of baby teeth. I held the cart to steady myself. I wiped my forehead. Real sweat. "Those can be our secret," she said.

The last thing I needed, another secret. But yes, anything for her. "It's you," I said. "The Chevy woman."

"I don't usually self-identify based on my car, but yeah. I'm the one, the only."

"Why are you here? *How* are you here?"

"I can't make a living, Celine, by driving around town getting hit by distracted moms."

I felt the impact of our crash all over again. "I actually never go by Celine. Forget Celine." It came out too forcefully. Relax. "It's a fine name; I just prefer Clove."

"Well, Clove. Seems like we're supposed to know each other or something."

I was glad she said it. I was thinking the same thing.

"I knew I'd see you again," she said casually as she straightened the Bach flower potions.

"How do you like grocery?" I asked, when what I really wanted to say was, *I've thought of you incessantly since we met, let's never be apart again.* Was I attracted to her? I was indeed, but it wasn't sexual. It was so much more than that.

"This is temporary," she said. "Some other opportunity will present itself. I can feel it."

"I came up in grocery," I said. "It's my favorite place to be. Maybe you'll find you really love it after a while."

"Why don't you work here, then?"

Did she know I fantasized about the peace of clean aisles? "Well, those little kids in the car you saw are the main reason," I said. "I want to be home with them." Had to be home with them, no other choice, or else something terrible would manifest. I also left out that somewhere along the line I'd been convinced working grocery was a lowly pursuit. Something the Glowing Woman herself would not do. I'd gone to college, like she'd instructed, educated myself. "But I miss it."

She laughed, and her charm wrapped around me. "I'm starting over in life."

"That can be really good," I said. "I know a thing or two about it."

"So, you've suffered?" she asked.

Before I could answer, a man passed by, bumping his cart into my hip. "Where's the senna tea?" he asked Jane in a grating voice. I had uncharitable thoughts about him, things my father would have said out loud. "I read about it online."

I grabbed a box off the shelf, tossed it in his cart. "Right in front of you."

He looked to Jane for confirmation that the tea was in fact senna, an herbal laxative that would tear him apart. "It says senna leaf," I said, "on the box. Though I'd proceed with caution."

"She used to work grocery," Jane said kindly to the man. "I trust her with my life."

He had little tufts of hair coming from his ears. It was hard to keep up my anger in the face of them, but still. Men in loud trucks, men with blowers stirring up dust on perfectly fine sidewalks, this man now, bouncing his need around the aisle. I glared. He made the wise decision to move forward.

"I have suffered," I said, picking up the thread.

"You're very pretty," she said. "I thought that when I first saw you. And then when I saw you come in the other day with your kids, just how beautiful you all are together. I mentioned you to Mike in coffee bar. I said one day I'm going to have a family like that woman. He said, 'Yeah, she's a total crushtomer.'"

"Crushtomer?"

"Customers we crush on."

I tucked this knowledge away to savor later. I had always wondered what the staff thought of me, if they noticed me. Now I knew. "Why didn't you say hi then?"

"Mike was drooling all over me. I didn't want you to see me like that and think I was a woman who enjoyed a Mike. You'd create a whole false idea about me when the truth is, I'm a woman who *uses* a Mike. An important distinction."

"Indeed," I said, and smiled. It was sunny summer in the sky. I was an adult in my favorite space with another interesting adult and no one was interrupting us. It was time to shoot my shot and ask her to be my nanny. It was all leading to this. But something stopped me. I could rationalize it as wanting more time to get to know her, vet her for red flags, make sure she knew pediatric CPR. But something else held me back, something selfish, a beating desire, and while desire was a foolish pursuit considering everything, desire pressed its way in. Seeing Jane, I wanted to stock aisles together. I wanted to be in this world, just this way, with her, again and again. Time stopped during a grocery shift, I remembered. And that was all I wanted, for time to stop.

"Are they still hiring?" I'd just see.

"This place is constantly hiring, seems like," she said. "High turnover on account of the fact that so much bullshit goes on."

"Grocery-based bullshit?"

"You would not believe the creepers buying bananas and commenting on employee ass at the same time."

Child's play. I could withstand that if I was with Jane. I looked at her belly-button piercing. I, too, had once had a belly-button piercing. One of Velvet's girls did it during an empty afternoon before I'd been hired at the market, before I'd decided to live. The girl was training to become a body piercer and needed practice. When she was done, two fake aquamarine stones glistened up at me. Later, the Butcher would kiss me there, fake-bite the metal. The first acupuncturist I went to see after I'd moved to Portland implored me to take it out, said that by wearing it I was constantly stimulating my umbilical connection with my mother. That I was, in a sense, torturing myself. I'd taken it out right then on her table. But the scar tissue remained. Jane likely had no idea what would happen to her belly button if she got pregnant. That the cute piercing wouldn't really shrink back after it had been stretched, I could tell her, I could *warn* her. Then I could tell her of the weaning sads. I could tell her what no one had ever told me. It seemed insane to embark on motherhood without another mother farther down the line holding your hand. I saw completely the way I'd be able to give her what I'd so badly needed. The way it would correct something. We'd start together in grocery, where all good things were born, and then we'd meld. With time, perhaps I would tell her about you.

"You don't have a mother anymore, do you?" I said. It wouldn't work if she did. Or if she was one of those women who said her sister was her *best friend*. Those women were unavailable for the brand of trauma bonding I was after. When she didn't answer I filled the air with more words: "You said your mother wasn't stylish the other day. The way you said it made me feel like maybe she wasn't around."

"My mother did a lot of damage and then she died. That's her life story in one sentence."

"As sad as *For sale: baby shoes, never worn*."

She didn't pretend to know the reference. "There's no way you want to work here. Don't you have a husband? Don't you want to be around your cuties all day long? I know I would. Aren't you rich?"

Sweet Jane. "It's a common assumption that pretty people are rich," I said. "People think I've had a nose job but it's not true. This is really my nose. It's my father's nose."

She slid a finger down the bridge of her own. "Does your father like being a grandfather?"

I pictured him holding your wrists. Leaning you over that rail. So high up. So high. *Let's end it now, Alma. Let's end it now.* Had he lived, would those same hands have held my children? Would I have allowed them to? "That's a long story."

"I'd love to hear it," she said. I considered that perhaps she'd be hearing it soon enough, with or without my telling her. Depending on what you decided, Mother, everyone would be. Next to my sacred Earthside checkout line would be my face on every newsmagazine.

I felt the hot throb of my cell phone in my pocket. The Butcher. *Seen,* now maybe a reply. And here I was making new friends.

"Well, I'm in shopping a lot. So I suppose I'll be seeing you."

"Don't crash into anyone, mom."

I normally hated when other adults referred to me as *mom* or *mama,* as if I had no identity beyond my role as a caretaker. But out of Jane's mouth it seemed playful, some kind of inside joke. *I'm calling you* mom, *but only because I know you are that in addition to containing multitudes.*

"Okay, bye." I didn't want to leave her, but I had to; the clock of motherhood persisted, and the clock of you, Mother. As I turned to go, she placed her hand on my lower stomach. I held still. "Get the air down here. Let your body do what it's meant to do, which is breathe."

A tingly warmth oozed from my crown to the small of my back. "Thank you."

I broke into a light run to the front, looking back at Jane every few steps to make sure she didn't evaporate. Around other adults I usually felt several degrees outside myself, performing a part in a play. But I hadn't just then with her. And I hadn't when we'd talked outside our cars that first time. This was valuable; this was rare. Not to be mishandled.

At the checkout, Sandra with her short bleached hair seemed to be waiting for me, no line. "Where's the kiddos today?" she asked. She usually liked to give them several stickers apiece that they would mount on my car windows, leaving permanent residue behind.

"Just me," I said.

She made an exaggerated disappointed face. I loaded my shots onto the belt with some B_{12} supplements I had no memory of selecting and an ashwagandha golden milk latte mix. In the reflection of Sandra's quirky glasses I saw a future chatting with Jane, my new best friend in Wellness. But what about my kids? Who would watch them while I spent many secret hours vetting their future nanny in my favorite place? My heart fell. What made me think I could do something like this? But this was a necessary means to an end. I remembered one of your sponsors telling you to take the body and the mind would follow. My body leaned in. "Can I get an application?"

"A what?" she squawked.

"An application."

"We already have a mom making granola out of her kitchen." I didn't react. I'd let her find her own way. "As far as local vendors go. You're trying to be a local vendor, right?"

A line had formed behind me, and in it stood a father from Nova's class who was a real writer. Last I'd heard he was penning a long, important pastoral American novel that might actually be one of a trilogy. But what did he know about America? A profile I'd read of him mentioned his wife brought him tea to his *study*. America was my mother trying to take a community college class and my father beating her up before she could get out the door. This writer reminded me of the thing I'd learned at college that nearly broke me, nearly derailed my plan of forward success and normalcy: no matter what I did, I would never catch up to the very apparent generational wealth all around me. I wasn't talking about money, though that mattered too. I was talking about the wealth of familial love. The leg up of a trauma-free or low-trauma childhood. The students around me had parents who called every other day, who beckoned them home for the holidays, where their childhood bedrooms were still intact, like shrines. They had not had to bloody their hands to get a seat at the table. And this man in line, this real writer. I could only imagine how much he'd been encouraged, nurtured, connected, and exposed early in life to the arts and sciences. Above all, given access.

He gave me a small wave. He'd probably win a Pulitzer Prize. I offered a mouth smile and turned back to Sandra.

"An application for a job," I hissed. "A regular job. In the Wellness department."

"Oh," Sandra said.

"I'm sure most crushtomers don't ask for a job." I thought I said this in my head, but I'd said it aloud. It was time to go.

She reached behind the counter and handed me the paper. Paused and touched my wrist with tenderness. Said too loudly, "You know, it gives a mother purpose to work outside the home."

"Yes, as opposed to my utter purposelessness in the home." Let her suffer, let her feel shame. But then I cut the tension with a laugh. Light, fun Clove for hire.

I hid the application next to your letter in my purse, next to my cell phone with an unread message from my first love. What surreal items I carried on these strange summer days.

In the dark of the Earthside parking garage, my belly full of electric possibility and ginger, I locked myself in my car. Silence pressed into my ears. How long since I'd been alone in a parking lot without my kids hassling me from the back seat? I couldn't recall. I imagined Jane next to me, supporting me kindly but firmly: *Own your fears before your fears own you. Read the fucking message already.* Okay, if you say so, Jane.

> I never thought I'd hear from you again. I'm in shock. I only ever wanted to protect you. Give you a happy life. I'm sad you're out there imagining I would do something with the intent of hurting you, or as you say, ruining your life. I figured you'd come around eventually, that you'd want to see your mom, to talk about things in a real way. I figured we had time, a lifetime really, but then you left me. I was heartbroken over you, but also, you left me to carry some guilt about what I knew. You left me with a part of yourself that for a long time I felt burdened by. But I've grown a lot since then. And now that you've reached out to me, I feel I can tell you that I think we need to talk. I thought I was at peace with our silence, with your disappearance, but I've known for a while that I'm not. There are things you need to hear. That I need to hand back to you. Let me know if you're interested in a conversation, a real one. Face-to-face and not on this app.
>
> And C-Love, I was right back then. I think of you every single day. It was nice seeing your message even under these circumstances.

This was not at all what I had expected. There were things the Butcher needed to hand back to me? Face-to-face? But what things? The Butcher said he would never do something to hurt me. I did believe that. I just couldn't be sure we had the same ideas about what would hurt me.

CHAPTER 12

Back at home, Tootsie wore a crisp white button-down blouse over pressed chambray slacks, white Keds adorned with tiny rhinestones. She had a small Stars and Stripes flag pinned to her shirt and red-framed glasses that magnified her already large eyes. She loved the United States of America. I took stock of the house, imagined what she saw. It was husband-clean, meaning half-assed clean, meaning good-try clean but did you get the toilets, the sinks, the dust in the corners? No. Things were tossed in closets and floors were unswept, pillows unpoufed, but "good enough." She was the only grandmother my children knew. This really killed me. That for all my attempts at inserting myself into a normal and adoring family, ensuring my children would have what I never did, I had still failed in the grandparent department. For Tootsie was busy with her other grandchildren who lived within a five-mile radius from her in eastern Washington. She was, as she told my husband, an "out of sight, out of mind type of person." And her other grand-children were in sight, she reminded us. She never texted and she never called. You would have loved my kids, Mother.

I set my purse down on the foyer table and saluted her. "Tootsie." She regarded me from the couch with a small twitch of her eyebrow. The children swarmed her, did what they did best, preventing potential adult interaction. It seemed she'd arrived just minutes before me.

When my husband and I were newly dating, Tootsie loved me. I said all the right things, I brought little gifts each time we visited, which was at least once a month back then, so much free, childless time. She was kind to me in a very basic way. But it seemed that with each step forward—engagement, marriage, first child—she took a step back.

I learned then it had been a wild miscalculation to think a motherhood of my own that included support from my mother-in-law would somehow replace my need for you. This was confirmed in the months that followed Nova's birth as my desire to cry on your shoulder swelled, every time I saw a woman with her baby and her own mother, every time a woman at my new moms group mentioned her mother. They were everywhere, these held women. Meanwhile, Tootsie faded from view, visiting only once during Nova's first year.

I often wondered if maybe she smelled it on me, my desire for a mother, and it repelled her. She once said she thought it was ridiculous when daughters-in-law called their husband's mother *Mom*. I took note: never call Tootsie *Mom*. I never would have. But still, it felt like a rejection. It must have taken a lot for my husband to get her here. What had he said? How crazy did he think I was?

"Surprise," my husband said. He looked like he wanted me to high-five him. When I stared back coldly, he guided me to our bedroom and closed the door.

"When did we decide on this?" I said.

"Listen. You won't research childcare, you won't find a nanny. You say you need more balance and more space, but you're too scared to let anyone else in. I'm not going to wait around all summer for you to be ready for help. This is for you. So you can write. So you can do yoga. All the things you want to do. So you can stop hating your life. I'm sort of ready for you to not hate your life again. Honestly, I'm worried about you."

"It's not"—I started sharp and then caught myself, continued in a whisper—"it's not like I've abandoned anyone here. You act like you're some savior doing more lately, but they are your kids! You aren't *helping* me. You don't get a prize for being a good *helper*."

"This right here is why I asked my mom to come. You don't factor in that I have a full-time job. Full-time. That pays for our life. What do you want me to do, quit? You make the money? Doing what?"

"Well, that's the design of this system isn't it? We'll never get to find out."

He sucked in a tight breath. I imagined him lunging at me. Pushing me into the bookcase, the books falling on my head. My body sliding to the floor. I hadn't ever caused problems before now. Was it possible to unlock aggression in him? Could violence ever truly be off the table?

"She's never shown interest in the kids. Especially Lark. It was like he was never born," I said. "Where has she been all this time when we could have really used her support? Now she wants to swoop in?"

"Well, she did visit after he was born."

Right. The time I'd requested Tootsie and his father show proof of getting whooping cough vaccines after a terrifying presentation at the midwifery clinic on the dangers of whooping cough to newborns. When she offered a shoddily written doctor's note on my own notepad from my own kitchen, I told them no holding the baby. My husband's father didn't seem to care, a passive and nervous man who spent most of the visit pacing the hallway, jangling the coins in his pocket. But Tootsie sat across from my nursing station in the living room like we were in a standoff. I guess she thought I'd give in eventually, have to use the bathroom and set the baby down. But by then I was no rookie mom; I could pee—hell, I could take a shit—with the baby still latched, I could do it all myself, all the time.

She left after two days of this, and I never asked my husband for details about the harshly whispered talk they'd had by the door before my father-in-law drove her away in their Suburban.

"She could have stayed and helped, made food, played with Nova, taken her to the zoo, unloaded the dishwasher. But all she cared about was smothering him with infectious kisses. You do realize your nonchalance forces me to carry the entire load of worry. It's a heavy load."

"She's the only grandmother. It could be worse."

"Yeah, it could be my mom."

He didn't like that because it didn't make sense. My mother was dead. And it was sad to him that I had no parents, deeply sad. I assumed, though he would never say, that on some level we were both reckoning with the fact that we had married people whose families were total bummers. To think, I'd been horny about camping!

"I'm not doing this," he said.

"Good, yes, let's ramp up the tension now so we can be in a full-fledged fight in front of Tootsie. That will be fun."

"You want family but you reject my entire family. You want community but you barely ever see friends anymore."

"I tried with that one babysitter, the one who broke our two-year-old daughter's leg? Remember that? Or maybe you don't because I was the one who dealt with it. I left her to write in a coffee shop for two hours and in two hours she was returned to me literally broken. Sorry, never again. Not worth it."

It felt good to remind us both that I *had* tried that one time with the babysitter who had let Nova climb a jungle gym while she stared at her phone, only looking up once my child was screaming on the ground. "I don't know what's wrong with her, but I know she fell," the highly recommended young woman had feebly tried to explain when I'd returned home to find Nova in shock, pale and staring strangely at the wall in her room. Jane knew better than to be on a phone while watching a small child, I could tell.

"So now it's worth it to you to make yourself insane being the only one who can take care of them. Ever heard of *it takes a village?*"

My jaw tightened. "The village is a lie."

"Our son almost choked to death and you were standing right next to him."

"Are you kidding me?" How dare he mention the time Lark's lollipop had come off the stick and he'd sucked it back in his throat. A piece of Halloween candy. "That was one of the worst moments of my life, and you're rubbing it in my face?"

"I say it only to show you it can happen to anyone at any time. Even you. You rear-ended someone with them in the car a few weeks ago."

"You have no idea what I've been through. What I've seen. What I've lost. There's a reason I'm like this." *Too far.*

"Well, you never talk about it, so how would I know? The past is the past. Are you going to let it ruin our lives?"

"Wise up," I said. "The past is right here, right now."

Nova was suddenly next to her father, the door ajar. How long had she been listening? "Stop fighting!"

"Oh, sweetie, this isn't fighting," I said. I meant it to sound comforting, but it came out like a threat. "You've never seen fighting. Neither has your father."

Then my own father was in the room, reaching over and picking up our nice jade lamp, hurling it, narrowly missing Nova's head and leaving a permanent gash in the wall. Next he would fixate on a small thing. Like the time you bought new jeans that had a tiny pink heart sewn on the corner of the back pocket.

"Trying to pick up all the guys at work?" he had started in. You were in the kitchen and he was leaning against the fridge, eyes squinted, taking you in. You were so cute. He hated how cute you were. He lived in fear of another person recognizing your cuteness. So did you.

"Here comes Alma, whoring around in her new jeans. Wearing those jeans so all them guys at work will stare at your ass when you bend over to take a pie out of the oven?"

"I don't even take the pies out of the oven, asshole," you'd whispered. I felt instantly mad at you for calling him a name. *Why did you have to provoke him like this?* I remember thinking.

He dragged you to the back bedroom, held you to the floor on your stomach, took out a pocketknife, and cut that heart right out of the denim. You didn't move. Play dead, you'd instructed. But if you were in the open and a man had a gun, run in a zigzag pattern. There were so many rules to survival and you wanted me to know them all, the way some people's mothers pass down recipes.

I'd stood in the doorway hoping the heart cutting was the climax, watching, calculating what sort of risk we were dealing with. The floral dress was safe, I knew. And while the level of public influence was indeed higher in a densely populated high-rise apartment building, more people around than at The Pines in California, my father had adjusted, had learned to enact his violence in near silence, an unnerving thing to watch, like an action movie on mute. He shredded most of your wardrobe that night in one determined streak. I walked back to the kitchen as he did it, my hands twitchy. I grabbed the now melted bowl of ice cream I'd been eating when he started in. Came up behind him and broke the dish over his head.

Later you recounted this story to Christina, telling her about my violence, how it hadn't fazed him. How he'd kept going. You threw up your hands. "Good excuse for us to hit the Goodwill again, at least, right, Calla Lily, get a new bowl? Maybe we can convince these two to go on an outing for once."

"I won't be caught dead in the Goodwill with my medically fragile daughter, are you crazy?" Christina waited. Stared at you. This was a few months after we girls had gotten our periods and Christina had grown less tolerant of your excuses.

"What?" you said. "Give me a break, I've been through it."

Christina looked at me and shook her head. At first, I thought she was upset with me, that she perceived I had done the wrong thing. But her anger was for you. "Guess what kind of man she's gonna end up with one day? Bingo! Just like her daddy. You're putting her through hell."

You took a long drink from your grape juice with vodka. Pointed at me, incredulous. "Her? Imagine how I feel. All my clothes are ruined."

But why was it your duty to keep us away from a monster? Why was the question never—*Why is he doing this to you both?* I didn't tell any of you that as I'd cracked the bowl over his head, when his scalp had split enough to bleed, I had floated above myself looking down at the scene, at my parents. I thought, *You are not mine and I am not yours.*

But somehow, we were each other's.

"He's diminished you," Christina said to you. "He's dimmed your light so low I can barely see it. Soon, he'll snuff you right out." She turned to me. "You're going to end up watching your mother die. But you already know that. Your mother's the only one who doesn't seem to."

I looked to Celine, who had been quietly listening. I pressed my toe to her elbow. "What do you think?"

She turned her pale face from you to me and back to you, Mother. "I wish I could save you, Alma."

But Christina cut her off. "Every woman's got to save herself. That's what no one tells you. But it's the whole truth."

I looked at Nova now, her hands in fists at her sides. So young. She knew nothing of real fighting, but her body was strung up by our tension nonetheless. And though I'd long feared becoming like you, it struck me now that I was much more like my father. My cunning, my heat, my lies. Perhaps I was the danger I worried so much about.

"Okay," I said to my husband. "Tootsie can stay." Nova whooped in victory, a sudden mood change, and threw the bedroom door open to reveal Tootsie in the hallway, listening. She stepped back, pretended to be looking for the bathroom.

"Sorry," I said. "We were just getting on the same page." My husband patted his mother on the shoulder and then scurried off, presumably to exchange observations about the weather with his father.

Tootsie let out an exasperated sigh. "You were speaking loudly. Anyone could hear you. You were upsetting the children."

"We *were* speaking loudly. Anyone *could* hear us. You were definitely not pressing your ear to the door to listen." I used my toddler communication skills: nod and affirm their reality without taking it on as your own. The kids pulled on their grandmother's arms, starting up the game of *who is getting the most attention.*

"I won't need you hovering around while you, while you…get yourself together. I'm perfectly competent with children, despite what you may think. I raised the man you're married to, in case you forgot."

"You *are* competent, Tootsie," I said. "You raised my husband."

She softened, looked like maybe she was gearing up to say something kind. Instead she said, "Women these days are so delicate."

My children began chanting, "What did you bring us, what did you bring us?" switching Tootsie into grandma mode then. She disappeared into the guest room, returning with a nearly bursting plastic bag of toys, dumping them out onto our organic wool-and-cotton-blend rug: bubble guns and water guns—*no real guns in there, right, Toots?*—the plastic figurines of entire Disney movie casts, a life-sized Barbie head for Nova and a fleet of trucks, trucks, trucks for Lark. I felt myself become unnecessary to the scene. My children were not tuned in to me, not even Lark, who was so excited to see this elusive grandmother that he could barely catch his breath.

"Best grandma ever," he squealed, pressing a button on the back of a talking Elsa, releasing a high-pitched scream song. Button cell batteries were back.

"You should go," my husband said quietly behind me. "Just try it out. Leave for one hour. Come back, see that the kids are fine, leave for another hour. I know you can do it. Trust me. Look, they're already having a blast."

He was a good man. I had not been wrong about that so many years ago. He was steady, predictable, slow to anger if he ever angered at all. He didn't know what he didn't know, sure. But he was good. The question soon would not be about goodness, though. It would be about darkness. It would be about resilience. It would be a test of what a man like him could withstand.

CHAPTER 13

I did not write and I did not do *my* yoga and I did not call a friend to get tea. In my first moments of having someone else in charge of my children, truly in charge, I found myself driving back to Earthside, the job application humming in my purse. The same day I found Jane, Tootsie had appeared like a cosmic permission. So why not stay in that flow, sit in the parking lot and fill the application out now before I lost my nerve? Was it desperate to return the very same day, or was it showing initiative? All I knew was that I had to act.

The automatic doors welcomed me, my second time in, not unusual; I came in three times a day if my anxiety called for it. The smoothie bar emitted its comforting Vitamix whirr, the produce section twinkled under the bright but not bothersome lighting, and the long aisle of bulk bins, the contents of which were 25 PERCENT OFF TODAY ONLY, told the story of wholesomeness—everything here is good, everything here is safe. The cashiers scanned and smiled, punching in the item codes of wet cucumbers and ripe nectarines, knobby thumbs of ginger and turmeric root, codes they had memorized, codes that would be rooted in their subconscious forever, and the meatpackers in their gloves and black coveralls playfully hassled one another, bandanas on their heads, toothpicks between their teeth. The show of grocery played on with grace and precision, each person a vital part of the production. My diaphragm released the slightest bit now in the safest place on earth. Grocery, the opposite of violence.

There was Sandra at her usual checkout station. "Back already?" she said.

But I would not be embarrassed. "I'm being proactive," I said, handing her the application.

She assessed my information and nodded a lot. "A writer." I felt a thrill at the suggestion that my English and creative writing degrees made me a writer in her eyes. Had she said this to me just weeks before, I would have objected, but since receiving your letter, Mother, I found myself overflowing with words in response. "I like writers in grocery. You all do a good job with those staff-pick cards. Customers love that kind of thing."

I briefly imagined a whole Instagram page called *Writers in Grocery,* maybe an off-Broadway musical. "I can start today," I blurted out, for a moment feeling as bare as I had that day at the market, standing before the Butcher for the first time, asking him to choose me.

Sandra mimed a series of exaggerated thinking expressions. Finally: "I guess we could get going on training while we run your background stuff."

Celine's background stuff. It never failed to produce panic. Every record from my marriage license to my children's birth certificates had her name on it. I tried to remind myself that I had accepted the gift of Celine's information to *not* feel like this, though. This was the freedom Christina had offered. Yet why had it never quite felt that way? "Great. Sounds perfect."

In the staff room, I claimed a locker. I had never been in this area of the store before and it was just as lovely as I'd imagined. Sandra brought me an apron, an employee packet, a hat, and a complimentary reusable water bottle.

"I'd love it if Jane could train me," I said to her, sinking into a handsome green velvet couch. A fiddle-leaf fig tree hulked in the corner and a tray of gluten-free cookies were arranged on the coffee table for the taking.

"Jane practically just got trained herself," Sandra said. "She's definitely still in learning mode."

I knew at Portland's Kindest Grocery Store they had to take my mental health pleas seriously or face a potential lawsuit. I assumed this from the many self-identifying stickers the staff wore (PLEASE BE PATIENT, I AM _____ ☺) and the fact that at least two employees walked around with emotional support kittens in small clear-domed backpacks.

"Honestly, I'm suffering from post-weaning anxiety," I said. "It's a real disorder despite total medical disregard. It's vital I work with someone I already feel comfortable with."

Her face softened. "We've got you, Clove. Every one of us has stood where you stand today, nervous to start a new job. It's like the first day of school, isn't it?"

I couldn't remember a single first day of school before college. "So I can work with Jane?"

"That part's not up to me. Stephen's the main manager. I just get people settled in. But I can put in a word, of course. If you think it will really help you."

I was about to pivot and ask about discount benefits when Jane walked in with long, powerful strides, glancing at me, not allowing herself to appear surprised, though I could tell she was. She untied her employee apron and plopped onto a tasseled meditation cushion below a sign that said QUIET, PLEASE, REGULATION IN PROGRESS.

She grinned at me, sipping her free break-time employee smoothie. "You don't fuck around."

"Their grandmother is in town," I said. "Tootsie."

"Thanks, Tootsie," she said. "Now I get you to myself."

"And I get you."

Something passed between us, something important yet hard to define, made impossible to define because Mike from coffee bar, maker of the best coconut milk matcha latte in town, snuck in and tickled Jane's side. She let out a squeal, sprang up, and collapsed theatrically into his arms. He wore a trucker's hat with the state of Oregon emblazoned on it in silver glitter, his flannel shirt working overtime to cover his burly middle. His long brown beard was oiled and his eyes were tiny twitching marbles in a bowl of pudding. *Move on, buddy. No chance here.* But then as Jane's hand snaked around and pinched his butt where his boxers came up over his belted jeans, I remembered her comment from before. How was she using him? She was certainly putting on a convincing performance of a woman going below the standards set for her by nature.

"Got a backstage pass?" Mike said to me. The fourth wall between crushtomer and staff, shattered.

"She works here now," Jane told him as she playfully pushed him away. His eyes moved up and down her body, performing an unabashed physical exam. I felt like the protective father sitting on a porch with a shotgun in a country song. I remembered then a boy I'd had a crush on in school. I was only thirteen, and I relaxed one day around my father, wasn't wearing my two sports bras — Christina had suggested I do this to flatten my chest, knowing it was best for my father to continue to see me as a child — and made the mistake of mentioning the boy to him. Nothing about the crush, just merely mentioning that a boy in my English class liked to fish, and didn't my father like to fish too? He swigged his beer. "Look at you, a slut like your mother. Thought you were different."

I'd cried, tried to make him take it back. Tried to convince him how different I was. But it was too late. He'd glimpsed it. My sexuality, my form taking shape into another *crazy woman*. I worried my womanhood would make him focus on me during beatings. On the one hand I thought it would be good to give you a break. On the other, I was terrified. But more and more I saw the fear went two ways: when he looked at me, he looked into his own eyes.

Mike turned his examination my way, appraising me tits down. I could see those little eyes doing math: he worked with hot Jane *and* the crushtomer? I cleared my throat. "I bet there's a long line forming at your station," I said. "Wouldn't want you to get behind."

He shook himself like a dog coming out of water. I couldn't help but consider the ways his fantasy of what was under my smock stacked up against the reality. How neither he nor Jane could rightly imagine my body, all that had happened to it. For instance, my breasts, two smashed cupcakes. If she wanted children, she'd need to know what a diastasis-recti abdominal separation was.

"Fall on hard times or something?" Mike asked me. How little I cared for his presence now that my daily warm beverage wasn't part of the transaction. Silence was often the best course with men. I swam my hands around the large pockets of my new apron. Mommy was not playing dress-up in our pretend store with wooden fruit at home. I was in the world. My and Jane's world.

"You got kids, right?" he continued. "Cuties."

I warmed slightly. Anyone who was nice about my children got points.

"Yeah, the grandmother is watching them," Jane told him. "But Clove doesn't know what she's going to do once Tootsie goes back home. I guess she'll have to quit her job here."

"You talk about wanting kids all the time," he said to Jane. "Why don't you be her nanny? See what it's really like. Me, I got six nieces and nephews. It's no joke."

Her face lit up, and it was then I saw his utility; the universe was good! The universe was strategic, unexpectedly using boorish manimals like Mike for the greater good. "I'd love to nanny those smart little babies. Hello, dream job."

I did not know her, I reminded myself. She could be anyone.

But the vision was already rooted: Jane and I floating together, wispy women ghosts, nearly conjoined we'd be, unshakable amid the demands of children, of household, breezing above it all, embodiments of ease and plenty. What could not be done with two hands could be done with four. Two laps to sit in, two chests in which to smother tears. I could visualize my children delirious with it, drunk on communal love. Of course I was not enough for them. I was never meant to be.

Children, we would muse under the shade of the weeping willow. *For whom play is the only true work.*

Shocking, then, when Sandra guided me upstairs to the indoor/

outdoor eating space, far away from Jane and my healing journey, and deposited me with Stephen, the hiring manager, who wore a very tight black Ramones T-shirt and jeans with holes on his upper thighs and Chuck Taylor sneakers and heavy black-framed glasses. His hair had been recently dyed black, the rim of color still visible on his skin. He was probably older than me but spoke like a concussed teenager.

"So we have an art wall," he said. But it sounded like, "Sooooo. We have an art walllllllll?" Like he wanted my confirmation, but none was needed because we were in fact standing before a large orange wall with a series of beach watercolors hanging from it. "Sebastian's gonna be here soon with his collection and he'll help you hang it. For now, take these old ones down and put them in a box."

"Who's Sebastian?" I asked, my rage mounting with each second away from Jane.

Stephen squinted at me over the glasses and nodded. "Oh yeahhhhh. You're new? I mean. He's rad? He does rad stuff? You can look him up on Instagram or whatever it's called. His name's Sebastian Bliss."

Or whatever it's called. Yeah, right.

"I'm on Instagram. I actually have a lot of followers. People really like my aesthetic," I said, and nothing, *nothing* could have sounded worse.

I began taking down the paintings. They were labeled at ninety dollars each, which seemed a high price for art the likes of which Nova and Lark produced daily. When I was nearly done, a middle-aged man appeared next to me in a maroon collegiate sweatshirt and jeans, fine blond hair combed straight back. He held a large flat portfolio.

"These are barely allowed in this country," he said like we were in on some conspiracy together.

I refused to look interested, could not give that satisfaction. He moved the salt and pepper out of the way and set the portfolio on a table. "Kombucha scoby art," he explained, holding up a large laminated flat that looked like a pressed human organ, burnt orange and red and translucent with veins running through it.

"Looks like a placenta," I said, remembering giving birth to my own, how my chamomile midwife held it up for me to see like it was a prized cut of lamb, and proclaimed, *It's a beaut!* while my legs shook and I wondered if I was dying. Sebastian Bliss gestured for me to take it and I stepped back, my hands clasped behind me.

"That's your basic scoby," he said, unfazed. "I've also got earrings I make out of them if you're interested. Dried everything in an Earthside pie pan."

"Excuse me," I said. I went back into the locker room. I felt acutely that I was going to cry but I couldn't now, because there was Jane, looking like she'd been crying herself, typing furiously on her cell phone.

"Everything okay?"

She sighed. Raised her eyes. "It's Stephen. For a hot second I thought maybe he'd be a good dad, but I overestimated him."

"Stephen? I thought maybe you and Mike…"

"I tried at first with Mike but he's a grade A fuckup. And he didn't get me pregnant. So on to the next."

"And the next is *Stephen*?" I said, aghast. She needed me more than I realized. "Jane, you should be dating, like, grounded, cool dudes. Dudes who have done some emotional processing. That guy is pulling a heavy suitcase."

She stood straighter. "I'm sick of being alone, and my clock is ticking. Once I have kids I'll be needed. I'll belong to someone."

I remembered the nights alone before I'd met my husband. My paranoia. The way I'd set booby traps for intruders, make escape plans in my head as I fell asleep. I, too, had fantasized about the noise and distraction of family as a means to avoid personal suffering, not understanding that one could never truly escape oneself.

"I get it, I do, but you can do a lot better."

"I'm done imagining life is going to work for me in a traditional way," she said. "Things aren't going to come easy for me like they have for you."

I pictured Jane living with us, experiencing the chaos of actual real-life parenting. Maybe she'd still want it. More, even, because, vital to the continuation of our species, she'd convince herself she could do it better.

"Some things came easy," I said. "But most of it was very hard-won."

"Sorry, I didn't mean for it to come out that way. I'm just overwhelmed by the fact that Stephen has been showing my nudes to all these slavering dogs around here without my consent. Mike just told me."

I tried not to show my shock, not that Stephen had betrayed her, but that she had trusted him in the first place. "If it makes you feel any better, I'm pretty sure everyone in this store has seen my tits at some point. I've nursed in every aisle. Now that I think of it, maybe that's why I'm a crushtomer."

She looked at my chest. "Are they different now that you stopped nursing?"

"Oh yeah."

"Show me."

"Show me a nude."

She held up her phone to reveal a picture of what seemed to be her, peering back over her ass on a bed, mouth in an O. The photo struck me as a bit porny, an energetic mismatch for the woman who stood before me. I shifted my smock over to one side and pulled up my top. Out popped a tired boob, my nipple sort of flattened into the breast skin. "Now it's this."

She was unfazed. "Gorgeous. All boobs, gorgeous. That's what I say."

"Sag," I observed, plucking the nipple and lifting it to demonstrate the way the boob flesh didn't readily come along.

"Do you think on your death bed you'll be worried about saggy tits from nursing?"

"Actually," I started. She should know it wasn't the act of breastfeeding that pulled buoyant breasts to the floor; it was the hormones that came with pregnancy and postpartum. It was the whole package. You could choose to forgo breastfeeding entirely and still your boobs could change wildly. This is what I wanted to say, the truth to another woman.

But she cut in. "You'd never cheat on your husband, right?"

She didn't care about breastfeeding. "I don't have the energy even if I wanted to."

"See, that's the kind of stability I'm looking for."

I hadn't said much about my husband to her yet. I wondered what made her assume stability. A part of me was proud, though. It's what I'd been after all these years.

"Never fuck that up," she went on. "My father was stable and my mother trampled him."

"Was he around?"

"Left when I was little. Well, she pushed him out. That's the truth. I was there. But that's not the story she fed me after."

"Do you talk to him now?"

"He's dead."

I wondered if she was lying. The way she said it. I had to remind myself that just because I was a liar didn't mean everyone was.

"Well, the important thing with men is to find one that won't kill you."

"Jesus," she said. "You're so intense."

"There's a hundred ways these fuckers can take your life and only one of them is literal."

"I just need the sperm. It's like a free sperm bank in here."

She had to be joking. "You really want a kid bad."

She sighed. Maybe I had gone too far and she'd tired of me. But then she perked up. "What are you supposed to be doing right now?"

"Well, there's a man out there who wants me to hang his scoby art."

She laughed. "Forget that freak. Let's play today." She took my hand and we walked out of the locker room back into the frigid air of the store, *together*.

We wasted the next four hours high on rhodiola tinctures, bouncing around the store, opening boxes and trying things, Jane leading the charge. I told her about the market in general terms, nothing too personal, just the palm-sized spiders that would sometimes emerge from banana boxes and how we played nostalgic eighties music to make customers feel happy and buy more. How there was something satisfying about standing for so long, watching the community collect their necessities. Then, like an out-of-body experience, I heard myself telling her about the sexy butcher boyfriend I'd had.

Jane listened rapt, asked all the right juicy questions, but somewhere in my retelling, I felt I'd revealed too much, felt like I had on that first date with him. I wanted to suck my words back in, keep them for myself, but this was what I'd wanted with Jane: transparency, sisterhood. *It's okay, Clove. Baby steps.* "Anyway," I said. "I'm sure you don't want to hear about that."

"Oh, I do. I live for the details." She looked deep in my eyes. Finally she said, "What's wrong? Isn't your husband as good in bed as your grocery guy?"

"It's different," I said. "It's good, it's just…without urgency. You know?"

She looked at me expectantly. "Say more."

"All you need to know about my husband is what he looks like so you can hide me if he comes in." I showed her a picture of him. "Remember, this is my secret job."

"Is this some adult game for you guys?"

"He doesn't normally set foot in grocery stores," I said. "Especially not if his mother is around. And she's a Fred Meyer person. Safeway maybe. Grocery Outlet. She's not about the… experience."

"What about your friends, or other parents from school?"

I could barely visualize their faces. I simply didn't care about them anymore in the face of my entire life imploding by summer's end. "I'm undergoing something major. I'm in the birth canal. And grocery is going to help me transform into a better version of myself. You are."

"You have a lot of faith in me."

The rhodiola sped up in my veins. "I want you to hang out with my kids. You never know, you might like to help us out a bit. But not as a nanny. That's not it. Something more. You know, we could sort of…do life together." What was I thinking? This was way too soon. But I couldn't help myself. Maybe the village could exist after all. "I think you'd be amazing with children," I went on. "And one day make a great mother. I could help you."

She smiled. "I just wish my body would cooperate."

"Say more," I echoed back to her.

"Well, I've been trying to get pregnant for ages. I keep thinking finding the right sperm is the issue. But no dice. I went to a doctor a few months ago and she told me it was very unlikely I'd be able to conceive, but I figure why not still try."

"I hope this isn't overstepping, but have you considered that maybe your body doesn't want to procreate with a Mike?"

She rolled her eyes. "Maybe."

"What will you do if you can't get pregnant?"

She put her hands over her womb. "I'll find a way. In fact, I can feel myself changing already. Maybe it's all your maternal hormones rubbing off on me." We laughed, but I felt a slight unease, a judgment rising in me I wasn't proud of. I wanted to ask questions like, Who will watch your baby while you work this time-consuming and relatively low-paying job? What makes you think your body is ever going to cooperate without more invasive assistance? But I didn't say those things. Because all of that could be solved if we joined forces. It was July. We were going to need each other more than I thought.

★ ★ ★

Eventually Stephen said I could clock out and print my schedule and I'd be good to go. Somehow an entire shift had passed and I hadn't worried about my children. It was like they existed in another dimension. Was this how parents with childcare routinely felt, shape-shifting between two disparate worlds?

"Did Jane show you the ropes?" he asked.

Jane had shown me how to position my body so when I opened the bulk bin of organic chocolate-covered sprouted almonds and shoved a handful in my mouth I would not be seen by customer or camera. She had shown me how to put bags of CBD gummies in my purse before they were logged into the system. She had explained I could forage organic bones from the meat counter for free to make homemade bone broth and at that I had stopped in my tracks and said, "You know how to do that?" and she said, "Sure, don't you?" and I fell in love. Quite simply, I'd had fun with Jane, untethered fun, worrying for no one's safety, for the first time in years.

"You're going to schedule us together all the time. We're going to do whatever we want."

"We'll see about that," he said.

"I wonder what corporate would think of you showing Jane's naked photo around to, like, Mike over there."

He pretended to be confused. "What are you talking about?"

"You know what I'm talking about."

"She's an adult woman who can handle herself."

I pulled out my phone and opened it to my Instagram profile. I hadn't even realized my follower count had crept up another ten thousand. So many people loved my faceless anonymous photos with their meaningful captions. I turned the screen toward him. "Imagine your face right here, shamed for all to see. Lots and lots of local mamas and businesses follow me." For a moment I considered how disembodied it felt to have so many connections online while not a single friend had called or stopped by the house to check in. They sent me crystal ball emojis instead.

He tried to pretend like he didn't care, but I saw the flicker. Felt the shift. "She sends the pictures to everyone. You'll probably get one soon if you haven't already."

"You mean nothing to me," I whispered. "I'm here for Jane. This is a stop on a much longer ride."

"You sound like the predator here, not me."

"Stephen," I said, leaning in close, "I'm desperate. And maybe you are too. Maybe this wouldn't be your first brush with a sexual harassment complaint." Now I was taking chances.

"That chick got jealous and quit on her own terms."

"I'm sure." A tingle ran through me. You and I rarely talked back to my father. It was so much safer to stay quiet. But now I saw the flaw in that logic—all that silence had gone back into us as poison.

I looked at Stephen now and saw him, the good and the bad, and wondered why it was, as a woman, so often I was forced to parse out bad men's goodness and allow it to override everything else. To take the *whole picture* into consideration. Like my father, for instance. Why couldn't he just be a monster? Why couldn't I settle myself in that truth, let x equal x and cherish the simplicity. It would be easier. But I still held out hope for my father, despite him being dead, hope that the good parts of him were at peace. The bad parts too. Especially those.

I walked away from Stephen and clocked out, my pockets full of stolen GoHealth bars. The world still owed me small treats.

"Brown rice syrup is the first ingredient in those, you know," Stephen said to my back, almost kindly. "It's just sugar."

"Actually," I said, "brown rice syrup is an easily digestible vegan and macrobiotic glucose-based sweetener metabolized by all the body's cells without overtaxing the liver like its fructose cousins, honey or maple syrup. Or, god forbid, white sugar."

He didn't flinch. "What about the arsenic found in rice?"

I tore one open and took a big chewy bite. "I'll take my chances."

CHAPTER 14

Toward the end of my father's life, he began to think in absolutes. In order to overcome his dark traveler, he would have to kill us first, then himself. Finally put an end to what we had not been able to solve. This was not what he'd envisioned for a family life. The traveler had ruined us all. He sat at the kitchen table explaining his theory as I made toast, my fingernails still wet with purple polish we had bought at the dollar store. Even purchases like this had to be schemed about—if asked, I was to say a girl at school had given it to me. You were napping off the latest fight in the back bedroom.

"It's not right the way we are," he said. He spoke as if all this, "our situation," as he called it, was a collective failing.

"What if you *are* the dark traveler?" I asked him, taking teenagerly chances. I was sixteen.

"That's the problem," he said. "I used to think me and the dark traveler were two separate entities, but now I can't be sure. Ending the whole thing is the only way."

"Leave us out of it," I said. He stood up and got close to me, beer and cinnamon Altoids.

"I can't do that," he said apologetically. He put both heavy hands on my shoulders. I searched his blue eyes for the real him, but he wasn't there anymore.

"Why not?"

"Because I've infected you both," he said. "And it's too late for you. We have to take it with us." He looked for his traveler in my eyes. Cringed when he found it. "My own father should have done us the favor when he had the chance. But he was too chickenshit."

"Back up," I said to him. "I'm choking on your beer fumes."

"Do you think you're funny?" he said.

"I don't know what I am."

That wasn't entirely true. I knew I was a person who would do anything for you, Mother. I knew protecting you was why I existed at all.

But now I know better.

Please consider how lousy my eyewitness account would be. My memory of the night my father died is an ever-changing hologram. Sure, I could explain that Hawai'i wasn't what we hoped it would be. That the abuse got worse each year and we marked time by your injuries. Two broken wrists not months after we moved. The next year, a skull fracture that would forever change the curve of your brow on one side, which you downplayed with expertly placed bangs. A ruptured bowel when he kicked you too hard, and the resulting sepsis that required several surgeries to resolve when I was thirteen. We really thought you were going to die that time. But you survived to see me turn fourteen and for him to push you hard enough into the bathtub to shatter your pelvis and leave you with a permanent limp. Fifteen brought the first time he dangled you over the wall of the lanai by your armpits, and we knew, didn't we, that we didn't have much longer?

But I could never be sure how you felt, if you saw reality as I did. Or if you had settled into this life so deeply that there really wasn't a way out, even if the exit signs were clearly marked. All of it was baffling to you, Mother, each assault, each cruel word, surprised you as if it was the first. "It would be surprising if he *stopped* hitting you, Mom," I'd say, and you'd shrink a little bit at my tone, which by then was very much a replica of my father's. You would remind me that it was my father who nurtured you back to health each time. Kissed your wounds and grew soft with you, accommodating. Our best times all together were usually on the heels of a hospital stay. Meanwhile my peers at school played sports, read books, made out in movie theaters.

My father died at night is what I know. I remember you had seemed clear and cheerful that morning, which meant you were due for another injury. The last ER nurse, a woman, had looked not at you but at me when she said, "This won't go on forever, you know." You heard it as *One day he will have to change,* and I heard it as *Next time you will die.*

"Can you help us?" I'd asked this nurse in the hallway.

She didn't look as disturbed as I thought she should. "Your mama want the help?"

But that cheerful morning, we headed to the beach. My father and I swam out far in the ocean, and there in the depths something happened that changed me forever, something I will tell you about in detail, but not yet. I do remember that part well. I wish I didn't.

We came home exhausted, and my father got drunk, while I fell into a thin, anxious sleep punctuated by the cracking sound of beer cans opening. I awoke to you and my father on the lanai. You stayed low on hands and knees begging him, begging God. "How can you do this to your daughter?"

"You think I can forgive you for leaving me?" he said, crouching on that concrete ledge with the freakish nimbleness he only possessed while enraged. "I tried to trust you again, but it's over now. You've done it."

We'd tried leaving for the first time when I was thirteen while he was working a night shift, driven aimlessly around the island until the tank ran low and we sat in a parking lot, trying and failing to come up with a real plan. We spent one night in the car. Went back.

We tried again the following year when you took me to school but really we went to the Salvation Army. Spent two nights and left after a woman pulled a boxcutter on me saying she would slit my throat in my sleep because she claimed I used all the toilet paper. We drove home, again, defeated. You wrote in your journal that day, an entry I later read as you showered: *No wonder. No love. Just a hole in my gut. I walk from room to room. We've already ruined Calla Lily. I told him we might not see it yet, but her adult life will show. What chance does she have?*

The third time we tried to leave, which almost worked, remains my sweetest memory of us. But it led to the night my father died. That was what the fight was about, of course, that we'd nearly escaped. That we'd basked in freedom.

As I watched you both on the lanai, I considered the logistics of what would happen if he finally succeeded in his dark traveler's promise. The anticipation was exhausting, the unbearable anxiety of waiting for the next big one, when I'd return home from school to find you gone, or watch you be taken away by ambulance thinking *Is this it is this it is this finally it?* Your death ran in my veins day and night. At school, I bit my nails to the quick, desperate to get back to you. I have few memories of being in class. If anything, getting older made me more absorbed in your and my father's world. Our secrets hemmed us in. Christina's was my only retreat, Celine the only girl who knew me. I could not articulate it but felt in my body there could be no greater relief than for it to end. Maybe we *were* all meant to die together.

I almost settled into this idea. I imagined us all leaping off the lanai, holding hands in the sky. But in life I do think we're offered a few moments that stun us into something new. And there, standing in our hallway, my finger tracing an old rust-colored stain, I thought, I'm done living in a place with my mother's blood on the walls.

CHAPTER 15

A family outing, my husband proposed, was what we needed to celebrate one week with Tootsie, one week of me writing every day, one week of nothing horrible happening to my children on someone else's watch. We went to the gross pizza place with the pinball machine the kids loved and they ordered the meat-lover's special and I watched my husband turn into a boy again at a pizza parlor after a soccer game eating greasy cured meats that he would normally never dare eat in front of me, and Tootsie played the game I used to find interesting and sweet, the game where she recalled every last memory of how special my husband was, tallying each romantic interest he'd had in his entire life that did not include me. "Remember your crush on Mary-Kate and Ashley?" his mother said, winking at him, I guess implying he could have dated Mary-Kate and Ashley Olsen if he hadn't slummed it with me? Well, surprise, Tootsie! I might also be famous soon, but for entirely different reasons.

"My, oh, my," I said. "Think how rich you'd be."

The father of my children, who never, ever beat me, looked

up at me now as Tootsie droned on about how he was the most talented on the soccer team and mouthed, "I love you," and I felt a rush. When was the last time he had done something like that? He smiled. He was happy I had come with them to dinner. He was happy his mother was helping. He looked at his life and saw that it was good.

"We're glad you're here, Mom," he said.

She took a deep breath. Her mood darkened. "I can't stay forever, you know. What's the plan here?"

My husband looked to me. "Well, Clove is working on it. We're working on it."

"Clove is working on it?" She spoke as if I wasn't there. "Oh, come on."

"Tootsie," I said, "I'll have you know that I have a very good lead for a nanny. It may be a perfect fit."

"What are you waiting for, then?"

"I have to make sure that she's not…" Careless, unsafe, that she wasn't going to put my kids in the back seat of that Chevy and drive them all off a cliff? How could you ever really know? But I was trying. I was trying so hard to do what other mothers did all the time. "I have to make sure that the timing will work out."

"Clove has a way of seeing the tiny details other people miss," my husband said. "You know, about other people. She has a real intuition." How nice of him. He was trying. He had clearly watched that Brené Brown video I'd been sending him for two years.

"Tiny details?" Tootsie snorted into her soda. "Is the person competent or not? It can't be that hard. But, Clove, you have impossible standards. I'm not afraid to say it. You can't find an organic nanny."

I held my palms together at my chest in prayer position. "Tootsie," I said, "I can." *I have.*

The waitress refilled my water. "You look familiar," she said.

I smiled. "We live around here."

She frowned. "No, that's not it."

I forgot about her until we were walking out, and there she was near the door. "I know, you work at Earthside."

I pretended to busy myself wiping Lark's face. "I must have a twin."

"Are you saying you don't work there?" she said. "Because I don't forget a face. I have, like, the opposite of face blindness. You told me my adrenals were zapped and gave me that free bottle of Gaia herbs. Spot on, by the way." Today's youth was so bold and sure of their correctness.

"That does sound like you," my husband offered merrily. "Clove loves talking about adrenals."

"I'm in there so much I might as well work there," I said to her. I tried to communicate *back off* with my eyes. "And I've been known to get pushy with my supplement recommendations."

"Service people know service people. You were wearing an Earthside smock."

"Well, I don't work there," I said more forcefully than I wanted. My husband ushered me out, looking at me strangely.

"What?" I said to him. "I don't work there! How crazy."

"Maybe you have a secret job we don't know about."

"Are you serious?"

Lark jumped on his foot, and my husband let out a fake yowl, picked him up, kissed his cheek. I loved that he kissed their cheeks every time he picked them up.

"No," he said. "I'm not serious. Are you?"

"Let's move on."

We got in the car and I strapped the kids in. That was too close.

Much too close. But I barely had time to catch my breath before Tootsie started in again.

"I've heard about your grocery store spending, Clove, and it's not my place, but I have to say, it's totally out of control," she said from the front seat. I sat squished between two of the world's safest car seats.

"Mom," my husband said, "let's just have a good night here."

"You're letting her get away with too much," Tootsie snapped.

"Tootsie, you're totally right. I do spend too much on groceries. I'm working on it." So my husband had noticed. Maybe I wasn't as covert as I'd thought. "I'm working on a whole lot right now." I reached forward and touched her shoulder tenderly to see if I had anything left for her, any last bit of kindness in my heart that I could apply to making her love me.

It felt like freedom to learn I did not.

The next morning, lying in bed next to my sleeping husband, I reread the Butcher's message. Why did I feel paralyzed, unable to respond? At times his words were comforting to read, but then they doubled back and became menacing. Was he saying he one hundred percent had not spoken to the feminist lawyer, or was he leaving it a bit open-ended, was he evading my question, distracting me with his adoration and his own personal quest? I felt like I needed a translator. Each time I reread the message I knew less of what it meant. I should probably never contact him again. But now he was involved. He knew more than he was letting on about all this, I felt sure. I had to be armed with all the information, didn't I? And more than I could admit, I *wanted* to see him. But how? My husband rolled over and draped his arm around me. I put the phone under the pillow. Left the message unanswered.

My husband wasn't one to mistrust me, would never look through my journal or my phone. I couldn't imagine the thought even occurring to him. This was one reason it worked between us, his general incuriosity, lack of obsessive tendencies. I touched his hair lightly. He was still that young man I'd first met. Every day he challenged me to believe a person could live like he did, with total positive regard for life, and every day I felt maligned because I could not quite believe it. He kissed my neck. I pressed my ass into him and his hand went down the front of my shorts. Alright. I got up and locked our door and slipped back into bed. He pulled my underwear to the side and I grabbed his dick from between my legs, angling it right. Okay. For years now I reached orgasm by visualizing my *highest self,* the version that was finally free of you and my father, but today I saw the Butcher's hands, the way we fit together, the way he knew me. I pulled my husband into me harder. Said, "Harder." He had to be told the harder part before he'd do it, like he didn't trust my need to have my thoughts fucked away, if only for a few minutes, to release mind from body and allow for a corporeal railing, but what else was sex for in my life if not for this departure? I saw the Butcher's face between my legs and came instantly, and my husband, practiced after all these years, came at the same time and then we lay there for a few minutes in silence.

He stretched his arms overhead, kissed my cheek. I cupped a hand under my crotch and waddled to the bathroom.

"My mom has got to be nicer to you," he called after me. "I hated how she treated you at dinner. I feel like you really deserve an apology but I'm not sure she's capable." I sat on the toilet. He came in and started brushing his teeth. "It made me feel weird watching her. Everything was an undercut."

"I don't like the kids seeing her talk to me like I'm a pile of trash, but I need this. I need this time."

He nodded slowly. "It feels like we're in something." Post sex he was malleable, as open as he got. *You could tell him now. Right now. How about now?*

"I really might have found a nanny," I said instead. "I wasn't making that up."

"Yeah?" he said. "That's amazing."

"Don't you want to meet her first?"

"Clove," he said. "I trust you."

CHAPTER 16

Every year the Waikiki Marie Callender's waitresses planned a summer employee barbecue at a beautiful grassy park near Kailua Beach, and the day I am recalling now as I try to finish my letter back to you, my cease and desist letter, was the day of the last one we ever attended, weeks before my father died. I believe it's important to revisit this day, however painful for you. As a mother myself now, I can imagine just how painful. But we have to look at it. I hope it helps you understand something vital I'm trying to say, and I fear I can't say it in any other way. Because I know by now you are thinking, *How can my daughter do this to me?* And I want to say, this is why. This is how.

The sun was bright, it was windy, the sky was that perfect cerulean punctuated every so often by rolling gray clouds on their way somewhere else. All day you'd been saying we might as well not go, that it looked like rain. But my father had the day off and kept insisting. "Don't you want to show me off, Alma? Aren't you proud of me?" He turned to me in the back seat with a scary grin. "Or maybe she doesn't want all her boyfriends to see me, huh?"

"I've worked with them for years," you said, raking a pick through your home-permed hair. "For god's sake." You knew better than to pull down the mirror and primp. It was best for you to arrive places looking unfinished, a bit frazzled, so he could then complain about not having a woman who put in the effort, a safer gripe in general and not one that usually led to things getting physical. But he'd suggested you wear your floral dress, a setup that could go either way. "When we talk it's about replacing old ketchup bottles."

"You can't pull the wool over my eyes," he said. "I know how you are."

"Dad, stop," I said.

He put his hands up. "Hey, I'm ready to have a good time with Alma's sweethearts."

I fumed as you covered the bruises on your arms with your cheap stick concealer in the front seat.

"Mom, you should quit Marie Callender's and get a job doing makeup for movie sets. You could be their official bruise coverer for all the other ladies who get hit by their husbands."

Your shoulders inched up toward your ears. "Calla Lily."

My father nodded as if he agreed, was considering this potential path.

"What? It's the truth," I said. "One day when my husband beats the shit out of me, I'll know just what to do."

At this my father jerked the steering wheel, swerving across two lanes of traffic as he slammed to a stop on the side of the road. He turned back to me breathless. "Some fucker ever pushes you around, I'll kill him."

"Your dad really would kill him," you mused as you both stared at me lovingly, protectively. I wish I had a photograph of the two of you at that moment. I'd frame it. I was your daughter.

"I would," my father said. He looked at you for a moment and you nodded. Did he see the irony? Did you?

A car blared its horn at us. Our tail was still in the road. My father flipped off the other driver with his big hand. "Fucking fuck." We peeled out back onto the highway and the moment was over.

When we arrived at the park, your coworkers beamed at you. Your boss, a pug of a man named Gary, folded you in a full-body embrace, lifting you off the ground. "Jesus Christ, Gary," you said. You said it a bit too nice, though. He wouldn't learn from it. *Close, but no cigar,* as you liked to say.

I eyed the many varieties of beer on the table. "Yeah, Gary," I said. "Jesus Christ, you're gonna get us killed here."

The adults laughed at me with confused faces, this teenager making a joke about the thing everyone knew but wouldn't talk about—that my mother was a *battered woman.* I didn't understand why violence in a marriage seemed somehow without risk to others, without risk to society. Why my father's jealousy and his intensity and his anger were so often mistaken for passion. I still don't get it, when every other day there's a new mass shooting on the news that, bingo, was preceded by years of the dude beating his mom or girlfriend or wife. But even then, I was already running out of patience. So when no one was looking, I slipped two beers into the pockets of my dress and took them to the bathroom on the other side of the park. I drank them one after the other. I'd never drunk anything before, hating alcohol on account of you two, but I heard other kids at school were drinking at the parties I didn't go to. I think I wanted something new to happen.

When I came back to the party, my father was in a friendly conversation with Gary. You looked at me, and we both knew what was in store later. Now the game was to see if we could fix it in time. Trick my father into forgetting that stupid hug. He put an arm lovingly around you.

"Glad you keep her busy," my father said, as one of the younger waitresses gave him the once-over. My father's beauty allowed for so much. Every time he bought me ice cream, the lady behind the counter gave him an extra scoop. Even I would soften toward him in these moments, revel in the display of what our family could be, what we looked like from the outside.

The sun set and the park lights flickered on and I felt a steady buzz behind my eyes. I'd had three beers by then and no one seemed to care. My father drank and drank. Even you decided one couldn't hurt, though you normally never drank in public. A pig roasted on a spit. A man named Lagi gave a speech about how he loved his Marie Callender's family and you stayed quiet, occasionally whispering something to me, vibrating messages. But I didn't want your messages. The beer was telling me to ignore you and make a plan of my own to leave you and my father to your destruction.

My father had sequestered himself on the outskirts of the park at a picnic table with the young waitress, and you kept glancing at them and then at me as people finished eating and dancing commenced.

"And he gets on my ass for that shit," you said, as if something about how things were going was a surprise. I had little hope for you.

"Christina says you have Stockholm syndrome."

You looked annoyed. "What does she know? Cooped up in that apartment with that sick baby doll all day. She's too scared to even date. There's something fundamentally wrong with her."

"She said you've become conditioned to the abuse, you think it's love, and you'll never leave."

"I'd leave if there was a way," you said. "I'd leave in a heartbeat."

"Get someone to drive us to the airport. You have money. Let's get on a plane. Right now. Prove it to me."

"You don't know how money works, honey." You glanced at my father. "Besides, it would break his heart."

You launched into describing the way it felt to be with my father when you'd first met: like everything you had ever known had been wrong, like you were a stuck drawer whose wheel had finally clicked over into the right track, you were someone's. You felt nothing could be more romantic than to be owned fully and fiercely. You said when you were in public together, his whole body leaned into you, shrouding you, encapsulating you. His his his. You called my father a powerful drug.

"Maybe Christina is right. I'm addicted to booze and your father."

Here's the thing I'm just now understanding, the thing I want you to know. It's the reason why I can't help you, won't upend my life for you, the reason I'm begging, *begging* you to go to trial and leave me out of it, completely out of it. It's this: you didn't protect me.

And yes, yes, I understand all the reasons you couldn't, all the ways your behavior could be explained. But my body doesn't understand those explanations. And my body is angry. You looked in my eyes year after year and fed me reasons why we had to stay. You were so distracted by your bad love that you didn't notice me get drunk that night, you didn't notice the way Gary pulled me onto his lap and I could feel his erection through his board shorts. You didn't notice the way he reached into my dress and massaged my boob, the same boob I later nursed my children with. When I went to the bathroom you didn't notice him follow me, try to close us into a stall together. I mean, come on, Mother. He'd tracked me all night, chasing the scent of my particular isolation. Girls like me wore a target for men like him. He'd noted you drinking, your hyperfocus on my father. He'd noted my father move on from beer to drugs with the young waitress. In the bathroom he'd said, "Come here, pretty girl." And something reared up.

I smashed my beer bottle against the brick wall. The sound sobered me. I lodged it into his thigh and he cried *yelp!* like a cartoon character. I walked back to the party with his blood spattered on my dress. Even now, when I piss in park bathrooms, I hear his voice, can still feel the ghost of that skinny chicken dick, the fabric of his cheap trunks. I want you to know that. I need you to know that.

And imagine, upon my return from the bathroom, finding that both my parents had left me at the party without a word. I took two buses home and fell asleep outside our door in the hallway.

You ended up in the hospital that night. You relived the story two weeks later at Christina's after you'd finally been released, Celine and I watching *Jerry* while I ate a bag of sugar-coated gummy worms so sweet I could have unzipped my skin. You said it was nice that after he beat you in the parking lot, my father had driven you to the hospital because if not you would have bled to death internally, according to the doctor.

"All I did was ask him why he was flirting with that waitress. Just couldn't keep my mouth shut." You smoked your cigarette near the cracked window, blowing it out into the sky. You were still a bit swollen, and your bottom lip was weird, like it had come off completely and been sewn back on. It would never look the same.

Add it to the list. Some women your age were getting procedures to turn back time, while my father was remaking your face for free. Well, nothing is free. You made a joke about your lips finally looking plump.

"You look terrifying," I said. Christina snapped her fingers in agreement.

"That doctor said there was a hole in my back. Said he'd never seen anything like it."

You had almost died. Again.

"You know what this means," you said to us. Yes, now we would leave. Surely now we would leave. You were stiff, your body so sore. "It means no more company parties."

You must have seen my face fall, because later that day in the communal laundry room as you paired my father's work socks, you said, "Listen. We'll figure something out."

"Do you care about me?" I asked. I was older now. The day wasn't long off before I could leave you alone with him, set off on my own. My whole life I'd been a buffer between my father and his true violent potential, and I feared what would happen if I wasn't there to defuse and distract him, to defend you. I knew you feared this too. I knew you thought of me as your protector. And there was really no freedom for me unless there was also freedom for you.

"I'm sorry we've been living like this," you said.

"Then let's go."

"Well," you said, looking around the room, lowering your voice, "there might be a way."

You told me you had an old AA friend who could help. Someone you'd run into during your time at the hospital. He'd stayed sober, become a nurse. You recognized him as he changed your gauze. Of course, it took him time to recognize you, your face so altered. He said he understood your situation. That his sister owned a small house in North Shore on a big piece of land she rarely used. Very private. Not visible from the road. That he had a heart for women like you. He saw too many of you come in to be treated and go back out, come in and go back out, until there was no more going back out or coming in anymore, depending. We could stay there while we figured out next steps.

"What's in it for him?" I asked.

You shrugged. "I think he's a good guy."

"Why didn't you tell me right away?"

"I knew you'd get your hopes up," you said. "But your face today. I want to make you proud of me for once." Or, maybe, your injuries had finally scared you enough.

But who cared about the reason? I hugged you hard, knocking my father's socks to the floor. You cried into my hair and we stood holding each other for a long time and I never wanted to stop. But of course, eventually, I let go of you, and you let go of me.

CHAPTER 17

I printed off my letter to you in the early morning while my husband was on a run, while Tootsie clanged around the kitchen with the kids, and slipped out of the house without saying goodbye to anyone. I felt proud of the weight of the pages in my hand, all I'd written, these words my only defense against the past. My bargaining letter, my please-proceed-without-me letter. My whole life I felt like I could never give you the right thing, give you enough; I was perpetually failing. But in these pages, I had articulated something of worth. Here I had let you know me. And now the question was, Would you understand? Would you be convinced that true love can be, despite what we're told, a forgetting?

Could you choose to forget me, Mother?

At the post office, I tried to open the glass cabinet on the Lego display, maybe snatch a mini fig to bring home to Lark, but this time it was locked. Not only that, but in the corner was a small new bookshelf with kids' books and two little chairs at a little table covered with crayons. A child Lark's age colored there, content. It appeared the scene I'd caused had made a difference. I took it as a good sign. Things turning in my favor. A sign that if I was lucky, you would find the people who could help you. Just not me. I allowed myself to slip into fantasy, that if you followed my directions now, that maybe one day in the long-off future I could get in my car by myself and drive to where you were—I imagined you in a little house by the sea—and I could see you and we would figure it out again, no, we'd figure it out for the first time: how to be mother and daughter.

I slipped my letter to you into a mailer, wrote your address on the front. Don't imagine I felt callous to the fact that I was addressing a prison and not a home, Mother. I felt nothing but devastation for you, a constant and unshakable sensation of sadness over your days. Yet still, at the counter I mailed the words you did not want to hear. I collected my various packages, most of which I only faintly remembered ordering. I had to stop with that. What was wrong with me, thinking finely crafted ethical fashion would somehow fix me, control my situation? I resolved to quit cold turkey.

Upon my return, Tootsie requested a break. Time alone at the Hobby Lobby in the suburbs. "Of course," I said. "Please, have the best outing." She nodded curtly and the children stood on the front lawn to watch her drive away, crying as if it would be forever.

"Is she coming back?" Lark kept asking.

"There are no guarantees in life," I said finally when he wouldn't let up. "But yes, she's coming back."

I thought I would revel in my morning with Nova and Lark, but it wasn't clicking. Lark styled my hair in painful twists that wrenched my neck. Nova pretended to record a yoga video looking up at me every two seconds to make sure I was still watching her and if I wasn't she'd scream *MOM*. Lark sang "John Jacob

Jingleheimer Schmidt" over her. I popped my wireless headphones in as stealthily as possible and pressed play on an audiobook that muddled "John Jacob" and drowned out my daughter. But it was not enough. My fingers marched their way to the Instagram secondhand clothing page and claimed a grandfatherly Spanish-wool sweater for $240.

No, no, no. I deleted my claim. Why couldn't I simply be with myself, with them? With my irritation? All I had to do was submit, but that felt no longer possible. You were in the room. My father, in the room. I considered the sweater once more but imagined what Jane might say about my shopping. *Switching seats on the* Titanic, *Clove.*

Tootsie came back to find me sprawled on the living room floor covered in nontoxic play makeup, my hair a swarm of fifty barrettes. The audiobook turned up high, the subpar dialogue obscuring whatever judgments she might be offering. The children dropped me and ran to her. At least I had made it through the morning without buying anything, a small win. I got ready for my shift as fast as I could, practically leapt out the door.

At Earthside, as we unboxed the various superfood powders and lined them neatly on the shelf, I asked Jane if she felt loved by her mother, something I was always curious about in others, sourcing back to the fact that I wasn't always sure how to answer it myself.

She thought about it. "I did, I guess, but I wised up eventually."

"How?" I asked.

"One day the thought came to me to try things differently than she said they had to be, and so I did. But it wasn't easy letting her go. It was a death."

"Powerful." I felt relieved to have sent off my letter, but now the anxiety about when I'd hear back was already creeping in. Would my words, just measly words, work? Make you understand?

"Some people will do anything to survive, and I'm one of them," Jane said.

"The things I endured at my kids' ages were unimaginable," I said. "I had no innocence. I think that's my issue. Like, the older my kids get, the more fucked-up I realize I am, and I feel so angry at my parents. I look at my daughter and relive all the things I saw at her age. Lately I feel jealous of her life, how easy it is, and annoyed that she'll never understand that."

"Did you have friends as a kid?"

"There was one girl who knew me pretty well. She knew my mom too. She was the only person who understood our life."

"All you need is one."

"Like you now," I said. "I feel like you get me. I feel totally open with you." *Almost.*

"But I hardly know anything about you," she said.

"I mean, at this point I tell you more than my own husband."

Her eyes were downcast. "Yeah, but that's a low bar. You don't tell him anything. Who are you really?"

I expected her to laugh, but she remained serious. Maybe I was losing her trust. She needed more from me, that was clear. I drank the Maca Blast Mike had made me, the closest thing to a milkshake I could imagine. It was suspiciously creamy.

"I think Mike dairied me." I handed the smoothie to Jane.

She swished it in her mouth. "Oh yeah, that's some whole-milk goodness."

I took another sip. "I don't know, cashew milk can be deceiving."

I contemplated throwing the goodness in the trash.

"I know we love a maca smoothie, Clove, don't get me wrong. But when was the last time you got wasted?"

The image of my father's hand lazily holding a sweating bottleneck. The way he would smack you without even setting it down. "My father was an awful drunk."

Jane put her arm around my waist and led me to a display at the front of the store, pointed to the sign touting a new kombucha called *Flower Palace*. "How about botanicals?" she said, holding up a pretty floral can. "L-theanine?"

The last time I drank was with the Butcher, a time that predated the botanicals that were now trending. The taste memory of rum leapt into my throat. The beers I'd had at the Marie Callender's party. The dangerous way alcohol worked at first like your friend—making you free, making the world seem better, making people safe—but it always warped. Called spirits for a reason, it invited possession. I hated alcohol and what it had done to you, to my father.

But this was not that. "I love L-theanine," I said.

"Great," she said, picking up a six-pack. "Tonight we timeline-hop. We compress years of bonding into a span of mere hours."

Maybe it sounds silly, but when she spoke like this, I felt like I'd found my soulmate.

We gathered our things from our lockers and left without paying. We got in our cars and drove separately to Mike's rental house, where he was hosting a summer Earthside staff party. On the drive, real life intruded—what business did I have going to a house party when I had children at home who hadn't seen me all day? Whose cells were likely yearning for my touch, the tenor of my specific voice. But I needed to be near Jane. She allowed me to live in possibility, and possibility was more important than ever now. I parked and took in the leaning old Portland house. A skeleton was propped in a window, paint peeling around the frame. The whole thing looked soggy. I made a note to tell Jane that she shouldn't spend time here, what with the obvious mold problems. Mold wreaked havoc on fertility, she must know that. Party sounds and car-crash music streamed out into the warm night air. I had almost no experience with parties. When I was single in the several years between the Butcher and my husband, I was concerned a party with alcohol was the exact place I'd be most at risk for attracting someone like my father. Best to abstain entirely.

Jane handed me a kombucha as we walked in, and I downed the small can quickly, my nervy throat so parched, and opened another. It was good, had a strong fermented zing that was balanced by lavender. Mike enveloped Jane's body into his as Stephen walked in, shotgunning a Coors like a fool. I stood next to him.

"I can't believe Jane wanted you to father her child," I said.

"Joke's on her. I have a kid already and I got the snip right after."

"The snip?" I gripped his shoulder. "Jane was trying to make you her baby daddy and you'd had a vasectomy?"

"Sorry to disappoint."

I looked at Jane, who was still enduring Mike's flirting.

"Does she know?"

"Look," he said, dropping the slow-speaking stoner act. "I don't owe her my medical records. Anything in her mind about what we were is her responsibility. That should be a warning label on my dick."

Jane sidled up to me, handed me another kombucha.

Stephen eyed her. Looked back to me. "Jane ever told you where she lives?"

I smiled at Jane, searching my mind. How had I never asked this?

I was pretty sure we'd covered where she was originally from…the Midwest I seemed to recall, but must have gotten sidetracked when it came to the day-to-day. "Where she lives is the least interesting thing about her," I said.

She shot him a look. "Clove knows I just moved to town, that I'm still getting settled."

"Yup, getting settled in my bed, or in Mike's or whoever's free that night."

"Is that true?" I said.

"I'm saving money right now. You aren't looking down on me, are you? A woman with your kind of privilege should only be asking yourself, how can I help?"

She was right. What Jane was doing was a revolutionary act for a woman. Starting over could be bumpy, I knew firsthand. I had benefited from the random care of so many people. I thought of Velvet and wanted to run back through time and throw myself into her arms. How grateful I was for her ability to look only at who I could be, and not dwell on who I'd been before. All of this primed me to say what I said next:

"Come live with me."

Jane tilted her head to one side. Smiled as if amused.

"I'm serious. Tonight. Don't stay with any of these douche-bags." I looked around at the cluttered, grimy house; did they even have a radon mitigator? I couldn't stomach the thought of Jane needing these men in any capacity. "Stay with me and my family. And help me with the kids. In exchange for rent. We have an extra room. You can live with me and help us. And then I can help you with your baby. And then we'll keep helping each other on and on."

The room grew claustrophobic; time was moving so fast. I

had until the end of summer and no more, for god's sake. Jane living with us made more sense than I had even first realized. If I was whisked away and had to go to trial, or imprisoned for stealing an identity or who knew what else, someone would need to be there to watch my children. Someone would have to be able to mother them, really mother them, someone available and nurturing, who wasn't required five days a week in the detached-garage office on a headset, someone who wasn't frothing at the mouth to get back to her other grandchildren. And who was more available than Jane?

Stephen snorted. "What is this?"

Jane looked at me squarely. This close, I could see she wore colored contacts and wondered what her real eye color was. It wasn't blue. "You really want to help me have my baby?"

Stephen threw up his hands. "Actually, I don't want to know."

"Of course I do!" I said. "I'll do whatever I can to support you, whatever is needed. We just need to get the fuck out of here."

"Well, if you really wanted to help, you could be my surrogate."

I laughed. The thought of being pregnant again, doing all of that again. Ridiculous. But who knew, maybe anything was possible. Maybe this was a way to pay penance to the world for abandoning you, Mother. Something was owed, and this was how I could settle my debt. Help someone the way Celine and Christina had helped me, give a life. My voice sounded weird and soft and not mine. "You never know," I said to her. "You never know what could happen."

"This is such a relief, Clove. Meeting you and feeling so close to you. I'm so grateful."

People were staring. "Manifestation is real," I announced to them.

I hung off Jane. I felt very peculiar—was I reaching kundalini?—but also, everything was right. She hugged me hard and a little vomit came up into my mouth. "Okay, I need to go home. *We* need to go home, I mean. You don't need anything, Jane. I have everything you could need. I have, like, so many linen jumpers. Do not bother these asscracks for shit."

"How'd you like that smoothie, Clove?" Mike said.

"I fucking knew it," I said, walking toward him. "Unforgivable."

"Oh boy," Jane said, pulling me back.

"These kombuchas are creating a great thirst in me," I said. "I need another one."

"How about some water?" Jane said, guiding me down the porch steps and settling me into my own passenger seat. "I'll drive us."

"You're acting like I'm drunk or something. Honestly, I do feel kind of drunk. Do these have CBD in them?" I looked closer at the can. The letters took a moment to focus, but when they did, *Hard* was right there, apparent to any common fool. I'd missed it somehow. We'd missed it. "Oh my god, I drank alcohol accidentally," I said. "Oh my god!"

She seemed unfazed. "Maybe it's good for you to let loose every now and then. I mean, look how amazing the night turned out. Look at all you offered of yourself. You think you would have asked me to live with you without a little encouragement?"

My body was tainted, impure. I imagined the alcohol ruining the finely tuned brain of my microbiome. "I don't drink. Ever," I said. She started the engine and did a few deep yogic breaths. I tried to join but let out a jagged cry. "Jane."

"Wow, this is a huge deal for you," she said. "You never told me how important it was to stay sober. This proves we could be a lot closer."

But I had told her I didn't drink. I'd told her that very night in Earthside. Had she not heard me? I had said it, right?

"Listen, let it go and lean into the sensation for now, knowing it will soon be gone. Maybe even ask yourself how it can serve you while it is still here."

I nodded. Okay. Yes, I would try. What else could I do?

"What do you think your husband's going to think of me? I guess that's the part I'm most nervous about. Meeting him, and hoping he likes me, and is, you know, into this whole idea."

"He's been begging me to get some help with the kids for a long time."

"He's probably expecting a teenager to come around a few times a week to fold laundry and take the kids on a walk."

"I'd never let a teenager take the kids on a walk, are you serious? Too many crazy drivers."

"Why do you think you're like this?" she asked. She put on some of my lip balm from the center console. "So scared, so cautious."

I sighed. "There's something wrong with me, that's why."

"Yeah, but what is it? I mean, you perceive there to be something wrong with you, you're scared in both rational and irrational ways all the time, but I don't know, if you had to name one reason."

"There's something inside me," I said. "My father had it too—it turns up different in me, but it's part of the same thing." We drove in silence as I fought back my urge to cry. She pulled the car over in front of my house, cut the engine. We sat in the dark. I stared at her profile. Her long straight nose, the curve of her lips. "I've seen things that make me cautious. I want to be this ultimate protector of my kids. If I fail at that, if I slip up for even one second, if I were to lose them or hurt them or if something happened to me to leave them motherless…I just live in terror. I've always felt this way, but lately it's become overwhelming in the midst of all these fucked-up weaning hormones."

"You're avoiding the question. I can understand all of that, but what things have you seen? I don't like how vague you are with me. If we're going to get anywhere with each other, that has to change."

"It's too much to ever explain. Trust me."

"Nothing is too much for me."

"Well, that's what you say, but…" I trailed off, the hard kombucha cracking the door on what had been locked away for so long. The potential release of telling another person. Just one other person. Right now, Jane. The thought of her genuinely knowing me was rapturous, the temptation immense.

"Clove," she said. She only had to say my name like that, in that tone, to push me over the edge.

I whispered, "Jane, my mother killed my father when I was seventeen. He was a violent man my whole life and she finally killed him. It was self-defense. We lived in Hawai'i, in a high-rise. He fell from a long way up."

I saw her shock, her full-body flinch—she would never want to be around me again, she would now be able to see my father's traveler in my eyes—but she recovered fast, pulling her face back to neutral. "And you've told your husband?" She glanced toward my house, at the glow of light and life coming from the windows.

"No."

"None of it? Nothing? He literally knows nothing?"

"I told him they died in a car accident. I told him they were great and then they died tragically." She shook her head. Disapproval? "I don't need a guilt trip about it. Listen, it's not my job to carry this story around with me my whole life. I want people to see me, and only see me, not Clove's crazy story. Then people pity you, decide things about you. I didn't want my kids to grow up with that kind of lineage."

"I have so many questions," she said. "I mean, can't he, like, google you?"

"He doesn't even know my real name. Technically I'm missing."

"What would happen if I searched your real name online?"

"Oh, you'd see a lot of inaccurate articles making my mother seem like a homicidal maniac, and you'd see some pictures of me when I was young, making myself small next to my father, who looked like a movie star, by the way. That was not helpful for my mother's case. It would say I was a missing person, presumed dead."

"So how do you, like, legally function?"

I could tell her about Celine and Christina, their remains somewhere in the ocean. What happened to bones in salt water?

But only the Butcher knew about that, and he was more than enough. "You're a very curious person."

"I hate feeling like I don't have all the information. Makes me feel like my brain can't relax. I require the whole story. That's why if I read a novel, I have to read it continuously, like two days blocked off, so my brain can have immediate resolution."

"Sometimes it's easier not to have the whole story."

"Whether you have it or not, it still exists. Not telling me doesn't make it go away. I think you know that."

"I was doing fine before my mother wrote to me," I said. "Brought it all back. I probably crashed into you because I'd just gotten her letter and was losing my mind. I doubt we'd have met at all if she had kept to herself. But she found me. She wants my help. I have until the end of summer before she and some lawyer expose everything and then my kids will have this trail them forever. I did some things to escape that might not be looked at kindly, from a legal standpoint. All because a man couldn't sort his emotional problems out, all because a man couldn't control his anger. This is all because of one man's violence, leading to another man's violence, and to another."

"Wow, okay. So your dad's dead. Your mom's alive. Been in prison since you were a teenager." She paused, putting it together. She probably wanted to bolt from the car. "Do you think your mother deserves to be in prison?"

"My butcher boyfriend I told you about thought I was a monster for not helping her. But here's the thing I could never make him understand. My mother did damage to me. The cost I've paid my whole life to be their daughter, *her* daughter. And I knew my mother would never change. That as sick as my father was, she was sick too. That kind of violence infects everything. It's easier to just cut off the infected limb."

"There could be hope now, maybe. Don't you think after all this time she might see things differently?"

"If there was a way that I could help her, I would have done it. Believe me when I tell you, I love her deeply. But I don't love her more than my children."

"You aren't at peace with that," Jane said. "I can tell that much."

She was sounding a lot like the Butcher. "I told you my secret. Now you tell me yours. I mean, you show up in Portland not knowing anyone, you don't live anywhere, you live everywhere, and you're a bitch of indiscriminate age with no wrinkles."

She studied her rose quartz bracelet. "I didn't have a good childhood either. I ended up working as an escort when I was young, flying all over the world, traveling. For a lot of years I did that and then I had this one older client who was very rich and he paid for me to live a comfortable life, he got me a nice apartment in LA and took care of all my food and bills and he helped me get different surgeries to make me look…better. I'd had a rough life and I didn't want to look like myself anymore. For a while I was able to relax and not work, aside from when I'd see him once or twice a month. That's when I got into spirituality. I got my yoga-teacher training certificate and became Reiki master certified. I started figuring out what I really wanted in life."

"I could tell you were Reiki certified."

She held up her hands, smiling, then dropped them into her lap and sighed. "But then he died and didn't leave me anything—you don't leave your sugar baby money, I guess, you leave your wife money—but I was still shocked. I had to decide what was next. That's when I realized I really wanted to be a mother. I wanted to reclaim myself in a way. I never imagined myself this old. I never imagined what I'd do in life, you know. So I started trying to have a baby, but it didn't work. And now here I am. With you."

There it was, why she was special. Why we were drawn to each other. In the car my darkness met hers and neither of us was backing away.

"I don't pity you," I said.

"I don't pity you either."

And as we walked up to my front door, the porch light on and beckoning, I realized I'd never told her where I lived.

CHAPTER 18

Inside, I led Jane to the basement, where I put fresh sheets on the pull-out couch with my clumsy buzzed hands, assuring her this would just be until Tootsie vacated. Jane was quiet, her mouth set. I reached out and touched her shoulder. "Are you okay?" I said. She smiled and held my wrist. Was she going to cry? Of course, she had realized this was a mistake, that she couldn't live with someone like me. "It's just...your house is so pretty," she said. "I love it."

I felt so lucky then, maybe even luckier than when I'd gotten married to my nonviolent husband in an expensive rent-by-the-hour barn, surrounded by his family and his friends and no one who knew me other than through the ways I was involved with him. But Jane was for me. I would mother her and she would mother me and we would both mother my children. I felt a deep spiritual knowing that with her here, this whole mess with you and the feminist lawyer would come into alignment.

I went to the kitchen for some high-mineral-content water and noticed Tootsie's door ajar, a light still on. Unusual for her to be up at midnight, a woman who tromped to bed around eight to recover from a day with my kids. I stepped closer and peered in. Tootsie sat at the desk, staring intently at something out of sight, my purse at her feet.

My purse. I had forgotten my purse, had left for my shift with only my phone like a total idiot.

I stepped back and the floor squeaked. She turned around and we locked eyes.

"I didn't mean to startle you," I said from the doorway. She stood up, on guard. "I was looking for my bag. Thought maybe the kids dragged it in here."

Surely that's all this was. But then I saw the letters in her hand. Selby's and yours. Tootsie's eyes looked like she'd been clawing at them. "What do you think you're playing at?" she said.

I moved to snatch them and she scrambled awkwardly, took a step backward and then another, and then fell on her butt. She looked up at me with fear in her eyes.

"Tootsie, those are mine."

"You've lied to us all, made us feel so sorry for you all these years. Poor Clove with no parents."

"You don't know what you're talking about," I said.

"I've been telling him all week, that wife of yours is up to something. I thought you were having an affair. I was sure of it. But it's worse. You have a mother."

I reached again for the letters and she reared back, knocking over the standing lamp behind her. She held her arms across her face like I was going to hit her. Was I?

I didn't have to wonder long because Jane's voice broke through my desperation. "That's enough," she said, stepping into the room quickly and closing us all in together, putting the lamp right side up.

"Who is she?" Tootsie hissed.

I needed to make Jane quickly understand. "Tootsie has my..." I paused. "She found some of my fiction writing and is... misunderstanding."

"Tootsie," Jane said. "Why don't we get you off the ground. No need for this level of dramatics." My stunned mother-in-law accepted Jane's help onto the bed. Jane plucked the letters from her and without even glancing at them handed them over to me in what felt like a move of pure solidarity. I shoved them back in my purse.

"You can't go snooping around in people's things. You know that, don't you?"

"I know what I saw."

"You saw Clove's fiction writing, and let me guess, you don't read fiction." Tootsie said nothing. "So you wouldn't understand the sort of thing Clove is writing. What she's doing is art. It makes sense you would be confused."

"Who are you?" she said.

"Oh, my mistake," Jane said cheerfully. "I'm the nanny."

"You're manipulating me," Tootsie said. "I'm not stupid. She has a mother in prison. Her mother wrote to her, I read it."

"You're not going to say anything," Jane said.

"What's stopping me?"

"I mean, I think that's obvious, right? Don't you ever want to see your grandkids again?" Jane smiled with ease, but I wasn't sure this threat would work seeing as it had taken an extreme situation to get Tootsie here in the first place to see Nova and Lark. Still, Tootsie's story of herself included being a good grandparent, and preserving this story would likely win over reality.

"I won't be spoken to this way."

"You're going home tomorrow," Jane continued. "And I'm moving into this room. And you can forget whatever it was that upset you about Clove's fiction. It's really that simple."

I heard the creak of my husband's steps coming down the hall. In the doorway, for a flash, he looked like his mother and I couldn't help feeling a slight revulsion.

"This is the *nanny*," Tootsie said, pointing up at Jane as if accusing her of something.

"Soul nanny," I clarified.

"We're still working on my title," Jane said, holding her hand out to my husband. He had explained to me once that his philosophy for how to deal with life's challenges was to pretend everything was fine and eventually it would be. I could see him practicing this now. He shook Jane's hand.

"Are you okay, Mom?" he said. "I heard a crash."

"Your mother found some of Clove's fiction writing and it made her a little upset and she fell," Jane said. "But we're getting it all sorted out."

Jane was quick as hell and I could almost see Tootsie considering whether perhaps Jane did have it right. Could this all just be an artistic misunderstanding?

"I'm leaving. I won't stay another minute in this house."

"Mom, what's the problem?" My husband, bless him, crouched down so his eyes were at her level like I'd told him the parenting podcasts recommended for communicating with kids.

"This is why everyone should read more literary fiction," Jane said. "You know, there's studies that show it increases the capacity for empathy in the brain."

"I'll talk to her," he said. He looked up at me, tired. We had definitely woken him. "Have you been drinking?"

"Kombucha," Jane and I both said at the same time.

"This is plain weird," Tootsie said to us. "This random woman. Bringing her into the house like this."

"Yes," I said. "It's so wonderful. Tootsie, it's all thanks to you. All this time you've given me to find her. What a gift you are. I love you so much."

"Is she on drugs?" Tootsie said to my husband.

"Mom, she's just happy. Look, your help has made her happy again."

"I'm very concerned about my grandchildren."

"There's nothing to be concerned about," my husband said, though a glimmer of his own worry passed over his face.

But then Jane was beside me. "Go be concerned in the comfort of your home, Tootsie," she said with the tone and cadence of a guided meditation. "Let it all out. Punch a pillow or something. It's not good to keep that feeling stuck in the body."

This was sisterhood. This was community. I'd finally found it.

"Clove, you are going to ruin my son's life," Tootsie said. She looked to her son. "Where did she come from? Why doesn't she have any family? Huh? Why doesn't she have any pictures of her parents? Maybe you need to be asking more questions, buddy boy. She's not who she says she is."

"Mom, please don't call me buddy boy."

Tootsie got up and began shoving things in her bag.

"She does have a family," Jane said, putting her arm around me. I let her pull me in close. I pretended she was you, that you were hugging me, Mother. "You're looking at it."

Jane and I walked out of the room into the kitchen, leaving my husband with Tootsie.

"Thank you," I said, handing her a glass of water. "You saved me in there. This situation is so fucked. As you can see."

"Don't worry about your husband," Jane said. "I could tell he believed everything we said in there. I mean, it would be quite a stretch for him to imagine what you've done. He'd really have to be hit over the head with it."

"Well," I said, "good thing that's not going to happen."

My husband joined me in our bedroom after calming his mother, convincing her not to start her four-hour drive back home in the middle of the night. He went on for a bit about how shocked Tootsie was by my writing, how she couldn't imagine where I'd come up with the ideas. "I told her, 'Mom, Clove is writing a thriller. Her parents died when she was young. It makes sense she's writing about a mother character who comes back into the picture.' It's probably, like, your biggest fantasy. She didn't get it. She kept saying you were hiding something from me. I told her she was being crazy."

"Not wise to call a woman crazy," I said. "But, in this case, if it fits, it fits."

"She is right about some things. Why didn't you tell me Jane was coming to stay tonight?"

"She's had a hard time, but she's amazing. I promise. She will truly be able to be her best self once she moves into the guest room tomorrow."

He laughed. He thought I was kidding.

"She's the one I was telling you about. She's our new nanny. Like live-in."

"This night just keeps on keeping on," he said. "I'm down there defending you to my mother, but you really are pulling some strange shit."

"You told me to hire someone."

"Yeah, like a few times a week."

"Well, maybe you don't know this about me, but when I finally choose to do something, I go all the way."

His face registered concern, apprehension, and—unless I imagined it—a little thrill.

Lark came into our room a few hours later, climbed into bed next to me, and vomited on my pillow. From there the night was a series of short naps punctuated by wake-ups and cleanups and more wake-ups. Nightmare upon nightmare and by the time morning came, my husband and I were fully destroyed. Lark was feeling much better, though, more concerned with Grandma being gone than anything. Yes, Tootsie had left without saying goodbye, something that no doubt hurt my husband, though he would not articulate this hurt. Instead, my husband drank his coffee. Instead, he was cool and silent toward me, which was his defense mechanism and would pass, though I sometimes wondered if he knew the real me, if he had access to the things I'd seen, if he would still punish me this way, remove his warmth from me at will, or if he would decide I had been punished enough. I hadn't wanted the Butcher's or anyone else's pity, but I was starting to think recognition could be separate from pity. That in recognition there could be a healing, perhaps, but I was not able to be recognized, and because my husband didn't beat me, and in his coolness my body was still safe, I let it lie.

The kids watched Jane set things out for almond flour pancakes, slowly inching closer to her, their curiosity compelling them, won-dering probably if this new woman was different from their mother, if she would allow them to make messes, big, great messes. I wanted to be relaxed in that way, but I wasn't. Cooking with my kids often ended in tears, Nova storming out when I corrected her too much, Lark rubbing raw egg on the countertops and me shrieking *Salmonella!*

"Can we help?" Nova dared Jane. But Jane seemed utterly pleased at the proposition. She turned to them and bent down. "You're seven and you're three, is that right?"

Their faces fell. Surely they were too young for the culinary pur-suits their hearts desired. Nova replied, "Yes, but I'm wise beyond my years. My brother, I don't know, I think he's just a plain three."

"Aha, well, a plain three and a wise seven is plenty old enough to be fine young chefs." She set them up on their Montessori stools, gave them each a job, and soon sounds of a pleasant busyness filled the air. Whatever hesitance my children possessed upon waking to this new person in our kitchen was quickly replaced with total openness. I was amazed at the way Jane could fold so easily into us, the way my kitchen seemed more her kitchen, as if she'd been there long before me.

And still, even though there was a chill between us, I knew my husband believed me. His own mother was telling him the truth and his brain couldn't even entertain it. He trusted me that much. I wanted to reach out to him, to hold him in this moment.

I caught his eye and smiled. Mouthed, "She's amazing, right?"

He looked into his coffee. Muttered, "One week."

I set down my mug, gestured for him to convene with me out-side in the backyard. "What do you mean *one week*?"

"I think this is weird. She's wearing your clothes. I mean, where did you meet her again? What are we paying her?"

"We're not paying her at all. She's living with us in exchange for childcare. It's a trade. Mutually beneficial." I knew he'd be proud of me that I'd taken finances into consideration.

"She needs a paycheck or she's not going to know her place."

"Her place?" I repeated. "She's not a dog. She's a friend. She wants to help. She's new in town and needs a place and doesn't want to live somewhere shitty or with some bloodsucking dude. God-dammit, why are you making this hard?"

I felt a panic attack coming on. My diaphragm got tight. Some-times I felt like I would just stop breathing.

"We're going from nothing, no help ever, to someone here all the time. Someone we don't know. In a scenario we did not even discuss. My mother thinks you've gone off the deep end."

"Your mother is not a barometer for my well-being."

"She can't comprehend a thirtysomething-year-old woman floating around with no place to live who just moves in with a family. Neither can I, honestly, unless there's something stunted about her."

I reached out to hold his hand and he crossed his arms over his chest. "Jane wants to be a mother someday. But she's going about it all wrong. I'm going to help her. She's going to help me. This is the design. Women helping women while men go out and kill animals and bring home the meat. Where's all your village talk now? This is the village, my friend."

"Where's all your *Dateline* talk now?"

"Knowing that today I will share the weight of caretaking on my own terms—not a full Tootsie takeover—but the ability to be present yet supported, makes me feel a little bit better. That I'll be with my kids but not be totally dysregulated, yeah, makes me feel great."

"Where did you meet?"

Catch up, *buddy boy.* "I hit her."

He looked at me in a way he never had, a flash of pity? "Oh my god, this is the woman you rear-ended?" No, not pity, fear.

I couldn't tell him that we worked together at Earthside. "That's how we met, but we've gotten to know each other super well. I feel like we took a crash course in each other and now I can honestly say I'm closer to Jane than any of my friends."

"I want this to be okay," he said. "But I'm skeptical. I can't help it."

"You don't understand women," I said, looking toward the house where Jane watched us from the window, Lark on her hip, natural as breeze.

Later when my children were nourished and dressed and happy, Jane and I glimmering from the beautifying tonics she made, we got in the car and went to collect the Heavenly Chevy, as I'd begun to call it, which had spent the night in front of Mike's. The drive there seemed less magical than the drive the night before, and I felt a sudden wash of shame that I'd allowed myself to drink those hard kombuchas. I'd told Jane so much, too much.

"I can't believe I was sort of drunk last night," I said.

She smiled beatifically. "Never again, never again. But I do think the loosening up was beneficial for you. Imagine the inflammation swarming your cells from all that secret keeping. Gotta release the valve every now and then."

"I love kombucha," Lark said from the back seat.

"He's so cute," Jane said. "I can't handle how cute he is."

"How did you know where I lived last night?" I said it lightly.

She studied her long nails. Pulled down the mirror so she could put on her lipstick. "You talk about your neighborhood and your street all the time. You've described your blue house on the corner, the archway, your cross streets, the bike greenway. I didn't need to be Sherlock Holmes to find it."

"Oh," I said. Did I really talk about my house that much? It was possible. I was very proud of my house, astonished most days I lived in a house at all and not the dingy apartments from where I originated. "I guess you're right."

"You assume people aren't listening to you when you talk. But I listen to everything."

I started to object—did I assume this?—but we pulled up to Mike's. The house looked even rougher than it had last night, knee-high grass so overgrown you could barely see the heads of his flock of garden gnomes. Crows sat in a line on the fence cawing out their bad desires.

I parked behind the Chevy. "Where did you get this car?" I asked. "It looks like something off a movie set."

She popped a ginger digestive into her mouth. "I stole it. I mean sort of. It was a gift from the old man I worked for. I drove it out of LA when he died, figuring his kids would come looking for anything they might be owed."

"Did you pick it out? Like, did he say, you can have what you want, babe, and you picked this?"

"We were driving down Sunset and I saw it parked with a For Sale sign in the window and I said I want that, and so he bought it for me. That's how things were between us."

"Wow. Sounds ideal."

"Clove." She glanced back at the kids and lowered her voice. "I was doing things with a seventy-year-old man with a ball-sack hernia. Everything was earned."

We got out and she unlocked the Chevy and opened the heavy door. A hairbrush fell out onto the street and an In–N–Out wrapper floated away on the wind, but Jane did not eat meat that was not pasture-raised and organic and Jane did not go to fast-food drive-ins. Besides, the closest one was an hour away. A tattered box sat on the back seat that looked like it had lived through a hurricane. "Jesus, did someone break in and trash it?"

Jane seemed flustered for a moment. "Mike must have taken it for a joyride last night, that fucker. Go on, I'll meet you at home."

Home. Our home. "Did I catch you eating fast food? Is someone embarrassed?"

"How dare you even imply. This is definitely Mike's work."

"Sure you don't want help?"

She stuffed something under the passenger seat. "I'm good," she called.

I got back in my car and watched Jane clean out the Chevy a bit more while pretending to text. It was a car my father would have loved. It seemed clear she had been living out of it. Holding my phone, I felt the urge to call you, Mother, tell you about my day, a fantasy so ordinary, so common, but not to me. That should be what a phone was for, for calling one's mother, but my phone functioned only as distraction. I would have liked to call you now and tell you about Jane. When my own daughter piped in, I stepped back into my place. I was not the daughter. I was the mother.

"Is Jane weird?" Nova asked.

I pulled away from the curb. "What do you mean?"

"I don't know."

"We're all weird in our own ways."

"Why can she take her hair off?" she said.

"What are you talking about?"

"I peeked in the bathroom this morning while she was taking a shower and her hair was by the sink."

I pictured Jane's gorgeous copper locks, how shiny and cared for they were, how she looked like she'd just stepped out of a salon. I assumed it was due to the CoQ10 gummies we'd both been taking by the handful.

"Are you sure?" I asked.

"Full hair sitting by the sink."

"It might be a wig." Did Jane wear a wig? Was Nova alright? I made a mental note to schedule her annual well-child visit, maybe check in with her pediatrician about when imagination crossed the line into delusion. "Anyway, it's probably not our business what someone's doing in the bathroom with the door closed."

"I was trying to see her boobs," Nova said.

"Jane have Nonnies?" Lark asked.

"You can't open the door while someone is showering because you want to see their boobs," I said.

"How do you see someone's boobs, then?" My daughter. Did I ask questions like this, Mother? I don't remember being so carefree.

"Sometimes you have to live in the mystery."

"She said she wants to be a mommy and have a baby and I wondered if her boobs would look like they could milk."

"I'm sure they can milk and if they can't that's fine too. All bodies are beautiful and fine the way they are."

"You say that stuff, but what do you really think?" Nova said, exasperated.

"I think Jane is very nice, so who cares about her hair? Or her Nonnies."

"I love Jane," Lark said.

Nova scoffed. "You love everyone."

A week flew by in a blur of small adjustments, mainly me adjusting to relinquishing control, allowing Jane to do the things I had always done for my children, a reality I'd dreamed about but that was difficult in practice. Luckily Jane was the perfect alchemy of kind and directive, soothing and stable. "I got it, Clove," she would say as she plucked things out of my hands in the kitchen to make their meals, or, "Now would be a good window for a meditation," when I was caught in the weeds of Nova and Lark bickering over a toy. My husband warmed up day by day until the episode with Tootsie and the shock of Jane's arrival were a long-gone chapter of the past requiring zero processing. I was almost afraid to believe it, but it seemed like this could be working. Jane and I were working; the family was working. My instinct about her had not been wrong, and this was a relief.

That morning Jane had gone out on an errand to get bulk nettle and raspberry leaf to make infusions. I'd recently realized my hair had thinned considerably with all this stress and weaning, and Jane knew just the fix. In her absence I paced the house waiting for the mail. Despite this new domestic bliss, I could not forget that Jane's main utility was to offer me the mental space to stay sharp, stay on guard, and always be ready to intercept you. This moment, I knew, was critical. Relief and safety in reach, my fantasy about to manifest that you'd read my letter and finally understood. Seen me. The confirmation from you, Mother, that you would honor my request would arrive any minute. I could feel it.

I went to pee and when I came back to the window, I saw

our mail carrier with her long braid bent over in front of our appointed secret mail bush. I ran outside but spotted my husband from the corner of my eye emerging from the backyard. Really? Why was this the moment he magically didn't have to be on a call? Jane had only been gone an hour and everything was falling apart.

I could not let my husband see the mailwoman. Not when I was so close to putting this all behind me. I jumped into his arms. Hugged him like I used to, full frontal press. "Hi," I said.

"Hey," he said. "Where's your friend?"

"Herbal voyage." He nodded as if he understood and stepped around me toward the mailbox.

"What are you doing?" I said, putting myself in front of him again.

"Supposed to get something from work today."

"I'll bring it in when it comes," I said. The mailwoman was playing along, bless her, frozen solid behind the bush just out of his sight. "Actually, want to walk and get a coffee or something when Jane comes back? We can do things like that with her here. Little day dates."

A sneeze erupted from the bush and my husband turned. "What's she doing?" he said lowly to me, as if trying not to embarrass her as she emerged awkwardly.

"Must have dropped something, I don't know," I said. "Who cares?"

I ran over to her and took the remaining normal mail from her hands. She waved at my husband and looked back at me. Raised her eyebrows like *sorry.*

"Thank you so much!" I said with a wide smile.

I handed the mail to my husband—a flyer and an auto insurance ad. An envelope from his work, as promised. "Go get your wallet,"

I said, but then Jane pulled up—yes, Jane, fulfilling her duty as not only a wonderful source of childcare but a supreme distraction for my husband as well. That beautiful car. He lit up and bounded down the driveway to inspect it. Maybe today he'd even look under the hood, take it for a drive around the block, really detach himself from the fact that his wife was waiting for the moment he turned away so she could creep to the bush and snatch a letter from her supposedly dead mother in his own front yard.

The kids went to greet Jane and I stepped out of my life, watching them all together for a moment, content without me, a reality that was both terrifying and relieving—terrifying, the way I wanted to be with them, but relieving because if something happened to me, if I had to go away because of all this, they would still be four. My childhood with you and my father had given me the ability to think this way, a curse, a blessing. I dashed inside and locked myself in the bathroom with your letter.

Mother. Oh, Mother.

Dear daughter,

Selby saw your letter and said, that's long enough to be a book! You're a good writer. I see why you like writing fiction. A lot of this felt like fiction to me. Being right there with you during your escape, your time in San Francisco. It pained me to watch you walk through the world without me. See, I was spared from that when they told me you were dead. Maybe it was easier to believe you were, because then I didn't have to imagine you getting older. You were frozen as my child and nothing beyond. To be relieved from worrying about your child can feel like a vacation. But only at first.

It was nice to read about your children. My grandchildren. To first learn about them even existing and then to hear about your time with them. I very much agree that motherhood is hard. Just because we lived like we did doesn't mean you were never a difficult child. In fact, you were quite draining. You didn't like the little diced onions on your happy meal cheeseburger and you'd scream until I picked them all off. Once you hid in a clothes rack in JCPenney for hours and I had to have security shut the mall down. I thought here it is—she's been abducted. You even kicked the priest in the shins when I tried to have you baptized. You were very stubborn and did things that shocked me. Like when you told your father I had a boyfriend who took you for ice cream after I'd denied you ice cream and he beat me senseless. You were five. I forgave you and I forgive you still. My own mother wasn't around to help me, and her mother wasn't around to help her. I guess we come from a long line of that sort of thing. So I can understand why you don't want to risk losing what you have. You have so much.

I am turning to dust in here. You really don't want me to ever meet your children? I eat my dried noodles and I marvel. My daughter, alive. I'm sorry about Gary. If I think too long about the things I've done wrong, I can't lift my head. You poor little girl.

But you're not a little girl anymore, are you?

My lawyer thinks if you tell the truth of that time and of that night, really tell them what it was like for us, there's a genuine chance I could be freed. You were so young. How could anyone not take pity? You can't run away forever, and I won't give up on this. If I could, I would. But there's parts of this story that only you can tell. They are the most important parts.

Mom

CHAPTER 19

The summer ran through us. My children's feet outgrew their shoes. I loved my life wholly and freely now that it was ending.

Whenever my mind drifted, I imagined how it would all go down. Would I be contacted by police? Would they surprise me at home? Would I be taken away by force, my children watching? The confusion they would feel. And then the media onslaught. I wasn't confident like your feminist lawyer. I didn't see much evidence that things had changed for women. What they had done to you back then, the villain you became. Why would it be different this time? It was driving me crazy that my letter to you had not worked. That now I had to regather myself and prepare for the worst, continue living in a world where this was all actually happening. See, for a little while with Jane around, I'd tricked myself into thinking it would all go away. Tricked myself into thinking you would do what was best for me.

If you were going to involve me, expose me, I had to be armed with everything. I couldn't avoid the Butcher anymore.

I didn't show Jane your latest letter, didn't tell her anything about it. It felt too intimate, and I was scared if she saw it she would abandon me and feel sorriest for you. It was best Jane and I form a seal around ourselves, continue to settle into each other. She seemed to sense a psychic change in me, though. Maybe my worry seeped through more than I realized. Jane would smile, hold my hand. "Here if you ever want to talk about anything." But I didn't want to talk. I wanted to bask in our hours in the yard while Jane played music on her phone, songs to elevate our vibrations, while we danced and the kids waved ribbons across the lawn. Morning glory muffins with crispy tops and tart spirulina lemonade. Meanwhile we kept one secret shift a week at Earthside to maintain our discount, the perfect balance of work in and out of the home, achieved at last.

Then one morning in early August Nova came storming out of her room, shook me. Her face looked full of something. But what? What did she know? I sat on the couch and put my head between my legs, tried to re-center.

"Mom, Mom!" I looked at her.

"I'm so sorry," I said, preparing to apologize for everything, for my life.

"What's wrong with you? Did you even look at the calendar?"

The calendar. She knew it was almost time, *the summer and no more.* Had you written to her, Mother? My mind scanned all possibilities.

"What's on the calendar?" *Just the end of everything.*

"Mom." She threw up her hands like a tiny adult. "It's music class."

Jesus Christ. Music class. The late-summer session of parent-child music class I'd signed them up for months ago, when I was a different woman, started today.

"I'll be in the car," Nova informed me. "So hurry up."

Lark emerged from the hall and hugged me. "I just love you, Mama."

On the way to music class, fortified by Jane, I forced myself to be a present mother. We hadn't left the house much since the post office incident and look how far I'd come, driving along now, the Chevy woman literally in my car! Despite my mounting terror, maybe I was in the vibration my podcast women had described. Everything was under control if I just told myself it was. And then about a mile from the community center, Lark screamed that he had to poop now, now, NOW.

"My butt hurts!"

"Almost there, honey," I said. I sped up.

But he had started unbuckling himself. "It's coming."

"Mom, stop the car!" Nova shrieked.

"Pull over," Jane said. "It's for real."

I pulled over and jumped out. Grabbed Lark, who already had his shorts almost off, and held him over the curb, where he released a ten-inch log onto my sandal. It slumped over my foot in a languishing position, as if it had fainted. It was warm on my skin. Lark laughed. Jane stared in amused shock, her mouth open.

"Oh my god." Without moving my foot, I wiped him with a paper towel from my pocket and maneuvered him back into the car. "Oh my god. It's on my foot."

Jane heaved in silent laughter. My various mothering podcasts would probably advise me to praise the shit right now, congratulate him. *You must feel so much better! Your body is doing its perfect work, and I am at peace with the fact that you've ruined my overpriced lambskin slide.*

"I'm going to cry," Jane gasped. Her face looked so different laughing this hard, a glimmer of her at another, easier time. Or maybe it was just her now, present, having fun with us. I liked thinking this, that the work of reparenting ourselves in tandem was indeed under way and working.

"Come here," I said to Nova.

She gave me the annoyed look.

"Do it, unbuckle and come look at this." The corners of her mouth twitched into the tiniest smile. She leaned over and we all gawked at the enormous, seemingly expanding shit.

"Wow," Nova said. "No wonder his butt hurt."

"I want you to remember me like this," I said. "With this poo on my foot. Please remember it was your mother who held your little bodies over the side of the road to poop on her. Will you? Will you remember this when I'm old and you're trying to find me a nursing home? All the things I did for you?"

Nova was hysterical now, slapping her knee. Jane reached out and held Nova's hand. I imagined Nova as an adult with Jane still in her life, some supportive aunt figure, a part of her feminist fight club. All I wanted was for my daughter to start life on a different path, to have an expanded view of herself, know her worth, possess a regulated nervous system. She could dodge what we'd been through, Mother. But not if you bring it all back. Not if you color her world with it.

"What am I supposed to do?" I asked them in a sort of legitimate way.

"Kick your leg up and send it flying," Nova said.

"Fly it!" Lark cried out with glee.

I was in a neighborhood; I couldn't fling shit onto someone's lawn. I'd leave it near the curb and pray for forgiveness. But then I looked around and realized the house before me was familiar. A sort of unique house for Portland, pink stucco and Spanish architecture and I knew who lived there because once when I'd decided to walk the kids in the stroller all the way to music class, Lark had gotten out to get a closer look at a clay dog statue on this exact sprawling lawn and the woman who lived here had scolded me for letting him onto her property, letting him touch her things. I had tried to explain he was so little, he was just saying hi to the dog. But she wasn't having it. "You're trespassing," she'd said.

"I didn't want him to scream and disturb you so I was giving him time to keep walking on his own."

"Get off my property," she'd said like I was a criminal.

"We're going." I carried a screaming Lark away that day, tears in my eyes, imagining what it would have been like if the woman had said, "Hi, my name is Brenda. I've seen you walking with your kids before, always alone. Are you okay? You're doing your best and your best is good enough. Would they like a graham cracker? Would you like five minutes of adult conversation?" But that rarely, if ever, happened in real life. I felt the familiar dislocation; I was welcome almost nowhere with my children. Almost no one saw me and saw someone who was at work. For I was at work every day with them, wasn't I? Didn't everyone get tired of work? It baffled me that people could grow up and forget they, too, had once been children, dependent on others and curious about clay dogs on lawns. I thought of you in those moments, Mother, how few resources you had. How much of a survivor you really were.

I didn't see that woman today, though I hoped she was watching me from an upstairs window as I kicked my leg high and flung my son's shit in the air, as it broke in two and landed on her lawn at the feet of that smiling dog who knew all and saw all.

We made it to the community center, where Nova sauntered ahead and joined in preparing for class, sorting shaker eggs alongside the teacher, a warm woman whose long bare toes, stacked with silver rings, seemed too erotic in this space. Lark and I plopped down in the circle with other toddlers and their parents. There were several mothers in tight athletic ensembles and ponytails, sweat still drying from a workout they had just done before this at the park, squatting and gyrating and burpee-ing around their strollers while their kids ate pretzels and snoozed or screamed. A non-workout mother sat apart from them in a stained tie-dyed sweatsuit looking like she'd just dug up a grave.

A few dads were sprinkled in. I assessed their propensity for violence—did they beat their wives? Berate and control? Without their other halves around it could be hard to tell. At music class at least, the dads were on their best behavior, lively and happy in the circle, kiddos in laps. I imagined the Butcher here with us. I had a strong matcha buzz and combined with the leftover adrenaline from the poop launch I felt suddenly able to respond to him. So many drafts I'd typed out and deleted, long, convoluted messages that doubled back on themselves, winding, winding, up an endless mountain, but I could just keep it simple. I would do it right now, in fact, before I could change my mind. I pulled up his picture on my phone, him standing next to the Home Grown sign boasting half-off-hummus day, and showed Jane.

"This is him," I said. "The one I told things to. He wants to meet."

"Oh wow," she said. "What are you going to do?" She seemed a bit aloof; it was unlike her not to comment on how obviously attractive he was.

"He said there's something we need to talk about."

The aloofness was a pose. I could tell she was interested. "What is it?"

The opening sounds of the "Hello" song tinkled in and I lowered my voice.

"Well, I don't know. That's why I have to see him. I still think he might be lying about being involved in all this. Now that you're here, I feel like I can handle it."

She shrugged. "Just don't fuck up your marriage."

"It's not about that. It's about something deeper. He knew me. Like, really knew me."

I typed out Yes, let's meet. I agree we should talk.

Within seconds the Butcher responded. Wow, I thought you weren't going to write back. I'm so glad you did. I'm supposed to come up there at the end of the month for the northwest grocery expo. Maybe then?

"Are we working the expo?" I whispered to Jane.

"Stephen said it's time and a half, so yeah."

I know the one. I'll be there, actually. I work in grocery again.

I can't believe I get to see you.

Yeah, it will be good, I typed out. I looked at Jane. And true.

The teacher cleared her throat, looking directly at Jane and me. I tried to come back to the room, to the all-important present moment. Lark settled in Jane's lap for the chorus of the "Hello" song. He really liked her. *Helloooooo, everybody...so glad to see you...* Nova sat next to the teacher, mimicking her, and I winked. She returned a half smirk that let me know she was ultraproud of herself for being a leader and happy Jane and I were witnessing it. Everyone stood for the folk-dance segment and I hoisted Lark into the air with all the other parents and wondered if the stroller-workout moms felt pressure in their vaginas with each lift. They jumped around a lot. A *lot*. How was it they were able to do this without pissing themselves? Jane watched the other mothers and fathers and her demeanor seemed to wilt with each song. It made sense that being in a space like this might be difficult for her. But she played it off well, sending the kids silly smiles as she pretended to know the lyrics. I felt overcome with responsibility for her, a suffocating love.

We kept singing and shook the noisy eggs in our hands and with Jane around, my mind didn't pummel me with images of what would happen if I dropped Lark's body accidentally or if Nova ran out of the building and into the road. I didn't see my father kicking you and the way your body would fold around his steel-toed work boot. Him pushing me into the wall, the sound of a beer can opening. Always another beer. I smiled and sang.

Finally, the teacher invited us to lie down for the lullaby. Lark used this time to race from electrical outlet to electrical outlet trying to touch the deadly hardware beneath. I called to him and he returned, hugged me with force, then collapsed into my lap. Nova settled next to Jane, their knees touching. I liked to be still while the lullaby played—*su la leeeeee…*—and gear up emotionally for the "Goodbye" song. *Goodbye to your mom and your dad, or the one who takes care of youuuuuu.* I held Lark close and kissed his pointy little chin. He still had all his baby teeth, so small in his still round-cheeked face. "Goodbye, everybody!" he screamed in my ear over and over. My eyes met with one of the dads for a moment and his eyes became the Butcher's eyes. I felt a shot of warmth in my center. Lark wrapped his arms around my neck and announced, "Time to go home and wash my poop off your shoe!"

* * *

In front of the house, I let the kids and Jane go inside ahead of me. On the porch, I opened my messages to stare at the Butcher's writing and this clear proof of further synchronicity. Surely it was no accident he would be in Portland soon. Your letter was the worst thing I could imagine, Mother—you weren't letting up—but perhaps the universe had another plan. The universe desired wholeness for each of us, my podcasts said. Maybe things were going to work out. Maybe I was going to come out of this with more than I started with. If I could really dig deep I could see everything anew through the lens of abundance: I had Jane, I had contact with my first love, and I had, for the moment, a mother who was writing to me. You could still come around to understand that this was your moment for abundance too. To find freedom, yes, but also, to do what you'd never been able to before: protect me.

CHAPTER 20

After the Marie Callender's fiasco and the new permanent indentation in your back to go with your limp, but before our final attempt at escape, my father went to a support group for the first time. He meant to go to Anger Management but messed up the schedule and wound up at a Battered Men's meeting, where he found himself in a room of men telling stories of household terror, their wives and partners holding court over them, being physically and emotionally manipulative, beating them, weaponizing sex. I can only imagine he wanted to align with these men, imagine himself a victim. So he told a story of his own. A story that later, the facilitator of that meeting, a ruthless mouse of a woman, would use against you in court. She described my father in accurate detail—she had the paper where he'd signed himself in—and she repeated the harrowing story he'd told of being trapped with an alcoholic madwoman who wanted him dead all while trying to raise his daughter, who was starting to display violent tendencies of her own. Who had, one night, cracked a bowl over his head.

"If I turn up dead, go looking for my wife," he'd told the group.

The woman wrote it all down, *verbatim,* she kept stressing. "Men don't lie about abuse," she'd said. "Not when ego is concerned."

She said he'd shown the other men in the group the scar that creeped down past his hairline from the bowl to prove it. Was quoted as saying, "All I ever wanted was a normal family."

I'd come across the Battered Men's pamphlet in the glove compartment of the Jimmy while looking for gum. We'd given him a ride to work that day and brought the Jimmy back so we could clean it. We did this once a month and usually snuck in a secret trip to the McDonald's drive-through on the way to get him. You were in a light mood as we drove. Happy to be out, such a luxury for you to drive a car without my father breathing down your neck, but you were mostly happy because my father was being so kind, so sheepish and loving, and, most thrilling—"You'll like this, Calla Lily"—you'd talked on the phone with the old AA friend you'd reunited with at the hospital, and we had a date coming up. A real date in just one week when we would leave, escape to the man's sister's house in North Shore, my father none the wiser. You weren't drinking and Tina's "What's Love Got to Do with It" played on repeat, your favorite song. I held the pamphlet up. "Battered... men?"

I knew you were *battered* because shortly after we'd met her, Christina had given you a book she'd special ordered called *The Battered Woman,* a pioneering feminist account of domestic violence from the seventies. I devoured it, felt a tingling of hope that people were writing about these things. That we were far from alone. But you merely flipped through it, fixating on a story that described a forced act involving a dog, and then threw it across the room. "Your father has never treated me like that!"

"Not yet," Christina replied, mixing the chalky protein powder

Celine hated into her yogurt. "Your mother can't see sense," she'd said later just to me, because we knew the book had backfired, made you feel lucky instead of motivated.

In the car with you, I read the stages as outlined in the Battered Men's pamphlet, which were the same as the women's version. First the abuser dropped a *love bomb,* defined by grand romantic gestures, compliments, and lavish gifts.

I asked you: "Did he ever bomb you?"

You smiled. "Of course. Why do you think I fell in love?" I hated that you could still be starry-eyed. "We actually met doing something called cocaine," you said. "Don't ever do drugs, Calla Lily, but we did, and it sort of set us off on a fast track, you could say." I knew all of this already. I wanted to hear something new. Something to make me understand for once.

"Then the tension stage."

"Eggshells."

"Then intimidation. 'Will punch a wall next to the partner or slap instead of punch.' "

You nodded vigorously. In this you were the expert. "Yeah, yeah. Your father hasn't met a wall he didn't eventually punch through. We've never gotten a security deposit back."

"Then the violent event. Eruption. Following eruption, the calm," I read. "Winning the partner's trust back again."

"What we're in now."

I thought of the times my father would bring home lobsters and we'd eat them with our hands, butter dripping down our chins. When he'd take us to the movies, and we'd all share an extra-large popcorn, me in the middle. A major pastime of the calm phase was talking about all the fun things we were going to do in the future, mostly never doing them, but then one day, boom, we'd wake up and he'd have the Jimmy packed for a surprise surfing lesson, a trip to the zoo. We never knew.

"The cycle begins again," we both recited.

You squinted into the sun. "Let's get shave ice, kid," you said. "They have McDonald's everywhere, but our days might be numbered for real shave ice in Waikiki."

"Where will we end up? You know, after North Shore? We can't just stay there forever. Eventually he'll find us." I was ready for more of the plan. I wanted things signed and sealed. The island felt sickeningly small.

"Well, I guess deep down I'm a California girl," you said.

"That's not far enough. He'll know to look for us there."

"I don't know. We can't leave the country. Not yet anyhow. Where do you want to land? New York City?"

"Be serious."

"I'm not joking. Maybe we'll live in New York. See a play on Broadway. We'd have to get you a real winter coat. I bet you barely remember wearing closed-toe shoes."

"What if this doesn't work?" I thrust the pamphlet at you. "It says most victims get stuck in the cycle and then they die."

You parked. Took the pamphlet from me and put it back in the glove box, where later investigators would find it. "He won't ever kill me."

Why didn't you see? "He's killing you now."

And the pamphlet reminded me that my father, for all his affection post attack, had not yet reached his apex. Not with himself, and not with us.

We crossed the street toward the hotels. Some man looked you up and down and whistled. I watched you take him in, reward him with a smile. I was alone in this world.

You got the shave ice and we sat in the Royal Hawaiian garden on our favorite bench near the young hula dancers, who swayed while tourists looked on. Tears streamed down my face into the treat that, like everything else, was a secret.

"Don't cry," you said. You put your arm around me. "I hate when you cry."

The ocean was all around. Trapped. I desired an airplane, our airplane that would take us away.

"I can't help but think of how much I'd miss him," you said. "The good parts."

"I'll miss you more," I said. "When you're dead. I'll miss you so much."

"Honey," you said calmly. "You're not old enough to understand this. But your father loves me. Why else do you think he gets so mad?"

"Stop buying things like this," I said, slamming the shave ice down between us. "We have to save every penny for our new life."

"Living a little is necessary to survival. We can't hate life in the meantime."

"We do hate life."

You looked thoughtfully at the beautiful dancers. Flowers of every color dripped from the beams above. "I don't hate life," you said. "Every day I get to spend with you, I love."

Your AA friend picked us up from around the corner of our high-rise in the middle of the night during one of my father's double shifts and dropped us off at the North Shore house, promising to return in a few days with our plane tickets. He felt it was best to wait a bit before getting on a plane in case my father immediately checked the airport. We lay across the back seat the entire ride there and I heard you softly crying.

Do you think of those days with me, Mother? Two bedrooms, but we slept entwined together in the larger room under a dark quilt with bright white flowers in a double bed with a starched white bed skirt. Each night we checked under that skirt to make sure my father wasn't hiding there. Opened all the cabinets, looked in the shower, looked in places we knew he couldn't fit but we had to look anyway. We brought enough groceries to survive a week so we wouldn't need to leave. During this time you barely ate, drifting past a box of dry cereal and taking a handful every couple of hours or so.

"His work buddies could be watching. He always said, 'Don't bother hiding from me, Alma, I got eyes everywhere,'" you said when I suggested a walk to the beach. Said again later when I suggested we do like Julia Roberts in our favorite movie when she finally escapes her husband and immediately cuts her hair off, changes her looks. "Then we could do whatever we wanted." I was eager to start our new life.

"Your father would still find us," you said. I could see you weren't ready for that part, the action of what would come next, and okay, I thought, I'll give you this little time in this sweet house to ease in. Not everything all at once.

We watched soap operas and movies and you cried about how much we'd miss Christina and Celine, how you wished we could take them with us. I didn't see the utility in crying for them. We'd had them all these years. And wasn't it wonderful, the way they were helping us, had agreed to divert my father by telling him we'd flown to Maui in case he started asking neighbors where we were? "We can see them again," I said. "Once everything settles down. Don't get distracted."

You shot me a wounded look. "I used to call your father *my darling.* If I wrote him a note, I'd actually kiss it."

"You want me to love him the way you do," I said.

"There were good times too. Promise me you'll remember some of the good times."

"Yes," I said. Thinking of all those good times. To me they meant little. But to you they meant everything.

"I failed you," you said. "I failed my daughter. I think a part of me always knew I would."

I let it sit. I wanted you to feel this way, to let it motivate you. I kept miscalculating how you worked.

Those days at the North Shore house you stayed sober. You began to unfurl your sloped shoulders, walk taller. We would sit outside in the sun and you let me drink coffee and I felt utterly grown. We were doing it. Together. All this time the problem had been that I was a mere child, but now you could rely on me. Now I could really help. From here, if we could get on that plane before he found us, we'd be gold. Your AA friend said he'd asked everyone at his home group meeting to donate to our cause and had collected enough to get us to New York. I knew nothing about New York. It sounded like another world because it was.

"Your father would hate New York City," you said many times over those days. "He hates crowds. Hates weather. Even if he wondered if we were there, he'd never go. Trust me, he likes his island life. Pretty soon he'll have a cute Hawaiian girlfriend, you can mark my words."

"I hope he never has another girlfriend."

"Ha," you said. "That man can pull any woman he wants, and

he knows it. That's the worst part. He'll barely miss me once I'm gone."

It was as if you had no long-term memory about why we were doing this. We just had to get on the plane.

But I know what it's like to live a dream: your friend arriving like he said he would, handing over two one-way tickets to what he called *the Big Apple,* said we would leave the next night. He would pick us up at dusk to take us to the airport. I hugged him, this man who was doing this for no personal gain, only to help. He brought along a baby name book, told us to start looking because once we landed we shouldn't go by our actual names anymore. It would be a good idea for you to try to find a job that didn't involve too much paperwork, register our phone number under the landlord's name, something to give ourselves a chance. He said he'd seen stuff like this on TV, and it was important to lie low.

"Are you listening?" I said. You touched the tickets and looked as sad as I was happy. I could miss my father later. In fact, I looked forward to missing him.

"Listen," the man said to me, eyes clocking the windows, the doors. He wasn't excited like I'd first thought. He was terrified. "Take care of your mother, alright, keiki?" Sweet of him to call me *child,* and I savored it, knowing it would be the last time I'd hear it said to me this way once we left the island.

The next morning I got up before you, too wired to sleep in—we would leave that night!—and stood in the kitchen in an old shirt of my father's with a tractor on it. It was still darkish outside as I ate my cereal. I could see my reflection in the tall sliding glass window, a girl, almost a woman, about to leave for New York City. That feeling, Mother. All that potential. Us. Together. I finished my bowl and started to clean up. Today we'd tidy and pack, get everything organized. Then we'd fly over the ocean, over the entire United States. The house was quiet. Birds rustled outside. The tall reach of the banyans surrounded us. Our own private getaway. I rinsed the dish. Looked at the window one more time. There was my face. My hand raising.

But it wasn't me.

"Hello," my father mouthed.

He stood calmly outside. We stared at each other for what felt like a long time. My feet were suddenly wet. No. I ran to the front door to make sure it was locked and slipped in my piss, hit the back of my head on the tile floor, felt warmth spreading across my scalp. Got up, made my way to the door. Of course we had locked it. Ran back to the kitchen to grab the phone, I was such an idiot, I should have done that first. How had he found us? But then a blast and the window was gone, glass all around me. My father stepped through the hole he had made with his shotgun.

"There you are," he said. "And here I thought I'd lost you."

CHAPTER 21

Mid-August now, and thanks to Jane my kitchen was labeled and organized, my bathroom floor gleamed in places I assumed would never be clean, and my husband was his lighthearted self with an extra spring in his step, taking evening rides around the neighborhood on his longboard like he had before kids. My children had cooled down their sibling bickering, seemed eager to help. Jane made everything, including chores, fun. She was good for us. And she was happy too. Thriving. Today she wore one of my matching yoga sets and her skin gleamed. She looked up when she saw me standing in the doorway.

"The mister and I were just talking about you," she said.

My husband smiled. "Jane made juice."

She handed me a glass of it, tart and bright green.

I put my arm around my husband and pecked his cheek. An arm around Jane. This was balance. Two opposing yet congruent energies on either side of me, holding me in place.

"What were you talking about?" I asked.

But Nova popped in. "Mama, okay. So I made a playlist for my birthday party and…" She went on with very elaborate birthday plans for a koala-slash-mermaid pool party with pizza but also an ice cream cart with a person serving ice cream, unlimited cones for everyone…Her birthday was the same weekend as the grocery expo, and I had not done a single thing to prepare. But I could not fuck this up. Her birthdays were very intense holidays to her. She loved a party. I scooped her up in a hug and she wrapped her legs around me like she used to when she was so small. She squeezed my cheeks and centered my face to look at her. "Are you listening?"

"Yes! I'm right here. I got it all. Jane can help us make it the perfect day too. And Daddy."

Nova looked skeptical, and I couldn't blame her. I'd never accepted help from anyone before. "Jane's going to help with my party?"

Jane laughed. "Sure. In fact, why don't we plan it together and surprise your mom and dad?"

They looked at each other conspiratorially. "A secret?" Nova said.

"That's right," Jane said.

"Well, I gotta work," my husband said. "I'll be out there if anyone needs anything." He never said that to me when I was alone. In fact he often locked the office door so if we did need him, he was unreachable. But with Jane around we could afford to be more generous in all ways.

She smiled at me. "And you are writing today. Go on."

At the coffee shop, I tried. On my laptop I searched for the right words. Mother, *you* could tell the story of my father. *You* could explain how he was, and why you couldn't leave him. *You* could explain the things I never could then, and still cannot now. That night flashed through my mind, all its unorganizable fragments, the sound of you wailing, Christina's face as she took me in. My imagined images of the aftermath, my father, his blood, you in a courtroom standing alone. I felt suddenly dizzy and light-headed. I realized I'd been holding my breath for some time.

I closed my laptop and stared out the window at the beautiful summer day. A couple walked by hand in hand, teenagers trudged to school wearing low-slung backpacks, a skilled unicyclist with a neon green mohawk smiled and raised his arms overhead as if in worship. If any one of them turned, looked in at me, what would they see? A mother who was here while my children were else-where, a careless woman. What if there was a drive-by shooting, a break-in, an abduction? How could I, a mere mother, protect my children from anything if I was writing alone in a coffee shop? How could I protect them even when they were in my arms? I couldn't even control my own mind.

And I could not control you either, Mother. I could not make you see, and it was infuriating, devastating, demoralizing. Celine said all you wanted was to be loved, but I loved you. I saw you and I spoke the truth. You didn't want to be loved. You wanted his love. You wanted him to love you so much he wouldn't hurt you. If you could change him, you'd win the game. My love was never enough because my love was never in question.

I returned home to Jane making lunch for my children, who were still very much alive and unharmed, a happy and easy energy sur-rounding them. They ate ravenously, SunButter and jelly sand-wiches, now garnering two enthusiastic thumbs-ups. I went to the bathroom and splashed cold water on my face, willed my own energy to shift. I was exhausted. Every time I let myself ruminate on my old life, I came back to the present feeling jet-lagged.

I collapsed into the couch, and Jane joined me. Maybe I'd tell her more of what was going on. The weight was certainly wearing me down. But before I could speak, she said, "You know, it's been awesome hanging out and settling in, but I think—and I hope you feel this way too—that this time together has really proven that we should definitely go forward with everything."

I looked at the kids finishing their sandwiches. If they sensed an important conversation was about to transpire they would come up with a sudden laundry list of needs.

"Why don't you go play in the back for a little while," I said to them. "The sidewalk chalk is out. Draw me a picture. A surprise. Who can get there first?" That did it. They raced out of the room, arguing over who was going to win.

"Sorry," I said to her. "What were you saying?"

Her face brightened and she seemed a little nervous. I had the sense she'd rehearsed what she was about to say next. "It's time to talk logistics. Get a general timeline."

"In terms of?"

She cracked her knuckles. "If you get pregnant now, that's, what, a May baby? I'm fine with that. Honestly, I don't really care when."

I was hit with the memory of the lemon-sized hematoma in my vaginal wall left by Lark's fast and furious descent through the birth canal. No one discovered it for weeks. I'd had to have it surgically drained. Each childbirth had been a miraculous scrape with death and I knew I'd had it relatively good. I felt relief every day I'd made it, made them, and now it was over.

"You mean when *you'll* be getting pregnant," I said. "Oh gosh, you scared me for a second, you said it funny."

"I can't get pregnant," she said. "I told you that. I've been having unprotected sex for years and nothing. My ovulation is all over the map if it happens at all. Clove, you said you'd carry my baby."

Here was that feeling again I'd had all summer, the feeling of holding an orange in my palm and being told it was an apple. "Well, if you're referring to that night at Mike's, I was more than half in the bag."

Her brightness drained. Jane wiped her forehead with the back of her hand, causing some wispy hairs to spring up around her hairline. I looked closer, remembered Nova's observation about Jane's wig on the bathroom counter. Why wouldn't Jane be open with me about something like that? "You said you'd do anything to help me become a mother."

"Sure. Of the baby *you* will have. Or if you choose to have a surrogate, of course I'd be there for that too. Or adopt. I just can't be the surrogate. That time in my life is over."

"Says the woman who got pregnant so easily she chose her children's astrological signs."

"Why would you want me? I'm a wreck. Look at what happened to me from simply weaning. I feel like I've lost my mind most of the time. And everything going on with my mom. Jane."

"You promised you would help me at Mike's party. I mean, look at all you have to give. The kombucha wasn't that hard."

"I'm giving you a place to live, complete access to my closet and refrigerator, and anything else you could want."

"I'm not freeloading off you, I'm working. You don't view my time with your children, my housework, as work?"

"I value your work, Jane. I'm sorry. I just don't get where this is coming from. I'm sorry we had a misunderstanding. But I'm not going to carry a child for you. I mean, who would even be the father?"

"Ideally I would use your eggs and your husband's sperm. And then I'd raise the baby as my own while we continue supporting each other as a soul family. Like you claim to want."

"You want me to have another kid and give it to you? That's literally what you just said. Am I understanding you right?"

"The child would be mine."

"Jane."

"But you love talking about how women have helped one another have babies for centuries. Isn't it you who wanted to create this happy little commune? Or is it really that you need me to do the grunt work of parenting while you write your poor mother long letters about why you can't help her."

"Out-of-bounds."

She wiped away her tears, smearing her foundation and revealing pink mottled skin underneath. What was now very clearly a wig had slipped to one side a bit.

"Why wouldn't you tell me about your wig?" I asked.

She touched the top of her head lightly. "My hair's not natural enough for you?"

"I have no judgment about it; it just seems odd of you to never mention it. We've told each other so much."

"We haven't told each other anything, Clove."

I sensed a current of danger. But Jane wasn't dangerous. Jane read auras and knew all varieties of amethyst and was planning to buy Nova a rock tumbler for her birthday.

"I can't have your baby," I said softly. "You have to know that. I was caught up in that moment with you at the party. Maybe I confused you. I want this to work so much. And it *is* working."

She was still for a moment. She looked into my eyes. I couldn't read her. I had the urge to break out of our locked stare, but I held on, strained to make out the real color of her irises.

"What will happen when your husband finds out about you?" she said. "Do you think he'll still love you once he realizes he doesn't know you?"

Did she mean for me to feel frightened? I didn't have time for this, didn't have time to find another source of childcare if she left. I didn't have time to invest in someone new, someone who would never understand me the way she did. And, truthfully, I didn't want to. For a moment, I touched a fingertip, Mother, to what it might have been like to excuse bad behavior to stay in a relationship. I had thought myself above it.

"You're upset, but we can work through this," I said.

She forced a smile. Shook herself a bit. "I knew this would happen. I knew I'd get too involved. Get ahead of myself. You know how hard it is when you want something to make you whole. To love you unconditionally. You become blind to everything else."

"I want to help in any way I can," I said. "Just not the way you were envisioning."

"I need to think a little," she said. She got up and gathered her purse, closed the front door softly behind her. From the window I watched the Heavenly Chevy glide down my quiet street, a rarefied gem among the many identical Subarus. Every time I saw that car drive away I had the sense I would never see it again.

I went to the backyard and found the kids playing with chalk as instructed. I lay down on the cement and they traced my body like a crime scene while I replayed the night at Mike's party over and over, each time more disorienting than the time before. How could we have miscommunicated so wildly? But I couldn't wonder long—my children needed snacks, they needed help building a block tower as tall as the ceiling. Tears were shed when it fell and tears dried when I built it quickly again. They cycled through the full spectrum of human emotion in mere minutes, repeat, repeat. Hours passed and lifetimes collapsed into each other. Someone once told me when they ran out of things to do with their kids, *just add water.* This was, in fact, somewhat practical advice. We went back outside and I turned on the hose. My body laid itself down on the grass. Water rained on me and I didn't care. "What now? What now?" they shrieked. From my back I offered them the task of filling the mini pool my husband hated because it ruined the lawn. My kids became seals, mermaids, sharks, oh my. I tried to create silence where there was none. I tried to remember Jane's exact tone as she'd contemplated aloud what my husband would think of the truth.

That's when my mind offered instruction: *You need to have something on her. Something to even things out.*

I was just entering that very dark place when I sat up to see a bee on my thigh. I was not gentle like my husband. Instinctively I slapped it and as I did so it stung me. As the pain registered, I heard the Chevy's engine roar back up the street and cut. The sting would wait. The sting meant nothing. Pain, a state of mind that was thwarted by Jane. I ran to the front to meet her. All of my defenses fell away.

"Please," I said. I felt myself drop to my knees on the concrete driveway. My hands involuntarily found prayer. "Please don't tell him."

She braced before me. "I wear a wig because my hair looks like my mother's," she said. I could tell she'd been crying. Her face was bare now, no trace of makeup. The wig still looked like it needed adjusting.

"I'm sorry," I said to her.

"About my hair or because you won't have my baby?"

The kids' voices grew near. I stood up just as they emerged from the backyard, ran to Jane. "Oh my gosh, aliens!" she play-screamed. "Oh no! You got me!" She bent down and hugged them, Lark's sweet face nestled in the wig hair, but Nova's eyes were on me. She could tell something was off. I hated knowing I had such a deep effect on her. But of course I did. I was her mother.

"How about a show?" I asked them. "One show, and then we'll start dinner." They ran to the basement for their one show, which now wasn't so much a treat as a solid part of our routine. Jane and I were alone again. If one of my neighbors was watching us, perhaps we looked like two sisters trapped in a decades-long tension, something ordinary, a kerfuffle about whether to grill salmon or chicken or who was doing the salad dressing, who forgot the shallots.

"I thought becoming a mother was going to reset me," I said. "That it would erase the past. But, Jane, it doesn't. It's an express highway back in time. You look at your kids and you see your-self too. I mean, you can't even look at your own hair because it reminds you of your mother. Imagine if you had to stare into her eyes all day."

"But if you had my baby, I wouldn't be staring into my mother's eyes. I'd be staring into yours."

I felt loved when she said that. It was priceless to be loved by another woman. Yet I could not give her what she wanted. "You'll still remember it all, each thing. Relentlessly."

"My journey will be different." There it was, the reason humans still existed.

"Maybe. But even beyond all that there is the very real fact that my vagina will fall out onto the floor if I have another kid. I can't physically do it again."

She sighed. "You're manifesting physical ailments to distract yourself from the fact that your mom's in prison begging for your help and you're fucking paralyzed, alright? Someone's gotta say it."

We sat on the porch stairs. An immense sadness emanated from her. She looked up at the house, the flower boxes outside the window.

"You did it," she said. "You got what you wanted."

What I wanted...

I wanted everything I was giving my children now.

But we had apartments with broken doors, holes in walls, work boots lining the hallways. Shotguns in closets, mismatched plates and plastic forks, smeared windows lined with remnants of duct tape after Hurricane Iniki. Musty old carpets and scratchy furniture. Eau de cigarette. A smoke childhood. Fear in the air, in our lungs, in our blood.

I don't tell you this to shame you, Mother. I tell you this to let you know that now as a mother myself, I finally understand the magnitude of what my father took from you.

We did have, we did have, for the worst years of it, the ocean.

And your strength somehow, your body with my body in space, your hand in mine while we raced across the sand among a mass of people sunbathing—we could have been them. We could have had a room key and a towel with a hotel logo and we could have gone into the pink hotel and ordered the pink pancakes with the tourists and we could have drunk the guava juice and we could have been anyone out there, the sun the same in everyone's eyes, the sun obscuring us into normal people. Day ticking away, we were free on that beach, and I would wonder why when the sun set on that bliss you would still pack us up and take us back to him.

I held Jane's hand. "Did I get what I wanted?"

"See," she said, blue. "You don't even know it."

CHAPTER 22

The next night I poked my head into Nova's room, where she had placed bowls of water and cereal on the floor and was busy lining up her stuffies in front of them. Lark had wised up, didn't want to play puppy anymore. She wore a nightgown from Tootsie, a shimmery plastic-looking thing that gave off a chemical perfume. No matter. Let her wear it.

"Hey, want me to read to you?" She looked up, startled out of her inner world. She was so little but could seem so old.

It had been weeks since I'd done bedtime, pre-Tootsie, pre-Jane, and it felt almost awkward to be in her room alone with her. Beethoven streamed from her little speaker. I imagined us adults together, having lunch. How I'd yearn to tell her everything. But I'd stop myself, take a bite. Remember there was a cost to quelling generational trauma. I suspected more and more, though, that I'd gotten everything wrong. It was possible—likely, in fact—that all the lies I had told to keep her safe were in fact creating new and wildly complex issues for everyone. *The only way out is through,* Jane loved to say. But wasn't there any merit in digging a tunnel in the opposite direction?

"Sure." She brightened. "But first I want to show you something."

She took me on a tour of her room, showing me all the stations she'd set up for her animals. The hospital for when they got run over by a car, the wing where they dealt with choking cases, and the lost-puppy archive for when the babies got "napped." Great, she was as paranoid as I was. But then, the grocery store—"Earthside, of course"—where they got their dog food and their smoothies. A sign she'd written that said PLANTS ARE POWERFUL!

"I love all of this," I said. I got down so our faces were close. "Honey, I know I've been sort of not myself lately. And I'm sorry."

She combed the hair of a wonky-faced horse. "Did you know cows have four stomachs?"

"Cool," I said. "I didn't know that."

"Imagine all the probiotics they have to take," she said. And we both dissolved into a nervous and relieving sort of laughter, mine telling her I was doing my best, hers telling me that she saw me, knew me, all seven years of her could point to me and say with confidence, *That's my mother.* Narrative of the past unneeded. I was Nova's and she was mine.

I could not make you see, Mother, but I could tell you about my daughter in this way. I could beg. Please don't take this from me.

Later that night, the sky clear and dark, the kids finally asleep, my husband reading the novel I'd been telling him to read for several years, Jane and I drove to our mandatory Earthside graveyard shift. I felt a little thrill, my first Earthside graveyard, but Jane was annoyed. "I knew they'd start scheduling me shitty once I wasn't doing them anymore." But I couldn't help feeling excited for the physical work to come, unloading pallets, stocking shelves, purging and renewing the store: it was barbecue season and every little detail in the front, Stephen said, needed to scream *Grill, motherfuckers!*

"This is great," I told her, putting our bags in our lockers. Sandra nodded a hello before answering a call on her walkie, leaving us alone. "Now no one can be like 'they get special treatment, they never work, wah wah wah.'"

"Why do you insist on us still working at all? We have acquired basically our own complete natural wellness pharmacy by now. How much backup chlorella do you need?"

"I need money," I said. She snorted. She didn't believe me about that one even though I'd tried to explain my spending problem several times. "And I like it."

"I'd rather actually go to a women's moon circle like we tell your poor husband, than turn into a zombie doing product face-outs until two a.m."

"We'll leave before then," I said, fully intending to stay the whole time like the good student I was.

My husband had hugged me sweetly before we left. "You seem a lot better, Clovey."

He wasn't wrong. I hadn't been ordering clothing. I'd stopped buying supplements, and the money I'd made at the store wasn't a lot, but it was something. I had paid down almost two thousand dollars of my secret debt. The problem now was that Jane couldn't stop talking about you, Mother, imagining your life. "Prison really would be the ultimate hell," she mused, tying her smock. "Sitting around, innocent, knowing your daughter is out in the world. Out there, but not *there* there. Totally crazy making."

"I think you're really taking too much of this on, Jane. I'm worried I've stressed you out. Maybe try to forget it." I handed her a tin of Rescue Remedy pastilles.

She popped two and handed the tin back. "I care about women. I care about what happens to them, you know. Don't you? This is your mother."

"You have no idea the life we lived. Honestly, you're starting to annoy me."

"You're all distressed and blocked and convinced something's wrong with you physically, mentally, spiritually. You want me to be this mirror for you, to usher you along in your ascendence, and I'm here, telling you the block to everything. You and your mother will never be free until you do the right thing."

"It feels like you're on her side."

"There's no sides. There's only truth."

"Okay, Ram Dass. How much special bread did you eat today?" Jane had been making what she called *healer bread,* which was chock-full of eleuthero and astragalus powder. Slathering it in ashwagandha-infused ghee. "Maybe the right thing isn't what you think it is, but it's still right."

Jane held up her hands. "I just don't believe justice has been served in this particular case."

"What does justice look like here? My father is dead. He'll never go to jail. That's over. If this turns into some sensational story... Forgive me if I want to avoid a total bomb going off in my life on a very public level."

"But that's the whole thing, Clove. You don't want this version of your life. If you did, you would have never asked me into it. You would have never run away to work a secret job. True friends tell each other when they're crying out for help, so I'm telling you now. You have, like, colic."

"How can you say that? I'm doing everything to keep this version of my life. This version is just fine. I'm doing the hard work here, even if you don't realize it. I have taken action. I have a plan."

"Yes, your ex. You're going to see him. Somehow that will enlighten you."

"It's about figuring out some things for myself. I need all the information. I'm running out of time."

Admitting this out loud was sickening, the bare truth that you had rejected my plea and probably no amount of further begging from me in letter form was going to do anything, not with the feminist lawyer at your side.

I thought of the times I'd gotten drunk around the Butcher when the past was closer at hand. Sometimes I felt on the cusp of knowing the things I'd said, but then the film went fuzzy.

"He's not going to tell you anything you don't already know."

She was pushing too much, assuming too much. This was not how I imagined receiving her support. "Jane, no offense, but you couldn't possibly understand."

"There's something closed off about you. I can never read you. I thought I could when we first met, but now I can't."

"You're not so transparent yourself," I said. "Maybe you're hiding something. Maybe you're on the run."

"What are you trying to say?"

I imagined her old boyfriend, his thin-skinned hand snaking up her thigh. Maybe she'd poisoned him, finally grown tired of the arrangement that required her obedience, her submission. Maybe she began to feel raped by him.

"How did you say your old-man friend died again?"

She slammed her locker door shut and faced me. "Do you think I'm capable of murder, Clove?"

"If you did kill him," I said, "I would understand."

She maintained eye contact. Those electric-blue lenses. "If I killed him, do you think I'd be driving around in a car he bought?"

"You said he bought it in cash." She had not said this, but I tried it out to see if it was true.

She didn't object. Red splotches appeared on her chest. She put her hand over them. "You're zeroing in on the wrong thing here," she said.

"You're so focused on my secrets because you have secrets of your own."

"Here's what I know," she said. "You're not scared of being on the news. You're not even really scared of your husband finding out you've lied all these years. It's something else."

She was wrong. All wrong. She didn't get it, just like the Butcher hadn't been able to. "Tell me, then."

She opened the break room door to the security of grocery beyond her. Paused and then turned back to me. "You're scared of what it means to have her in the same room as you. You're scared of your mother."

CHAPTER 23

Jane avoided me during our shift and the work felt like work, nothing magical, and by the end my bones ached despite the curcumin capsules I'd swallowed. Jane went home with Mike that night citing possible ovulation. "The shatavari is working," she said, by way of explanation for why she was going to go sleep with a man with a collection of *Star Wars* action figures on his bedside table. I drove home alone assaulted by images of you, the loving moments, which in their own way were hard to stomach, you holding me, the feeling of weightlessness; the longing this provoked in me felt dangerous in its intensity. Was Jane right? Was I afraid of you? Or was I afraid of who I was around you, who you made me become?

I shook you off, or tried to, as I entered my front door. Even that late, I could feel the shift in the house without Jane there. Lark, who had been mostly sleeping well in his own bed, came crashing in next to me, commencing the night dance of displaced bodies, my husband to the couch, me in my husband's space, Lark stretched out fully into mine, little feet nestled into my back. I entered the shallow mindscape of bad water dreams and my father's hands. Then pure wakefulness. The time you brought home a Richard Simmons workout tape for us to do while my father was at work. It was time to get strong, you'd said. We did it every day for several weeks and I felt hopeful, felt our energy aligned and building toward something. I would look over at you doing the moves, your smile, and your body, which was in fact quite strong. But it didn't take long for my father to discover and destroy the tape. To get jealous of Richard Simmons.

I made a breakfast that was not as good as what Jane would have made—which everyone was all too eager to inform me—and laid out that day's plan to Nova and Lark, a plan that by the looks on both their faces seemed incredibly disappointing—eat, clean, maybe a gratitude meditation, eat again, and make healthy smoothie pops that they would likely not touch since they were not Jane's creation. And if all that went well, maybe we'd go to the community center pool.

But as soon as I said the word *pool* my nervous system made an announcement, which was that I could not, under any circumstances, go to the pool. The pool where I'd see other mamas I knew, who would have questions about the chrysalis, or worse, would have no questions at all and coax me gradually to death with small talk. No possibility, no curiosity, no discovery, no deepening with them. And yet I *did* understand why it seemed relevant to dissect the rules and regulations for every registration process of every children's activity, for instance, the swimming classes that filled up in thirty seconds, how you had to have multiple browsers open and better yet if you did it across several devices—that shit *was* hard, was a maze no doubt created by the patriarchy to misdirect women's talents—I could never go back to subbing that in for conversation after being around Jane.

"You know what?" I said to the kids, pretending to poke at my phone. "Pool's closed today. So weird! Well, we'll do other stuff."

"Really?" my husband said, not catching on. "Did someone poop in the pool? Shocking the water shouldn't take too long."

"Liar," Nova said, reaching for my phone, ramming my jaw with her head in the process. There was never an end to rage; it filled from behind. What a disappointment this truth must have been for my father, who probably sensed if he could just express his rage fully enough, beat you hard enough, finally it would be spent. I took a deep breath. At times that felt like the only difference between my father and me. My ability to take that breath.

But then there was Jane coming in the door, looking as luminous as the day I'd run into her. I couldn't play it cool; I couldn't hide my relief she was back. "Do you ever get tired of people staring at you because you're so shockingly beautiful?" I asked her. The kids engulfed her in hugs.

"Hmm," she said, play tossing her hair. "No, I don't." I could forget the tension of the night before in exchange for the ease her presence would bring to our day. "I think," Jane said slowly, setting down her purse. She sent a little wink to my husband. "That we should all get in the car and drive to the beach!"

My smile faltered. Spontaneity was for other mothers who didn't need to consider winding roads, and what if their hands slipped on the wheel? Pressed the gas instead of the brake? And what if Jane *had* killed that old-man boyfriend and then we'd be toting a black-mailing murderer around in the car.

Jane looked to me for confirmation about the beach, but the kids had already decided. Nova and Lark ran to their rooms to get their swimsuits and my husband made his way to his office for the day. Jane smiled at me. "I know exactly what you're thinking," she said as the door clicked behind him.

"You definitely do not."

"I didn't kill that man, Clove. I can tell you're looping on it."

"My mind is a dangerous neighborhood, what can I say?"

She laughed. I laughed. We relaxed. In the light of the kitchen, it did seem silly.

"But if I did," she said, turning serious, smoothing out that vintage top. "I'd make sure he suffered a little. I don't understand murder if there isn't suffering involved."

"I'm not sure I understand murder at all."

"But your mother murdered your father. I mean, you must have some philosophy you've worked up."

"That was self-defense," I corrected. "I don't think of it as murder."

"So you agree she's innocent?"

"I can tell you were an insufferable child," I said, "asking endless questions."

"I wasn't, actually," she said, following the kids outside to the car.

I threw snacks into a bag, swimsuits for me and Jane, sunscreen, and hats. I popped into my husband's office to say goodbye. He sat, dutifully typing away, Bob Marley soft in the background. He liked to joke that given his real choice in life he'd live on the beach and own a pizza shack and wear tie-dye and grow his hair out. I hadn't recognized that part of him when we'd met, too focused on whether he was concealing an untamable rage. But maybe he should be working at a pizza shack on a beach. Had we led each other to the wrong lives?

"When do you think Jane's going to get bored of us?" he said.

"Like, is this a three-month thing, a six-month thing, is Jane actually your life partner and soon I'll wake up drugged in another town with no name?"

I gave him a laugh. "You seem pretty happy with her here."

"Sure, it's been nice. But I don't know if we need this much help. Maybe when the kids go back to school, you know, it can be *as needed*. I feel like you're really wrapped up in her. I wish you looked at me how you look at her."

"I look at you fine."

He smiled at the wall. "No," he said. "You don't."

His needs tightened around me. "When school starts up, we'll readjust." Readjust to your wife's face all over the news, in jail for stealing a dead girl's identity. Really, the more I understood what the future could be, I saw that Jane was the best gift I could offer him.

"I wish I was going with you guys."

"Can you?"

"No, I gotta get shit done. Have fun. Call me when you're there."

"Okay." I kissed him quick and dry, but he pulled me into his lap, went in again, deeper and with a surprising amount of tongue. I leaned back and we looked into each other's eyes. "Onion," I said, reporting what his mouth tasted like, a single word to bring potential sex energy and connection to a halt. I had nothing to offer him at this moment. I stood and pressed on my deflated chest with my palms, gave him a look like, *Sorry I suck.* I wished there were no kids in the car, no weaning from anything, just pre-milk titties and a stretch of unoccupied afternoon so we could reset each other's bodies.

My anxiety told me to kiss him one more time in case I died in a car accident on the way to the beach, in case this was the last time I'd ever see him, in case the news broke while I was gone and you rushed in, Mother. But I walked out, no kiss. I got in the car.

The kids were already bickering in the back seat. Jane looked at me, showing the first creeping signs of maternal drainage. "They are…talkative today."

"If I was talking in the car my dad would reach back and pinch me. Or he wouldn't let me eat that night. I learned to stay quiet. Kids these days are too well treated to ever be quiet."

"My mom liked to pinch too," she said. "Little secret stings."

I drove us down the road and toward the highway. "Just big babies masquerading as parents, having tantrums."

"Oh, that was just the cream cheese on the bagel of shittiness." Jane had her whole body turned to me, the strap tucked under her arm. I imagined how I would defend myself if she tried to strangle me. Stop. I would not latch on to anxiety about Jane. I would not. I would continue to embrace help. I would lean into this new supported reality.

"What are you guys talking about?" asked Nova from the back.

Jane leaned in to me. "Listen, I had a little talk with her about Grandma in jail. And she felt so bad for her."

I pulled over to the side of the highway. Other cars zoomed past. Nova and Lark shrieked about stopping, why were we stopped, *oh my god the beach, Mom, go to the beach!*

"First, put your seat belt on right," I said to Jane. "Second, what did you tell her?" I turned up the music in the back seat.

She took her time fixing her strap. "See, I wasn't even going to mention it, and now I know I shouldn't have."

"I told you no one knows," I hissed. "You are the only one."

"It was like your mother came into my body and wanted to talk to her grandchild. It channeled right through me. I can't help it if I'm a portal."

"You're supposed to be a portal for me, for my sanity, not for my mother. What exactly did you say?"

The kids cried and whined louder. Nova kicked my seat forcefully. "Driiiiiive," she wailed.

"It was barely anything. I said it must be hard having a grandma you've never met. And she was like, yeah. And I told her that her grandma loved her so much, then I swear to god she got distracted and we moved on. It was nothing."

"She registers everything."

"It was nothing, trust me. She probably thought I meant Tootsie."

"She's not stupid."

"Let's have a good day," Jane said.

"Why don't you have friends?" I hissed. "Why are you with us all day?"

She smiled and stared at her hands. She seemed embarrassed. I'd gone too far. But then I saw she was embarrassed for me.

"Because. This is my job."

Of course. I was providing her a home, which in turn was payment for her cleaning, her listening, her childcare, her friendship. But I wasn't paying for her preoccupation with justice and whatever cartoon idea she'd drawn up about you in prison. "Let's go to the beach," Jane said slowly. "I think it will be good for you."

Jane handed the kids Veggie Stix and the crying that ripped sense from my brain stopped. My vision heightened and prickled. I felt hyperaware yet exhausted in a deep clinical way as I veered back onto the highway. Visions of my tires popping and us skidding into oncoming traffic littered my mind while Jane took selfies with her pouty lips.

"Tell me those aren't for Mike."

She smiled. "You will never believe in one million years who these are for."

"Hmm." I pretended to wonder and then listed everyone we worked with.

"I *have* slept with half of those people," she said, considering. "But no."

"Someone stable and your own age who might make a good father?"

"It's online right now. But we dated in real life before I came up here. I don't know."

"I can't believe you never mentioned this to me."

"Is Daddy coming?" Lark asked over us.

"No, honey," I said and then whispered to Jane, "Who are they for?"

"Watch the road, alright?" She shooed me away. "Anyway. Little ears, remember?"

When we arrived in the quaint beach town, I parked in a pay-all-day lot and Jane popped out of the Subaru, that tight body, her skin so smooth. Full of collagen and natural moisture, and likely lots of Botox. No vitamins were that good. I fought back a feeling of jealousy that she'd been connecting with some person from her past, that maybe she'd leave to be with him in LA, that this time with her would soon be just a blip of memory.

I got Lark out of the car and held him on my hip. "Mommy, are you a bird or am I a bird?" he asked softly in my ear.

"Both."

He giggled. "Just me."

"Okay, just you. Are you a seagull?"

His eyes were the pale blue mine had once been. He clung to me with his small legs and peered out at the Oregon coast that would never be Hawai'i. Would never be palm trees and that particular warmth and the rolling rains that came and went in minutes. The Oregon coast was an unwieldly rocky beauty, ice fog and cutting wind. Once when I had been here it was so foggy I could not see the water at all from the sand. I felt like I was on the moon. Today, though, it was clear and gorgeous and still. We walked past shops to the entrance of the beach and Nova and Lark ran ahead. Not Hawai'i, but the ocean was medicine regardless. I watched them play and Jane piled her long hair into a bun, ran out into the water, and started breast stroking. She kept her head dry, but you always went all the way in. It had never occurred to me to swim in the water in Oregon. What if she drowned? The kids called for her as she swam out farther and farther. A little too far.

My father always swam out too far. The day he died he told me to hold on to his shoulders. It was a game we hadn't played for years, since I was that ten-year-old girl who had arrived on the island. We called it *personal dolphin*. "Come on, I'll be your personal dolphin," he said. You were barely healed from the North Shore attack by then. He thought this beach trip was meant to break the tension we'd been living in. Start fresh. We knew it was our last nice day with him before we left forever.

After shooting through that sliding glass window, he'd dislodged one of your molars and harassed you for what felt like hours before he marched us into the Jimmy at gunpoint, our plane tickets left ripped up on the floor. He was going to kill us all, he said. But it wasn't going to be in your "boyfriend's house." He was sure whoever had helped us was the boyfriend he'd long been certain you had, confirmed at last.

But back at the apartment, we had entered the eerie coolness that followed my father's violence where it was unclear if he'd make good on his promise for more, or if there could be a possible reprieve. The sense that we could choose our own adventure if we did everything just right weighted us. You needed to go to the emergency room, but first you made mock lobster, cod rolled around cheese and baked, and we ate in silence—well, you moved your food around, you couldn't open your mouth. One side of your face ballooned cartoonishly and your eyeball was completely red. My fingers returned again and again to the matted hair on the back of my head. The cut from when I'd slipped on the tile had stopped bleeding by the time we left North Shore, but it still throbbed. My father finished his meal, complimented your cooking, and got up to look at my head with a calm remove. I felt him gently part my hair and press around the cut. He'd been trained as a combat medic in the military. I heard you ask if he needed the first aid kit and I left my body and set my mind to our next getaway plan.

We still had a stash of money saved. He hadn't found it. I'd been smart to tuck it inside the lining of the fanny pack. This time we wouldn't hesitate. It would be straight to the airport. I would never let my father nurse the wounds he'd inflicted again.

"Take her now," I said to my father when he was done patching me up. You looked wrong; you looked like at any moment you'd fall over. He got up, did what I said.

So, weeks later, our courage built up again, my father was none the wiser to our new plan. We'd played things just right. He didn't suspect anything. We brought a cooler with sodas and Spam musubis. You read a book about dreams under a straw hat. My father wore small European-looking shorts. His hair was wavy to his shoulders and his beard was full and I hate the overused description of eyes twinkling, but his did, they twinkled, and his gold back tooth winked in the sun. The signet shone from the nest of his chest hair.

"I'm too big for personal dolphin," I said. "You won't be able to swim."

You shot me a glare. *Do what he says.*

"What, can't play around with your dad? Maybe you'd rather get a new daddy like the—"

"Alright." Anything to avoid him bringing up your *North Shore boyfriend,* who was now a full-fledged character in our lives. I clutched his strong shoulders and he began to swim. I kicked hard to compensate for my weight, but he pulled me easily. I let my legs relax, stretched out. I would miss this when we left him. But not that much. Gliding in that water, I visualized us showing up at the airport with the money. Christina had given you a strong sleeping pill to crush into his beer if we needed it. We would take nothing, leave without a trace. Material things mattered not at all to me then.

This, I decided, would be my final nice moment with my father before we took up these new lives. Just one last swim.

"I'll believe it when I see it," Christina said when we'd been over the day before. But I could tell she took it all very seriously. I could tell she had hope for us too.

But Celine wavered, fell in line with the doubts you'd been vocalizing every chance you got. "Maybe Alma's right. Maybe it's not safe. I mean, look what's happened every time they've tried."

Christina had gotten up, fixed a spoonful of medication. "I feel fine," Celine protested. She must have been in immense pain but wanted to be with us, to stay awake and talk. I wanted that too. I didn't know when I'd see them again.

"Gotta stay ahead of things, my sweet gift. You know that," Christina told her. Celine finally took it down and soon she fell asleep and we didn't hear any more from her. I pushed down my sadness for her ailing body. How I'd wanted to imagine a day she would be healthy. I'd never seen her outside their apartment. But I couldn't linger on her pain when our escape was at hand.

My father swam out and out. The salt on my skin made me feel strong. At North Shore the mistake had been allowing you to be in charge. We'd stayed much too long at the house. Your friend was kind but not skilled. Now I knew enough to take care of it all. It was about quick forward motion, about not sparing a second. My father stopped swimming. I opened my eyes. We'd reached the quiet part of the ocean, past the breaking waves, past people with common sense. No one paddled on surfboards nearby. We were far beyond them. I could no longer make you out in the crowd on the beach. The water was dark now and the sky came down into it. I was a good swimmer, I reminded myself. But it had never been tested.

"Let's go back," I said, cheerful. Never show fear. I thought of sharks circling below. My father took a long while catching his breath, long enough for me to catch my own. Now we would swim back together; what an adventure we'd had. A seagull swooped lonely above us. "Look at that gull," I said. "He seems lost."

My father looked only at me. His necklace glinted in the ocean. He let water flow into his mouth and he spit it at my face. His eyes had turned. You called this the Dr. Jekyll and Mr. Hyde moment, the lowering of the scrim.

I strained to keep sight of the sliver of shore.

"You and your mother must laugh all day about how stupid I am."

My mind started doing this weird thing, folding in and in. Goodbye to the sky and the water, goodbye to the seagull. I thought of the money we'd saved. The money would go unused. My things thrown away. What a useless life I'd led. I thought of the way Celine laughed at my jokes in a high-pitched giggle, how once I'd promised her I'd never leave her, knowing as I said it I was a liar. The saccharine zing of Christina's grape juice. This was it? Just this? I started to shiver in that perfect water and my legs felt numb and not mine. There was zero public influence around me. I reached for my father but he leaned back. "We love you," I said.

It's only water, I told myself. It was impossibly deep water with a bold waving current, but it was still water, and I could do this. I turned toward shore. I would swim and not stop. I started but he pulled my foot back toward him, then pushed me under. Like this? Like this I was going to die? He was going to get to do it? Pitiful. My own father.

I wanted to say goodbye to you, Mother. You would be growing worried. Realizing we should be back by now. He pulled me up and close to his face and I gasped for air.

"I found your little notebook," he said. He pushed me under again. This was a game. Water torture. Brought me up. "Your whole stupid plan written out." Writing really was trouble. Why had I written down everything we talked about? Why had I listed out our plan to Celine? But I'd wanted her to know each detail about our new life and what it might be like so that one day she would be able to find me. "It was a paper," I told him. "For school. Just made-up."

Under again, his hand on my head. You said when I was a newborn he could hold my entire body with one hand. My heart burned. Maybe dying was best.

But no. I twisted out from under that hand and came up and spat in his face like I'd seen him do to you a thousand times. "I lied. We hate you," I said. I felt my jaw lock down, my neck veins bulging just like his. I was him and he was me. He grabbed my shoulders, all the intensity in his body meeting all of mine.

"What are you going to do about all this, girl child?" he said. "I see it all going on behind those eyes. They're my eyes, and I see it. So what are you gonna do?"

"I'm going to take her away from you."

"That won't work. I'll find you every time."

"I would do anything for her," I said.

"Anything?"

We stared at each other for what felt like a long while. *Love me,* I thought. *Do one thing right.* "Anything," I said.

"Then do it." His anger turned to pleading. His shame bared. He sounded like a little boy when he said, "Then fucking do it already."

Could it be true? Was this his permission? Permission to leave, for me to finally take you away and put out the flames between you. It would be the greatest gift he could give you, give me, and now I saw, give himself. Let me return to the shore without him, leave us alone in our apartment, women together, safe. The ocean was loud in my ears as he swam away from me toward shore, abandoning me in the waves so far out. But I swam hard behind him with renewed energy. I believed we had finally understood each other.

He was so much faster than me. I collapsed on the dry sand gasping for air, coughing up water. I couldn't see either of you in any direction. I lay there and people walked around me as if I were a beach chair. No one noticed me. Even now, no matter where I am, I look for the woman abused. There is usually one. No one sees her, but I do.

I couldn't see my kids. I couldn't see Jane. I jumped up and ran toward the water. I screamed. I ran up to people on towels, frantic. "Have you seen two young kids, a girl and a little boy?" No one had. My god. I gasped. I screamed their names. I ran and ran. I turned in circles like that would fix something.

Then, "Mama!" It was Nova. They were just behind the umbrella we had brought, making a sandcastle. Jane was nippled out in the bikini top I'd packed, looking clear-eyed and joyful, and the kids were blissfully fine.

"We didn't want to bother you," Jane said. "It looked like you were praying there in the sand. I was like, 'Let's let Mommy have a nice time in the solar therapy.'"

Praying, when I felt like I'd just fought for my life again in the ocean with my father. But there was no danger I could reach out and touch. He was gone, wasn't he? And what danger was there in memory?

Nova and Lark danced in the sand, ran up to their knees in the water and back out screaming. Jane went for a walk to the tide pool. I wanted to dive into the water and swim unencumbered. I had never swum in the ocean again after that day with my father. And now, if I went, I would worry about my kids on the sand. But if I didn't go, I would resent them. My resentment took second place as a risk, but now I knew there was danger in that, too.

"Jane," I said when she came back, body gleaming. "Can you watch them close while I jump in real quick?"

"Sure," she said. "See, this is good for you."

I took off my sundress. "Brings back a lot of memories."

She handed the kids fruit snacks. "There's no hiding from the sea."

What would it be like to lie next to Jane in the sand and tell her about my father? Really tell her. I waded in slowly instead, the water ice. Nothing like Oahu, the place I longed for even though so much bad love had happened there. I went under. I wanted the story to go like this: I got in the water and my sads went away. I got in the water and I came up different. After all, it had happened to me once before, after that swim with my father.

Sun-drenched and weary, we drove home to Portland, the curves of the road not daunting this time, the tall trees forming a canopy of safety over our car.

The kids slept hard. Jane wiggled Lark's foot. "They're out."

"Such a good day. Thank you for suggesting it."

"You know," she said, stretching her arms up overhead. "I've been thinking about your plan to meet up with your ex. I'm worried you're losing sight of what's important here, and that's helping your mother. Seeing him seems like a massive distraction."

"You're as bad as Tootsie," I said.

"If you cheat on that nice man that fathered those beautiful babies, you're an idiot."

"I have no intention of cheating. And besides, our bond was much more than sex. Sex is far from my mind right now."

"The longer I'm around you, the more I'm certain I was sent to remind you to be grateful for what you have."

"I am grateful, Jane. That's why I hired you, so I don't ruin it."

Darkness was just beginning to edge out the sun. It was quiet for a while, and then she said, "I really care about you, Clove. Please remember that."

After we carried Nova and Lark inside, Jane went to bed, and I stayed up remembering a diary of yours I once found and read when I was fourteen, voracious for clues on what being a woman was like. The entry was dated from when I was young. *What are you supposed to do with a kid all day?* you had written. You skipped a few lines, as if to signify yourself thinking. Then: *I drink.*

I imagined myself writing the same lines, slightly askew: *What are you supposed to do with kids all day?...I think.*

I looked at my social media messages. So many messages every day, lots of women asking me questions or for advice on ingredients, brands, parenting philosophies. Maybe I was a better storyteller than I'd ever known. I had certainly told a story on my page all this time, concocting a mosaic of anonymous magic. There was a new message from the Butcher.

Will I still see you this weekend?

This weekend. How was it already time for this weekend? Planning on it.

I was so in love with you I thought it would kill me. I've never felt like that again. I thought of Jane's warning. Don't cheat.

I think our astrology lined up or something.

Yeah, something.

Is it better to not meet? I wrote. My heart pounded. Of course it was better to not meet. He didn't answer right away.

Then: I don't think we have a choice. We need to see each other. And it will be a bonus to heal that old "she went out to get some milk and never came back" wound.

I was a kid. A really scared kid. I still was.

I forget that. We were so young. You especially.

I loved you. I sent it before I could think. I had loved him. I hadn't said it much to him because he was always saying it to me, breathing it into my mouth, into my ears. But I did.

Thanks for saying that. I think I just wanted to know I meant something to you.

I would not let him know how much. My legs wrapped around his waist. His drowsy stare. The ache in my chest that had never really gone away. He had preserved the real me all these years. What would it mean for him to hand her back to me?

CHAPTER 24

At the grocery expo, Jane and I helped Stephen unload the Earthside truck. He was surprised we'd begged to come to work at the convention center, and I felt a pang of remorse for not trying harder during shifts, for being surly and teenagerly. I wasn't proud of myself, but my behavior at work seemed so small amid everything else going on. Jane tired of unloading within minutes and sat on a box, painted her nails with nontoxic polish. She hadn't brought you up since the beach day, which had been a relief, but she seemed adrift.

I sat next to her and held out my hand to be polished. When she didn't reach for me, I folded it in my lap. "Thank you so much for taking over Nova's party tomorrow," I said. "You have no idea how nice it is to have that off my plate right now. Even under the best circumstances I'm not a natural at that stuff. I bet it's going to be so cute."

"I'm thrilled," she said flatly. "It's going to be fucking magical."

"How are things with the mystery man?"

"He's been busy. Haven't heard from him much."

"Well, I hope it works out. Gotta be better than this lot." I glanced at Stephen.

"Well, when it comes to luck in dating, I'm no Clove," she said. "You've currently got your husband around your finger, and your ex too. Look at you."

"Once again, today is a necessary catch-up. Not a date. You're acting like it's some sexcapade. This is part of my healing journey, alright? Part of me helping my mother. It's all connected." I scanned my surroundings, my radar set for the Butcher. Jane said something under her breath I couldn't hear. Didn't have time to hear. The thought that I could see him at any moment unnerved me but also made me feel celestial, beyond the confines of just this one life. "I'm gonna walk around a little, see if I can find him."

"Wait a second," Jane said. She took a breath and reached into her bag and pulled out an envelope. Motioned for me to step behind a stack of boxes and handed it to me.

"What is this?" I said. But I could clearly see it was another letter from you, Mother. It had been opened.

"You read this before me?"

"You're asleep at the wheel and someone has to take control," she said with a sudden sharpness. I'd been right to think other people would never understand me, my place in our story. "What are you going to do about this? The more I think about it. I can't sleep. It's on my mind all the time."

"Too far, Jane. Way too far. You care too much, and you need to stop." I turned from her and unfolded the letter to see just one line written so shakily it looked comical, like a Halloween font.

This isn't fair. —Mom

An angry heat crawled up my neck. Nothing was fair,

Mother. Why would you expect fairness? My father's rage flew into my hands and I ripped the letter up. Dropped the pieces at Jane's feet.

"You and me, we've become weird. Codependent," I said. "It's not what I wanted."

"It's exactly what you wanted." She gripped my arm, her long nails pressed into my skin.

"After Nova's party, we need a reconfiguring, a clearing of the decks. I don't blame you for getting swept up in this. I know it's crazy. I know it's sad. But you need to stay out of it."

"How are you not completely haunted?"

I shook her hand off me. "Haunted would be the mildest possible way to put it, Jane. Do you think I haven't lived every day in this cell?"

"You could help her now. Why do you not see that?"

"You are delusional to think there is help for women." I thought of Christina, how right she was about the world. "What, because you've seen a few men called out recently? Because you really handed it to your sugar daddy? Play the tape forward. Nothing happens to them and the women absorb it all."

"You make the help. You become the help. We can, together. You're not alone in this."

"I know what I'm dealing with here. I know what's at stake. You will never truly understand."

"Hate to interrupt this little catfight," Stephen said. "But, Clove, can you saunter around and see if anyone is slinging some new state-of-the-art organic diapers or something? We need to spice up the kids' care section."

"Stephen," I said. "I don't really work for you and we both

know it. Think of me as recreational support from now on. I'll be keeping my discount, though, and you know why."

"Whoa," he said, stepping backward as if offended, but quickly softened. "Fine, you can keep your discount."

"Just focus on Nova's birthday party," I said to Jane. "I'll pay you for it. We'll talk about everything after that."

"Your husband doesn't even know who he's married to." She looked like she was going to cry. "Your kids will never actually know you. This is all just too much to witness."

"If you try to tell my husband anything, I'll find that old man's kids and tell them where to come get their father's car."

She bent to pick up the strewn pieces of the letter. Held them softly. Your handwriting, your sadness, your need, your intense pulsing need, all in Jane's hands. My past had now infected her just like it had once infected the Butcher. "Alright," she said. "If this is how you want it, fine. I'll let you make your own mistakes."

"That's the only way it can be," I said, but she had already turned away.

On the event map I found Home Grown and charged toward it. You were concerned about fairness, Mother, but what was fair about what you and my father put me through? My entire life devoted to the war of you both. It seemed to count for nothing, but it had led me to the man who was now before me arranging his booth. I paused and watched him. Soon he'd look up, see me. He'd feel the weight of my gaze; it would startle him. Yes, now his eyes were on mine, a chill down my spine. He walked toward me. His long stride, his arms. I smelled him and there it was, instant pheromonal recall. Jane faded from my mind. Even you, Mother, for the moment, faded. Because near him, I was someone else.

I was me.

I threw my arms around him. He laughed. He lifted me up off the floor. "Oh my god, Oh my god," was all I could say.

"It's really you," he said. "I wasn't sure if I'd actually see you or if I'd pass out instead."

"I'm glad you didn't pass out."

I remembered the careful way he'd position me across the bed, stare at me until it was unbearable. I don't know if I loved my body then, but I knew when I watched his mouth on me, I glimmered. I hadn't felt like that in years, since motherhood at the very least, but probably longer. I was so apart from that version of me now. I wanted to step back into her.

He led me out of the convention center, out the tall glass doors and into the sunshine, through the vortex of time and space, stripping us back to our primary forms by the time we reached his car.

He opened the door to the back seat and we closed ourselves inside. It took everything I had to look at him. His eyes on me felt so exposing. I had shut my emotions off to leave him. It was the only way I could do it. But everything was back. He cocked his head at me.

"I'm feeling it all for the first time," I said. "Feeling myself leaving you. Feeling all I did to make it here. I never let myself grieve, not really. I feel so, so sorry."

He smiled. "But online you seem so well-adjusted."

I scooted closer and put my hands on his face. "I wanted to tell you. I wanted to explain it. Why I left like that."

"You did what you had to do."

"I'm sorry."

His hands were nervous as they pulled me into him, my hands in his hair, muscle memory, the way I remembered how to touch him. I could not inhale him deeply enough. But these details don't matter. You've already made your judgments about me, Mother. Where's the line? If I kiss him? I just did. Your greatest pride was that even though my father accused you relentlessly from the first days of your relationship, you never cheated on him.

We pressed into each other. My family was in another realm. They thought I was helping Jane prepare for Nova's birthday party. But this was not connected to my husband at all. The Butcher had seen me, you must understand, he had seen me fresh from my father's death and he had pulled me up and shown me what my body could do, had shown me pleasure where before all I'd known was pain. It's a long way back to seventeen, but I was there now.

We paused.

I looked at him. "I feel like I'm high."

Of course I was high! The blissful oxytocin that had drained from me when I'd weaned my son now charged through my body. The Butcher put a palm on my heart.

Mother, I was afraid of balconies and heights when I met him, and after him, I wasn't.

"You saved me," I said.

"I was so mad at you after you left, I made something of myself. Something better."

"I'm glad."

"What did you make yourself into?"

"Depressed, repressed, unable to rest. Well, lately."

"Have you tried Suntheanine?" he asked, morphing into his co-op grocery store owner self.

"Child's play," I said.

He laughed. "You have two kids. I always knew you'd be an incredible mother."

"You never wanted kids."

"I would have come around. I mean, I did come around."

"Don't do that," I said. It was too hard to hear.

We were both quiet.

I wondered when he would tell me what he had to tell me. I didn't want to get there. I wanted to stay here, in his neck. He grabbed my ass like he used to, it was his ass again. Maybe you think you know what is going to happen and how sad it will be once we have sex in this convention center parking lot, how after that I will be such a disappointment, but right now, please imagine the feeling. One plus one equals more than two. The equation was never: do I love the Butcher and not my husband? I loved them both, it turned out, and that love, the expansiveness of it, made me feel light for a moment, hopeful, that maybe everything wouldn't be torn away by the end of summer. Wasn't there enough love here to solve something?

"Why are we here?" I asked. "What do you need to hand back?"

He gripped my arms and then pulled his energy away. Looked out the window. Sea change. We sat up. The hot, carnal pressure shifted, became careful, cool.

"What?" I said. "What is it?"

"C," he said. "Honey."

Anger entered me. "Alright, enough. Did you go to that lawyer, did you go visit my mom? Tell me. Tell me what you did." I had always been angry at him. His stupid optimism, his desire to help when help was not asked for. For seeing me as damaged as I really was.

He wiped his eyes, his nose. "No, no," he said. "None of that. I would never have done that."

"There's no way anyone could have found me. You were the only one who knew about my identity. Velvet and the girls never knew. It had to be you."

"I wouldn't do that to you, and you know it." I wanted him to be lying. For something to make sense. But he wasn't the liar. I was.

"This is so fucked."

"Listen, I thought I could let go of it, or forget, but in the past few years it's felt relentless," he said. "I've been in therapy over it. I even hired a guru, and I realized I'd been in a weird holding pattern because I'm totally alone with this awful thing. I knew the only way to put it to bed was to talk to you. But I couldn't find you. I never could. You totally vanished. I even did a whole cord-cutting workshop in Taos."

"Did it work?"

"If anything it created new cords," he said. "I thought maybe our resolution would have to come in another lifetime, but when you found me, it seemed so clear it had to happen in this life. That for both of us, it was time."

"So what's the awful thing? What do you need to put to bed now? You want my blessing to go stage a march for my mother outside a courthouse or something?"

He breathed in through his nose and out his mouth a few times. Pressed his palms together. "It's about the night your dad died."

"You always wanted to talk about that stuff, always fishing for details. Maybe for people who have never gone through shit this is all entertaining, but for me, believe me, it's anything but."

"I thought we were going to be together forever. I wanted to know you. And honestly, I could sense that everything you'd been through was always going to stand between us if we didn't tackle it head on. I was young but I knew that. It was like a shadow trailed you."

"It was too much to tackle. That's what you didn't understand."

"And now?"

The car was too small, too hot. I felt the GoHealth bar I'd eaten that morning rise into my throat. Reminders of my old San Francisco death wish prickled over my body, that easy fantasy, a sure way to turn all of this off forever, always available to me, such comfort. But I could never solve it that way now. My children had stripped me of that option. I had a daughter and her birthday was tomorrow.

"I don't know. It seems like life is telling me I don't have a choice."

"I've always wondered if you think about what you told me."

"That's the thing. I don't remember what I told you. I mean, the basics maybe. But not a lot. Whenever I'd open up about it, I was very drunk. I can only imagine the things I said. I missed my parents so fucking much, and I was ashamed of that."

He reached for my hand and held it, our pulses attuned. "You always said your mom pushed him," he started. "That was it. She pushed him and you ran. You felt so bad about running away from her."

"I live with my guilt every day over leaving her. It's like you never believed how sorry I was about that. That was the worst part for me. But I didn't have a choice."

"That's the thing we'd get caught on. Why you felt like you didn't have a choice."

I could see you, Mother, your back as you ran away from me to the elevator. I'd stood for a moment in our doorway, unable to follow. Ran down one floor to Christina's, the only safe place.

"You thought I should have been with my mom every step of the way, but there's dynamics you don't understand. I knew even if my father wasn't in the picture, it was never going to be a good life with her."

"That's not what I mean."

"Say what you mean, then."

"A few times you weren't sure," he said. Maybe this was the resolutely calm tone he used with his daughter. He was probably a great father, just like my husband was a great father. Just like my own father wasn't. But then his face broke open into an expression I'd never seen on him. I saw death on his face. "You couldn't be sure of what really happened."

But I couldn't locate compassion. "This is what you're haunted by? You're haunted by the worst night of *my* life?"

"You weren't sure about the logistics of everything."

I put my hand up. "Stop."

"You were so traumatized," he went on. "You said you felt scattered. You felt like…I don't know. You were scared."

"Of course I was scared."

He held my wrists. "Listen to me. This is the part. You have to listen."

I looked away. I'd get out of the car and walk back to the expo. Why had I expected this to go well? The Butcher was still a person who couldn't shoulder the burden of my story, just like Jane.

But then his tone changed. "Come back." He said it like he used to, in bed, when he could tell I'd departed from myself. It jolted something inside me. Something cleared. I nodded.

I heard him when he said, "You felt like maybe it wasn't your mom who did it."

My father's Jimmy joined us in the parking garage. Suddenly I was no longer with the Butcher. I was with my father in his car. My father held the box out to me. It was time to look inside.

I took it from him. It was heavy in my hand as I undid the ribbon. I understood without him telling me that the box contained a truth.

Open it.

CHAPTER 25

After my father left me far out in the ocean, I lay there on the shore feeling, for the first time in my life, that I had escaped death, that he had released me. Released us. I smiled in the sun with my eyes closed. A luxurious moment alone before we'd take up our new life as unencumbered women. Then there you were, pulling me to my feet.

"I think he's gone," I said to you. "I think he's going to leave us alone. He told me. Out in the water."

You squinted toward Diamond Head. I hugged you, my entire body shaking, fatigued but electric. Could we be free? We were on the edge of it.

"He's watching us right now," you said into my salt-mangled hair.

"No, Mom. He said for me to take you away. In the water, he said that. This is it, Mom. I think he's letting us go. We can have our own place, just us."

You gestured with your eyes to the alleyway alongside the pink hotel where normally a man placed parrots on people's shoulders and then demanded money. The man was not there today, but my father was.

"We have the public influence," I said. "We have to stay in the public influence. We need to stay right here. Let him give up. He wants us to leave. I'm telling you."

You took another look at him. "He's your father," you said.

Mother, do you replay this moment like I do? The moment you led us back to him?

"I'll run. I won't go with you this time."

"I talked to him," you said. "He's alright. His feelings are hurt. It's best to get through it and then we can start saving up again."

"He pushed me underwater. He left me all the way out there. I almost drowned."

You looked at me oddly. "You know how to swim just fine."

They say divorce is the closest some people will ever come to war. But it's not. Not even close. War was getting in my father's car.

Back at the high-rise, I fell onto my bed. You cleaned as if everything was fine, while my father drank in the living room, staring at the wall. I would rest for a moment before going out there to tell you both I'd finally had enough. No more sneaking, no more secrets. Head high, I was done. I'd look him in the eyes, and as he had in the water, he would fear me. Revere me. Let me go. Let us go, if you wanted that.

But I fell asleep, woke some hours later, and it was night, 11:11 on my Goodwill digital alarm clock. I heard your voice from somewhere far away. I felt nauseous. I'd swallowed so much sea water, was I going to vomit? Had I eaten that day? Maybe there was a pie in the fridge. I stepped into the hall but went rigid when I saw myself already standing there. This self was watching you and my father on the lanai, such a small space for two.

Was I dead? I really did wonder that. Maybe my father had drowned me after all. But that didn't feel quite accurate. There I was, shoulders tense to my ears, there I was, taking you in, my parents. Your blood on the walls as I advanced down our hallway that was void of family photos, yet I saw memories drift by: You in the hospital with that hole in your back. You birthing me, the Anita Baker tape all you wanted. Me as a baby cradled in my father's hand. *In Hawai'i things will be better. In Hawai'i things will change.* My father was threatening to jump, threatening to take you with him, take me too. And there I was, as tall as you, an almost woman, possessing you both in my face, my limbs, my stance. I felt affection for that girl who was made of you and him, but also some other flickering thing.

The dark traveler greeted me as I stepped into the living room. I'd never felt I had any choices, but there was one to make now. My father pulled you up and over the ledge of the lanai as you kicked and fought. So high up. I looked at the front door. Now, I thought. Now. Now. Someone come in and save us, now. He leaned you farther and you screamed in a way I'd never heard before. *Now.*

But no one was coming to save us. *My mother. My mother.* I thought, *That's my mother.*

The Butcher held me as I shook. I leaned over and opened the Prius door, vomited, his hand on my back. Something was coming out of me now. "It was someone else," I said to my old love. "It wasn't my mother, it was someone else."

And then I watched myself run.

Toward my father's body, squatting on that concrete ledge, balancing with freakish ability, his arms hooked under yours. I reached for his neck, surprising him enough to drop you. The gold signet hung down. I was thinking of airways, if I could slow his breathing, bring him back inside, leave him unconscious while we left, one last escape, this was it. But my hand got caught in his necklace. He tried to swat me away. The chain snapped. He lost his balance, then regained it. He made a grab for your hair, and I felt the thud of my hand against his chest, my hand colliding with the tattoo of a human heart with our names in script. The last thing I saw were his eyes, my eyes. Was there a moment of peaceful resolve as he realized his fate? I couldn't see it.

You didn't understand at first. You looked around like he was hiding somewhere. But then you did. Your howl that wouldn't stop. The howl I hear at night. I tried to quiet you, to hold you in place, but you ran out the door. This I see now: I didn't leave you. You left me.

So I rushed to Christina's. Did she see by my eyes what I'd done? I had not yet pushed it down; my brain had not yet altered it. It must have been all over me. "He deserved to die," she'd said. I remembered it now. "He deserved what he got. You've suffered enough." But did I say the words to her? Did I say, "I pushed my father. I killed my father"? Maybe she'd always known I would. Maybe she'd made me into a person who could.

How I wanted to say goodbye to Celine, to thank her, my only friend. Her life for mine. But Christina ushered me out. "Everything is paid for now," she said. "Every wrong is right."

"I thought my mother would tell them I had done it," I said to the Butcher. "I thought she'd defend herself. But she didn't." I looked into his eyes. I'd left him alone with this torment.

"You were both in shock. And you. C, you were just a child."

"I was never a child."

"That's the thing, though. You were."

"I was going to lie low for some years, settle into my new identity, and she was supposed to be free. Then when the time was right, we'd be reunited. Why did she tell them she did it?"

"She was protecting you," he said. "From everything, but maybe, also, from herself."

Mother, you sat in prison all these years, remembering. All these years, protecting me. You had been serving the sentence of motherhood all this time, not wanting me to live with this truth. I'm sorry about your dead mother. I think if she had not died when you were young, you would be a different sort of person. And me. If we had not been separated, if we had finally escaped, left my father behind. Imagine us in some grocery store, somewhere, reading ingredients in the wellness aisle. Imagine us in New York City.

But I killed my father. My hands had done it. *This isn't fair,* you'd written. You'd always known it. And you wanted me to know it now too.

"I can't go home," I said to him. "How can I ever face my kids again? My husband?"

"Let's be together. Just a night. I don't think you should drive anywhere."

I texted my husband that I was feeling a lightning bolt of inspiration and needed to immediately get it all down right now or else it would drift away.

He texted back, *Would have been nice to have a plan. I know you're going through something right now, but throwing this at me feels wrong.* Was I supposed to feel guilty? I didn't. Instead I thought of all the business trips he'd taken, leaving me alone with the kids for days, even weeks at a time.

I'm asking for one day, I wrote, and turned off the phone.

★　★　★

The Butcher's hotel was downtown, a trendy place with a pool, a photo booth in the lobby, and colorful velour couches, but I saw nothing but the blaring red of what I'd done. He carried me past the front desk as I sobbed into his chest. "Is she okay?" I heard someone say. The public influence was all too ready for endangered women now. Maybe. "Her father died," he told them. Good enough. We went up to the room. The Butcher laid me on the bed and collapsed next to me. Held me. My body seemed to convulse for a long time, the integration of this old truth. This truth my body had shut out in order to survive. And then stillness. I said, "What am I going to do?"

"Memory is tricky. Are you sure this isn't just your worst fear, and your mind made a story around it? I always wondered if that was possible."

"When I told you about it back then, did you believe me? Did it sound like what I just told you now?"

He reached up and touched my father's necklace. "Yeah, the part about you watching yourself in the hall especially. But I didn't know what to believe. I didn't want to bring it up again. You only said it the one time and it seemed like the alcohol let you finally release some things, but I couldn't be sure if it released the truth or your fear."

"Truth or fear."

"Two different things."

"Truth *and* fear. I think it released truth and fear."

"Oh, C," he said. "Is this why you left me? You didn't want to be with someone who knew?"

He kissed my neck in the specific way I remembered. I closed my eyes and saw my husband's face, my children's faces. "My kids, they will know about this and they will never be the same. They'll carry it."

"One day you'll be able to explain it to them, and they will understand. Why do you think an easy life is a better life? You watched your mother get beat nearly to death. You were really brave. There's value in what you did. I want you to see it that way."

"It was him or her that night. I felt that so clearly. It was him or us."

"You saved her. Can you think of it like that? You didn't kill your father, you saved your mother."

Maybe I haven't conveyed it properly, but I loved my father and his eyes and the way he laughed and I loved him so much, but I did not love his dark traveler. He did not love his dark traveler. It scared him. I loved my father's nose and his eyebrows and I missed him still every single day. That moment in the ocean between us, I saw now I'd gotten it wrong. He wasn't telling me to leave, to take you away, to finally *do it* and abandon him. He was asking me to finish it. Finish him. He knew it was the only way. He knew my love for you made me capable. My love for him too.

Then do it.

"You've been running a really long time," the Butcher said. "You don't have to anymore."

"I'm sorry," I said. "I'm sorry I left you with that."

"I'd do it all over."

"I can't leave my family," I said. "And I love you. Two truths."

He smiled a sad smile. "We'll try it again in the next round, C. We'll take a long sleep, and I'll find you again."

★ ★ ★

We lay there as day turned to night and I thought perhaps I wouldn't sleep at all, but I fell deeply into a dreamless place on top of the hotel comforter. Early in the morning I woke up to my phone dinging, many texts coming in. I stared at the screen, confused. My own legal name was in the little message box. *Celine iMessage (8).* I tried to swipe the messages open but the phone wouldn't unlock. I was disoriented; why couldn't I open the phone? Why wasn't my face recognition working, or my code? Another text chimed in. Finally, the phone locked for a five-minute security break.

Then I realized why: I wasn't holding my phone. My phone had been off since yesterday. I was holding the Butcher's.

I shook him awake. He smiled like he always had upon waking, seeing my face.

"Who's Celine?" I asked, holding the phone up to him. "Who is she?"

"Whoa, what's going on?"

"Who the fuck is Celine?" I raced around the room gathering my things. "Who? Just tell me now." It wasn't a totally uncommon name, I considered. He could very well know another Celine, no big deal.

He picked up his phone. "Oh her. She's this woman I met at Home Grown. We dated for a few months back in, like, March, I guess. Didn't take off. She wanted to settle down really fast."

I was C-Love to him. I always had been. He never knew me as Celine. Only the old man who owned the market had seen my employment forms.

"What does she want from you?"

294

"Why are you freaking out?" The Butcher stood up, put his clothes on. "Are you mad at me?"

"Do you have photos of her?"

He shrugged. "Maybe a few."

"Let me see."

"They aren't really—shareable. Hold on. Maybe there's some."

"I don't fucking care right now about nudes. Let me see her face."

He pulled up a picture of a woman, taken in the natural light of day. Blue tank top, perfect smile. "Show me another one."

He shuffled around the phone. "Alright, here."

San Francisco, holding a dripping pink ice cream cone. Straight black hair framing her face. *I didn't want to have hair like my mother's.* The contacts, the plastic surgery. When I'd known her she'd been so emaciated, so frail, so ill all those years. A sick girl trapped in her own malfunctioning body. Then a dead girl in a Polaroid. And yet. There she was. My old friend.

"I have to go. I have to go right now."

CHAPTER 26

What lies beyond anxiety? Mania, insanity, madness? Celine was Jane. Jane was Celine. Still, I searched for another explanation. Some way I might be wrong. Celine was dead. I'd had proof in the Polaroid Christina had sent, but now I understood I'd seen what I needed to see to believe in the lie, in Christina's story. To believe in the life I had taken. All this time, Celine was alive, and doing what exactly?

Maybe looking for me.

The Butcher kept talking as he drove, but I was thinking of my husband now, my family, the crushing responsibility I carried for these lives, four seats at the dining room table each day. You only find out in the trenches that babies turn into people who will always need their parents, that your soul will never sleep again. I could almost understand you not leaving my father simply because he was just that: your daughter's father.

I tried to turn my phone back on but it was dead. It was possible Celine had already told my husband everything. But today was Nova's birthday party. Even with all of this going on, my mother brain would not let go of my daughter's birthday party. I wanted to think Celine wouldn't either. She would wait. She was furious with me, but she wouldn't ruin Nova's day. It was a thin hope to hang on, but a hope nonetheless.

Once we turned onto my street, I could see the Heavenly Chevy was nowhere. Maybe my husband was already on the way with them to set up the party. The Butcher parked, turned, and held my face in his hands. I allowed myself a long look, no words. His face, the first face I'd loved. And now he delivered me to my fate.

Inside, the house was silent. I ran out to the office and found my husband by himself on the computer. He raised his eyebrows when he saw me. What did he know?

"Where are the kids?" I said.

He finished typing. Casual. Took his earphones off. Shrugged. "With you and Jane."

"I haven't seen Jane since yesterday," I said.

"What do you mean? She came by around dinnertime to get the kids last night. She took them to the hotel wherever you were for a sleepover. She said you texted her about it, for them to come swim. She said you'd gotten your writing done."

"I never told her to do that."

"She had their swimsuits in the pool bag."

I plugged my dead phone into a charger on his desk. Certainly, the answer would be there. "Did we cross wires somehow?" he said, calm, cool, but I heard the slightest tremor of fear underneath. I had never seen him scared, and it made my heart race. "Maybe this is part of the secret surprise party she and Nova have been cooking up."

"Call her on your phone while we wait," I said. She didn't pick up. Then my phone came alive, but there were no texts from her, nothing. I called her twice more, no answer. I texted her. *I know who you are. It's all fine, just bring them home. Bring them home now. Celine, please. They are my life.* I screamed into my hands.

"Relax, this is just a misunderstanding," he said. I watched as my good, pure husband, who had never had to entertain tragedy, reached for a harmless explanation. "I'm sure it's all fine. Why are you freaking out? It's Jane."

"Jane is not who you think."

"What do you mean?"

Before I could explain, there was a knock at his office door. Through the glass I could see the Butcher. I opened it and stood between the two men in the small office.

"I was going to leave but I felt worried." The Butcher looked at my husband. My husband looked at me.

"Jesus Christ," I said to him. "This is my ex. My only ex before you."

My husband smiled faintly. He was so very lost. "What?"

"I'm sorry, man," the Butcher said. "I just came back to tell C I remembered something. I'm not sure if it's helpful." He looked at me. "But Celine talked a lot about volunteering. She was big into helping out at the women's prison in Chowchilla. She'd drive down there a lot. But I always pictured your mom in Hawai'i. I never made the connection before now." I could tell his mind was spinning too, trying to put it all together.

"Her mom is dead," my husband said to the Butcher. "What are you saying right now? What is this?"

"I'll explain in the car," I said. "We have to go." I turned to the Butcher. "She has our kids."

298

My husband continued to search. "Did I miss something important here?"

"No," I said, "I did. I missed everything."

He eyed the Butcher again. "Are you guys fucking around? Was my mother right?"

"She was right," I said. "But not about that."

My husband raced past the Butcher and into the house. "Thank you," I said to the Butcher before running after my husband. I reminded myself Celine was intense sometimes and impulsive, but she loved the kids. She would never hurt them. She felt owed, though. Maybe she felt owed her whole life. Who knew what someone in her position would do? I mean, look at all I had done.

"You've lost your fucking mind," my husband said. He was an animal I'd never seen before, slamming drawers, looking in closets as if our kids could simply be hiding. "You really have."

"Listen to me," I said. I pulled him by the hand over to the couch, guided him to sit. "What your mother found in my bag. It wasn't fiction. I do have a mother. She's in prison. We've been writing to each other all summer."

He looked annoyed. The truth was not sinking in. From the window I could see the Butcher get back into his car. Pull away. I was alone again with my truth, but I didn't have to be. Couldn't be now.

"I lied to you. I lied to you from the first second we met. I'm so sorry. I wanted to tell you a different way, but this is happening now."

"This guy showing up at my house? With your name across his knuckles. You've got to be kidding me." I was impressed he noticed that. "You're telling me my kids are gone and you don't know where they are? It's my daughter's birthday and you let her get abducted by some psycho nanny?"

Maybe he would hit me now. Now would be the time. "Please listen to me. My dad was abusive to my mom. They were fighting and she went to prison for pushing him off the lanai thirty-three floors up."

"Come on," he said. "Be serious."

"Listen to me." I grabbed his hand. It was limp. "This part is important. The most important part. She didn't push him."

"What the fuck, Clove."

"I pushed him. I thought he was going to kill her. I thought my father was going to kill my mother. He was. So I pushed him. I blocked it out for a long time. I wanted a normal life. Please. Please, you have to understand."

He looked at me as if I was a stranger, the most vacant of looks, all the years of us wiped away. The truth was now between us for the first time. "You blocked out killing your own father?" he said. "What are you even saying right now?"

"Do you remember when Nova was first born? We were watching that *Snapped* show and I got upset?"

"I don't remember that, no."

"Yes, come on. We watched it. I was so angry and you didn't know why. You didn't realize that was me on the TV. That was my family."

"Where are my kids?"

"Jane isn't Jane. She's Celine, she's a neighbor I had in Hawai'i. She was my only friend. I thought she was dead. Her mother let me take her social security number and start a new life. I know. It sounds crazy." My own voice rang out as if it were coming from a speaker in some other part of the room.

"Your spiritual transformation has gone too far."

"I don't know what she wants exactly. Maybe she wants them. She thought I was going to have a baby for her. But I can't do that. Obviously. But it's her. She's mad at me." And I knew she was currently with you, or on her way to you, Mother.

He stood up, looked bizarre to me then, taller from the anger, bolstered by it. "You're a liar, all this time lying to me about your entire life?"

I could try to explain the many times I'd wanted to tell him. Birth drunk, Nova in arms, her face your face. She was so miraculous it seemed there was not a single hardship her perfection couldn't stamp out. Then again, Lark newly out of me, dusky blue on oxygen, would he be okay? All that hospital drama can make a person reckless, feel too connected to love, get too soft. But I'd held it back. The first time we'd had sex, how my husband had looked at me, how I knew he was in love, how I knew I'd accomplished it, and then seeing his love, I allowed myself to feel love of my own for him. How I thought, *Wait, wait. I want him to love the real me,* but by then it was too late. He already loved the version I'd showed him. He'd already chosen her.

"My kids are missing!" he yelled. He gripped my arms. "Missing!" He got up and went into the bathroom and closed the door. I heard him groan into a towel.

I grabbed the keys. "You can't leave me yet," I said on the other side of the door. "You have to be right with me. For whatever this is. For them. For the kids." He cracked the door, gray-skinned, ill with my lies. *Come on, follow me.*

"I think I know where they are," I said.

He opened the door at that. Followed me to the car.

"I think my ex was right." My body buzzed with action. "You have to trust me."

"This is a misunderstanding," my husband kept saying as I slammed it out of our driveway. "This is just a big misunderstanding," he said as I sped us south down the I-5. "She's in a powder-blue Chevy. A powder-blue old Chevy." As if at any moment we would see her car and everything would make sense.

About two hours in, he put his face in his hands and cried. A real cry. The first I'd ever seen. We'd made an entire family together and I'd never seen his face contort in exactly this way. Never heard him sob. I put my hand on his back. He looked at me like I'd eaten his heart. "What does she want?" he said.

"I think," I said, "we have to let her tell us that."

CHAPTER 27

We drove all day, my terror transformed into purpose. I knew Celine, and yet, I didn't. I could allow myself to believe she would never harm my children in one moment, and by the time we'd reached the next town I could imagine her doing something horrific, something that would continue in line with my awful lineage. Who had each of us become since our years together? She had become unrecognizable, and me. Well, my husband could barely look at me.

Eleven hours of road behind us, we exited in Chowchilla, the middle of California. Air thick with the heat of summer, smog and pesticides floating in through the vents. The prison was closed to visitors by now, but they were somewhere here, they must be. The sun heavy and low on the horizon, the day almost done, but it was still my daughter's eighth birthday. Maybe they were finishing dinner, celebrating in whatever way they could. By the time I was eight I was fully indoctrinated into my father's world, holding ice to your temples, throwing myself between your two warring bodies. And now my own daughter was spending her special day abducted. We cruised restaurant parking lots, peered in the lit-up windows. We kept the news on in case.

"We should have told someone," my husband said. "We should have done, like, an Amber alert or something."

"Please," I said. "Let me try this first." What my husband didn't know, but I did, was that Celine loved you, Mother, a deep love. The way she looked at you. How she favored you, understood you. Her love was the reason most of me believed she would not hurt your grandchildren. She seemed so healthy now, so vital, and it was hard to square with the image I carried of her sitting weak and limp in her pink chair; how had she gotten out of that apartment, away from Christina?

After twenty minutes we'd seemingly been everywhere in the town, and still nothing. Maybe I had miscalculated, driving us so far away. By now Celine could be a thousand miles away in the opposite direction. I imagined her disguising my children— *let's play dress-up!*—as she drove them across the country, perhaps herding them onto a plane to start their new life with her. Maybe that was her ultimate goal. Maybe that's what she thought I deserved.

But then I thought back to the In-N-Out wrappers flying from the Chevy, not Mike's at all. It was clear that Celine had studied me, had become exactly the person I wanted her to be. But who was she really? I searched my phone for the nearest In-N-Out. There was one twelve minutes south in Madera. I steered back to the freeway. It was worth a try.

"This is the plan?" my husband said. "We're just going to hop from town to town looking for our kids in fast-food places?"

Admittedly it was a feeble idea. But what about signs? I had noticed those wrappers, clocked them for a reason. Maybe everything had meaning. Maybe nothing did. It made more sense to me—what did they say in your meetings, Mother?—to *act as if.*

And then as we approached the glowing yellow arrow, he started pounding on the window. "Oh my god, the Chevy." My husband pointed to the parking lot where the Heavenly Chevy gleamed.

The relief that overcame me was indescribable. I didn't realize until that moment that a part of me had died thinking they were truly gone, and now that part had come back. My whole body shook. I parked directly behind the Chevy, blocking it in, and began to cry, to wail, to howl. My husband placed his hand on my back. It wasn't to comfort. It was to awaken. After a few moments he said sharply, "Clove. Get it together."

I straightened. Of course. I would get it together. I would do the right thing. I would do what good mothers do.

As I opened the car door I saw them walking out, Lark and Nova holding Celine's hands, wearing little white-and-red In-N-Out hats. Celine wasn't holding them at gunpoint; I didn't see a knife behind her back. They were having a lovely time. A surprise California birthday. I had never wanted to hold my children more than I did right then.

"I'm going to have her arrested," my husband said.

"You can't do that," I said. "Just wait." When Celine registered us, she stood still. Held the kids behind her. I felt my body pull toward them.

"Mommy!" Lark broke free and ran to me. I opened my arms and engulfed him. Celine squeezed Nova's hand. My own daughter looked at me warily. What had Celine told her about me? "Honey," I said. "Honey, I'm so sorry."

Nova's face brightened. "It's my birthday!" she announced, breaking away from Celine, jumping into her father's arms. "Daddy!"

Celine stood alone, small and defenseless.

"What is wrong with you?" I said through my father's set jaw. I checked Lark's body to find it all in one piece, kissed Nova's face. "You stole my children."

"They visited their grandmother. She deserved that. To see her grandchildren. You won't help her, and she at least deserved that."

"How dare you take this away from me," I said. If anyone presented my children to you, Mother, it should have been me.

I could almost see the Celine I remembered now under her procedures. I set Lark down by my husband and stepped toward her. Rage entwined with love. She knew me. I wanted to slap her, but I found my arms embracing her instead. "It's you. I'm so mad at you. But it's you."

Her body softened into me. In my ear: "You left me with her. You left me to die."

I pulled back. "You were so sick. I didn't know what else to do."

"I wasn't sick. I was never sick. She made me sick. She made me weak and sick so I could never leave her."

"What?" All Christina ever wanted was for us girls to be strong.

"After you left, after you got out. I realized it. I started pretending I'd taken my medicine. Slowly I got better."

"But she wrote to me, she said you were dead, and that she was dying too. That she didn't have long."

"My mother was the original great liar."

All those days spent with them, all I didn't see. And you, Mother, you missed it too. "What happened to her?"

"Well," Celine said. She was trying to be tough but I saw her crack. She hated all of this as much as I did. "I took a page out of your book."

"What do you mean?"

She pulled me in again so my husband and kids couldn't hear. "We're really more like sisters than friends, aren't we? We both did what we had to do."

"You knew?"

"I heard you that night with my mother. I heard your voice when you came in. The sound of it. I knew you'd done something. It was enough to realize what happened. All this time, I've wondered, does my old friend really not remember that part? Is she really going to let her own mother, sweet Alma, rot in there? I used to be weak, but I'm not weak anymore. It's time for things to be properly sorted, Clove."

"You aren't weak."

"I didn't have it easy like you, though. No one handed me an identity. I had to do unspeakable things to get out of there, get my feet on the ground. I've really struggled all this time while you've had it made. On my name, of course."

"How did you kill her?"

I heard my husband buckle the kids in their seats and close the car doors. He stood beside me, our arms touching. He was still here.

"She sure drank a lot of grape juice, didn't she?" she said with an odd, hard smile. "But she didn't have much tolerance for the stuff she'd been giving me. Was surprisingly fast."

Christina and her principles. Her hatred of bad men. Her encouraging me to leave, to make change for myself. All the while she wanted to trap Celine with her forever. She was so terrified of her daughter out in the world. Of those bad men finding her. Why had we never thought it was strange, Mother? Because everything in our life was wrong? My father had created a chaos so all-encompassing that we couldn't see the world clearly.

It's all a part of the same disease, Mother. This is what I've been trying to explain this whole time. Are you seeing it now? How it infects everything?

"I never knew," I said. "Please believe me, that I never once imagined she was doing that to you."

"At first I thought there was no way you didn't know. No way you could have been in our apartment all those years and not sniffed it out. I was angry with you for a long time. But then I had to remind myself that I didn't know it either, even though it was happening to me. It allowed me to have some compassion for you. For your mother. It made me want to find you both again, to help you."

"I could only see what was happening right in front of me," I said. "It never occurred to me that someone was going through something just as bad."

"Not a lot has changed. You're still incredibly self-focused."

"It takes so much to keep up with all this normalcy. You know as well as I do, the past is in every room."

"Well, it's time to change that. We're going to end it. Together."

"Celine," I said. "I have a family. They don't deserve any of this."

"Sure, you've got this beautiful family, but it's all built on lies. On my name. And I guess now, I really want my name back."

"What are you going to do?" I said.

She took a jagged breath. "It's not what I'm going to do," she said. "It's what you're going to do. Get in the Chevy. We've got work to do at the Holiday Inn."

"I don't think so," my husband cut in. "This is too much. I'm calling the police."

I turned to him. "It's okay. Just follow us."

Celine smiled at my husband. "She's in debt up to her eyeballs, by the way. There, now everything's out. Happy to watch the kids while you two go to marriage counseling."

He looked at me with a deep exhaustion, this man who had been there for so long, who was now being forced for the first time to understand pain, deceit, sorrow. He would run from it, get in the Forester, and drive away with my kids. Take them from me forever. I wouldn't blame him. "Please," I said to him. "Let me make this right. Let me have some time alone with her."

"How do you know she's not dangerous?" he said, looking at Celine.

"Because I know her. And I know she would never hurt me." I did know this. I had always known this. The friend I had never stopped grieving. I felt Calla Lily step back into me.

Maybe she hadn't been waiting in that high-rise apartment all these years for you to come get her, Mother. Maybe she'd been waiting for me.

My husband pulled out, unblocking the Heavenly Chevy. He followed close behind as Celine drove to the hotel. I stared ahead. Where was my anxiety now? It seemed it had finally crested, fight and flight joining together creating a definite current of purpose in my veins. Didn't one of my parenting experts say *The catastrophe you fear will happen has, in fact, already happened*? Was it meant to comfort? How could I access comfort when I was very likely cruising toward a new and unimaginable catastrophe in that very moment?

In the parking lot I looked at Jane. Not Jane. Celine. "I wonder what the feminist lawyer will think of all this."

"Clove," she said, putting a hand on my arm. "I am the feminist lawyer. I'm the one who visited your mother for months, once I finally felt like maybe the world was ready to help her. And I've always known where you were. I had your social security number. *My* social security number, remember? When I came to Portland, I wasn't sure what my plan was. I certainly never imagined things would get so entwined, but it was like, doors wide open with you. It was almost like you'd been waiting for me. You even ran into my car."

Had I been waiting for her? It was possible. I'd been waiting to not be alone. I thought back to that first moment seeing her but not really seeing her. The crunch of impact. The spiritual pull. "I was so drawn to you. Now I know why. Did you stop in front of me on purpose?"

"I had been following you that day, witnessed the entire post office debacle, figured it wasn't the right time to meet you, then I drove alongside you, watching your whole breakdown. I was worried you weren't going to make it home. But then you seemed to be calming down. I figured that was enough for one day, so I got ahead of you and then that man with the cat walked into the road. I thought you'd know who I was immediately. I thought the whole thing was ruined. I considered speeding away, but then I had to talk to you. I couldn't stop myself. I wanted to get to know you. I saw then you needed help to see all this clearly. To help your mom. And when you didn't recognize me...Once I knew that for a fact, I admit, it made things more interesting than I thought they'd be."

"You look nothing like you did as a kid. Nothing."

"I know," she said. "But I figured you'd still see me. If anyone would be able to, it's you."

"Your plastic surgery is too good for that."

We broke into nervous laughter.

"For a long time, I liked knowing you were okay in the world. I never wanted to intrude. But when I found out I couldn't have children...When my old man died...I guess that's when it all became too much for me. Too much to bear. I retraced your steps to San Francisco, got to know you through your first boyfriend.

Started visiting your mom. Between knowing Alma was in prison for something she didn't even do and that you were living this life, this life that didn't really belong to you…I started feeling like you owed me something. And then the women on TV, on the internet, telling their stories finally. I wanted that for you, for your mother."

"It wasn't my idea to take your identity."

"When I heard my mother give it to you, I knew I was going to die. I knew I was never getting out of there if I listened to her."

I thought back to Christina's rough childhood stories, all that had been done to her. How it became a sickness. Her need to keep Celine safer than safe. And what could be safer than death?

I wanted there to be one person wholly at fault, one evil person, but it wasn't so simple.

"And now you want me to confess, you want me to turn myself in. For what? So my own children can suffer, be motherless too?"

"You're not listening to me."

I glanced back to see my husband getting out of the car with the kids, but I followed Celine past the front desk and into the elevator to her room on the third floor. I could see it was just a room, no balcony. Not so high up.

I stepped over my children's sweet backpacks, their clothes. The coloring books on the bed. "I want to fix all of this. But I don't know how," I said.

She pointed to the desk where my laptop was already sitting. "I do."

"What are you talking about?"

"You're going to write it."

"Write what?"

"Write the story. Write the story that will free Alma. That will reclaim your own identity and return mine. Free us all. You're the only one who can do it."

"What makes you think anyone would understand what I did?" My body was weak; my father idled in the Jimmy, the box on the seat. Inside the box, the clear fact of what I'd done.

"What if they take my kids away?" I said to her. "I killed a man. I stole your identity. How safe can I really be?" But even as I said it, I knew the truth. That everything I had experienced in my life had only made me safer. Had only made me a more vigilant, diligent parent. But vigilance had only gotten me so far and would not get me any further now.

Celine sighed. "I didn't say write the truth, Clove. I said write the *story*."

Celine paced behind me as I typed. I had no memory of her pacing in our childhood. She was always reclined, covered in blankets. Now she was a live wire. She peered over my shoulder, weighed in occasionally. Cut lines. Added details. And finally, when I felt like I had something, she read it. Turned to me. Looked disappointed. What I'd written wasn't good enough. It was over. I wondered how to tell my children their mother might be going to jail and never coming out. I wondered how to tell them who I really was, who they really were.

"Something's not clicking," she said.

I knew she was right. "Wait," I said. "I have a better idea." When I told her what it was, she had to agree. "But one condition," I said.

I had to see you first.

★   ★   ★

312

The next morning at the prison you wore a white two-piece cotton set. I had expected a different color, something neon or drab. Your skin was tan and lined, your face a map of what my father had done to you. It was all there. Yet you held an elegance. Your hair was long and straight and parted down the middle, pure silver. You looked like a healer of some kind, a witch in the desert. Your trademark Wild Orchid was applied perfectly but your mouth was different, seemed to pull into itself.

You covered your face with your hands, hiding like a child. Peekaboo. Mother. You were still mine. My husband hovered next to me, poor man, a friendly smile plastered on his face, his posture straight and firm. He was meeting the mother for the first time. A moment I never imagined. Our children seemed comfortable, bored even, having already been there the day before. "Hi, Grandma," Nova said. My throat constricted. I never thought I'd see you and my daughter in the same room. I should have reached for you, tried to hug you, but oceans of shame, yours and mine, stood between us. My desire to feel your love, to have you at last, was treacherous in its depth. But in that desire my whole world hung. You stood before me, maker of that whole world. My mother.

You looked at my husband, didn't make a motion to meet his outstretched hand. He slowly dropped his arm. "Does he hit you?" you said to me.

"Never," I said. "Not once."

You nodded as if skeptical. "I guess I've learned to be wary of men," you said. I thought but didn't say: *About time.* "Your little ones are gorgeous," you said. "They remind me so much of you. It's like looking right back into the past."

"I want to help," I said. "I want to get you out."

You nodded. "I've had good behavior in here."

"Of course you have."

"I'm going to get them a snack," my husband said nervously. He turned and walked toward the vending machines, where he spent a long time letting the kids pick out chips and candy. Since our car ride it seemed a valve had opened in him and he couldn't stop crying. He sniffled now as he opened their packages. My kids were at a prison visiting Grandma. So much for my ideas of normal.

"I have to say something," I whispered.

"It's not private here, if you need it to be private."

I took a deep breath and a cry escaped me. "I'm so sorry, Mom. I'm so sorry." How little the word *sorry* meant. How useless it was in the face of everything. I could say it all I wanted and it didn't change a thing.

You looked at your hands. "A lot happened that night." You paused. You motioned for me to lean in. You got so close I could smell your skin, it was you, still your skin. "He almost killed you that day," you said. "He almost drowned you. When I found you on the sand, I saw death in your eyes. In the end, what needed to happen happened. I do believe that."

"You were supposed to find me," I sobbed.

"I messed it up. Without you helping me, I messed it up."

"It was always rigged against us," I said.

"It's like you wrote in your letter," she said. "'The world is not made for mothers.'"

"Why didn't we leave?" I said. I held your hand. Adult Clove understood why we never left. But this part of me, young Calla Lily, still didn't.

"He would never have let us go," you said. "That's how much he loved us."

"That isn't love."

"That's what everyone tells me. That's what everyone always said. But your father did love us. Underneath it all. He really did. You were always smarter about it, though. You understood him, and I never did."

"I have a lot of anger."

You looked around. "I know. But I still don't deserve this place."

We could agree on that.

"Don't say anything yet," I said. "I have a plan."

"Can you believe that Celine? What a firecracker."

"It's because of her I'm here."

"I didn't recognize her all those times she visited," you said. "I really thought she was a lawyer."

"We missed a lot back then," I said.

You considered this. "I guess we did."

So much I wanted to say. I wanted to go back to the beginning.

"When I get out, if I do," you said, "I won't bother you. I read your letter, and I understood that part. I understood how you want life to be. You want it to be tidy. But I don't drink in here. I don't. And maybe, with time…" You bowed your head, began to cry. "I just never thought I'd see you again. My baby, my daughter."

I threw myself at you then. I heard a guard yell a warning, but I held on to you and you held on to me. "Mama," I cried. Mama. Mother, mommy, mom. So much had been stolen from us. Eventually, you leaned back and showed me your mouth where the teeth were dissolved and soft. Where once your strong teeth had been, the gap between them I loved the most. "Maybe you can help me fix these."

It was a place to start.

CHAPTER 28

That night, as my family slept in their hotel room down the hall, Celine and I were two girls awake past our bedtimes. The television played *Jerry* reruns. Celine brought in that tattered box from the Chevy's back seat I'd seen the day she'd moved into my home, something bundled on top. She set it down in front of me and unfurled an impossible dress. Floral. Yours.

"How did you get this?" I marveled.

"After you left, my mom went out to look at the scene. She wanted to see your father's body. She wanted to be sure he was dead. And I got up and made it to your apartment. The door was wide open and I remembered where you told me you always hid Alma's favorite dress. I grabbed that, and the box. A part of me wondered if you'd want these things someday. If we'd see each other again and I could hand them to you."

I held the dress to my body. The same as I'd remembered. And your picture box. This kindness felt disarming to me, too much to hold. The ways Celine had cared for me even as I'd abandoned her.

But I had to work toward forgiving myself. I wouldn't survive if I didn't.

We took our time choosing the photograph and eventually landed on one of you on the beach that I had taken. It was one of those endless ocean days when we could pretend we were tourists, a mother and daughter, extravagantly loved and enormously worthy. You had turned and smiled, holding your book, and the camera caught your black eye.

I wrote the caption, used all the right tags. See, Mother, I realized I couldn't wait on someone else to tell me our story was deserving. And I couldn't let anyone else try to tell it. It had to be me. It had to be us. On our time. In our words. Now.

I posted the picture to the many followers I had amassed over the years who knew nothing of the real me. The first face on my profile was yours, Mother. The carefully written caption expanded into the comments.

Not the truth—Celine was right. We did not owe the world a truth that would be used against us—we would use the story that would work. One more lie to get things right: Christina, the neighbor who had walked in on the fight, who got between us and my father, who pushed him to his death. The daughters who ran in fear, and you, the battered mother who took credit for the push to protect the friend who had saved you. I saw in Celine's eyes that despite herself, she was proud of her mother for this imagined act of bravery.

Sometimes it's okay to believe our own stories. If we're lucky, these stories help us survive.

And before sleep overtook me, I thought of my father, his necklace caught in my fingers, my love for him guilty, angry, consuming.

He had taken my joy, my life, my mother. He had taken my inno-cence, left me a made-up person. But now I saw his death could mean something beautiful. A long-standing cycle had ended with his fall. The cycle ended with me.

CHAPTER 29

I spent the next morning with my phone off, my husband quiet, the kids compliant, watching cartoons with abandon, eating hydrogenated oils and god knew what else from the continental breakfast offerings. My life was my life. All I endured had led me here. All I had seen and all my heartbreak held a meaning beyond anything I could imagine. Looking at them, I knew this to be true.

I did not imagine that just because #MeToo had taken flight, this would be a cure. I did not think my primal rage that had been collecting over years and generations of women was enough to undo what had happened to you, to us. But I found myself hopeful that morning. I knew, at the very least, that I would not go back to being who I was before, a self in secrets. My husband stole glances at me. I imagined he would be contacting one of his many lawyer friends to ask about a divorce. I did not want that. But I would understand.

Finally he spoke. "I'm so amazed by you."

"You are?"

"I can't believe everything you did to survive. I'm in awe." He saw me, the real me, and said that.

"We still have a lot to talk about. I get it if you don't want to be with me anymore. I really do." Tears rose to my eyes. I loved him because he was mine, and I was his, and most of all, we were our children's.

"We do have a lot to talk about," he said. "And a lot of time to do it." It was as if I'd held my breath all my life and had finally let it go. I was no longer alone. Whatever happened from here, this was true.

Celine burst through the door. Wig off today. Her short black hair didn't remind me of Christina, as she'd worried. In fact, Celine looked simply like herself. "Holy shit," she said. "Are you watching your phone?" My children clung to her legs as she scrolled and scrolled. "Seriously, how are you not watching this?"

"Are people commenting?"

"Are people *commenting*? This is what I believe they call *viral*. People are going nuts. I think this is going to work. Oh my god. I think it's actually going to work!"

I turned my phone on and opened the app. It appeared to be self-destructing inside the glass. Message after message and comment after comment. I made my way to the photo, where tens of thousands of likes were flooding in. My followers had risen into an army. Something was happening. A post was being shared and I was tagged. A pink square with the photo of my mother zoomed in, my words quoted below, the hashtag in block letters above it: #FREEALMA

There were many, many messages, all requesting interviews. People offering support. Several real feminist lawyers who wanted to provide legal assistance. People offering solidarity, sharing their own stories. There were so many stories. I sensed the heads of many women nodding. I clicked the phone back off. I had turned the most private thing about me public. And I could not undo it.

But then I thought of all the times the cops had come to our door, your blood on my father's hands, me in the corner screaming the truth to a dead crowd. And how they looked past me to you, asked, "Is everything all right here?" and when you said it was, that everything was fine, they told you to keep the noise down and left us alone.

I don't know what I can really offer you, Mother. I don't know if we will ever be okay. But you should be free. I will make sure of it. We will see the ocean again.

If you or someone you know is in a dangerous situation, please know there are agencies and resources that can help. And if you'd like to be part of the solution, please consider donating to the organizations below and supporting local efforts. There are so many people doing this vital work, and this is only a small list:

Women experiencing any kind of domestic abuse can call the National Domestic Abuse Helpline: 0808 2000 247

Men experiencing domestic abuse can call Men's Advice Line: 0808 8010 327

For further information and help, please visit
https://www.nhs.uk/live-well/
getting-help-for-domestic-violence/

ACKNOWLEDGMENTS

First, I'd like to offer special acknowledgment to the countless individuals, predominantly women and children, who are affected by domestic violence every day, and the many who have lost their lives while isolated and without protection. Sending solidarity, love, and hope for healing. A special thank-you to my mother, Mary Glim, who died in September 2022, to whom this book is dedicated. I miss our phone calls when I would tell you about this story, and you would say, with all the enthusiasm in the world, "Well, what happens next?" This one's for you. For everything we survived, and everything we didn't.

It takes a special alchemy to bring a book into the world, and I am immensely grateful to the following people, who ushered *Madwoman* into the hands of readers: My brilliant agent, Samantha Shea, who pushed me in each draft to cut closer to the truth of this story. My editor, Jean Garnett, for her genius-level guidance and offering what feels like a kismet union—I hope we get to do this many more times. Katharine Myers, for working her magic and helping this book soar. Gregg Kulick, for this stirring, captivating, and original jacket that I love so much. To the entire incredible team at Little, Brown for championing *Madwoman* so enthusiastically from the jump, especially Katherine Akey, Ben Allen, Karen Landry, Craig Young, Marieska Luzada, Khadijah Mitchell, Eileen Chetti, and Marie Mundaca. I am so lucky to have a home for this book where it feels so deeply understood.

So much gratitude to Juliet Mabey and my stellar team at Oneworld in the UK for making my dreams come true and sharing *Madwoman* far and wide, and Valerie Borchardt and Rachel Clements for making it happen.

Thank you to my film agent at UTA, Kristina Moore, for your vision and ongoing faith in my work. I'm so happy to get to work with you.

To my writing group and soul family: Genevieve Hudson, T Kira Madden, Allie Rowbottom, and Cyrus Dunham, for asking all the right questions and offering unwavering support and love. It's the honor of my life to write books alongside you—BAWS forever. To my star, my fountain, Kimberly King Parsons, for your camaraderie in all ways. Thank you for the conversations and the laughter, and most of all for holding the vision. Thank you to Rachel Yoder and Ashley Audrain for your early support—it means so much. To Annabel Graham for reading multiple drafts and always offering her intelligence and encouragement, Anne Zimmerman for bringing Lenore E. Walker back from that San Francisco free library, Hannah Thomas for providing invaluable "crushtomer" intel, and Leah Dieterich for understanding Clove. Finally, my deep admiration and gratitude for the work of Nancy Price, Anita Shreve, Anna Quindlen, and Lisa Taddeo: your novels felt like North Stars to me.

Thank you to the booksellers who work tirelessly to support authors and get books into readers' hands all over the world. Kim and Sally at Broadway Books, and Kevin Sampsell, Katherine

Morgan, Stacy Wayne, and everyone else at my beloved Powell's: you all do the most, and I am grateful! Thank you to Portland Literary Arts, and especially to Amanda Bullock and Susan Moore, for creating a beautiful community of writers and readers in our great city. And thank you to every reader who has read my work, posted about my books, recommended them to friends, hosted book club parties, and reached out with your kind words. The sacred connection between writer and reader is never lost on me, and your support means the world.

I owe enormous thanks to Tin House for awarding me a Parents Residency. The gift of that time and space was integral to writing this book. Thank you for seeing mothers as worthy of support in the arts and connecting me to fellow writer-mother turned dear friend, Gina Balibrera. Thank you also to Portland Literary Arts for the Booth Emergency Fund and for supporting writers during the pandemic, and at all times.

Amber, I'm glad our roots are entwined as we grow in our powers. Sam, thank you for all the park days. Three witches fall asleep on a picnic blanket…and wake up and keep talking. I'm so lucky to do motherhood alongside you both. Thanks for letting me know about the game of life. To the F4, Anna, Hannah Grace, and Helen—my love for you is eternal.

To Jolene Kelley, you changed my life. Thank you.

Both my parents died while I was writing this book, and my community showed up for me in ways I will never forget. Thank you to the many friends, family, and neighbors who sent flowers, cards, and meals; showed up at my door; and helped me plan. I will always remember the gestures that got me through those early odd dark days of grief. Grief can certainly feel lonely, but thanks to you, I know I am not alone.

When my father was in his physical form, he told me to tell the stories I needed to tell, whatever they were, and however I needed to tell them. There is no greater gift he could have offered to me, and I am grateful. Wendi, you always know exactly what I mean. To the women in my family who loved my mother, we share the same stardust. And to my precious granny, by the ocean, you spoke the words that freed me. Do you feel my love for you? *I do, I do.*

To the grocery stores of my life, near and far, thank you for always being there, and to Gen for leading me to the Holy Grail those many years ago and changing my life forever in the wellness aisle.

Finally, to B, *the one who believed in me from day one*! ☺ and to our beautiful babies, Harper Jewel and Finn Ocean. Because of you, I can travel to these depths and come back up again. What an amazing *positive opposite experience* you've turned out to be. You are the loves of my life.

© Jessica Keaveny

CHELSEA BIEKER is the author of the debut novel *Godshot,* which was longlisted for the Center for Fiction's First Novel Prize and named a Barnes and Noble Pick of the Month and an NPR Best Book of the Year. Her story collection, *Heartbroke,* won the California Book Award and was a *New York Times* Best California Book of 2022. She is the recipient of a Rona Jaffe Writers' Award, as well as residencies from MacDowell and Tin House. Raised in Hawai'i and California, she now lives in Portland, Oregon, with her husband and two children.

N